Accidental or Designed

All Mine series, Volume 3

J.N. Crump

Published by J.N.Crump, 2024.

This is a work of fiction. Similarities to real people, places, or events are entirely coincidental.

ACCIDENTAL OR DESIGNED

First edition. September 16, 2024.

ISBN: 979-8227598813

Written by J.N. Crump.

Dear Readers

Just like the first two books, all translations will be at the end of the book--after the last chapter.

If you've come this far, and are enjoying your experience--Thank you! Hopefully you fall in love with these characters just as much as the others.

Please keep your mental health in mind while reading.

The song dedicated to this book is; Curiosity by Bryce Savage

Now, enjoy yourself.

There you are.. Are you ready for me?

Prologue One

Three years ago
Elizabeth

MY HAND BRUSHES AGAINST the smooth wood of the bedroom door as I push it open. Every muscle in my body strains from holding back the shaking trying to overcome me. My feet stay planted in the doorway as I look down at my father. He sits on the floor, leaning back against his bed. The only picture left of my mother is in his hand while his other holds onto his handgun. He clasps the picture so gently... Gentleness I never truly got to witness.

He looks up to me with bloodshot eyes and silent tears tracking down his face, then flicks his eyes back to the picture. This isn't the first time I've found him like this, but it is the only time I've found him holding his gun as well. I move to take a shaky step forward only to freeze when he points the gun at my chest. His eyes move to mine slowly, not wanting to leave my mom's beautiful face.

His pupils almost swallow the dark brown of his eyes, the pain in his gaze instantly making me flinch. His throat bobs heavily before he opens his chapped lips, "You're the reason she's not here. You ruined her, then ruined everything else."

My eyes shut tightly, his arm flexing to pull the trigger. I'll accept death as long as it's better than this.

The shot rings in my ears and I flinch on instinct, but the pain never comes. My mind is slow to catch up as I open my eyes and look down. My mother's picture is still gently held in one of his hands, the gun laying at the tips of his fingers in his lap, while blood soaks into the bed spread and the collar of his shirt...

My body jolts upright, my blanket falling to my waist. A cold sweat covers my face and back, my chest heaving with breaths that are too quick. I try to swallow past my thick throat as I look around my room.

Just a dream.. It was just a dream.

But it wasn't. It was only *one* of the bad memories I have of the monster who was supposed to be my father.

I groan and shove my palms into my eyes. These nights are less frequent than they were three years ago, but they're still too many for my liking. When my muscles finally relax and I can breathe without a weight sitting on my chest, I look to the clock on my nightstand.

4:44. *Great.*

My double at the diner doesn't start until seven, but I doubt I'll be sleeping any more tonight. I grab my phone from the charger and unlock it, seeing I have three text messages from Murph. My dazed mind flashes back to when I first came to this city, after my foster mother died. Rundown car, no job, no friends, and only fifty dollars in my pocket. I ran into him, literally, when I was reading through job openings on my phone. He gave me a gorgeous but lethal smile, and immediately decided to help me. Only, he didn't tell me he was the head of a small mafia until it was too late.

He got me the job at the diner which is one of their 'covers', and gave me a decent amount of cash to get myself a small apartment to stay in. Ever since that day, I've been stuck with him. Too chicken-shit to leave, and too alone to know what to do if I did.

He owns me, and after six months, I'm starting to doubt exactly how quickly I'll be able to get out of his grasp. Especially alive.

Prologue Two

One week ago
Elizabeth/Gabriel

ELIZABETH

The trash bag starts to slip from my hand as I lift it to toss it over the rim of the garbage can. My throat is constricting from holding my breath so I don't smell all the old food fermenting in the can. Once the bag is out of my grip, I drop the garbage lid quickly and let the breath rush from my open mouth. I look up at the night sky with a groan. *I can't wait to get a better job.*

I never wanted to work at a diner, but it's a job, and considering I don't have anyone else to help me out of this mess, I don't have a choice. I've been at this job longer than I wanted to be. My max was a year until I could get a better opportunity, and I still haven't left. Not that I think Murph would let me leave. Not only am I a waitress, but I've turned into his personal calculator/cyber geek, among other duties.

I look past the street lights in the alley and focus on the few stars in the sky that are visible. The stars in the city are nothing like the stars outside my childhood home. I used to love laying on the grass in the backyard, talking to myself about the constellations. Before my father got worse...

Shaking my head free of the memories, I tilt my head back down and turn to reach for the handle to go inside to finish my shift. Right as my fingers drift around the handle, I get pulled back harshly, my legs coming out from under me. My butt hits the ground roughly and a huff of pain springs from my throat. I look around with confusion as to why I just fell backwards. And it all makes sense when my eyes land on two brawny men on either side of me, their arms crossed and smirks lifting the corners of their mouth.

Fuck.

I smile sweetly and switch my gaze between the both of them, "Hello gentlemen, what can I do for you this fine evening?"

The one I think is named Ben chuckles, "Deciding to act nice this time?"

I fix my stare on him, blinking quickly in mock surprise, "Whatever do you mean?"

Ben full on smiles and squats down so he's eye level with me, resting his elbows on his knees, "Don't be a bitch Liz, you know why we're here."

My smiles falls and I pinch my eyebrows together in determination, "I told him I had a long shift tonight. I can't."

The other muscle-head squats down and my attention goes to him as he speaks, "And Murph told *you*, it's either tonight or he'll take another form of payment." His eyes snake over my body, my skin feeling as if bugs are following the trail.

Murph is a huge asshole that hid it so well in the beginning. The only reason I let him help in the first place was because I would've died in an alley otherwise. I needed money, and being so new in this city, he seemed like a beacon in the dark. I'd heard of a Russian mafia that controlled most of this city, but I figured Murph was safer to stay with.

I figured wrong.

I narrow my eyes at both men surrounding me, "I'm not done here yet." I think I sound strong and firm until Ben chuckles once more.

Ben grips my arm in a hard hold, yanking me to my feet. He keeps his eyes on mine as he talks to the other guy, "Bring the car closer to the alley opening, I'll wait with her. Don't need her trying to make a scene."

The second guy says nothing but I hear his heavy shoes clomping farther away with each too quick beat of my heart. When I no longer hear him walking, Ben opens his mouth like he's going to say something, but I do the only thing my brain is screaming at me to do. I don't break eye contact with him as I bring my knee up as hard and as fast as I can, slamming it into his crotch with all the power I have. His face immediately contorts in pain and his fingers loosen around my arm as he hunches forward.

I pull free and my feet start moving before I have to think about it. The cool air whips at my face as I sprint towards the opposite end of the alley. I have maybe twenty seconds before Ben recovers enough to chase after me. I get out on the street and run harder than I ever have before. Each pound on the sidewalk thunders from my heel throughout my leg, my thighs jiggling annoyingly and riding up the skirt of my uniform. Following footsteps start getting louder behind me and I turn quickly, cutting down another alley, praying to whatever is out there that I can get away before they catch me.

GABRIEL

My eyes start to burn as I look through the code Rick sent me earlier. I've been trying to find the mistake he thinks is in there but, so far, haven't come up with anything. I lean back in my seat and slump, lifting my glasses and rubbing my eyes roughly. Normally, I don't stay this late but, since moving out of Rick's house, I haven't liked being home at night. It's not the same living by myself. I miss training with Nat after work before trying to sneak bites of food as she cooks. Or teaching Rick my favorite videogames.

Sighing, I drop my arm and look at the screen. *I can finish this in the morning.* Closing everything, I gather my things and lock my office. Maybe I'll stop by the bar down the street for a quick drink before going home, take the edge off a little.

I step into the elevator and press the lobby button, once again rubbing at my eyes after putting my glasses into my jacket pocket. The ding of the doors snaps my eyes open. I give a clipped nod to the security guard as I make my way to the front doors and step out into the cool night air. I could've rode my bike to the bar, but my legs need the stretch of the walk there.

My mind won't shut off as my lungs breathe in the refreshing chilled air around me. The code Rick sent is going to bug me. I know I said I could do it in the morning, but I already know I'll probably be sitting in bed for the rest of the night looking at it.

Before I can start going through it in my head, a body slams into my chest. I grab their arm to steady us both, my free hand slipping to my back for my gun out of instinct. My hand freezes from pulling it out when I look down at the head of long brown hair resting against me. They pull back slightly to look up at me and my arm flexes with the urge to pull them closer as I take in their face. It's a beautiful woman—her cheeks and nose are slightly pink like she's been out here for a while. Her mouth is slightly parted, showing off her plump bottom lip. I look into her eyes that shine under the street light. My gaze bounces between her eyes to try and determine their actual color until the panic in them catches my full attention.

My brows lower as I let go of my gun and hold her other arm gently, "Are you okay?"

She takes a quick look behind her before turning back to me and shaking her head quickly. I lean around her and look down the alley she just came from, seeing a man turning to run down it.

Without thinking, I spin and pin her against the brick wall. My body completely engulfs her, the sensation lighting my skin on fire. Her breathing is hard and short against my shirt, warming the spot it lands on. Wrapping my hand around her jaw in a tentative touch, I push up so she looks at me.

I give her a light-hearted smirk and lean in until our noses almost touch, "I've got you, Shchenok[*]. Slow your breathing for me."

Her eyes flash with something too quick for me to grasp before she starts to breathe slower and quieter. Our breaths mingle between us in the cocoon we've created. The heavy footsteps of the man get louder as he gets close to coming out of the alley and I feel her body tense against me. My hand slides effortlessly down her soft neck, moving to cup the back of her head, her hair soft between my fingers. I push her tighter against the wall with my body to hide more of her, my hand against the brick flexing as the man rushes behind me. He stops near us, probably to see what's going on, and my throat vibrates with a low growl before I can stop it. The woman's eyes spark at the sound as my arms struggle to hold myself back. Whether he thinks my response is from anger or desire, he decides moves on.

The woman goes to move away but I push my legs against hers, tightening my fingers in her hair, "Not yet."

Her brows furrow but she nods slowly. The arms she's kept locked at her sides start to release the tension they hold, her body hesitantly melting into mine. I no longer hear the man running, but I can't get myself to let her go. I can't stop looking at her, and I realize I don't want to. She's stunning. Her cheeks still hold what most consider baby fat, but her cheek bones are high. Light freckles are speckled across her nose, thinning out as they get farther away from the bridge. Her eyes are bright and big as they graze over my own face with a faint flicker of interest in their depths. Her thick black lashes reach the bottom of her brows as she finally looks into my eyes.

"Is he gone?"

Her voice is quiet but it sounds loud to my ears. I could drown myself in that voice—it reminds me of what I believed angels would sound like when I was younger and hiding away from my father's booming lecture and violent hands.

She starts to furrow her brows and I realize I didn't answer her. I clear my throat and drop my hands, only moving back enough so we aren't completely touching. "Yeah, he's gone."

She nods and looks left and right, checking to make sure I'm correct. I smirk at her attempt at double checking around my shoulders. Her fingers slip her soft brown hair behind her ear as she looks at her shoes. *Is she afraid of me, or shy?* I take another step back to give her more room and that gets her eyes to snap to mine.

Giving her a half smile, I cross my arms over my chest, enjoying the way she tracks the movement. "So, who were you running from, Shchenok?"

She crosses her arms and pops out her hip, tilting her head slightly as she looks me up and down, "What's it to you?"

I have to hold back my chuckle at her sass. "Considering I kept you hidden, I think it's only fair."

Her head bobs slightly, "Some dumbass henchmen. They were trying to bring me to their boss before I was ready to leave work." She seems to take a second to register something, her eyes flaring, "Fuck! I'm supposed to be locking up the diner right now!"

She moves to go back the way she came but I catch her arm, and her head whips to me with a new fire in her eyes. I let go and hold up my hands, "I was just going to offer to escort you there, seeing as they could be going back to wait for you."

Her fingers twiddle with the hem of her skirt as she chews on her lip. She thinks it over for a couple of seconds. Then reluctantly, without looking at my face, she nods. I give a clipped nod in response and begin to walk at her side. We walk in silence before I get too curious to stay quiet.

"Who's their boss." I realize I don't have the tone for a question, but I don't like the situation, even without knowing her.

She keeps her eyes ahead and takes a deep breath before speaking, "Murph Silkon."

My steps almost falter. That's not what I was expecting. Dominic has been trying to get rid of Murph without starting a war. He's a thorn in our side keeping us from cleaning up the city like we've been trying to do for years.

I clear my throat, "I know him. Why does he want you?"

She stops dead in her tracks, I stop a step ahead and turn back to look at her with confusion.

"H-how do you know him?"

There's fear there, like I'm less trustworthy than I was thirty seconds ago. Something is happening where she's scared of his wrath. I try to reel in the anger wanting to take hold. For some unknown reason, I feel drawn to her. I want to help, if only just to get to see her more.

"Let me introduce myself. My name is Gabriel Morozov. I'm the second right hand to Dominic Mortelli, the head of the Russian Mafia in this city."

Her eyes practically bulge from her head and she takes a shaky step back. I reach a hand out to hold her in place but quickly pull it back when she flinches. I soften my stance and give her a light smile. Something must show her I won't harm her and she relaxes—*slightly*.

"I'm Elizabeth.. It's nice to meet you, Gabriel."

A shiver runs down my spine at the way she says my name. *Why does she have such an effect on me?* I smile bigger and give a small nod.

"Elizabeth, I would like to help you with your situation regarding Murph."

Chapter One

Present
Elizabeth

STANDING IN FRONT OF my floor length mirror I run my sweaty hands over the nonexistent wrinkles in my dress. *Why did I agree to this?* Oh, I know why, because I'm a desperate bitch.

My mind flashes back to the agreement I made with Gabriel a week ago. He helps me get out of Murph's claws if I meet him at some wedding. He didn't tell me who's wedding it was or why he was offering this deal. Honestly, it doesn't make sense to me. Gabriel would be doing a lot more for me than I am for him. But, I guess don't look a gift horse in the mouth. I'm sure there's going to be more to this deal but so far, all I have to do is go to this wedding and spend a little time with him.

After Gabriel made sure I was safe that night, I ended up calling Murph only to get yelled at and summoned for the following morning. I've been having to tread lightly around him since then, but I'm almost positive he's over it by now—considering all the work I've been doing this week.

I blink quickly and step closer to the mirror to check my makeup one more time. I didn't do much besides some glittery eyeshadow, mascara, and a pink-nude lipstick, but I look pretty good. I didn't do anything with my hair besides wash and brush it, letting it drape down my back and brush the top of my butt. My simple-sleeveless light maroon dress sits snug against all my curves and stops at midthigh. It shows a classy amount of cleavage with a thin v-line dip, and compliments my slightly tanned skin tone. My black heels make my legs pop even more as I twist and turn to look over my ensemble. Why I'm trying to make sure I look good, I have no idea. But, Gabriel gave me a certain feeling I haven't had around a man probably ever. He's *super* hot, plus seemed kind, and gave me a sense of comfort.

Before my mind can start to get into *other* feelings he gave me, I grab my tiny purse from my bed and head out the door. Time to see how all of this will play out.

The cab stops in front of what looks like the most expensive wedding venue I've ever seen. I saw lights and flowers strung up at the back of it when we were coming around, but the front? It has a mix of gothic and modern architecture, making me want to just stand back and admire it for as long as I can.

The driver clears his throat and I blink quickly, giving him an apologetic smile before handing him some cash and stepping out. He barely gives me the chance to fully shut my door before taking off. Standing outside of the venue, I take some calming breaths. *Who can afford to have a wedding here?* With shaky legs, I begin to walk to the entrance at the back, following the elegant signs. I know I'm cutting it close to the beginning time I was told.. I stood at my front door for twenty minutes second guessing coming before finally giving in to the risk.

When I turn the corner of the building I stop short at the beauty. Beautiful light grey chairs are set up around the bright green grass, the carpet between the section of chairs is a stormy blue and leads all the way to the double doors at the back of the building. I realize I've been standing here too long when heads start to turn to take me in, all of their eyes confused. Obviously, I don't fit in here. All of the guests are wearing designer suits and dresses and hold themselves with that rich posture. Some of the guests even have that dangerous air about them, tattoos peeking out of collars and sleeves of their dress shirts. *Seriously, who's fucking wedding is this?*

There's only one open chair near the aisle in the third row, and so I shuffle quickly to take a seat. I lift the flap of my purse to look at the time on my phone, realizing that there are only two minutes until the service starts. There's an elderly woman sitting next to me, and when I look over at her, she gives me a kind smile. I return the gesture before looking towards the front. I really don't feel like mingling. The officiant is already standing under a beautiful altar of lights and flowers, waiting patiently.

Before I can look over the faces in the crowd, music flows through the air and we all look back at the double doors. I almost stand before realizing I would be the only one to do so. The doors swing open and who I assume is the groom starts to walk down the aisle like he owns the place, looking like he'll smother anyone if anything doesn't go as planned. His bright blue eyes flick over everyone's faces as he walks towards the front. When he gets close to my chair, I see his brows start to draw in confusion before smoothing out and he smirks at me. Now I'm the one looking confused.

Does he know me?

I'm still watching his tall broad form take his place at the front, trying to figure out why he looked at me like that, until the older lady next to me gently taps my shoulder. I look over to see everyone is standing now so I quickly pop out of my seat, swaying a little in my heels. I turn towards the doors again and watch as the most intimidating man I have ever seen walks out with a gorgeous beaming woman. If they're a couple, I'm really intrigued to see how that works. Based off the slight scowl on his face and her bright smile, it looks like they're each other's opposites.

They walk past me without a glance and I keep my eyes on the doors. I still haven't seen Gabriel yet, and he never really clarified if he would be in the wedding party or a guest. Before I have the chance to look around for him, he steps out of the doors holding a toddler. My heart instantly kicks into high gear seeing the big smile he gives the small girl as they walk. My lips twitch with the urge to smile, but I hold it back. I still don't know him. They get about halfway to the front before the little girl grabs Gabriel's cheeks and squishes them together. This time, I can't hold back a small smile, it's just too cute.

He continues to walk while attempting to pry her tiny fingers from his face. When he gets closer to my chair, his eyes swing to mine. Surprise flashes over his features as his steps falter slightly. His beautiful green eyes seem to be brighter than the grass as they bore into me. I tilt my head to the ground quickly, pushing some of my hair behind my ear. The way my body seems to light up with his eyes on me is not something I'm used to, it's almost uncomfortable. I badly want to sit down and hide in the crowd but I know I have to be polite and continue to stand for the bride.

The music changes and I look up once more to see the bride beginning her walk. My jaw almost comes undone at her beauty. *Why is everyone is this wedding party so attractive?* I might be straight but if a woman like her ever hit on me, I'd probably do whatever she said. Her dress is simple but elegant, fitting her perfectly and flaring out around her hips. Her bright copper hair is pinned up, but curled pieces fall out and frame her glowing face. Her blue eyes almost match those of her soon to be husband, besides the maliciousness beneath his, and her smile is so wide I'm surprised her cheeks don't crack.

I watch her walk to the front, in utter awe of her shining beauty. I'm still taking in everything when a flash goes off and I see her maid of honor holding her phone pointed towards the groom with a smirk. That's when I look at him and see him with tears in his eyes.

If my man doesn't look at me like that when we get married, I'm turning back around. He's looking at her like she hangs the moon just for him every night, and my heart squeezes tightly in my chest.

The only time in my life I experienced even a small amount of love like that was with my foster mom, and I secretly long for it.

I sit down as the rest of the guests do, trying my best to keep my eyes on the bride and groom, even though I can feel a heavy gaze on the side of my face. Quickly, I flick my sight to where Gabriel stands behind the intimidating groomsman. He's already looking at me, and I don't hesitate to stick my gaze back on the bride.

The minutes tick by as the ceremony moves forward and I never once feel the weight lifted from Gabriel's eyes. I clutch my purse tightly in my hands, my spine stiff, and my lungs struggling to get enough air. I must not be hiding my nerves very well, because the older lady next to me reaches over and squeezes my white knuckles. When I look over at her, she gives me another kind smile and leans a little closer. Following her, I lean in until out shoulders touch.

Her voice is warm and low as she speaks, "You here with someone dear?"

I hesitate but nod slightly, "I was invited by one of the groomsmen."

I see her smile widen in my peripheral, "Don't worry, Gabriel is a kind man. He might be looking at you like he'll eat you, but I promise it's not in the malicious way."

My head swings to face her as my cheeks burn with a blush I can't stop. She smiles with her teeth on display and her eyes show nothing but playful-kindness in their depths. Her chest moves with a silent chuckle as she pats my hands only to hold them once more before looking back at the bride and groom.

This night is going to be interesting at best.

Chapter Two

Elizabeth

BY THE TIME THE BRIDE and groom kiss each other, my eyes are watering and my left hand is nestled in the older lady's lap with her warm skin surrounding mine. Do I know how we ended up holding hands like she's a close family member? No. Do I mind? Not at all. I'm glad that I have her next to me, she makes me feel not so alone or out of place around a sea of unknown people.

The bride and groom begin their exit as the guests around me clap and cheer. The woman next to me gives my hand a squeeze and my attention drifts to her, my small smile becoming more genuine at the sight of her broad smile and bright eyes.

"So, dear, what is your name?"

My spine straightens as I realize she's been acting close to me without knowing who I am. "Oh, I'm sorry, my name is Elizabeth. But you can call me Liz."

Her chins dips slightly before she speaks, "That's a beautiful name. I'm Marian, but you can call me Mar if you like. I'm Dominic's mother, the groomsman next to yours."

My brain bypasses the way she referenced Gabriel as mine, and sticks to who she's the mother of. *She's the mother of the Russian mafia head. I've been sitting at a* mafia *wedding, getting comforted by the heads mother.* Marian must realize my downward spiral, and her face softens even further as she chuckles almost silently.

"Liz, there is nothing to be scared of. You are safe here and around my son. By the look on your face I'm assuming you know who he is?"

I nod slightly, "Gabriel told me he's the head of the Russian mafia here..."

Her eyes shine with pride, "That he is. And he's done a wonderful job at cleaning up our city. Tell me, how long have you lived here?"

My throat clears at the attempt to get rid of my nerves, "About three years. I moved here after my foster mother passed."

Sadness creeps into her features as she responds, "I'm sorry for your loss, dear. I would love to talk with you more later on tonight, but I'm afraid you are wanted in someone else's company at the moment."

My head swivels so fast my eyes take a couple seconds to adjust. Gabriel is standing near the front of the aisle patiently with, who I can now identify as, Dominic Mortelli. Dominic is talking with him and the woman he walked with, but Gabriel's eyes are on only me. Marian taps my hand affectionately and excuses herself, leaving me sitting alone with my muscles tightly wound. Gabriel makes no effort to come to me. His body is faced towards Dominic, his head twisted to keep his sight on me. I take the opportunity to rake my gaze over him from a safe distance.

His eyes are darker than when he walked down the aisle, holding too many emotions for me to focus on. There's a slight crease between his groomed brows that suggests he struggling with something, and the tightness of his shoulders suggests I'm right. The light behind him casts an earie halo around his head of brown hair that sits perfectly. I skip over his eyes to look at his strong nose and prominent jawline. His lips are the right amount of plump, and are currently sitting in a slight frown which makes my own pull into a smirk. A part of me oddly enjoys his discomfort in this moment. My mind tells me to look away and go inside, but I ignore it as I look over his suit. It's flawlessly tailored to his muscular, tall form. It's an all-black suit that only has color from the flower in his breast pocket. His arms are crossed over his chest, showing just how big they truly are. I know he stands only about half a foot taller than me, but from this distance, you would think he would tower over me like a tree. His body looks like it's been built not just in a gym, but also from using his muscles for other reasons. *Reasons I'm not sure I want to learn about.*

I quickly look away from him once I remember the other dangerous man by his side. But that's a mistake, I realize, when my eyes meet Dominic's. My muscles coil tighter, getting ready for the flight response. His suit matches Gabriel's, but he holds a much more threatening air. There's a twitch at the corner of his mouth like he wants to smile but won't allow himself. I decide it's better to find a more friendly face and look to the woman at his other side.

Again, her beauty is eye-catching. She gives me a warm smile, and I can't help but to return it with a slight heat in my cheeks. Before I can regain a proper rhythm of breathing, she begins to walk towards me. Standing quickly, like a frightened child, I move into the aisle. I don't have the chance to turn and run before her arms circle around my shoulders and she pulls me into a hug.

I freeze against her with wide eyes, her soft floral scent wafting into my nose. "Hi! I'm Elliana, Dominic's wife. You must be Elizabeth."

My hand lifts and I give her shoulder a light tap before she pulls away and looks at me with a wide smile. "Uh.. Yeah. Yes. I'm Elizabeth."

She tilts her head slightly, looking me over, "This dress was an excellent choice. It's doing wonders for your figure."

I can't help the nervous laugh that squeezes past my lips. For a wife of a mafia head, she is super friendly.

"Thank you."

Elliana wraps her arm around mine and starts to walk me towards her husband and Gabriel, both of them looking like they're kings of hell about to pass judgment upon me. I try to dig my heels into the ground, but Elliana is stronger than she looks, pulling me effortlessly forward.

"Elizabeth, I do have to admit something..." She whispers loudly towards my ear, "You're not exactly what I imagined when Gabriel told us about you."

That stops me dead in my tracks. She allows us to stop, but doesn't release me.

"Wh—what do you mean?"

She giggles like we're friends talking gossip, "Well, he explained your situation and I've got to say, I wasn't expecting someone who's trying to get out of Murph's clutches to be so..." I raise an eyebrow waiting for her to finish. "Strong-willed."

Now both my brows race to my hairline before furrowing in confusion. She lets out that tinkling giggle once more before pulling me to walk again, only slower now.

"You came to a wedding, alone, where you know no one—including the bride and groom—and sat there looking unfazed and comfortable. Even while probably knowing that we were all tangled with the mafia. There aren't a lot of women who wouldn't have run. Especially after seeing my scowling husband come out."

This time, I join her in the giggling. Although mine comes out choked from nerves. I don't have the opportunity to respond as we stop in front of the men. Gabriel's eyes catch mine first, seeming to soften around the corners like now that I'm by his side, he's more at ease. But that can't be right. Moving to look at Dominic, I muster up my courage and smile politely.

My hand comes up between us for a hand shake, "It's nice to meet you, Dominic. I'm Elizabeth."

A single dark brow raises on his forehead as he slips his hand in mine, giving me a quick firm shake. "Pleasure, Elizabeth."

Gabriel smiles in the corner of my eye, grabbing my hand before it fully releases Dominic's. Elliana moves closer to her husband, letting me go, as Dominic gives a smirk to Gabriel. *Am I missing something?*

Gabriel twines our fingers together and steps closer as he speaks, "Not many people would say it's nice to meet him, Shchenok."

When I turn to look up at him, a playful but harsh smile tilts his mouth up. I'm hoping he's as close to Dominic as he suggests, because I don't think a mafia head would be very pleased to be teased. To my surprise, Dominic gives a rough short laugh.

"Now, that is very true, Gabe. But most of those people don't see the side of me that's nice."

Danger immediately strangles the air from my lungs as I unconsciously squeeze Gabriel's hand tighter. My grip loosens in his as he gives a laugh back, like that whole sentence is completely normal. Elliana grabs my attention once more as she touches my free arm lightly.

"So, Elizabeth, I saw you sitting with Dominic's mother. I'm glad you were able to meet her. She's the only person here that can truly put these men in their place when they're together."

Assuming she's trying to lighten the mood, I give her a light chuckle, "She was really sweet. I enjoyed being able to spend that time with a friendly face."

Elliana nods knowingly, her smile turning sad for a split second before brightening once more. She turns to her husband and pulls on the lapel of his jacket, "Let's give them a moment." She gives me a wink before dragging a far too eager Dominic behind her.

Only when they walk through the double doors do I let out a tight breath. When I look around the space, that tight breath immediately rushes back in when I see that Gabriel and I are now alone out here. My palm becomes clammy as Gabriel's thumb lightly runs over my knuckles, bringing my attention back to him and the fact that he's still touching me. I pull my hand from his and clasp my other behind my back, facing him fully but keeping my eyes down on his shiny black shoes.

His throat clears loudly, "You know, I'm a little surprised you came today."

My head snaps up at that, my brows furrowing, "Well I didn't have a choice, really, did I?"

He smiles broadly, his eyes seeming to burn a dark green, his head tilting slightly to the side, "Didn't you?"

A thick breath rushes from my nose, making my nostrils flare, "Not really. You offered your help *if* I came today. So I'm here. If there's a stipulation, I don't really have a choice."

Gabriel's eyes look over my body slowly. Every inch his eyes touch, my skin heats in response. I watch him as he looks me over, time seeming to slow as he does. He seems to be devouring me with just his eyes and my thighs push together with the unwelcomed pleasure that I get from it. I've had plenty of men look at me with gross entitlement, but I've never had a man look at me like I've always been his, made just for him, like Gabriel is. His roaming gaze isn't insulting but rather invigorating. Making me feel powerful.

He speaks so softly I barely hear him as he looks back into my eyes, "YA by pomog, nesmotrya ni na chto, Shchenok."[*]

I don't know what he said, but goosebumps spread over my arms at his hungry look. There's no longer a smile on his mouth, the fire in his eyes burning into my own. I feel like prey a hunter just set their sight upon. My body ready to flee as his coils with the urge to pounce. His fingers twitch at his side like the idea of touching me is almost too strong to keep leashed. Before I can blink, the scary-hot predator is gone, replaced with the kind gentleman I met in the alley.

"Should we rejoin the other's inside, Elizabeth?"

I swallow thickly and nod, turning to walk inside. His large hand falls to the small of my back, heating the area quickly, as he leads me down the aisle and through the double doors.

What have I gotten myself into?

Chapter Three

Gabriel

SHE'S HERE. I CAN SAY with complete honesty that I thought she would bail. We don't know each other and she already seemed pretty guarded when it came to being around me but, *she's here.* When I saw her as I walked with Tamara—Ell and Dom's daughter—down the aisle, I almost tripped over my own feet. She looked stunning standing there exuding quiet confidence, like she was fine in the unknown situation she wound up in.

Before Ell went to get her, Dominic was trying to warn me about helping her. Even though shortly before we started the ceremony both him and Rick were telling me they knew exactly how I felt when it came to her.

The weird sensation that she belongs with me.

The unnatural sense of protectiveness that overtakes me when I think of her.

The urge to touch her however I can, as often as I can.

Something screamed at me when we were talking on the way back to the diner that night... *Mine.*

But, Dom does have a point about being careful when I help her get away from Murph. I don't want to cause too much damage to the already tense dynamic between Dominic's reign and Murph. Murph has always been egotistical, thinking he controls more than he does, and is more powerful than he is. We don't want to blow his shit up, figuratively, until we know we can do damage control properly.

As we cross the threshold to enter the building, light music instantly dances through my ears. My hand flexes against the small of Elizabeth's back as I scan the tables. Part of me regrets asking this of her. There are multiple mafia affiliates in this room tonight. Both clean and dirty. There's already been a few that have taken notice of her, a wanting in their eyes.

I'm going to have to keep her as close as possible for the rest of the night.

I find the table near the front where our seats are and start to guide her in that direction. Looking down at her as we weave through the packed tables, I notice she once again has put on the mask of ease and confidence. But, I can see the slight fear hiding in her face with the way her skin is tight around her eyes and mouth. I'm oddly proud of her. There's no one in this room that couldn't easily kill or break her without breaking a sweat, but she handles it like they're all innocent little kittens.

A smirk curves my lips as we get closer to our table. Ell and Nat are talking close to each other, all blushed and giggling. Rick and Dom look ever the indifferent assholes they normally are outside of our close circle. Then there's our seats between Ell and Dom.

As we approach, Elizabeth's back tightens under my hand and I reflexively smooth my thumb over a small area. Her head swings to me quickly as I pull out her chair and motion for her to sit down. I see her chest move with a deep breath before sitting down, rising slightly over the seat so I can push her closer to the table. I take my own seat and look around at my family who are now completely silent.

My brows rise high as I look over their faces. Ell and Nat are trying to hide their smiles while Rick has a smirk and a single brow raised, and Dom's lips twitch.

"Why are you all looking at me like that?"

Rick answers first with a laugh in his voice, "Since when did you become a gentleman, pulling chairs out for women?"

My eyes narrow on him, "Fuck you, Rick."

Elizabeth jumps slightly in her seat and my hand finds its way to her knee, closing around it lightly but firmly. Rick looks over at her and smiles a little more, softening his normally fierce features.

"Hi Elizabeth, I'm Rick, Gabe's brother and guardian."

Her head tilts slightly to the side as she looks over what she can see of him. "You're the right hand to Dominic, correct? How did you get to be Gabriel's guardian?"

Rick's chest rumbles with his chuckle, his eyes flicking to me before returning to her, "Well, that's a long story I'm sure he will tell you. And yes, I am Dom's right hand. Though, we are more like brothers too." He bumps Dom's shoulder playfully with his own, earning a scowl in return.

Nat leans over the table to get Elizabeth's attention, "Elizabeth, I'm Natalie, Rick's wife. But please call me Nat. I'm sure we'll get to be good friends soon."

Elizabeth opens her mouth to respond but Rick cuts her off as he pulls Nat closer by her chair, "God, I will never get over hearing you say you're my wife."

Nat slaps Rick's chest and blushes, looking back to Elizabeth so she can continue. I look down at her to see she's smiling sadly at the two of them and I have to withhold the confusion wanting to contort my face.

"Hi Nat, you can call me Liz. I hope we can be good friends. If I'm honest, I haven't made a single friend since I moved here."

Natalie smiles sweetly and nods, "Well, it's a good thing you now have Elliana and I."

Elizabeth's hand falls on top on mine for barely a second before withdrawing quickly like I've burned her. I move my arm to the back of her chair and lean in to whisper to her, my lips brushing the soft strands of her hair.

"So everyone here can call you Liz but me? Is that what I'm hearing?"

I move my head slightly back as she turns to look at me, our noses almost touching. My breath freezes in my lungs as I see the green popping in her hazel eyes. She leans forward, looking at my lips, then moves before they touch hers so she can reach my ear.

"They aren't the ones making a deal with me for their help. Our relationship is professional. They just happen to be a perk that comes with that."

She starts to lean back with a winning smirk, but my hand quickly moves from her chair to firmly grasp the back of her neck. Her smirk falls and her eyes widen, making me smile with a little more fierceness than necessary. My fingers squeeze the sides of her neck as I drag her closer until our noses touch.

"There's nothing professional about us in my mind, *Liz*."

I let her go and face forward in my seat—acting like her closeness has no effect on me—seeing her mouth slightly open as she stares at me. In my peripheral I see her blink quickly, paste on a kind smile, and look back to my family once more. They, of course, aren't hiding that they just saw our little moment. Now, both Rick and Dom are smirking at me knowingly, making my hand fist on my leg.

Am I going to deny the things I feel towards Elizabeth? Fuck no. But, is it still confusing and strange how strong those feelings are? Definite yes.

Rick and Dom have been there to see the women I bring around. None of them stay long and none have gotten these reactions from me. Elizabeth is sassy, strong, and has a fire that she tries to keep hidden. The other women were submissive, easily took orders, and boring. I don't think it slips by them how different Elizabeth is and how different I am around her. I've never been the type to be protective *or* possessive over a woman. I've never gone along with a woman's attitude, seeing how much I can push before they give in to me. Elizabeth is... She's just *different*. There's a factor in play that I can't even put into words. Her fire ignites my own in the best way possible. That night when I protected her—and had her against me—I could feel her fear... But, she didn't succumb to it. She fought it, no matter how much I could see she wanted to let it lead her actions.

Slowly, the conversation comes clear again in my ears, pulling me out of my thoughts. I look over at Elizabeth and see a genuine smile on her face. The sight has my heart speeding. It's wide, showing off her straight white teeth and making her eyes squint slightly.

I want to be the one to get her to smile like that.

She must feel me staring because she looks up at me. Her smile dims slightly as a blush quickly comes to life on her cheeks. I give her a soft smile, not wanting to scare her away from me more than I probably already have, and am the first one to look away.

Chapter Four

Elizabeth

I CAN FEEL GABRIEL'S stare on the side of my face as I smile at his friends. They're telling me different stories, playfully making fun of each other, and I can't help the genuine happiness I feel in this moment. What I would give to have a close friend group like this. But, according to Natalie, I'm now apparently a part of it.

Gabriel's eyes are still on me, so I look over at him. His eyes are focused on my smile, and I instinctually make it smaller, my cheeks heating at the unrecognizable look in his eyes. He gives me the softest smile then turns away. I continue to look at him, not wanting to miss the reactions he has hearing the stories. He looks so relaxed that I would believe he's comfortable in this moment, if it wasn't for the way his fingers flex on his legs.

My mind begins to disassociate as I look at his long, thick fingers. *Even his hands look muscular. Could he kill me with just one or would he need both?* I try to pull myself back to the moment, but it's hard. How is me being here payment for him helping? Why was this even a part of the deal? *How* is he going to help me without getting himself or me killed?

It's thought after thought and scenario after scenario as I try to come up with his reasons for doing this or the turn out. I jolt in my seat when his hand grips my knee for the second time tonight. My eyes swing to his face and the confusion creasing his brows. I then look at the others at the table and notice they are all looking at me with a mixture of concern and confusion.

I clear my throat and stand up quickly, "I'm going to use the restroom."

Moving quickly around the other tables, I try not to stumble over my heels. Gabriel might have said my name but I can barely hear it over the rising panic that's overcoming my body. I can't be surprised that I'm having an anxiety attack out of nowhere. They've been happening since I was young, but I'm not sure what triggered it just now. Probably the situation I've put myself into.

I'm almost to the bathroom when I feel someone grab my elbow. My instincts usually switch between freezing or fighting. Well, tonight is apparently a fight night. I let my elbow get held back and swiftly turn around, aiming my clenched fist for the throat of the person behind me. Before I can make contact, their other hand grabs mine and uses the momentum to push it across my chest. My whole body is forced to stop moving unless I dislocate a shoulder or fall, and then freezing happens. My breath is short pants in and out of my nose, my whole body tight like a snake ready to strike, and my back is starting to sweat. My vision is cloudy but I can see someone around my height stopping me from moving.

Before my memories can start to flood, I feel fingers gently rubbing on my elbow. My vision clears as my breaths come more fully. Elliana stands in front of me, nothing but worry across her features. When she notices I'm becoming relaxed in her hands, she lets go but doesn't back away.

"Liz, are you okay?"

I shake my head and look behind her to see if there might be anyone else coming after me. There's an empty hallway behind her, and I relax further. "Where's Gabriel?" My words come out breathless like I just sprinted a mile.

She smiles sweetly, leading me into the bathroom, "I had him stay at the table. He can be a little.. much, sometimes."

I can only nod as she opens the restroom door and gingerly pulls me inside, leading me to the row of sinks. The clicking of our heels echoes off the dark green walls, and I use it to further stabilize my mind. We stop in front of the middle sink, Elliana leaning her hip against the ledge and crossing her arms over her chest.

"Do you want to talk about what made you run from the table like a scared puppy?"

A light chuckle trickles from my throat and I rest my elbows on the counter, avoiding her eyes. She lets me think silently, something I'm immensely grateful for.

"I just..." I take a deep breath and try again, looking into her eyes through the mirror, "I don't know what I'm doing. Especially here. Why did I have to come here to get Gabriel to help me? *How* is he even going to help? What if he decides not to? What if he can't get me away from Murph without killing himself or me? Is this all I have to do? Because honestly that makes no sense to me. Why would he only want to spend one night with me, at his friend's wedding, and then spend who knows how long getting me out of Murph's reach?"

My breaths are starting to increase in speed again and Elliana doesn't hesitate to rub soothing circles on my back, keeping eye contact, and giving me an understanding smile.

"Well, for starters, you shouldn't worry about *if* Gabriel will get it done. Because he will. Murph doesn't have as much power as he likes to portray. Dominic is the most powerful man in this city. Murph has the tiniest bit on control, which is a pain in our sides, but nothing extreme."

I nod, regulating my breathing, "But *why*, Ell? Why does he even want to help?"

She smiles bigger, "Why don't you ask him?"

"Uh, because I barely know the guy. I barely know *any* of you. Even though I'm currently venting to one of you in a random bathroom at a random wedding." I roll my eyes and drop my head on my forearms with a disgruntled groan.

Elliana's chuckle bounces off the walls surrounding us, her hand moving from my back, and I feel her move down next to me. When I look up into the mirror, she's in the same position as me, giving me a gentle smile.

"Look, Liz, I'm not going to lie to you. Neither Nat or I know the exact reason why Gabe wants to help you. It seems the guys understand but us girls are in the dark. So, I can't answer that for you, but I do know that Gabe is a good man. He wouldn't offer his help if he didn't have a good reason for it.

"In your case, it's either trust him and fix whatever mess you got yourself into or..."

I raise my brows when she doesn't finish, my voice coming out as a whisper, "Or what?"

She shrugs and stands straight, "Or risk your life by staying and doing Murph's bidding until he tires of you and kills you."

My lungs freeze and my muscles lock. Murph wouldn't kill me... Right? I've been the only one capable of doing the stuff he tasks me with, there's no way he would kill me. Unless.. he finds someone else to do what I do.

I force a deep breath into my lungs and stand straight, turning to look into Elliana's hazel eyes, "Well then, I guess I'm stuck with Gabriel."

Elliana smiles brightly and nods in satisfaction. She links her arm through mine and begins to lead us out of the bathroom and back to our table. Once we're halfway back she squeezes my arm tighter, getting my attention.

"Natalie and I train and spar with each other almost every day. Would you like to join us?"

I stop walking, but she keeps our arms linked, looking at me with that killer smile. "I don't know anything about fighting, I don't think you guys would want me there."

She rolls her eyes at me, keeping her smile, "Girl, you almost got me in the throat just a little bit ago. And that would've been a solid hit that took away all my air flow. So, I think you have more potential than you give yourself credit for."

"I don't know..."

"Look, when we get back to the table, we'll exchange numbers and I'll text you our schedule. If you don't want to come that's totally fine. But, if you want to learn, you're welcome any time."

She doesn't give me a chance to respond before dragging me back to the table and plopping me into my seat before claiming her own. I sit with my back straight, refusing to cower with a room full of danger, and begin to look at everyone in the eye. Natalie smiles at me and nods, turning to talk quietly with Elliana. Rick gives me a smirk and a wink, and Dominic wears what I'm starting to realize is a natural scowl but gives me a respectful nod. I finally look to my left at Gabriel.

There's still worry in his bright green eyes but he's smiling like my little escape never happened. I say nothing but smile slightly, instantly noticing the tension leaking out of his shoulders. He doesn't have a chance to ask or say anything before some waiters place our dinners in front of us.

Chapter Five

Elizabeth

I WAKE UP THE NEXT morning to a dull thumping in my head and the sun shining in through my bedroom window. My phone is vibrating nonstop on top of my nightstand and a groan vibrates my throat. I go to turn over and grab the obnoxious thing but roll off my bed, my arm blocking my head from the corner of my nightstand and taking the brunt of the edge. Ignoring the dull pain in my forearm and ribs from the fall, I get to my knees and blindly grab my phone. Cracking open one eye, the incoming call stops and the time smacks me in the face.

8:02 am.

I slept in.

I didn't even wake up from a nightmare, apparently, which is more shocking than anything. Climbing back into bed, I unlock my phone and check my missed calls. Gabriel has called me twice, Elliana once, and to my shock there's nothing from Murph. Before I can click a name to call back I get a text from Elliana.

Hey Liz, would you want to come over for some coffee and breakfast? Natalie left for her honeymoon this morning and Dom took our daughter to his mother's... I'm bored.

Should I be insulted that it seems like the only reason for the invite is because she has no one else to hang out with this morning? Before I can think more, I text her back.

I'd love to. Coffee sounds amazing right about now.

I drop my phone on my chest and rub my temples, trying to stop the thumping there. I definitely drank more last night than I usually do. Behind my eyelids, images flash by of Nat and Ell shoving shots into my hand in the middle of the dance floor. The way the three of us created a circle, bouncing and swaying to the music the DJ mashed together. The one slow song I danced to with Gabriel, my drunk body leaning into his warmth like it could cure every plague in my life... The way he looked down at me with a peculiar sparkle in his field-green eyes, his hungry smile luring me like my personal siren song...

Ugh, don't go there you idiot.

Getting out of bed, my feet drag across the carpet of my room as I reach my closet. There's no way I'm getting fully ready today, so I grab a baggy white hoodie from the left side and toss it on my bed. The black yoga pants and sports bra are next to land on the bed before I drag myself into the bathroom for a shower.

By the time I'm washed, teeth brushed, and my hair is French braided, Elliana has already texted me twice. I get dressed before opening our thread to let her know I'm about to leave but stop when I see her, now, three messages.

What's your address?

Nvm I got it! I'm sending you a car.

Whenever you're ready there's a car outside waiting for you!

Confusion draws my brows together as I go to the window and pull up my blinds. My eyes squeeze shut at the first flash of direct sunlight before I force them partly open and look at the curb in front of my building. There is in fact a car waiting outside, a very scary looking man leaning against the side in all black scanning the sidewalk. I can't deny it's weird but then remind myself who I'm now friends with and what they do. Of course there's going to be a driver they can dispatch for their needs and *of course* he's going to look like he could kill you within three seconds.

Knowing I have someone waiting on me, I rush to put my shoes on, grab my purse, and head downstairs after double checking my door is locked. Stepping out into the light of day, my eyes instantly want to shrivel and I put on the sunglasses from my purse. Being able to see a little better, I walk up slowly to the driver.

Wish I knew this guy's fucking name so I don't look as stupid as I feel.

He's only a few inches taller than I am, but his bulk makes up for it. He's wearing black sunglasses to finish his all black ensemble, and his hands are behind his back. I'm afraid to get too close, so I stop at the back of the car, a good six feet from him.

I don't even have the chance to clear my throat before the man turns to look at me. His face remains unreadable but I can feel him inspecting me.

"Ms. Greene?"

I nod but don't say anything as I watch him reach for the back door handle and open it. He doesn't say anything else and waits for me to get in, still scanning the sidewalk like someone could pop out and kill me at any second. *Little does he know, I'm not important enough for this kind of protection.*

This guy works for Elliana, so I have to assume that nothing bad is going to happen to me in this car. Holding my chin high with false confidence, I step up to the open door and slide in quickly. The driver shuts the door for me and I track him walking around the car to get into the driver's seat. The car starts and I feel his eyes on me through the rearview mirror.

"Seatbelt."

I hide my snort-laugh and strap myself in. Only when we're moving do I look around the interior. I've never been in a car this nice. The whole interior is black, the only color is the red accents running along the seams of the seats and along the dash. The car screams money but not annoyingly. Sometimes I forget there are people out there that not only can have super nice cars, but have the luxury of someone else driving them around—or having someone else watch their back.

It only takes twenty minutes for us to get to Elliana's house and I can't stop my jaw from dropping at the sight. The house is huge, elegant, and *beautiful.* But it's not flashy, which is different from the rich pricks I had in my home town. The driver pulls up the curved drive and stops in front of the steps leading to the front door. By the time my seatbelt is off, he's already outside my door and opening it. I avoid looking at him while I get out, but say a quick thank you before making my way up the stairs.

Elliana opens the huge front door with a smile too big for how much she drank last night, and pulls me into a hug when I come close enough.

"How was your ride here?"

Letting myself enjoy the human contact, I sink into the hug before stepping back, "It was good but you didn't have to do that. I could've taken a cab."

She steps to my side, interlocking our arms, and walks me inside, "Oh stop. What's the point of being the mafia head's wife if I don't use the perks?" I give a soft laugh with her until she stops us and looks at me with high brows, "Wait, do you not have a car? Why would you take a cab?"

Another soft chuckle leaves me as I lift my sunglasses and roll my eyes, "My car was a piece of shit when I moved here and kicked the bucket a year ago when I sold it, so I've had to either walk or take a cab everywhere."

When I look at her again, her perfect eyebrows are pushed together and her lips are pursed.

"No."

A loud singular laugh escapes me, "No? What do you mean, *no?*"

She's already shaking her head, continuing our walk through the house, "I mean, no, that's not safe or acceptable. You should have a secure way of getting to places. Especially in this city."

"I haven't had a problem yet." My voice carries laughter with it but it does nothing to ease her tense features or stop the shake of her head.

We say nothing else as we make a final turn into a big gorgeous kitchen and she sits me down at the island. She gathers some coffee cups, steam wafting from the top, and sits down next to me and slides one over. I take a sip and moan into the liquid.

"Holy shit. This is the best coffee I've ever had."

She giggles quietly taking her own sip before setting it down between her hands and looks at me, "Thank you. It took me way too long to figure out the coffee maker but I finally got everything just right."

"You made this?!" My head swings to her with shock. This is like high-end coffee you'd get at a café in like.. Paris or something.

She nods, "I did. Even though the beginning cups tasted like absolute dog shit."

Ell and I fall into an easy conversation, talking like we've known each other longer than a day. She talks more than I do, telling me about how her and Dominic met, how she grew up in the mafia and what that was like, and how her and Dominic's love got to the point it is today. There's bits where I have a feeling she's leaving out some things, like her father and how he died, and violent acts, but I don't pry. I'm so captured by her stories that I barely register when she refills our coffees, or how two perfectly made omelets end up in front of us.

When she finishes her story of her and Dom, my heart is close to leaping out of my chest with want. Their love story might have had a lot of downs but the highs outweigh those without a doubt.

I have the idea that she's going to ask me more about myself since she's warmed me up with her stories. Part of me wants to trust her with the details of my life but, another part thinks it's better left buried where no one can ever find it.

Before she can ask me a question, I ask one of my own that's been on my mind since the car showed up outside my building.

"How did you find my address?"

Her eyes go wide for a split second before she smooths it out with a small smile, "Oh, I asked Gabe what it was."

"And how would he know?"

She gives me a confused but amused look, "Uh, he drove you home last night. Do you not remember that?"

My face mirrors her confusion as I search my memories. Gabriel holding me up as we exit the wedding. Sliding clumsily into the passenger seat of a blurry car. A warmth on my knee while my face cooled against a window. Strong hands leading me into my apartment. But nothing after that.

"Fuck." The curse slips out on a breath and my wide eyes swing to Ell who's trying to hold back her laughter. "It's not funny! I barely know him and he drove me home when I was too drunk to even stand on my own! What if I puked in his car?!"

Elliana bursts out laughing, leaning onto the counter for support. I can't help but to laugh with her. I'm laughing because hers is infectious, *and* I've never drank to the point that I was that vulnerable with strangers. There's something about the fact that I did, that I don't want to dwell on.

We both finally get the laughter out and gather out breath. Our hands holding our stomach from the ache of laughing so hard. She looks over at me, wiping a tear from her eye, and pats my leg with the other.

"If you're worrying about the fact that you were that drunk and he took you home, don't. You should've seen him last night when we were getting a little too far gone. He wouldn't let anyone near you except Nat and me. It was endearing and hilarious at the same time. I've never seen him act like that before."

My remaining laughter carries into my words, "Well I appreciate the reassurance, but I'm not going to think on that second part."

"Why not?"

My shoulders lift in a tense not-at-all casual shrug, "We're just doing business. This is, and will stay, totally professional."

She snorts and side-eyes me while picking up her coffee, "Right, good luck with that."

Chapter Six

Gabriel

MY FOOT EFFORTLESSLY shifts gears and I tuck close to the tank of my bike as I speed down the highway. The music blasting in my helmet does nothing to stop my mind from wandering to Elizabeth.

The way her hips swayed to the music at the wedding. Her sharp tongue coming out to play even more with the alcohol buzzing in her system. Her shining hazel eyes that changed between more green or more brown with the shift in lighting.

The way she held onto me when we danced together...

I couldn't stop myself from calling her this morning to make sure she was okay. She could barely get inside her own apartment without leaning on me with most of her weight. I don't think she noticed how I knew where she lived or how I was able to get into her apartment—and I doubt that she would remember it today.

Getting her changed out of her dress and into more comfortable clothes had been the most agonizing thing I've had to do. Even though I was respectful in her state and kept my eyes either closed or averted, I have never been so hard in my life. The warmth of her skin under my hands and the breathless way she said my name...

I *know* she would never have said my name like that if she was sober, but it didn't stop my body from sending blood straight to my dick.

Elizabeth still hasn't called me back or even texted me today but I know she's been at Elliana and Dominic's since this morning. Since it's early afternoon and I haven't gotten a text from Ell saying she left, that's where I'm headed. I want nothing more than to spend casual time with Elizabeth but, we need to get things moving on our 'deal'.

Right as I'm coming up to the house, I see Dom getting out of his own car. The amount of shit I want to give him for driving a mom car is almost too much to resist. I park my bike next to him and turn it off. I swing off and start walking to the house without looking at Dom. I could bet a thousand dollars that he has a shit eating smirk on his face right now.

Pulling off both my gloves, I swing my backpack over one shoulder before stuffing them inside. Dom falls into step beside me as we climb the steps, only to stop me before opening the door.

I glare at him, only to realize he can't see my face through the visor of my helmet. "Can we go inside please?"

He shakes his head slightly and smiles smally, clapping a hand on my shoulder, "You know what you're doing, kid?"

"Of course."

He raises a brow, "You sure about that? How are you going to handle this moving forward, knowing that she doesn't want to get too close to you."

I take a deep breath, and shrug while I answer, "I'm going to try my hardest not to push her but I'm not going to hide that I'm interested in her."

"That doesn't sound like too bad of a plan..."

He wants to say more, I know he does. I begin to tap my foot on the tile lining their porch and cross my arms over my chest. I'm not in the mood to have this conversation, I just want to see her and make sure she's okay before taking the biggest risk I've ever taken.

"...But? I know it's coming just spit it out."

Dom sighs and rubs his eyes before pinning me with his 'boss' look, "Gabriel. You're in a place that both Rick and I were in. Not wanting to fight your feelings, but having a woman who is. Because trust me, she is. I saw the way she looked at you when she thought no one was looking, and the way she danced with you last night. There's a part of her that wants you, but... The other part, that is closed off and bricked in, is what's making her act like this is purely business.

"My advice? Take it slow, don't corner her, and try to keep it mostly professional until she feels comfortable enough to let you in a little more. Don't do anything stupid. This business you're taking care of for her? It's already dangerous, and both Rick and I agreed we'd help you how we could, but you need to be careful. Not just with her but with Murph too."

I sigh and tip my head up, closing my eyes. He's not wrong. Elizabeth seems like she's in a delicate state while also being in the worst situation she could have gotten herself into. I *also* know that both Dom and Rick did the exact opposite of what he just suggested.

There's not a chance to respond before the front door swings open, and my head tilts down to find Ell standing there with a bright smile and rosy cheeks. *What have they been doing in there all morning?*

Ell sets her sights on her husband and lunges towards him. Dom catches her with ease, giving her a full, sweet, smile. They start talking lowly with each other but I tune it out as I walk into the house, giving them their privacy. I make it only a couple feet into the foyer before stopping in my tracks as Elizabeth turns the corner.

"Ell, did you get distracted by your—" She stops mid-sentence as her eyes come up from her phone. Her socks have her sliding slightly with how quickly she stops walking, and I let myself smile behind my helmet.

I tilt my head as I look over her outfit. Her socks are black with skunks scattered around them, her legs being hugged deliciously by black yoga pants that accentuate the curve of her hips. Her top half is only covered by a sports bra, the sight tightening my muscles so I don't draw her into me and tell her all the dirty things I'm trying not to think of.

My voice comes out low and rough, "Elizabeth."

I see her throat work with a swallow and my smile turns hungry, even though she can't see it. My foot lifts without thought, taking a step towards her, and her own retreats a step. My head cocks to the other side, like a predator sizing their meal. Her hands are hanging limply at her sides, but her chest moves with fast breaths, a blush of dark pink racing through her cheeks.

A deep chuckle rattles my chest, the darkness in me seeing a game ready to play out. Again, I take a step forward and she retreats a step. I let my backpack slide down my arm and land on the floor with a thump. Elizabeth, my fiery-sweet pup, watches me closely like she is waiting for a chance to run.

"Cat got your tongue, Shchenok?"

She starts to say something but clears her throat and tries again, "I didn't think you'd be here."

I stand to my full height, taking another step and watching her retreat once more. "I came to talk to you about our deal. Time to start working on a plan." My voice is a version I've only heard a rare few times, dark and hungry.

She does another thick swallow and chances a look behind her, looking for someone she won't find. I use the moment to take a quiet step forward, and she jumps when she turns back around. All my muscles are tense, holding back from grabbing her like I want to.

Keep it professional, dumbass.

But I can't, not when I can see her tits pushing against the restraint of her bra with her fast breathing, or the wide pupils in the middle of her Siren eyes.

Her voice comes out soft, "Okay. Let's make a plan."

I hum deeply and take another step, almost close enough to reach out and touch her, but she retreats once again. My entire body prepares for a chase.. and I want one. *Badly.*

"Is there a reason you're walking away from me, Elizabeth?"

She shakes her head slightly, "No, not at all."

My head tilts, "Are you sure about that?"

Our feet do the same dance, the distance between us remaining the same even though we move further into the house. She nods but looks behind me, hope briefly flaring in her eyes.

"Elliana and Dominic are outside. There's just me right now, Shchenok."

A laugh rumbles up my throat as her gaze snaps back to my helmet. I watch with fascination as her pupils dilate further while she looks over my helmet and then down to my shoulders and arms. She seems like someone who would have some secret kinks.. and by the way her blush increases, I can only assume I'm correct.

"Run."

Her eyes widen, her shoulders tensing, "W—what?"

"I said, *run*, Elizabeth."

She only hesitates for half a second before turning and sprinting around the corner. I hear her quick footfalls as they echo down the hallway. I give her a total of ten seconds before following her, trying to keep myself from running at full speed.

I can hear the Dominic in my head yelling at me that this is exactly the *opposite* of what he said. But my ears ring with two words, those two words racing through my veins as my legs chase the distance between her and I.

Catch her.

Chapter Seven

Elizabeth

I KNEW DOMINIC WAS on his way home, but I didn't expect to find Gabriel tagging along. I wasn't sure that it was him at first, until he said my name. I'd know his voice anywhere, even with the helmet making it muffled and dark. Which is disturbing considering we've only talked a handful of times.

But, when he said my name this time, it was different. It was hungry... Almost sounding angry. Am I happy that he showed up unannounced when I'm in a sports bra and yoga pants? Absolutely not. Did my body get the memo? Same answer. I was wet within seconds after he said my name. Gabriel is already extremely attractive. With bright luring eyes, kissable full lips, a jawline that could cut marble, long thick legs, and arms that I could consider porn, he's practically a walking orgasm.

But with a helmet on, in all black, with a dangerous and sexy vibe rolling off of him in waves, he's a walking orgasm on crack. The kinky side of me couldn't stop my physical reaction.

Now, I'm running. I'm running like I would be eaten alive by a rabid wolf if I'm caught. I was confused when he said it the first time. But when he demanded it thickly the second time, I took off like my life depended on it. Because there's a part of me that thinks it does. I couldn't see the expression behind his helmet, but I could feel it. The desire, the darkness, the hunger, the *need.*

I have no idea where I'm going in this house. Something I'm willing to bet Gabriel knows. He could corner me without a second thought. I've rounded two more corners and am now in the den that Ell and I were watching tv in. His heavy steps sound off down the hallway, moving quicker than I expected. Looking around frantically, I see a door in the back of the room and sprint for it. My entire body is tense as I swing open the door.

I come face to face with a closet—half of the room stacked with shelves of blankets and pillows. *Looks like Elliana is a blanket girl just like me.*

Gabriel's quick steps are getting closer, coming in faint compared to my pounding heart. I shove myself into the closet, not trying to find the light, and pull the door closed behind me. I turn the handle at the last second so it closes with no sound and let my eyes adjust. Trying to quiet my breathing, I put my hand over my mouth and breathe deeply in my nose. I definitely need to exercise more.

He's in the room.

There's no attempt at hiding his loud footfalls, he wants me to know he found me. My thighs clamp together, only making my clit want more. There has to be something wrong with me because a deep dark part of me is thoroughly enjoying this. I back up as I hear him walk around the room. My shoulders start to push through some hanging coats and I slowly move further back, hoping I can hide.

The light streams under the door until two thick-black lines part it. *Shit.* The door opens slowly, inch after slow inch appearing of Gabriel's tall form. My breath hitches in my throat as the door finishes opening and he steps inside the closet. He doesn't remove his helmet, and he doesn't turn on the light. Gabriel stalks towards me, his energy palpable in the small space he's now trapped me in. There's a little to no chance of getting by him.

My body locks against the wall at my back as he gets within a foot of me. I can see my reflection in his visor—a whimper I can't begin to decipher wiggles up my throat and he freezes. A low animalist growl vibrates from his chest and I suck in a sharp breath.

"Not fast enough, moy malen'kiy lepestok[*]."

My hands fist at my sides, my breathing once again becoming erratic, and my irritation pushing through to the front.

"I bet I could've gotten away if I knew my way around this house."

He hums deeply, stepping closer until his shoes brush my sock covered toes. "We'll have to try this in a place you think you could win then, next time."

My eyes widen slightly, my lungs freezing on my inhale. He leans forward, letting his helmet rest against the bar holding the coats and shoves his arms in until they cage me against the wall. I want to close my eyes so I don't have this terrifyingly-seductive sight in front of me. I should be scared. I should be quaking. I *should* be taking advantage of his open body to get in a hit and make a run for it. But I don't.

Because even if it confuses me and I hate it... I want this.

I want this hidden moment. I want to see what will happen if I don't reject him and he loses even an inch of control. Against my better judgement, I want *him*.

"Who says there will be a next time?"

His low laugh sounds dark from behind his helmet, "There will be a next time."

I shake my head but freeze once more when his hand lifts towards my face. His arm is flexed with restraint as he trails a singular finger down my cheek, the gentle touch at odds with the tension in the rest of his body. I take a deep breath and close my eyes, allowing myself this second to melt underneath the strength and warmth in that one finger. He trails it over my jaw and to the side of my neck.

My eyes snap open as his whole hand comes around my throat. Despite my trauma, my body practically melts on the spot. He must notice that I relaxed in his grip, because he tightens his fingers, pushing into the sides of my neck and groans. A soft moan pushes through my lips.

"To, chto ya khochu sdelat' s toboy, lepestok[*]."

I have no idea what he means—but by the way he slowly releases me and steps back—I can guess that he would have me right in this closet if I allowed it.

The crotch of my yoga pants are soaked with the evidence of what he does to me. My thighs are still clamped shut, and they start to rub together unconsciously. His head shifts slightly downward and I have to force my legs to stop moving. His hands clench at his side, his chest moving with a deep breath. I look down to his pants, seeing his erection pushing against the zipper of his black jeans. My throat closes to hold off the moan at the sight of his dick wanting to jump out of its confines all because of *me*.

"Show me how wet you are, Shchenok."

Oh, god.

My sweaty palms press against the wall behind me, my brain fighting with itself on if I should obey. I must hesitate too long for his liking, because he leans forward and speaks with a growl behind his words.

"Show. Me."

I lift a single hand to the waist of my pants. Slowly, I slip past the tight waistband and move between my thighs. My breath catches when the pads of my fingers slide over my throbbing clit.

Gabriel shakes his head slightly and my whimper falls free between us as I continue forward. I swirl two fingers around my entrance, my eyes falling closed for a single heartbeat. I open them again heavily, pulling my hand free from my pants and holding my fingers in front of me for Gabriel to see.

His whole body tenses impossibly further, clearly restraining himself. He lets out a breathless 'fuck' and moves to come forward again, but stops himself.

"Yesli by ty tol'ko pozvolil mne prikosnut'sya k tebe, kak ya mechtayu[*]..."

I don't know how many times now he's said something, I'm assuming in Russian, in that low and gravelly voice. I'm tired of not knowing what he's saying to me. I want to know everything he says, whether it's good or not.

"If you're going to say things like that, you need to say them in English." My words come out a little more breathless than I would like, but I ignore that when his head tilts slightly. I'm sure he's raising a brow in challenge behind that stupid helmet.

"Alright, Elizabeth. You want to know what I'm saying to you? Fine. I want to touch you, to *break* you. I want to see everything that makes you tick. I want to see how your face contorts when you come. If I were a better man, I would tell you how I want to make love to your delicious, soft body. But, I'm not that man. I want to *fuck* you, to *own* you, to make you *mine*. To hear you scream my name is one of my top fantasies.

"I fall asleep picturing your soft-pink lips wrapped around my cock as I shove it down your throat, my thumb smearing the tears that streak down your rosy cheeks. If I could do with you what I wish, you would be tied up for only me to see and have easy access to."

I don't think I'm breathing. Never has a man said those things to me.. and I enjoyed them. Despite what my brain should be saying, all I hear is 'fuck yes'. I want everything he said. If there's one man who could make my wildest fantasies come true, I know it's Gabriel.

My mouth opens and closes, my tongue trying to move to speak back to him. I'm stuck picturing everything he said. Breaking in his arms, hoping he'll put me back together when he's done using me.

But, I need to fight it. I told myself that this would stay just business, and I need to continue to do that.

No matter how much I want to jump on him, right in this dark closet, where no one would know what happens.

My face is an inferno from my embarrassing arousal. We continue to stand in silence while my ears hear a loop of his words. His posture is still tight, like holding himself back from enacting those words is one of the hardest things he's had to do. I open my mouth to hopefully change subjects, but he beats me to it.

"Come on Elizabeth, let's go get you seated somewhere preferably more comfortable than this closet."

He waits until I'm no longer leaning on the wall before grabbing my hand and leading me to the couch in the den. My cheeks still burn as I look down at our hands. His hand practically swallows mine, the heat from his calloused palm oddly comforting.

Stop enjoying this, it needs to be professional.

But I can't bring myself to let his hand go. Gabriel deposits me on the couch and I look to my lap, wishing my hair was down so I could hide the blush on my face. He continues to stand in front of me, unmoving. When I still don't look at him, he grabs my chin between his pointer finger and thumb, and tilts my head up. I blink quickly at the bright lights shining down around him from the ceiling. Of course he looks like a fucking angel right now. *Fallen angel maybe.*

His helmet is finally off and his sweet smile is present, stretching his soft looking lips that I want to taste. He runs his thumb heavily over my bottom lip, biting his own. He groans as he closes his eyes, relinquishing my chin, and breathes deeply like he's trying to find patience. I take the couple of seconds he gives, and look at the dick outline between his legs. Yup, he's still totally hard. *Right* in front of my face. When he opens his eyes again, and looks down at me, the playful and hungry man from the closet is nowhere to be found.

Now, I'm looking up at the mafia man that could both destroy and save me.

"Do you need anything before we start talking about our deal?" I shake my head, his eyes dipping quickly to the generous cleavage my sports bra shows. "How about a shirt?"

I look around the couch and find my hoodie. I move to get up but Gabriel sees what I'm going for and grabs it quickly, holding it out to me with heat in his eyes. Putting it on as fast as I can, I keep my eyes averted until he sits down a few feet from me. When I finally look at him, he has a foot resting on his opposite knee, his arms spanning over the back of the couch. He looks so relaxed I would never have guessed he just chased me through this house and said those dirty things to me.

I clear my throat, "So... What do you plan on doing to help me?"

"Well, first, I need to know a few things." I nod, and he continues. "One, what do you do for Murph exactly, besides work in his diner. Two, how often does he require you to meet with him. Three, does he provide you with your apartment or anything else."

His tone doesn't exactly portray that he's asking these things, but more like demands the answers, and I ignore how much I actually like that.

"Well, I do a lot of cyber stuff for him and sometimes help him with his bookkeeping. He never has specific days planned out to see me, he kind of just calls and requests for me to meet him whenever he wants. And he originally helped get my apartment but I pay for it by myself now. He doesn't provide anything for me except extra pay for what I do outside of the diner, but it isn't much extra."

The more I talked, the more his face morphed, now he's sitting there with a full scowl and irritation is coming off of him in waves. He says nothing as he looks at me, his broad chest moving with deep breaths.

He finally slants his head, his eyes squinting slightly, "What cyber stuff do you do?"

"Um... Some coding or building his systems and occasional tracking of certain people."

His eyes flare with an emotion he masks too quickly for me to catch before humming deeply. Some people are surprised to hear that I can code because, well, I didn't go to college. But, you can learn a lot of things without the education system.

When he doesn't say anything else and continues to stare at me, I break eye contact and look around the room. I can't do eye contact for too long, mostly while I talk. It makes me uncomfortable. Gabriel lets us sit in complete silence for a little longer and I start to grow antsy. My leg begins to bounce on the couch cushion and I take a quick look at him. He's still looking at me, a certain expression that tells me he's thinking pretty hard about something.

I go to open my mouth but he beats me to it, for the second time, remaining perfectly relaxed against the couch.

"Okay. First, as much as I want to, I can't *fully* take you away from Murph right now. It will cause a lot of deaths that none of us want to deal with. So, the first step is going to be moving you into a different location that Murph won't be able to access."

I quirk a brow, "And where would that be? Granted, Murph wouldn't be able to track me without help, but I doubt there's many places in this city I can afford to move to and—"

Without breaking a beat Gabriel continues, "You'll be moving in with me."

Chapter Eight

Gabriel

ELIZABETH ONLY LOOKS confused for point three seconds before her confusion turns to an angry-shock.

"The *fuck* I am."

I can't stop the smirk from contorting my lips at her response. It's better than her full on losing her shit. I knew before coming into this talk that inviting her to live with me is the best first step, and also that she would fight it. But, she'll realize that it's the only option we can safely accomplish before I look into Murph's obsession with her a little more.

"Look, the only way to safely take you away from Murph's grasp is to first get you somewhere safe that he won't be able to get to you. Because if you don't think he's going to retaliate once we start to ease you out, you're mistaken."

She crosses her arms and leans back into the couch, staring at me with squinted eyes. I let her process her options, and my perfectly valid point. There's not many places she can safely go to, especially with how little money she has. I've seen her bank account, she makes about as much as my mom and I did when my father stopped giving us child support.. maybe less.

"Why do I have to live with you? Why can't I live somewhere else?"

I don't move from my casual position even though my body is fighting to touch her.

"Well, a good reason is one you just said. You can't afford to live anywhere else. Plus, my house is one of the safest locations in this city. Besides Dom and Rick's houses."

Her eyes squint even tighter, "Why can't I stay with one of the girls at their house? Elliana gave me a tour earlier, they have plenty of space here."

I nod slightly, "Good point, but, Rick and Nat just got married. I lived with them before they were married and I can tell you right now, you'll have trouble sleeping with their... Loud night activities. Ell and Dom on the other hand, they are busy with their own businesses and their daughter. Would you want to take time they don't have to make sure you're safe?"

Elizabeth relaxes her face and her shoulders slump as she looks to her knees, "No, I don't want to interrupt any of their time. Especially with their daughter." I go to speak but she looks back up at me with newfound strength, "There will be rules."

I smile broadly and motion forward with my hand, "By all means, set any rules you want, Shchenok. I already have one of my own."

"Which is what?"

"I won't touch you, unless of course it's to protect you."

Her brows push together and her spine straightens, "You won't touch me? Like you won't even try to flirt touch or hug me or anything?"

I shake my head once, "No."

"Why?"

There's a part of me that wants to relish that she seems a little disappointed that that's my only rule, maybe play on that a little bit. But, I can't let myself because then I'll break that rule. So, instead, I tell her the truth with no emotion attached.

"Because, Elizabeth. When you want me to actually touch you, you'll beg for it."

Her eyes widen but she remains quiet, slightly shimmying her butt against the couch. The way her ass jiggled while she ran flashes through my mind, but I remain in my relaxed position. She stares at me for a minute longer before nodding.

"I'll type out whatever other rules so that you'll be able to read them over. How soon do you expect me to move in?"

I tilt my head side to side like I'm thinking, knowing full well when I expect her to be in my home.

"Tomorrow morning will be fine."

She stands up quickly, "Tomorrow morning?! That's too soon. I need to pack. I need to end my lease on the apartment, because I'm not going to pay for somewhere I'm not living. I need to figure out how I'm going to get to work. Where do you even live? Will I have to go far for work everyday? Because I don't want to do that. Plus—"

I cut her off from her rambling and hold my hand up, "Elizabeth. Breathe. It's not too soon. You will have help packing. You apartment lease is already taken care of. The diner, which you won't be working at soon, is only a fifteen minute drive. If you have other questions, I can answer them, but I need you to calm your mind and sit down."

She plops down with little grace and crosses her arms, "What do you mean my lease is taken care of?"

"I ended it before I came over."

"You what?!"

I shrug, "I ended it. There's no penalty, you have a week to get everything out, and your deposit plus the left over rent for the month is already in your account."

She relaxes into the couch, uncrossing her arms in favor of hugging her middle and looks to the ground. Her chest moves with three deep breaths, mumbling something like 'stupid controlling mafia men' under her breath, before looking at me with calm strength.

"Thank you. It *very much* bugs me you did it without even making sure I would *agree* to this stupid-ass plan, but thank you nonetheless."

I nod, "You're welcome. Now, I know we have more things to go over but we can do that once you've settled into your new home."

Giving her a big smile, I stand and gesture to the entryway of the den. She takes my lead, without the smile, and stands to leave. We walk down the hall in silence, her steps quick to keep at my side, and I lead her into the kitchen where Elliana and Dominic are waiting at the island.

Chapter Nine

Elizabeth

ELLIANA IS HELPING me throw all my clothes and things easy to pack into boxes in my room. Gabriel and Dominic are getting a truck to carry my boxes, but we'll come back another day for my bigger items and put them in storage.

Now that I'm packing, I'm realizing how little I truly have. And how crappy my furniture is. I got pretty much everything I have from thrift stores, Goodwill, or other places that had preowned furniture or clothing. Comparing how I'm living to how my new 'friends' live gives me a type of sadness I haven't experienced in years. There's also a swarm of different emotions trying to push through to the top to be noticed. One of those is irritation that I'm having to do this, even if I understand why. Murph can be violent, even though I've never seen it—and I know that when someone betrays him, he never goes easy on them.

I'm throwing random shit from my dresser drawers into a box when Elliana grabs my shoulder and turns me.

"*Elizabeth*, are you okay?"

"Huh?"

She lets go of my shoulder, her eyes softening around the edges, "I said your name three times. Are you doing okay? Is this too much to handle right now?"

I shake my head, "No, it's not. I'm okay. I was just stuck in my head, it happens sometimes."

She nods like she understands and steps back a little bit, motioning around the room. I look around and see that pretty much everything is packed and the boxes are folded shut.

"You have the last box and then we're done. Do you want Dom and I to come over and help you unpack?"

"No, but thank you. I'm sure I'll be okay to unpack it on my own. Plus, I think I just want to hide out for the rest of the night. Snack on some junk food and binge some Netflix."

Ell gives me a sad smile and nods, "Well, if you need anything don't hesitate to call me. Dom and Gabe are waiting downstairs at the truck, they're going to load everything for us. You done with that box? Want to wait outside with me?"

I nod, folding the box up and closing my dresser drawer. I say nothing as I follow her out of my apartment and to the truck that waits for my belongings. Ell stands at my side as we lean against the truck, watching the guys carry boxes out of my apartment building. Every time Gabriel comes out with a box or two, I can't stop my eyes from watching the way his muscles bunch in certain places to hold the weight of the boxes. There's always been something about men's arms and hands that just does it for me, and his are a prime example.

I shift my gaze to the many cracks in the sidewalk as the guys load box after box in the truck. My mind starts drifting to when I moved into my foster mothers home. The way I only had two boxes and a suitcase when I was practically dumped on her doorstep. I was expecting a foster parent to be heartless, only in it for the monthly pay they got from it, and to pay very little attention to me.. but I was wrong. I got lucky with my foster mom.

She was the kindest woman I'd ever met. Her and her husband, who had died the year before I got there, weren't able to have children. She'd been waiting to become a foster parent and gave up her hope once he died. Then she got a call about taking me in the day after my father died. When she opened her door to me for the first time, there were tears in her eyes and a wide smile on her face as she pulled me in to the warmest hug I'd received in my whole life.

I thrived in her home. She treated me like she'd been the one raising me all along... Until she got sick...

"Elizabeth."

My head snaps up at Gabriel's voice and I give him a small fake smile, hoping I haven't been in my head for too long. When I look around us, Elliana and Dominic have already left, leaving me standing alone with Gabriel.

"Where'd you go?"

I look back to him with wrinkled brows, "What?"

He gives me a soft smile, "Where'd you go in that pretty head of yours?"

"Oh, nowhere that matters. Are we ready to go? Where did Ell and Dominic go?"

"They just left to go pick up their daughter. All the boxes are loaded. I have someone who's going to drive the truck to my house."

I nod and look around again to break eye contact, "How are we getting there then?"

"We're taking my bike."

My brows rise and I look to where he starts to point. There is indeed a beautiful all black sports bike sitting behind the truck. Nerves start to kick up in my stomach as I side-eye Gabriel. He's smiling fondly at his bike before turning it to me. Clearing my throat, I walk over to the bike and start looking it over. I know nothing about motorcycles other than the death risk you take when you get on one.

Gabriel grabs two helmets out of the truck before joining me and hands me a dark blue one with a black-tinted visor. I take it with sweaty hands and look up to him. There must be the question in my eyes on how to put this on because he chuckles deeply and takes it back. Holding the straps on the bottom, he pulls them apart and lifts it over my head. His knuckles brush down my cheeks as he slides the helmet over my head until it sits snuggly.

He tilts my head up with a crooked finger and begins to latch the straps together. Once he's done, he lifts up the visor and gives me a big smile.

"All snug?" I nod. "Wiggle your head around a little, it shouldn't be slipping around."

I do as he says and bob my head around, not feeling the helmet slip around on my hair. "Yeah, all good."

He gives me clipped nod, his eyes darkening for a fraction of a second, then turns and puts his own helmet on. He taps a button on a device connected to the side of his helmet then reaches toward me. My body locks but he continues to reach for me like he didn't see it. He pushes something on the side of my own helmet and a beep sounds in my ears.

"Can you hear me?"

I jump slightly at his deep voice coming in through the helmet and I nod.

"Good. You'll be able to talk to me on the ride if you need to, but I'm going to be playing music also so it isn't totally silent while we ride. Sound good?"

I clear my throat, "I've never been on a motorcycle before."

"Well, I'm happy to be the only one to take you for a ride."

My brows furrow and he winks before shutting both our visors and swinging his leg over the bike to settle into his seat.

"What do you mean *only one*?"

His deep chuckle comes through the speakers, causing my arms to break out in goosebumps. "YA budu yedinstvennym, s kem ty kogda-libo budesh' katat'sya, Lepestok.[*] Get on, put your feet on the pegs sticking out."

I look to see two tiny rectangles poking out from the sides of the bike. Taking a deep breathe, I move to get on. My hand rests on his shoulder, a tingle going up my arm, and I try to swing my leg over. I can't get fully on from the height of the bike and take my leg off the seat and look to Gabriel.

"How the fuck do I get on, it's too tall."

"Put one foot on a peg, use me as balance, step on it, and swing your other leg over."

Doing as he says, I finally manage to get on the bike. My hands squeeze the back of his jacket tightly when I feel the bike wobble a little. Without verbal instructions, he grabs my arms and wraps them around his torso. I squeeze him tightly and try to keep my nerves locked down.

Gabriel grabs my knees, instantly warming them through my yoga pants, and pushes them firmly against his hips.

"You'll want to keep your legs against me and your arms wrapped around. I'll give you a double tap on your knee if I'm going to speed up quickly, so you'll duck down with me. Don't lean away from a turn, you'll make it harder, so lean with me. Any questions?"

I shake my head, feeling the helmet brush against his back. I actually have no thoughts in my mind other than praying we don't crash. Gabriel turns the bike on, tipping it up straight and kicking up the stand. I press myself further against him, holding tighter. One of his hands reaches up and rubs the backs of mine. The bottom of the gloves he wears, that I didn't even notice he put on until now, feel scratchy against my skin. I welcome the body warmth he offers as my chest rests against his hard back.

Gabriel revs the bike and I feel his chest move with silent laughter as I hold him tighter. *Dear lord, please get us there safely so I can smack him.*

Chapter Ten

Gabriel

ELIZABETH HAS BEEN holding on the whole ride like she's trying to crack my ribs. She does pretty good picking up on my signals which brings a smile to my face. I expected her to be scared the whole ride, but after about ten minutes, she loosens her grip. We only have another ten minutes before reaching my house and a part of me wants to lengthen the ride just to keep her pressed against me a little longer.

When we stop at a red light, she leans back to allow me to fully sit up and stretch my back. One of my hands sneaks over and rests on her knee, my thumb rubbing over a spot lightly.

"You doing okay, Shchenok?"

Her soft chuckle barely comes through the speakers, "It's less scary than I thought it would be. I actually think I'm enjoying it. It's kind of.. freeing." There's a pause as I feel her foot bounce on the peg before she continues, "Do you think you could take me riding again another time?"

The smile that stretches my lips is nothing but pure joy. I could tell she started to enjoy it, but I didn't think she'd ask for another ride so soon.

"Any time you want, just let me know."

She says nothing but I feel her body shift like she nodded her head.

The light turns green and we both lean over in synchrony to go. When I get up to speed, I don't stop myself from reaching for her hands around my torso and holding them. Her body tenses for mere seconds before relaxing further onto me. I've never had to focus so hard while I ride. Even with her behind me, my body reacts to the feel of her pressed against my back and her arms around me. When she moves her thumb over my jacket like she's trying to reciprocate the affection, my chest lightens like I've never felt.

It's in this moment that my mind comes to a final decision.

I will kill anyone who tries to take her away from me.

I slow down as I pull into my long driveway. Elizabeth's soft 'wow' whispers through my helmet and I chuckle. My house isn't as big or glamorous as Dom's but it is quite a looker. I helped design it myself, wanting to put my mother's secret love of architecture into the build. Stopping my bike in the garage, I put the stand down and turn it off to help Elizabeth swing from the back.

Once her feet are back on solid ground, I swing off and move to help with her helmet. She lifts her head without prompting and I look down, trying to see through her visor to get a glimpse at her eyes from this angle. My fingers are slow as I undo the buckle and my mind conjures up images of Elizabeth on her knees, looking up at me with wide-teary eyes.

Clearing my throat, I finish unlatching her helmet and help her slide it off. I set hers down on the bike seat, taking off my gloves before undoing my own—the lower pads pressing firmly against my jaw as I slide it off. When I set my helmet next to hers and meet her eyes, my fists clench at my sides. She must not notice that I can see the way her pupils are dilated as she runs those forest-kaleidoscope eyes over my frame. A smirk slips over my lips as I fully turn around and lean back against my bike with my arms crossed.

"My eyes are up here, Elizabeth."

Chapter Eleven

Elizabeth

THE ADRENALINE FROM the ride and from holding Gabriel for so long is roaring so fast through me that it's an effort to keep myself from fidgeting. After he removed my helmet I had to lower my eyes just in case they showed him how much I wanted to jump him. Watching him take off his own helmet was like some kind of drug, the way his thick fingers worked effortlessly to unlatch the buckle had my thighs pushing together. I couldn't help myself from looking him over while he wasn't paying attention.

But I've been caught. My eyes snap to his, and the blush that spreads fire across my cheeks is only rising as his smirk deepens at my silence. I blink quickly and clear my throat, hoping to ease the tension that is slowly building between us.

"So, this is my new temporary home huh?"

I look out the garage and scan over the bright green grass and the high trees bordering the property.

"This is your new home, yes."

My ears don't miss that he didn't say *temporary* as my eyes swing back to meet his. "You forgot to say temporary, Gabriel. I'm only here until it's safe to no longer be."

His smile turns downright deviously-playful, his chin lowering slightly, "YA ne zabyl, lepestok. Teper' ty moy."[*]

My inhale catches halfway in. There's something about the tone he uses when he speaks Russian to me that my body can't help but to react to. With the foreign language confusing me and the deep-dark tone of his voice, a part of me wants to give in and please him in any way he asks. But the other—more smart—part of me smacks me into gear. I glare at him and cross my arms.

"You know I can't understand you."

He nods, "I do."

"But you choose to continue to speak in Russian even though it's things I need to hear."

His smile widens, "Not all things you need to hear."

I roll my eyes even though my blush deepens, understanding his meaning. Throwing my arms towards what I'm assuming is the door to head inside, I give him my best exasperated look.

"Are you going to show me inside or am I living in the garage?"

His eyes darken to a stormy green as he straightens, "You better watch that attitude, Elizabeth. Professional relationship or not, you *will* get a punishment if I see you roll your eyes at me."

My eyebrows shoot up my forehead as my muscles lock. I'm not anywhere near experienced in the bedroom, since I've only slept with one person, but I'm going to assume that punishment would definitely be sexual.. and scary.

He waits patiently for me to acknowledge his words, so I nod once. Turning his back to me without another word he walks to the door I gestured to, and I follow. The moment the door is opened a scent of coffee breezes into my airways and my mouth starts to water. I follow him through a short hallway, coming into a small eating area. He keeps his normal long stride through the room, my legs doing double time to keep up.

We make it into the kitchen and I stop short in the doorway. This kitchen would be a dream if I knew how to actually cook. A six burner gas stove, double oven built into the wall next to it, a double glass-door fridge that looks like it would be in a professional kitchen, all take up the wall to my right. To my left in a massive island with counter tops that look to be made out of the stars, holding a farmhouse sink. The black stools pushed under the island accentuate the forest green paint. Looking around, all the counters match. The cabinets, which there are many of, are all sleek and black, framed by the same forest green that covers the island. Some counter space is occupied by different appliances, that I'm sure cost way more than my annual income.

The whole kitchen looks to be pulled from a fantasy novel based in a magical dark forest. I'm already in love with this house, and this is just the kitchen.

When I'm done drooling over the luxury of the kitchen, my attention gets pulled back to the man that's exudes such strong energy my knees almost buckle. His face is back to looking indifferent to my attention to his space, but I can see in his eyes that he's enjoying my reaction.

Without a word, he continues walking to the entryway across the kitchen, and I dutifully follow. After another short hallway, we emerge into a much bigger dining room. This room is dark colors with light accents. The long dining table a dark wood, seating ten, and taking up the middle of the room, is the nicest table I've ever seen. The back wall has a liquor cabinet and table, while the side wall has a matching long table that looks like possibly a dessert table. I don't have much time to take it all in, because Gabriel keeps walking.

We finally get out into the foyer of the house. The huge front door to my right is mostly glass panes. The color in here is almost the opposite of the other rooms. It's mostly a light grey with darker accents, one of those accents being the black staircase to my left. I stop in the middle of the marble flooring and turn in a circle.

Never in my life did I think I would be around such money.

When I look up I find a black chandelier, the normal lights replaced with candle lights, giving this space an older feeling.

I jump at the sound of Gabriel's voice so close to my back. "You have a beautiful smile, Shchenok, when it's an honest one."

I turn to find him looking down at me like he's lost, his brows pushing together slightly.

"Thank you.." My voice sounds so small in the big open area.

Gabriel takes a deep breath and steps back, his face smoothing out and giving the same look as when we talked about the deal. All professionalism.

He gestures behind him to a set of black double doors, "That is my office, I ask if you go in that it's when I'm home and you knock first." I nod and he walks towards the back of the stairs, revealing an almost hidden hallway with another glass door leading outside, "This hallway leads to a library, guest bedroom, bathroom, and living room."

He turns back around, not giving me a chance to actually look at the rooms. We walk in silence as he ascend the stairs. At the top, the wall in front of me is barely a wall but a bunch of windows, showing off the huge backyard surrounded by a line of trees.

Gabriel turns left, not slowing his stride, "To this side is two more bedrooms, and a gym. You can pick between either of these rooms, they've both been cleaned and prepared just in case."

He opens the first bedroom door and I stay in the doorway, looking over the room. The walls are white, the floor is a cherry wood, and the only color is the navy blue of the bed sheets. When I step back, he leads me to the next room further down the hall.

This time when he opens the door I step further into the room, drawn in by the scene of color around me. The walls are covered in cherry blossom flowers, portraying that they are being blown by an invisible wind. The four poster bed is covered in white sheets in front of a wall painted with a cherry blossom tree. All the furniture is a dark-brown wood, completing the illusion that you're living with this tree. There's a double door with the same wood leading to what must be the closet, and another matching single door that must lead to a bathroom. I've never seen a cherry blossom tree in person, but I've always loved it's beauty. It could possibly be my favorite tree.

I turn to Gabriel with a smile on my face, "I like this one."

The muscle in his jaw ticks, and he turns back around to keep walking.

Over the next five minutes he shows me the very equipped gym, then over to the other side of the stairs which is another living room type space, and his bedroom (which he doesn't actually show me). As we're walking down the stairs, I catch how the muscles in his back are tense.

My voice comes out soft, but echoes off the walls anyway, "Gabriel?"

He stops at the bottom of the stairs and turns to watch me land next to him. My insides start to twist when he still doesn't smile, something I got the feeling he did more often than not.

"Is everything okay?"

He gives a clipped nod, "I have some stuff I need to work on, I'll be in my office until dinner. Your boxes should be here momentarily, the men will carry them into the room you picked. Feel free to explore."

With that, he leaves me with a knotted stomach in unfamiliar territory. I watch his office door shut quietly before sitting down on the bottom step.

Everything was fine before we started the house tour. He seemed to be in a good mood, I don't know what could've happened or what I did to get him to all of a sudden shut down like that. He's been so... *open* with me so far.

Is he realizing that having me here is more of a burden than what he wants?

Chapter Twelve

Elizabeth

MY CLOTHES AND NECESSITIES are unpacked, I'm showered, and I looked over the library and living rooms. Now, I'm sitting at the smaller dinner table with a plate of delicious-smelling food.

Alone.

I look over at Gabriel's food for the tenth time since I sat down. He said he would see me at dinner, didn't he? It's been four hours since he left me to go into his office and I haven't heard a peep from him since.

My bare foot makes a slapping sound as it bounces against the tile as I grow more irritated. He must know that dinner is ready and that I'm waiting for him. He either doesn't care, or expects me to eat on my own and finish the day like he doesn't exist.

I make a final decision and stand quickly from my chair. Grabbing his plate of food, I navigate to his office. Just because he's not coming to eat with me doesn't mean he doesn't need to eat. I stop outside of his office doors, hesitating with my hand lifted ready to knock.

After a deep breath to keep my irritation at a minimum, I slam my knuckles against the thick door three times. There's no answer. I don't waste my time with another knock and swing the door open, immediately finding him behind his desk across from me at the back of the room. The closer I walk the more his face becomes clear.

He's wearing dark glasses that somehow make his eyes pop, his brows pushing together to create a crease between them. His big hand is closed over his mouth and his eyes are moving back-and-forth over the screen quickly.

I stop on the other side of his desk and wait, plate in hand. He doesn't look up. He doesn't even notice I'm standing here.

Talk about making a girl feel invisible.

I walk around to his side of the desk, leaning over his shoulder to read what he's doing. Knowing I'm invading not only his space but his privacy, I keep my breathing soft so he doesn't all of a sudden notice me. When I focus on his computer screen my eyes almost bulge at the code there. I've never seen such magnificent work done.

Is this what he does?

He moves his fingers like he's going to go further down but I lift my free hand and point to a line.

"That's not correct."

His whole body tenses, just now seeing I'm in his space, and he swings irritable eyes to mine.

"What?"

I clear my throat and put my finger under the line I'm talking about, "This line, there's something wrong with it. Depending on what you're doing, there's either something missing or something extra."

His eyes calm and he raises a single brow, turning back to look over the line I'm talking about. He leans a little closer and says something under his breath. When he turns to look back at me I expect to find him mad that I'm correcting his almost impeccable work, but instead he's smirking and his eyes are shining.

"Well look at that. Moy malen'kiy lepestok, you found an error I've been trying to find for quite a while now." He eyes take a quick dip down to the plate in my hand then at the clock on his desk. "Shit, I'm sorry I've been in here so long. I thought I could pull away long enough for dinner but time moves differently while I'm working."

I shake my head and stand up straight, "That's alright. I figured I'd bring your food to you before it got too cold."

I let the plate plop down on his desk harder than necessary and walk back towards the door. I make it halfway before Gabriel calls my name and I turn to look at him over my shoulder. I try to keep my face bored while my heart is dancing from the way he called after me.

"Did you eat?" I shake my head. "Would you like me to join you? I could use the break."

I shake my head again, finishing my walk out of the room as I speak, "No, thank you. Enjoy your work."

I shut the door before he can argue with me and speed walk back to my own food. Part of me so desperately wanted to tell him yes. I wanted his company the first night I'm in a strange new home, for the third time in my short twenty-two years... But, then I think about the deal we made. How we are keeping it professional, and us eating dinner alone together in his house isn't exactly professional. I sit down in my chair and start shoving half-cold food in my mouth as I talk to myself.

No need for unnecessary alone time.

You are not dating, you can barely say he's a friend.

Keep it professional, *Liz.*

Chapter Thirteen

Gabriel

I STARE DUMBFOUNDED at my office door. I know why she's upset, but it doesn't make it any less disappointing.. or irritating. There's only so much time I can spend around that little vixen before I break my rule. Seeing her face light up at the different rooms in the house, and then her glow when she saw the bedroom she wanted, had my cock begging to be out.

I've never been so turned on by seeing a woman *happy*. And she had me hard as steel with that fucking smile. What I wouldn't give to have that smile directed at me.

My fingers tap against the wood of my desk as I look down at the food my cook prepared. I don't even know what food she likes, if she even wants to eat what was made. *Fucking idiot.* I should've asked what she at least wanted for dinner. I'll have to fix that tomorrow, ask her for a list of her favorite foods. I already know she has no allergies, I took the liberty of looking over some of her medical files to make sure I didn't have anything that could cause her to have an allergic reaction.

Pushing the food away, I pull up the files on her I have saved on my computer. There's been something bugging me about her medical history. She went in too many times for a child, the records stopping when she was thirteen. I want to ask her why she went in so often.

Why she went in so often when the official records say there was nothing wrong, except for the one visit with a sprained wrist.

I know her mom and dad are both dead, getting her put into a foster home at seventeen. But those official documents never went into detail. I want to know her background—all of it. I want all the bad and good things that she had to live through. I want to heal and break her all at once.

Closing my eyes, I lean back in my chair and breathe deeply. *She'll seek me out eventually.* I open my eyes and close down my computer, making sure it's locked before picking up my plate of food and walking out of my office to find my little petal.

I find Elizabeth sitting at the smaller dinner table, pushing her carrots around her plate. I'm still standing in the doorway when she looks up from beneath her lashes.

"You should keep working, seems like it's important."

She looks back down as I open my mouth. I shut it with a snap and move to sit across from her. Once I'm seated she still doesn't look up, and my heart silently pleads at her to show her intoxicating hazel eyes.

"Elizabeth, look at me."

"I'd like to eat alone, please."

My jaw ticks as I take one deep breath.

"Look. At. Me." Her chest stops moving as she lifts her head, bringing her eyes up to meet mine at last. "I would like to eat dinner with you. Whether that's in silence or with conversation. I need a distraction from work and your presence alone accomplishes that."

I see her shoulders tense before she nods, looking back at her plate to finally take a bite. My lips flatten in an effort not to smile at this small win. I know I could've handled the tour and afterwards better. She needs support right now with so much changing at once, and I didn't provide that. But that changes after tonight. I can be there for her and anything she needs, even if it tears me apart at times.

Chapter Fourteen

Elizabeth

AFTER GABRIEL FINALLY came out of his hiding space and decided to eat dinner with me, my body was coiled so tight I could barely finish my food. We ended up finishing our food at the same time and I excused myself quickly. Now, I'm sitting on my new bed in my new room, trying not to listen for Gabriel coming up the stairs. I'm not even sure I could hear him from in here, he could already be in his own room by now.

Shaking my head with a sigh, I force my legs to straighten and walk into the bathroom. I rushed my shower earlier and didn't let myself look over the space. The bathroom matches the room perfectly, with dark brown accents against white, and cherry blossom petals floating over the walls. Seeing how Gabriel designed this space makes me wonder what his own bedroom looks like. Since he didn't show me earlier, I assumed when he said 'explore' that excluded his personal space.

To my left is a huge clawfoot tub and across from it, an expensive looking toilet. In front of me in the middle of the back wall is a huge counter with an elegant sink in the middle. Then, to my right, there's a walk-in glass shower with three different heads at different heights. I've never felt water pressure so good.

Turning left, I reach for the faucet of the tub and turn on the water until it's coming out slightly below scorching, and push the plug down. There's a huge mirror taking up the wall behind the faucet for the tub and there's an intrigued part of me that wonders why he put one *there* of all places.

Once the tub is half full, I drop in some essential oils and soap for bubbles. Dropping each piece of clothing in the wicker basket by the door, I avoid looking at my body in the mirror. I've never been too confident about my body. With a permanent tummy-pouch, thick jiggly thighs, boobs that hang a little too low, and an ass that's hard to buy jeans for, I've never felt comfortable in my skin. *Though I rarely let that insecurity show.*

I pull my hair on top of my head into a messy bun and slowly step into the water, turning off the faucet. As I sink slowly into the deep tub, I close my eyes and let the sting of the temperature sizzle over my skin. With my butt firmly planted and my arms hanging over the edges, I lay my head back and sigh.

I could get used to this.

A sharp knock has my eyes snapping open and my body pulling straight. My muddy mind is slow to catch up as I look over to the closed bathroom door.

"Elizabeth. Are you in there?"

I look down at the now clear water and wrap my arms around my chest subconsciously.

"Yes." He's silent for so long I wonder if he walked away, but then I hear him shuffle on the other side. "Do you need something, Gabriel?"

His voice is low and muffled, like he's leaning against the door, "I was about to go to bed and wanted to make sure you had everything you need for the night."

"Oh, uh.. Yeah, I think so."

He's silent for a moment longer. "How long have you been in the bath?"

It's with those words that I notice how cool the water is, and how areas of my skin are wrinkled. My cheeks heat with embarrassment even though he can't see me.

"I'm not sure. I think I fell asleep after I got in."

I barely finish my sentence before Gabriel swings open the door, giving me a perfect view of his body now only in sweatpants. I don't have time to look over his perfect form sculpted with muscle before I notice the fire roaring in his eyes and the angry set of his lips. I take too long to realize he can see through the water before pulling my knees to my chest, my body heating in the cold water.

"What the fuck?! I'm naked Gabriel!"

He shakes his head, locking his jaw, and walks over to me with strong calculated steps.

"Why would you do that, Elizabeth. You can't just fall asleep in a full tub like that, you could slip down and drown."

I roll my eyes, squeezing my arms tighter around my knees as nerves tingle throughout my body, "I'm a light sleeper, I would've woken up the second my chin touched the water. Stop worrying, I'm obviously fine."

His chest moves with his deep inhale, like he's trying to find patience. He moves to stand behind me, keeping eye contact with me through the mirror in front of the tub. My body is so heated, I feel like I could rewarm the water. My chest is barely moving with my quick-small breaths as he squats behind me, draping his thick strong arms on the rim of the tub. His biceps brush the sensitive skin of my shoulders and I gasp lightly. *What is happening right now?*

The fire in his green eyes grows brighter as he looks over what he can see of me. A part of me is saying that this is inappropriate and to tell him to get out. The majority is chanting yes over and over. The pull I feel towards him is the most intense thing I've ever experienced. It's uncomfortable but exhilarating. When he meets my eyes again, he clenches his jaw and moves his face till I feel his exhales against my jaw.

His voice comes out gravelly and low, causing heat to pool in my stomach. "You will not, under any circumstances, put yourself at risk. Do you understand me, Shchenok?"

My breathing increases but I don't respond, my tongue feeling heavy against the roof of my mouth. He twists his face so his nose brushes against my ear, keeping eye contact. His mouth opens and my lungs freeze. His tongue sticks out, and he slowly licks up the side of my neck. My eyelids grow heavy, fluttering with the effort to remain open as my thighs push closer together. Goosebumps come alive all across my body as he finishes the lick with a flick on my ear.

"Do you understand, Elizabeth?"

I barely manage a nod, my voice finally working but my words coming out breathless and broken, "Yes, I understand."

He stands up, walking to grab the towel on the door and hands it to me, "Go get dressed. I'll wait in here until you're finished."

I don't hesitate to wrap the towel tightly around my body and shuffle out of the bathroom, careful to not brush him on my way. He closes the door for me and I hurry to pull on some baggy pajamas. My skin is so sensitive, every brush of fabric causes my clit to thump harder. When I'm sure I'm covered, I go back and reopen the bathroom door. Gabriel sits on the edge of the tub, resting his elbows on his knees, looking down at his bare feet. A slurping noise draws my attention to bath water being drained. *He must have pulled the plug for me.*

I rub my foot over my calf, lean against the doorframe and hug my middle, clearing my throat to make sure I sound more composed than I feel, "I thought you said you wouldn't touch me?"

Gabriel keeps his eyes down as he shakes his head. He doesn't say a single thing for a few moments, just stares down at his feet, his hands holding each other so tight his knuckles are white. Then finally, I hear the thickness in his voice, "I didn't touch you. I tasted you."

He looks up at me then, the tension in his body matching the heat and conflict in his grassy eyes.

"Gabe..."

His face remains expressionless except for his eyes, "That's the first time you've used my nickname." All I can do is look at him, realizing he's right. When I don't respond he continues, "I'm sorry for bursting in when you were quite fine... But I won't apologize for anything else."

I nod stiffly, my fingers digging into my arms to punish myself for loving that he 'tasted' me and not apologizing for it. He stands slowly, like he's trying not to alarm me. I step back to give him room to pass by, my back pressing against the inner doorframe. He goes to step by me but stops with his shoulder a breath away from my face.

His voice is rough as if it's straining him to talk, "Goodnight, Shchenok. I will see you in the morning."

He goes to walk by, a gasp tightening my throat as two of his fingers trail lightly over my upper thigh as he moves. I've never been so wound up and desperate for a mans touch. But, there's something about Gabriel that every part of me begs for.

Except my brain.

I'm smart enough to realize that women have needs. *I* have needs. But I can't satisfy those needs with him. We need to stay professional, at least until Murph is taken down. If Gabriel still wants me by then, then I have no problem giving him every fractured part of me. There's only one question my mind won't stop looping through my ears...

How long can I last before breaking?

Chapter Fifteen

Elizabeth

MY BREATH COMES OUT in quick pants through my nose, my hand closing over my mouth. The crack in my closet door giving me a sliver of light in the otherwise dark space. My other hand covers my heart, like he would be able to hear it from outside this small space.

I was home for only thirty minutes before something I did upset him. I don't even know what I did wrong. I didn't make a mess, I didn't talk to him, I didn't bring up mom… What could I have done this time?

His boots pound against the wood flooring as he gets closer to my room. I should've hidden somewhere else. Maybe that's why he calls me stupid, because I can't hide good enough.

My door creaks as it opens past the halfway point, and my body tenses. I keep my hand over my mouth as he steps inside and stops by my bed.

"You think you don't deserve to get punished? Running away and hiding like a stupid bitch? Get the fuck out here."

I shake my head even though he can't see me. My little fingers clutching my face to keep any sounds down. Daddy used to be nicer… Did I do something so bad that he actually hates me? Do I not show that I love him enough?

My closet door swings open quickly and my hand doesn't stop the scream that bursts from my lips. He stands above me, looking down at me like I'm a rabid puppy he needs to get rid of. His hand moves too fast and wraps too tight around my small bicep, yanking me from my safe space. My feet barely scratch the floor before I'm weightless, my back suddenly slamming against something hard, and my lungs struggling to catch air.

"She would be alive if it wasn't for you."

His words make my eyes widen. That's the first time he's said that.. Does he mean my mom? Did I kill my mom? He starts stomping his heavy boots closer to my body that's still slumped against the wall, each thump causing me to flinch...

I sit up quickly, a loud 'no' bursting from between my lips. My eyes sprint around the room trying to gather where I am. *Another nightmare.* Of course, the first night I'm in a new place I have a nightmare. It's almost like a tradition at this point. My clammy hands run over my eyes—sweat coating my forehead. I'm glad Gabriel is on the other side of the house, I don't need him hearing my embarrassing nightmares. *Especially if I wake up screaming.*

I let myself process the memory my brain decided to force on me in sleep. That was one of the worst times. He got less violent as I got closer to eighteen, and I tried my best to avoid him. *I was also too big to throw around anymore after thirteen.* That was the only time he actually had to let the record stay accurate at the hospital and couldn't pay them off to wipe it. I had a sprained wrist from when he threw me from the closet, the doctor said if I landed just an inch differently I would've broken it.

Blowing out a big breath, I flop back down on my pillow. My eyes look over my blank ceiling as I think of my dad. The older I got, the more I realized why he was blaming me for everything wrong in his life. Why the way he felt was '*my* fault'. He was too stuck in grief—lost his greatest love, and couldn't have room in his life or heart for something else. *Or someone else.*

I've ended up accepting that. I've accepted the only parent I truly ever had was my foster mother. That, just because my dad blamed me for my mom's death, doesn't mean he's right. She had her own problems, ones that I couldn't have controlled as an infant.

My acceptance doesn't stop my sleeping brain from running through the worst times of my life though. And that's *another* thing I've learned to accept—until I have enough money to possibly seek help to properly heal from my trauma.

I wake up again to the sun shining over my eyes. A groan vibrates my throat as I roll over and shove the pillow over my face. It took me way too long to fall back asleep after my nightmare. My phone starts ringing and I jerk up quickly, hair falling over my face, and look frantically for the source of the ringing.

Shit, what time is it?

I see my phone on the other side of the bed and grab it, missing the call coming through. Before I can see who called, it comes in again. Murph. He can't know where I am right now, it would be too soon. Plus, he isn't the brightest bulb in the bunch.

Taking a deep breath, I answer like I normally would, "Do you need me?"

His heavy chuckle has a spider-chill roll up my spine, "Unfortunately, no. We haven't made contact in a couple days. I'm just checking in."

"I'm all good. I have the evening shift tonight."

He hums and the line goes silent. I shift in bed so my back leans against the hoard of pillows. My nerves are raging that he could possibly know I'm going against him. My mind going through possibilities of what he would do to me if he managed to get me away from Gabriel.

"Liz."

I swallow thickly, "Yes?"

"I'll see you tonight."

With that, he hangs up. I hold the phone to my ear for a moment longer before dropping it in my lap. He normally comes in during my evening shifts to have me do some sort of *other* work for him, but he's never said he'll see me like *that*. I need to tell Gabe.

Throwing the blankets off, I don't even check to see how I look before jogging out of my room. I stop at the stairs and strain my ears to listen for any movement. I'm not sure where he could be in the house in the morning. Office, maybe?

My breasts bounce freely as I clamor down the stairs and head straight to his office. I knock twice before opening the door, my breath whooshing from my lips when I find him in a suit—minus the jacket—behind his desk. His glasses reflect the light from his screen as he looks at me with pinched brows.

"Elizabeth?"

I walk up to his desk, my lips parted as I breathe through my mouth. My hands grab onto the edge of his desk as I look down at him. I open my mouth to tell him about the call but stop when I notice his gaze is slowly rolling down from my face. His pupils dilate when they meet my chest. I look down and realize I'm not only not wearing a bra, but I took my shorts off to sleep and am in nothing but a baggy shirt that barely reaches my mid-thigh.

Looking back at his face, my legs flex together when his jaw starts ticking and his normally bright irises are slowly building into a darker green. His pupils threaten to consume the color as he moves his sight further down, finding what I just realized.

I'm one piece of clothing away from being completely bare in front of him.

Wetness starts to gather between my thighs just from the sight of the restraint he's placing on himself. I might have never been comfortable in my body, but he makes me want to strut around naked like I'm a goddess given flesh.

I take in a deep breath as I try not to think about the way his tongue felt against my neck, pushing my hardened nipples tighter against my shirt and catching his sight once more. He flexes his hands and closes his eyes, rubbing them with his thumb and forefinger as his glasses balance on his hand.

"Ty budesh' moyey posledney zhenshchinoy.[*]" He drops his hand and keeps his eyes on my face, "What do you need, Elizabeth?"

I ignore his tense tone and drop into one of the dark leather chairs in front of his desk.

"Murph just called me."

His eyes ignite as his face becomes impossibly hard, "And what did he say?"

"That he'll see me at my shift tonight." My fingers fiddle with the edge of my shirt, making sure it's still covering me properly.

His jaw pulses once. Twice. Then he looks back to his computer, his feigned indifference coming back to his face, "Then we'll see him tonight."

My brows slam down over my eyes, "What do you mean, *we*?"

"You're not going to be going into work anymore without someone there looking after you."

I scoff, my eyes rolling off habit, "I don't need a babysitter. He's never hurt me so I doubt he would now. There's no way he even knows what's going on."

"Even so, me or someone else will be there. And don't think I didn't see that."

I restrain myself from rolling my eyes again, just to see what he would do. My bottom lip catches between my teeth and my eyes move to where his sleeves are rolled up over his forearms. My breathing increases as I look over the muscle there, some veins layering over the top. His hand flexes, moving his muscles around, and I have to physically stop myself from fantasizing over what his strength could do to my body.

Gabe clears his throat and my eyes snap to his. He's not smiling. Not even smirking at me in his flirtatious way. We sit there in silence, holding each other's gaze, until he leans back in his chair and rubs his fingers over his soft-looking lips. Only then does he smirk.

"How are you feeling, Shchenok?"

My mouth is dry as I keep my eyes firmly on his, "Good."

He hums and flicks his eyes down to chest quickly, "You seem a little tense."

I want to say no, to shake my head, but I would be lying. I am tense. My whole body is on edge, wanting so badly to feel him on me, in me, *consuming me*.

When I say nothing, my chest heaving the only indication that he's right, he rests his hands in his lap—his smirk deepening.

"Do you need my help with something, Elizabeth?" I shake my head as much as I can. "Are you sure?" I nod once, and he copies the action.

Donning the mask of emotionlessly-dangerous, he looks back to his computer and begins typing. He says nothing and I take the chance to escape, his eyes burning into my back the whole way out of the office.

Chapter Sixteen

Gabriel

MY COCK PRESSES PAINFULLY against my pants as I watch Liz's ass bounce as she leaves my office. When she shuts the door I slump back and slide a heavy palm over my mindless erection.

Fuck, she is a walking sin.

I groan as my hand continues to stroke over my pants. Letting myself have a few more seconds of torture, I think to how she tasted last night. She had been sweating at some point in her bath, the essential oils she used helping give her a sweet and salty flavor I could've continued enjoying all night. I picture her laid out on my desk. That big shirt she's wearing pushed up beneath her chin, her perfect tits bouncing as I slam into her with her taste on my lips.

Goddamn, that woman.

I remove my hand from my aching cock and look back to my screen. There's no way I'm going to be able to focus now. Not with her sinful body somewhere in my home, barely covered. It takes about two minutes before I give up, my feet moving me out of the comfort of my office. I stop by the chair she sat in and look down. When I catch a slight sheen on the dark leather, my body locks and I close my eyes to breathe deeply.

No, dumbass, do not *lean down towards the seat.*

I force my legs to keep moving me out of the room and upstairs. But, instead of turning towards my room to take a cold shower like

I know I should, I'm headed towards Elizabeth's room. My steps are near silent as I approach her door. I lift my hand to knock, but freeze when I hear a soft moan barely break through the thick wood. My forehead rests against the door as I try to control myself.

Is she seriously getting herself off after practically torturing me down there? Another, more confident, moan answers my question.

I shouldn't.. I really shouldn't.. but, my hand doesn't listen as it turns the knob silently and pushes open the door. Elizabeth lays back on the bed, shirt pushed up over her hips and her slender hand between her delicious thighs. My cock leaks at the sight, my throat closing in order to shut down the groan towards the artwork before me.

Her head is thrown back in pleasure. Her eyes closed, lips parted with panting breaths, and her feet pushing into the soft mattress.

I lean on the doorframe and stuff my hands in my pockets so I don't pull myself out and join her. My body feigns relaxation as her eyes open to roll back. I watch with interest as her fingers work herself closer to release with quick circles around her clit. The sunlight beaming into the room crosses over her face, casting her pussy in shadows—tormenting me by not letting me see how her pussy looks or just how wet she is.

As she goes to close her eyes, they fly all the way open with panic and her hand stops it's efforts. She doesn't remove her hand as her chest moves quickly, her cheeks deepening their rosy color.

A growl I can't stop meets her loud panting, and she bites her lip, an almost silent whimper pushing past her teeth. My lips curve into a hungry smile, showing her I want nothing more than to pounce.

"I'll meet you in the kitchen for breakfast when you're done." I go to leave the room but stop, turning so my eyes meet hers over my shoulder. "You better be thinking of me, Shchenok."

I shut the door behind me, moving with solid steps towards my room. I need that cold shower now more than ever.

Chapter Seventeen

Elizabeth

"YOU BETTER BE THINKING of me, Shchenok."

Despite my better judgement, as soon as the door closes behind him, I continue. His low gravelly voice and hungry smile keep looping through my mind as I continue my efforts. I'm not sure how long he stood there and watched me, but the second I noticed, I was instantly more aroused.

I *shouldn't* want to hear his voice as I cum.

I *shouldn't* want to feel his rough hands move harshly over my body.

I *shouldn't* want to see his eyes on my face as I scream his name.

But that's all I picture as wave after wave of sensation washes over me.

When my body finally comes back down from whatever planet I was on, I open my eyes and groan loudly. That was one of my best orgasms and he didn't even *touch me*. He said he wouldn't.. but I was a little disappointed that he didn't even come closer, at least.

I try not to think too long about how deprived I sound at wanting him to watch me masturbate before rolling out of bed, and stepping in the bathroom.

When I double check that I'm fully, appropriately clothed, I head to the kitchen to meet Gabriel for breakfast. I just have to get through the next seven-ish hours before I can go to work and have the familiar movements soothe my mind.

When I get to the kitchen, the cold tile seeps into the soles of my feet when I stop. Gabriel stands at the stove with his back to me. His dress shirt is tucked into his pants perfectly, his sleeves rolled up to his elbows to show off the thickness of his forearms, and his head is bent over whatever he's making.

My voice comes out more confident than I feel, "I'm surprised you know how to cook."

His light chuckle pulls a small smile from my lips as I keep walking to pull a drink from the fridge.

"I learned a couple things from Natalie while I lived there. It's one of her favorite hobbies."

I smile bigger, taking my juice to sit at the island, "When you take out the mafia part, you guys are a pretty regular family."

He looks over his shoulder with a soft smile, "I think the *mafia part*, as you put it, is pretty normal. But, I also grew up in this life so it's a little different from an outside prospective."

I nod and take a sip of my drink, ignoring the swarm of lightness in my head from his smile. We sit in silence until he turns off the stove and gets two plates from a cabinet. I watch as his strong body glides through the movements of plating our food, taking another big drink to deny my dry mouth from saying something stupid.

He sets my plate in front of me with a fork, then sits down, keeping a stool between us. A laugh gets stuck in my throat at seeing the distance he deliberately kept. I can't tell if the space is for my benefit or his, but it's weirdly entertaining anyway. Could be from the undeniable comfort I find with him around, or the fact that I feel as if I could actually joke for the first time in a while, but I speak barely above a whisper.

"You know, you could sit closer. I don't bite."

My smile grows when a silent laugh breathes from his nose. He keeps his eyes on his plate, but his playful tone shoots straight towards me.

"No, but I do."

My smile falls as my eyes widen. *Not the answer I was expecting.* When he slides his eyes towards me, that sensual smirk tilts his mouth before he runs his hand over it and chuckles quietly. I swing my head to my own plate and start to shovel food in my mouth like it's my last meal. He only laughs louder and I direct my middle finger to him without looking, earning me another laugh. I smile around my fork despite myself. *His laugh is like sunlight on a gloomy day.* There might be a good amount of sexual tension between us, but there's still plenty of care-free air that lightens my body.

Gabriel finishes his food before I'm even halfway done and walks his dishes to sink. He rests his forearms on the counter and looks to me with a serious expression. I raise a questioning brow as I push another bite of delicious food into my mouth. His eyes track my lips as they drag off the fork, but his face stays calm and focused.

When he finally looks back to my eyes, I don't miss his dilated pupils.

"I have to go into the office today to go over some stuff. You'll be expected to stay here while I'm gone. You're not to leave the property, do you understand?"

My brows lower over my eyes and I swallow my bite before responding, "So I'm a prisoner unless you take me somewhere?"

He shakes his head once, "No. You can do whatever you like. Explore more of the house, walk the grounds, whatever you want. But you cannot leave the *safety* of the property. We don't want to risk Murph backlashing, even if you think he doesn't know, he could. There are always eyes and ears everywhere, Elizabeth. You need to remember that."

"Even here?"

His lip twitches like he wants to smile but stops it. Ignoring my question he keeps talking, "Elliana offered to come over to hang out with you while I'm gone so you don't get bored. She also told me about offering to train with you, and I think it would be a good idea."

My eyebrows push together as I set down my fork, breaking our eye contact for a few seconds to look at my plate, "You want me to know how to fight?"

He nods once, "Fight, shoot, use knives, whatever you can learn to keep yourself safe."

"Aren't *you* going to keep me safe?"

His eyes flare with an emotion briefly before his face softens and a gentle smile curves his full lips, "Vsegda, lepestok.[*]" Although I'm not sure what he means, I give a small smile in return. He flicks a quick look to my lips before clearing his throat and continuing. "There might be a time where I'm not there, and you need to know what to do to protect yourself or someone else. That's why I think you should take up her offer. Either way, it's your choice."

My smile stays as I nod softly. He gives me another gentle smile, nods once, and moves to leave. I watch him exit, unable to stop myself from admiring him while he can't see me. That is, until his promising chuckle runs over my body and his arm flexes as he scratches the back of his head.

"Take a picture, Shchenok. It'll last longer."

I scowl at his back and flip him off for the second time this morning. I have a feeling he's going to be seeing a lot of this finger.

Chapter Eighteen

Elizabeth

GABRIEL LEFT ABOUT thirty minutes ago, yelling a quick goodbye as he walked out the door. I've already walked the house twice trying to decide what to do with my time. Elliana texted and said she was going to be here in about fifteen minutes so I'm just biding my time.

My steps slow as I approach my room. I *could* go look at the gym again. I haven't been in there expect when Gabriel showed me around. I've been to a public gym maybe three times in my life before deciding it wasn't for me. I felt like I always had someone watching me and I couldn't do a workout without feeling like I was being quietly critiqued.

No one is here, so might as well have a look.

After changing into better clothes and slipping on sneakers, I make my way to the gym and stop in the doorway. There's a matted area in the middle with a rack of weights on the edge, two treadmills facing the three large windows, a bike machine, a—what I think is—a squat rack, and a good few other machines I'm not sure how to use. Everything looks so clean and expensive, I'm scared to even breathe near it.

Taking a deep breath, I walk into the room with false confidence and make my way to one of the treadmills. I look it over like it'll bite me if I move too quick. I'm not sure why working out is intimidating, but it is.

Are you supposed to stretch before or after?

Closing my eyes, I give my head a good shake, hoping to dispel all my unnecessary thoughts. My muscles lock with determination and I step on. I grab the scrunchy from my wrist and pop my hair into a bun, eyeing the buttons on the panel in front of me.

Once I figure out what each button does, I turn it on and adjust the speed and incline. It slowly builds up speed until I'm jogging and I laugh lightly to myself. *This isn't so bad.* Once my legs get comfortable, I up the speed until I'm running. I look out the window as my arms pump with my legs and my mind starts to wander. I let the thud of each step fill the otherwise quiet space and realize just how calming this can actually be.

I don't realize someone else is in the room until a knock on the wall across from me gets my attention. I snap my head to the side and turn off the treadmill, slowing down to a walk before stopping.

Elliana gives me a big smile as she walks closer, "I see you're making yourself at home pretty nicely."

A light laugh tickles my throat as I smile back, "I had to find something to do, so thought might as well workout. Did you just get here?"

"I've been here for a minute or two, I didn't want to interrupt. You looked pretty focused." I smile bigger and move to the watercooler on the back wall as she follows. "How long were you running for?"

I chug a cup of water before answering, "I'm not sure. I got on almost right after your text so maybe ten minutes or so?"

She gives me a little smirk and walks back over to the treadmill and looks at the screen. When she turns back around her eyes are bigger and there's a laugh in her voice, "You were running for almost seventeen minutes. Do you normally run?"

I shake my head, "Last time I ran, it was to get away from someone."

I laugh but she only gives me a knowing smile and we fall into a comfortable silence while I drink more water. I'm glad I have company, but I was kind of in a groove. I honestly could've kept running for a while. My lungs hurt and my legs feel a little weak but it was relaxing in a way. I got to let my mind go where it wanted, and let my muscles take over.

When I finish my third cup of water, I find Elliana on the mat stretching her arms. I chew on my bottom lip, shifting on my feet, before deciding to join her. As I stop in front of her she gives me an encouraging smile and switches her arms.

"You can stretch with me if you want. We can also stretch out our legs because of your run."

I nod and follow along with her. My muscles pull before relaxing with each stretch, the tension slowly moving out of my body and into the quiet air.

We continue for five more minutes before Ell sits cross legged and gives me a warm smile. "Did you think about taking up the offer for training?"

My stomach knots as I think. Gabriel made a good point about being able to protect myself or someone else. But, I don't think I would be very good at any of the things he listed. Knives, guns, hand to hand...

I give a tentative nod, "I think I'd like to at least start. I'm not sure how much success I'll have but I'm willing to try."

"As long as you're trying and putting in the effort, I'm sure you'll get the hang of it." I nod again as she stands and offers me a hand to help me up. I take it and return her bright smile. "We'll also be working your muscles. So we'll do about an hour-ish of weights, thirty minutes of cardio, and then we'll do techniques for hand to hand each day. We'll do weapons on a different day so you aren't learning too many things at once."

"Sounds good..." She tilts her head slightly when I hesitate. "I.. I've never worked out or done any self-defense so I'm not sure what I'm doing."

She holds her arms out to the side with a winning smile, "That's what I'm here for!"

We both laugh and she leads me over to the first machine to start on.

Three hours later, I'm breathing heavily and my hands sweat inside the boxing gloves I have on. I throw another punch into the pad Elliana holds up with a smile.

"Good, remember to move with your shoulder *and* body. If you throw it with just your arm it won't pack as much than if you're putting your weight into it."

I nod and do another combo she taught me. Her smile gets impossibly bigger and she nods slightly. I give her a tired smile and start taking off the gloves.

"I think I need water."

She laughs and takes my gloves from me, "Go get some. You're doing really good Liz. You already have the combos down and you're form is pretty solid for your first time. I think you'll get this pretty fast."

I give her another smile before downing a glass of water quickly. When I finish I walk back to the mat and lay on my back, looking up to the two big fans turning slowly. Ell joins me on the floor as I catch my breath and cool down. Her head begins to move in my peripheral and I look over to her with a small smile.

"Liz.. Can I ask how you got tied to Murph?"

I blow out a big breath and look back to the ceiling, "I moved to the city after my foster mother passed away when I was about to turn nineteen. I was surprised my car even made it this far, it was so shitty. I was walking around exploring and looking for jobs on my phone when I bumped into him. Like, I literally bumped into him. Walked right into his chest when I turned a corner. He gave me such a charming smile, part of me was shocked to see such a good looking man give me the time of day." I let out a scoffing laugh before continuing, "He asked if I was okay, and what was distracting me. So, I told him I was new to town and was too busy looking at jobs on my phone to pay attention to where I was walking.

"He asked if I had any experience waitressing and if I would be interested working at his diner. At the time, I was desperate for money so, I said yes. When he found out I'd been practically living out of my car, he gave me a loan to get an apartment. After I moved in, I sold my shitty car for what I could and started taking public transportation to work. Every time I had a shift, he was there, trying to get to know me. He found out I had an interest in cyber security and other things, and had me try a few things for him..."

We sit in silence while I flash through memories of my unwanted relationship with Murph. He showed up for each of my shifts, seeming so nice and gentle. Then I found out he was in the mafia. And that there was a Russian mafia that pretty much ran everything. He was so excited about my skills with computers and other things that he not-so-nicely got me to do some of his dirty work. He slowly morphed from the nice guy I thought he was, to a manipulative monster who controlled my life. The only thing he never did was try something sexually, even if he flirted from time to time.

I clear my throat and give her a quick smile, "It kind of grew from there. He found out I had no other family and took advantage of that. My own life was enough to hold over me, he didn't need to add someone else into the mix to get me to do his dirty work."

When she doesn't say anything I look over to see her looking at me with sympathy.

"I'm sorry, Liz. I wish you could've ran into me or anyone else that day."

I nod and give her another smile, "Me too. But there's nothing I can do about the past, there's only what I can do moving forward."

She matches my smile and reaches over to hold my hand, "How old are you?"

"I turned twenty-two a couple weeks ago."

"You're pretty mature for your age."

I laugh lightly, "My foster mom used to say the same thing all the time. I guess you mature faster when you have trauma biting at your heels."

Her smile saddens, "I understand... You and Gabe are probably the same in that aspect. Both of you have had to overcome a lot of demons to get to where you are today."

My brows crease as I think that over. I know he's about my age, but he does act a lot older. Now that I think about it, I don't really know anything personal about him besides his relationship to Dom and the rest of the group.

Ell sees the wheels turning in my mind and gives my hand a light squeeze, "You can ask him questions about himself, you know. I'm not sure how open he'll be at first, but I'm sure you'll both get there."

I nod and give her hand a squeeze in return. She looks like she's going to ask me something else but a deep voice speaks first.

"Am I interrupting something?"

We both lift our heads up to see Gabriel in the doorway giving us a smile. My lips twitch with the urge to smile back, but I withhold it. Elliana is the first to stand up, reaching back down to help me next.

"We were just talking. Liz did really good today with training." She looks to me with a wide smile, "I'll text you about working out a schedule for more, sound good?"

I nod and lean into her hug when she pulls me close. I squeeze a little tighter than necessary, reveling in the feel of a friends embrace.

She lets me go with a smile and makes her way to Gabriel, giving him a quick hug. I don't hear what she says but I see Gabriel nod at whatever it was. She walks out with a wave over her shoulder, leaving me sweaty and alone with Gabriel. Before he can say anything, I give him a small smile and speed walk out.

"I'm going to go shower." He doesn't respond as I make my way to my room, but I feel his eyes on my back all the way there.

Chapter Nineteen

Elizabeth

I SPENT THE REST OF the afternoon in my room just to avoid Gabriel. I know everything seemed pretty normal during breakfast but, I still feel a little.. I'm not sure if awkward is even the correct word... Self-conscious?

Now, I'm in my work uniform in the back seat of a blacked out sedan with the same guy who drove me to Elliana's, now driving me again. Gabriel is sitting in the passenger seat, doing who knows what on his phone. He hasn't said a word to me besides, 'it's time to go'. I'm not sure where his head is at, or if he's offended I hid from him after he got home.

I shift uncomfortably in my seat and lean forward to look at the guy driving, "What's your name?"

Before he can answer, Gabriel speaks lowly, "Why do you need to know his name?"

What kind of question is that? This is the second time he's driving me around and I don't know his name. This might be his job but I'm a nice person, and I want to call him by his name.

"Because he's driven me once before. I think it's only reasonable to know who he is, especially if he's going to continue coming around."

Gabriel still doesn't take his eyes off the phone. Before he can argue with me further, the other guy finally talks. His deep voice just as gravelly as when he spoke on the first ride.

"You can call me Sammy."

I see Gabriel look over to him quickly from my peripheral but I ignore him as I smile at Sammy, "It's nice to finally put a name to the face. I'm assuming this isn't your only job for Dominic, correct?"

Sammy's lips twitch, "No, it's not."

Before I can ask another question, Gabriel gently pushes my shoulder so I'm back in my seat, his warm hand causing suspicious goosebumps to track down my arm. In the mirror, I see Sammy smirk at Gabriel. I let out a huff of breath and look out my window to see we're approaching the diner. The parking lot looks mostly empty, save for three other cars. Part of me wants it to be a slow night, but the other part wants all the activity so I don't have time to overthink anything.

And then, there's the fact that Murph will be here at some point. When he called earlier I was uneasy with the way he said he was going to see me during my shift. There's also never been a moment in a phone call when he pauses like that. He always keeps it short and to the point, never lingering.

Sammy parks the car around the building and across the street. When I go to get out, the doors lock.

"Um.. I kind of need the door unlocked so I can go inside."

Gabriel turns around in his seat and looks at me with that emotionless face I'm starting to hate. "I won't be going in with you since there will be a big chance that Murph would notice me. So, Sam will be going in and keeping an eye on you and updating on the activity. If anything happens where you feel unsafe, Sam will be right there. Just give him a quick look."

Ignoring pretty much everything he said, I look to Sammy with furrowed brows, "I thought you said your name was Sammy?"

He looks over his shoulder with a smirk, "My name is Sam, only certain people call me Sammy."

When Gabriel looks at him sternly, I see Sammy's chest move with silent laughter. The doors unlock and I slide out without a goodbye to Gabriel. Sammy walks around the car and gestures for me to walk in first. I'm sure he wants us to walk in separately so we don't draw attention. Me walking in with a wall of muscle? Probably not the most inconspicuous thing.

I walk over to the side entrance like usual, taking a deep breath in the dark hallway, and walk in to get to work.

I'm already halfway through my shift and Murph still hasn't shown up. I keep sneaking glances at Sammy who has been sitting at the same table and reading a book. I've refilled his coffee a couple times and given him free food so it doesn't look weird with him *just* sitting there. There's only two other tables, and they both just paid. Once they leave, it'll just be me, the two cooks, and Sammy until Murph arrives.

I pull out my phone and face the kitchen window. Gabriel hasn't texted me once since I started but I have a feeling him and Sammy are communicating. I still feel a little guilty about ignoring him after he got home, especially because during breakfast it seemed like we were building a kind of rapport. I decide to send him a quick text.

Hey..

I flinch when one of the cooks drops a pot in the sink, and I accidently press send. Nerves buzz in my stomach as I wait for a response. I'm not going to double text him.. even though I wasn't even done typing.

Within ten seconds he responds.

You should be working.

My eyes roll, glad he isn't here to see it.

Duh. I just wanted to apologize for the way I bolted when you got home. It was... Unprofessional.

There. Apology sent. I don't need to give him the exact reason I left. Seeing as I bolted because just the sight of him in his suit with that smile made me want to do things I have no business doing. I tuck my phone back in my apron and start getting the rags to wipe down the empty tables. Before I can make it five steps, my apron vibrates with an incoming text.

I honestly didn't think he would respond.

Are you still trying to keep things professional?

My heart starts doing double time. If things were different, no, I wouldn't want to be just professional with him. I would do every dirty thing I've been fantasizing about. I haven't had sex since I was eighteen, so it's been four *long* years. I lost my virginity to some guy I had been seeing for a week during the summer. I decided it was time to get comfortable with my sexual needs and what I want. Did the guy shatter my world? Absolutely not. Even though he's the only guy I've slept with, I could tell he wasn't that great. The only thing he did somewhat good was eat me out. And even then, I had to fake my orgasm to get it over with.

But when I think of doing things with Gabriel? My legs shake, my panties soak, and my mouth dries. I know just by looking at him and hearing him say those dirty things, that he would absolutely destroy me.. he even said he wanted to break me. And I don't doubt that he would. Giving in to the temptation that is Gabriel Morozov, would utterly wreck me. So, as much as I want to let him have me.. I need to hold out.

I decide not to text him back and put my phone back in my apron. Right as I walk out from behind the counter, a door from behind the kitchen opens and shuts followed by heavy footsteps slowly making their way to the front.

Murph is here.

I act like I don't hear him coming, even though I've already started to sweat. Clearing my throat, I wipe down a table quickly before moving to the next one. I skip over Sammy's table, making sure not to look at him. When I'm about to finish the last one, body heat covers my back and I stand straight slowly. I try to keep my breathing casual as I turn around with the usual small, shy smile I give to Murph.

He's standing closer than usual and I have to step back to avoid touching him, my butt bumping into the table behind me.

"Liz. How lovely to see you."

I swallow thickly, losing the smile, and nod. Murph's eyes dart quickly to Sammy, who still looks wholly invested in his book. I want him to step back. Being so close to him has nausea surfacing. Instead of doing what I silently plead for, he steps closer and brushes his lips over my ear.

"Let's talk in the office."

Without waiting for me to agree, he grabs my wrist tightly and begins to walk me back behind the kitchen. I make sure to keep my eyes off Sammy. Gabriel said all I have to do is look at him if I feel unsafe. Which I do.. but, this isn't the first time Murph has held me like this, and I'm almost positive he wouldn't actually hurt me. If he did, I wouldn't be able to do the work he wants. So, putting my free arm behind my back, I wave downwards, motioning for Sammy to stay put hoping he's watching. Hopefully, I won't actually need him to step in.

Murph drags me all the way to the office in the back of the building, the only space in this place that looks brand new. He sits me down in my normal seat in front of the double monitor's spaced along the dark wood desk. I keep my hands in my lap and my eyes on the black screens. Normally, when he brings me in here to work, there's already some instructions waiting for me. But today, there's nothing. There's no paper telling me what I need to work on, no sticky notes with names, no device he needs me to hack into.

Murph's toned legs come into my peripheral when he sits on the desk beside me—his dress pants making little noise as they adjust to his position. I finally look up at him, making sure to keep my face blank. His black dress shirt is tight against his arms and stretches along his broad chest, the top two buttons undone and giving him a carefree rich-boy look.

"So, Liz, I heard you went to the Morozov wedding."

I swallow thickly and nod, not giving him anything he doesn't ask a question for. I'm not stupid enough to start giving details he might not know. The good thing about growing up around my shit father? I know how to not give anything away even in the moments before getting hit. Murph is definitely threatening, but I've been through too much not to stand my ground.

"Who invited you to the wedding?"

Now, I hesitate to answer. Do I tell him Gabriel invited me? Wouldn't that lead to more questions like how I know him or any of them? I don't want to put any of them in danger of Murph's retaliation. I also don't want to risk my physical safety.

I swallow thickly, "I'm not sure. I found an invitation under my door a few days before the wedding. I didn't know anyone there."

The second part definitely is the truth. I didn't know anyone, and I don't count knowing Gabriel at the time. I barely know him now if I'm honest.

Murph looks deeply into my eyes, and I don't lower them. I've never cowered in his presence. I might have always treaded lightly, but I've never backed down from his accessing stare. He tilts his head slightly and continues to look over my face, like he'll find a secret under my skin.

He nods once, "How was the evening? I, of course, wasn't invited and neither were any of my business partners. But, I'm assuming it was beautiful considering Rick's tastes."

"It was." He waits for me to say more, but I don't. He hums and stands from the desk, walking around to the back of my chair and setting his hands on my shoulders.

I tense slightly and hope he doesn't notice. I've never liked his touch, it's always felt gross. I always thought I didn't like it because he was a dangerous mafia man who had invisible blood on his hands. But, after feeling how Gabriel's touch makes my body turn into its own bonfire, I don't think that's the case. Murph's touch feels slimy, unbearable, and dirty. Gabriel's touch feels—

"Do I need to worry about where your loyalty is, Liz?" I shake my head. His cold fingers brush hair behind my ear and I try not to show the uncomfortable shiver that rakes my spine. "Good. Because I have a new task for you."

His hands leave me and I let out a silent breath of relief. I watch him walk around the desk to grab a metal box from the shelf by the door. My brows push together and I watch him open it with a key and pull out a small black flash-drive.

"What is that?" My voice is small, like how it normally is when he's suspicious about his tasks.

He brings the drive over to me and sets it in front of the keyboard, "This, my sunshine, is a drive that I bought from an acquaintance overseas. It's capable of automatically hacking into any server once it's plugged in."

Part of me is immensely intrigued by this. I'm not the best hacker by any means, but I do pretty good, and this little drive had to have been designed by someone who is *really* good at what they do. Then, there's the part of me that's scared at what he's going to ask me to do with it. I keep my hands limply in my lap, and my eyes on the drive.

I only glance up at him through my lashes when he continues talking, looking at me like I'm going to solve all his problems.

"What I want you to do, is get into one of their houses and—"

I cut him off with fake confusion, "Them, who?"

The corner of his eye twitches at my interruption but he plasters over it with a broad smile, "Rick, Dominic, or Gabriel. Preferably one of the first two, but Gabriel being so close to them could be helpful too. I want you to get into one of their houses and plant this drive in their home computers. From there, you just need to leave it for forty-eight hours before retrieving it and bringing it back to me."

"What will be on it?"

He smile turns utterly sinister and he leans down closer to my face, his fingers once again tainting my hair with their touch. "There will be all the information I need in order to take them down. The details you don't need to know. All I need from you, sunshine, is to plant it and bring it back," he lowers his voice, leaning closer so his breath fans over my lips, "Can I trust you to do this for me?"

I keep my breath shallow as I nod. He's a lot more touchy than usual and I'm wondering if it's because he knows I went to Natalie and Rick's wedding. I *do* know that I can't stand his physical attention. It has bile rising in my throat and my hands going clammy. There's nothing about him that I enjoy. I thought he was handsome and charming at first, but that was before he showed his true colors. Once you show how ugly you are on the inside, there's no longer anything beautiful on the outside.

He takes another moment of looking into my eyes before smirking and leaning back on the desk. A big breath rushes from my nose as I focus on not letting my shoulders slump.

I can't show him weakness or lack of comfortability.

"I have someone coming to finish your shift. I want you to get to work on getting close to the Mortelli's and Morozov's. And don't worry sunshine, you'll still get your full pay for the day." He lets his eyes rake over my body slowly, causing tiny little ants to crawl over my skin. "Don't get too close, Liz. You work for me and I'm the one keeping you alive. You don't know what they've done or what they're capable of."

With that, he leaves the office. I wait until I hear the side entrance close before dragging in a much needed deep breath and relaxing back in the chair. The good thing about this office is that there's no cameras. Murph never wanted any evidence about what I work on in here.

Before I have the chance to stand from the chair, Sammy comes barreling into the room looking ready to kill. I give him a small smile and stand up, shaking off the touch I still feel from Murph.

"Down boy. I'm fine."

Sammy gives me a little smirk and crosses his arms, "For such a small thing, you show very little fear."

Huffing a laugh, I look down at my curvy body and turn a skeptical look back to him, "I'm not small."

"You're small to us, malen'kaya lisa[*]."

I cross my arms over my chest and pop a hip, "Why do you all insist on talking or calling me names in Russian. I have no idea what you're saying and I always assume the worst."

"I called you little fox. Because that's how I see you. You're a small thing that seems timid but is full of life and violence. You might be scared, but you don't let it show to those you shouldn't. You're a fierce little thing..." He tilts his head slightly and gets a charming glint in his eyes, "I can see why Gabriel wants to keep you."

I open my mouth to argue against that last point but he cuts me off by walking out of the office, leaving me no choice but to follow. I roll my eyes, grabbing the drive off the desk, and follow him out.

How did I let my life get to this point?

Chapter Twenty

Gabriel

I WAIT IMPATIENTLY for Elizabeth to text back. I'm taunting her, and I want her to show that attitude she keeps hidden. She has intrigued me from the moment she ran into me. With her big beautiful eyes that swirl with brown and green, her puffy lips and quick tongue, and the most addicting scent I've ever inhaled, I've never wanted something so bad.

A groan vibrates my throat as I adjust myself in my pants. Just thinking about her gets me harder than stone. My little petal is something I never want to drift away, and want to preserve to end of time.

Before I can send her another taunt, a sleek-red car pulls up to the curb by the side entrance and my spine straightens. Murph steps out and pays no attention to the sedan I'm sitting in. My whole body locks in place as I watch him step inside the diner. The over-protective voice in my head is screaming at me to go look after what's mine, to kill Murph before he can even see her.

I take deep breaths to calm myself but keep my gaze locked on the door. If there's even a hint that something could go wrong, I'm going in. Consequences be damned. The seconds tick by slowly, my hands beginning to sweat from the lack of action. Before I can do something stupid, Sam sends me a text.

He took her to the office. I lost eyes. She motioned for me to stay.

My lip lifts in a silent snarl. Sam is one of our best guys. Him and I have gotten close over the past couple years and we could be considered best friends. But, if anything happens to Elizabeth because he wasn't fast enough, I *will* kill him.

Sam doesn't send me another text as I keep track of the minutes going by with Murph alone with Elizabeth. As I get ready to say 'fuck it' and go inside, the side door swings open and Murph struts out with a smug smile. The urge to shoot him in the head from here is great, but I close my fists in my lap instead.

I swear to whatever is out there, that if he touched her...

He drives off quickly, his tires squealing as he rounds the corner. I wait another thirty seconds before swinging open my door and stepping out. I make if halfway across the street before the side door opens again and Sam steps out, followed by Elizabeth.

My chest lightens at the sight of her and my eyes travel over her body to check for any injuries. She stops quickly as I continue to barrel towards her, her eyes building wider and her body locking. I'm sure I don't have a very pleasant expression on my face.

I grab her arms lightly and continue to look her over, "Are you okay? Did he touch you?" I barely recognize my voice but I ignore it and lock my sight with hers.

Her eyes twinkle as she gives me a light smile and tries to step out of my hands, "I'm fine, Gabe. He didn't hurt me."

My words come out as a growl, "I asked if he *touched* you."

Her eyes widen further, her smile slipping. I don't lower the intensity that is flowing from me, I can barely contain my urges at this point. She gives a barely noticeable nod and my grip instantly tightens around her arms. When she winces I loosen my grip and do my best to relax my face.

"Where did he touch you?"

She shakes her head as she talks, "He only touched my wrist and my some of my hair."

I take a deep breath and nod. She relaxes in my hold but locks back up when I trail my hands down her arms to her wrists. I rub my thumbs over her smooth skin and give her a smile.

"We'll talk about it more at home."

I don't wait for her response as I walk her to the car, moving my hand to interlock our fingers. Another smile stretches my lips when she doesn't pull away and tightens her fingers around mine.

The whole drive home is silent. I continue to check work emails and tasks on my phone as Sam drives. Occasionally peaking in the back through the side mirror, I notice Elizabeth doesn't move from her seat by the window. She continues to look at the scenery we pass with a tortured expression creasing her features. I'm not sure what Murph talked to her about, but I'm not going to ask her about it in front of Sam. She seems uncomfortable with the topic as is.

Sam makes a small grunt as we pull in my driveway and I look up from my phone. Dominic, Elliana, Rick, and Natalie are all standing outside their vehicles waiting for us. A sigh breezes from my nose as I rub my temples. Of course, they're going to be here to discuss what happened. Elizabeth and I aren't the only ones who could get backlash from Murph, but I didn't think they'd show up when I told them she was seeing him tonight.

Once parked, I hop out quickly and open the door for Elizabeth. She barely turns her legs to hop out before I step between them. She doesn't look at me or attempt to keep me out of her space and I'm immediately more worried. I slowly and gently grab the sides of her face and lift her gaze from her lap.

Giving her a small encouraging smile, I brush a thumb across her cheekbone, "What's going on in that head of yours, moy malen'kiy lepestok?"

She shakes her head as much as she can in my hold, her voice the smallest I've yet to hear, "I don't know what to do..."

My stomach sinks and my heart lurches, wishing to jump from my chest to comfort her. I told her I wouldn't touch her, but she looks so fragile in this moment and so conflicted, I can't help but to do a small something.

Leaning forward, I press my lips lightly to her forehead. Not quite a kiss, but a brush of affection. Her shoulders fall forward as she leans into my hands and I take the second to smell the soft lavender fragrance of her shampoo.

I push my hands closer, my lips brushing her soft skin as I speak, "We'll figure it out together, Elizabeth."

She nods in my hold before her muscles tighten and she pulls out of my grasp. I drop my hands from the cold air she left behind and move from between her legs so she can step out. Keeping my eyes on her as we head inside, I can't help but to hurt for her struggle. Whatever Murph asked of her, it had to have been something with me or my brothers. I don't think she would look so confused otherwise.

I give a stern look to said brothers as we walk by, warning them to keep their fucking mouths shut. No one should make Elizabeth talk before she's ready. And when she is, we'll all be there to support her. She might've just come into our lives, but she's accepted. She's one of us now.

And we do anything to protect our own.

Chapter Twenty One

Elizabeth

THE RIDE HOME WAS A blur. The more I thought of what Murph wants me to do, the more worried I become. Of course, I'm going to tell Gabriel everything that was said. But, that doesn't mean we're going to have a solution to the problem. The problem being—how are we going to deal with the flash drive? Murph will know I didn't do it if he doesn't get it back. It's not like we can actually put the drive into one of their computers, especially because we don't even know how this thing works or what it's going to pull.

I barely see everyone waiting for me to walk inside as I keep my gaze trained on my feet. My mind is running over every angle we could do this, tuning out the world around me. I don't register walking to the downstairs living room, or sitting on the couch, or who sits next to me. I block out the voices around me as my eyes move over invisible possibilities in the air above my lap.

Only when I feel a warm finger brushing over the deep crease between my brows do I look up. Gabriel stands in front of me with a glass of a deep amber liquid and a soft smile. Without a word, he passes me the glass which I down in one gulp. It burns all the way down to my stomach but I ignore it, and the rasp in my voice, as I lift it back up and ask for another.

He leaves and comes back, again without a word. Patiently waiting for me to get my thoughts in order. This glass, I take smaller sips, letting it warm its way down instead of burn. Clearing my throat, I finally look around the room.

Elliana sits next to Dominic, both looking over different papers in their lap on the connecting curve of the couch. Natalie sits with Rick on the love seat across from the couch, whispering intensely to each other. Everyone's drinks sit on glass coasters on the dark brown wood coffee table in the center.

I'm glad I'm not the only one drinking.

There's a coldness to the room when I notice Gabriel isn't here. I open my mouth to ask someone where he went, but don't get the chance when he saunters in like nothing is wrong. He flashes me a cocky smirk and a wink before taking a seat closer to Ell and Dom. I try not to let the disappointment show on my face at his seat choice as I smile back.

Clearing my throat again, I wait for all eyes to be on me before I begin.

"Alright. Murph knows I was at Natalie and Rick's wedding. He thinks an invitation just showed up under my door one day and that I didn't know anyone there, which is pretty much true." Nat and Ell both give me a soft smile. "He asked if I'm still loyal to his side and I don't think he thought I was lying when I said yes. Then, he gave me a mysterious flash drive with the instructions to put it in any one of your guys' computers. I'm supposed to leave it in for forty-eight hours before taking it out and giving it back."

Rick is the quickest to ask a question, "What is this drive supposed to do? Where did he get it?"

I shrug, "Someone overseas. He said that it will give him what he needs to take you guys down and it can hack into any server once plugged in."

No one says anything, all looking around at each other in silent conversation. My leg starts to bounce from the tension in the air as my teeth chew on my bottom lip.

Dominic clears his throat, catching our attention, "He wants you to put it into any of our computers?"

"He said yours or Rick's preferably but that Gabriel's could work too."

He nods, "Then we plug it in."

My eyes widen, "*What*? How could we plug it in knowing that it can pull everything off your computer for him to look at?"

Rick chimes in, "Is there anything identifiable about the drive? Could we replace it with one of our own with certain documents?"

I look between the guys, all of whom are looking at me with intense, focused features.

My head starts to shake side to side as my leg bounces faster against the soft cushion, "I'm not sure. I barely looked at it. It looks like a normal flash drive, but it could possibly hold a certain security or something when it's plugged in to its home drive. If that's the case, we wouldn't be able to switch it out without him knowing. And we can't know if it has something like that without the home hub."

When I look around the room, everyone is looking at me with wide eyes. I shrink in on myself, not sure why they're looking at me like that.

My shoulders straighten when Rick lets out a soft deep chuckle and I turn to face him with high brows, "Who knew Gabe would bring home someone possibly smarter than him."

Heat flushes my cheeks as my eyes swing to Gabe's. He's already looking at me, but instead of shock or offense, there's a softness cradling his vibrant green eyes—a soft smile lifting the corners of his mouth.

We must have been staring at each other too long, because someone clears their throat. I look back down to my lap, feeling my blush increase from embarrassment. There's a discussion on what next steps to take that I'm too in my head to listen to.

Dominic calls my name and I look up, squaring my shoulders and hoping I show strength I don't feel. "What do you think we should do next, Elizabeth?"

I look over his sharp features as I think. *What can we do next?* We either need to plug it in and hope there's nothing Murph can actually use against them, or find a way to see if there's a home hub for this drive that we can take and put back before Murph notices.

Dom waits patiently, with no judgement on his face, until I'm ready to answer.

"Well.. we either plug it in and hope for the best, *or...*" I take a deep breath, hoping I don't sound stupid with this plan, "We can sneak into Murph's main office, see if there's a home hub for the drive, and take it. If it's there, and we have it, we can use it to look further into the drive Murph gave me to see if we can really replace it with a fake. Depending on how it works, I could look into it without even taking it from his office if I have enough time."

I'm breathing slightly heavier than normal with adrenaline from the idea. Dominic is smirking at me, same as Rick, but Gabriel and the girls look worried. Gabriel doesn't even have the opportunity to voice his concerns before Dominic stands, buttoning his suit jacket as he does.

"Do it."

Rick nods in agreement but Gabriel shoots from his seat, looking ready for a fight. Dominic gives him one look, that look holding more power and danger than I've ever seen, and Gabriel relaxes his stance but doesn't back down.

The glass burns against my palm and I gulp down the rest of its contents. I don't know how much trouble Gabriel would be in for going against Dominic's wishes, but I don't want to see it. As much internal conflict as I have towards Gabriel's and my relationship, I don't want to see him get in trouble or hurt.

No one moves as the two of them have their stare down, so I push my glass onto the coffee table and move to stand between them. Facing Gabriel, I grab his forearm in a soft but supportive touch. Slowly, he looks down at me, his face relaxing slightly almost instantly. I give him a tentative smile and step closer. His chest shifts with aggravated breaths and I rest my other hand above his heart.

"I want to do this. It's pretty much the only option if we don't want to stir shit up with Murph in this moment. You know we can't. I *need* to do this, Gabe."

His hands clench and unclench at his sides, but he doesn't move to touch me as he takes a deep breath. I let my hands fall on his exhale and move from between them so I'm by his side. He doesn't look at me as he responds, but looks at Dominic with a warning fire in his eyes.

"Fine. We do it. But if anything happens to her, I will never forgive you."

Dominic nods and grabs the back of Gabriel's neck, pulling him forward until their foreheads rest together. "We'll protect her."

Gabriel's jaw clenches but he nods and pulls away from the brotherly embrace. Dominic looks to me and softens his stance along with his face.

"Alright, Elizabeth. Let's make a solid plan."

Chapter Twenty Two

Elizabeth

EVERYBODY LEAVES, SATISFIED with the plan, sometime after nine. When the front door closes, I hear the echo all the way in the kitchen. I've been in here hiding out for the last ten minutes. I might be able to show them I'm able to do this but inside, I've never been more scared. So many things can go wrong.

I could be going in for no reason.

One of Murph's men could find me.

I could not even be able to get in at all.

If there *is* a home hub, it could not even be in his office.

So. Many. Things. Could. Go. Wrong.

I'm staring at an empty glass when Gabriel walks in looking for me. I don't look up, even when I feel him sit beside me. I twirl the glass between my fingers, trying my best to focus on the warmth he's providing instead of all the mistakes I could make with this plan.

"Elizabeth..."

I don't look at him, only give a slight noise of acknowledgement. He says nothing for a couple minutes, but I feel his eyes looking over my profile. When my skin starts to heat with a blush from his gaze, I finally look at him after an eyeroll.

Fire flares for a brief second behind his eyes at the eyeroll, but he just clenches his jaw and continues to monitor my features. When his face starts to soften, I realize I never put my wall back up before giving him my attention. All my worries and fears are laid bare on my face, and I have to force myself not to close back up. Despite the smarter part of me, I like letting him see this deep. Letting him see what's been going through my head for the last fifteen minutes.

His hand flexes against the counter like he wants to touch me, but he doesn't, and a little more disappointment sinks its way into my heart. He said he wouldn't touch me until I asked. But, I'm clearly struggling... *Why do I need to ask to be comforted?*

"What, Gabe? I just want to eat, drink, and pass out."

The muscle in his jaw ticks as his nostrils flare with a deep breath. "Are you sure you want to do this? If Murph comes in to find you there, snooping through his office.. he'll know you aren't loyal to him as you said."

Anger starts to boil beneath my skin, "Because I'm *not* loyal to him. I'll be fine. He won't be there."

He smirks irritatingly and my hands squeeze my glass tighter. "You're angry. Why?"

"Because I'm not a useless little girl you need to coddle! I know what to look for, and I know what I'm doing. I don't need you to be hovering like I can't handle this."

His smirk turns into something more evil. The danger is pouring from every inch of his skin as he stands slowly, hovering above me.

"Did I say you couldn't do this, Elizabeth? I'm just trying to make sure you stay safe. I don't want to see you get hurt. That's all. My concern—or anyone's concern—for your life, shouldn't bother you when it's warranted."

I do my best to keep my irritation showing even though my body wants to slump. He's right. I shouldn't let his or the others concern for me bug me. There's nothing wrong with them caring about what happens to me. But, that damaged part of my mind and heart doesn't want it. I've only ever been cared about by one person, and it didn't last as long as I wanted. I'm not used to people caring about if I die or get hurt, and I hate to admit that it makes me uncomfortable.

Taking a deep breath, I push my chair back enough so I can stand without touching Gabriel.

"I'll be ready. Thank you for your concern. Goodnight."

He doesn't turn to watch me leave, but his voice follows me anyway—sounding defeated and tired, "Goodnight, lepestok."

I spend the rest of the night hiding away in my room, thinking over the plan for next week. Murph never *actually* gave me a time limit for returning the drive, so next week will be when I break into his office. I'm supposed to text him tomorrow, telling him I won't be able to work for the week while I try to get into Dominic or Rick's house. Knowing how much he wants this to succeed, he shouldn't have a problem with it.

When I'm on the brink of falling asleep, I hear my bedroom door open. My body begs to tense but I force it to stay calm, pretending like I'm actually asleep. As soon as the person steps close to the bed, the familiar warmth I get only from Gabriel seeps through the sheets, and I relax further.

His weight settles down on the edge of my bed, the heat of his eyes searing through the blankets that are pulled to my chin. The struggle to keep my eyes closed is great, but if I open them now I might not know why he came in here.

He says nothing for a few minutes, but his eyes never leave my face. His thick fingers swipe hair away from my face and behind my ear, and I can't stop myself from chasing the touch, causing him to sigh.

His voice comes out rough but soft, "My little strong petal..." There's a long pause before he continues, "I barely have you, I don't know how I'll handle losing you."

An unexpected sigh leaves me when he brushes his knuckles along my cheek, and he matches it. I feel his touch slide down my covered arm, still somehow leaving goosebumps in its wake.

"Pozhaluysta, ne ostavlyay menya.[*]"

With those final words I don't understand, he stands and leaves my room as silent as he came in. I fall asleep racing after his invisible touch, mentally begging him to do more.

Chapter Twenty Three

Gabriel

IT'S BEEN A WEEK SINCE we made the plan to break into Murph's office. I've spent the whole week doing my best to keep distance between Elizabeth and I. There wasn't a chance I could get closer to her and not try convince her to let one of us go in instead.

She hasn't made an effort to get close to me either, and I don't really blame her. Her time has been busy training with Nat and Ell, who say she's picked up a lot of stuff fairly quickly. If she isn't with them, she's been walking the forest surrounding the house or watching movies while working on her computer in the living room upstairs.

I'm either in my home office or actual work. I leave early, and come home late. There's only been three times I've seen Elizabeth around the house, and each time I give her a pleasant smile and a simple hello before moving on.

So, in other words, I've been torturing myself.

I sneak into her room every night for a few minutes, just to look at her. I might not be able to see the vibrance of her eyes or hear the melody of her voice, but it's something. There's been a few nights where I've had to force myself to leave so I don't wake her up with my head between her legs or my roaming hands. Or from just crawling into her bed to hold her. I told her I wouldn't touch her, and I meant it.

But I'm regretting that promise now. I'm by the front door, waiting for her to get ready to head for Murph's office, and there's a massive part of me that regrets not talking to her this week. It regrets not laying with her in bed. Regrets not claiming her mouth in a kiss that would show her how much I need her...

It regrets not talking to her about how she's feeling.

When her shoes start to echo off the walls, I look up to find her walking down the stairs. She's wearing a short top with a very deep V, a mini skirt I can almost see up—showing her thick thighs, and knee high heeled boots. *She's fucking stunning.* I wait for her to look at me but she keeps her addictive eyes on her feet. My body coils with the urge to pin her between the door and me until she finally gives me the hit of attention I need. I definitely don't deserve it with the way I've kept away from her this week, but I didn't think I could control myself with her around.

She stops in front me, still not looking at me. Clearing my throat, I tuck my hands inside my jeans so I don't touch her.

"Are you ready?"

She nods, but says nothing. My shoulders sag and I step closer. My heart beats harder inside my chest when she doesn't back away.

"Elizabeth.. please look at me."

Her chest moves with a deep breath, and then she's lifting her head. When her shining hazel eyes finally meet mine, a weight lifts off my shoulders I didn't know I was carrying. I give her a smile but I think it comes off as a grimace when her shoulders flinch upwards and her eyes wither slightly.

Releasing one of my hands from my pants, I tug on the back of my neck, "We'll do everything we can to make sure you're safe while you're inside. You're going to be getting an earpiece so we can keep tabs on you since I can't risk going in with you."

She still says nothing, and only nods. I squeeze my eyes shut and let my head droop down.

"Please, lepestok, talk to me. I... I've missed you."

I can hear her breath catching as my words register.

"You're the one who stayed away from me for a *week*, Gabriel."

Her voice, although irritated and hurt, makes breathing easier. I finally look at her and do my best not to flinch at her expression. Not only is she hurt, but she's angry. At me.

I nod and pull my neck once again, "I didn't think I could be around you and not want more."

She scoffs and pops out her hip, crossing her arms over her tits that are giving a rare appearance in her low cut shirt.

"Want more? Seriously? You can't be around me because your dick takes over? How flattering."

My muscles tighten with irrational anger as she moves to walk around me to the door. I can't control my next moves as I grab her arm and pull her closer, her back slamming into my chest. I don't need her seeing my face, I'm no longer looking the part of the gentleman who opens her doors. I look like the demon that's come to steal her soul and keep it for myself.

"You think that's all I want? Granted, I want to sink into your tight pussy more than I want to eat, but I also want to *know more.* I want to know how you grew up, if it was as shitty as my childhood or better. I want to know what happened with your foster mother. I want to know if you ever wanted to go to college. I want to know your favorite food, drink, ice-cream, color, soap, hell even your favorite fucking pajamas. *I want to know you.*"

Our heavy breathing is the only sound in the space. Telling myself to worry about my actions later, I stuff my nose into her long brown hair and smell my way down to her neck. I don't give her the chance to move her head on her own before I'm holding her throat and tilting it myself. When my nose reaches the soft skin of her neck, I lick over her pounding pulse and groan. I wrap my free arm over her stomach and pull her flush against me, grinding my erection against her ass and back.

"Do you feel that, Shchenok?" Another groan, that's dangerously close to a growl, vibrates my throat. "This is what even the thought of you does to me. Sexual or not. I want all of you. Every thought, every breath, every heartbeat, and every word. I didn't just keep away because I can barely stop myself from fucking you on every surface of my house," her inhale of shock comes between my vomited confession, "but also because I want to ask you so many questions, I fear you won't want to answer."

Her body is practically vibrating in my hold and I realize how tightly I'm holding her. With much effort, I loosen my hold on her throat before letting go, but leaving my arm to lightly drape across her middle. I lean forward and rest my forehead on her temple, letting my nose stuff itself into her lavender scented hair that's hanging silkily down her back. I want to kiss her, to let her know I'll be there for her tonight.

Well, I've fallen this far...

I swipe her hair over her shoulder with a softness I force into my fingers, and kiss the back of her neck. I want to do more but convince my muscles to loosen their hold on her. As I step away, I keep my eyes on the door so I don't have to see the consequences of what I did written on her face.

"I'll be in the car with Rick when you're ready to go."

As soon as the door closes with a resounding thud behind me, I close my eyes and breathe in the cool night air with a deep inhale. Trudging forward with heavy steps, I manage to slip into the passenger seat and pull all emotions into the safe in my mind. My face is utterly blank as I look to Rick in the drivers seat. He knows me too well to fall for my mask and shakes his head slightly, sympathy brightening his blue eyes.

"What did you do, Gabe?"

I shrug with indifference I don't feel and look forward, "I told her things I probably should've kept to myself."

I see him shake his head on a sigh in my peripheral but ignore it, choosing to look at the trees surrounding my house. He doesn't get the opportunity to chastise me as Elizabeth opens the backdoor and plops down. I don't see her face, but I can hear the smile in her voice.

"Let's do this thing."

Chapter Twenty Four

Elizabeth

THE CAR IS SILENT THE whole way to the building that holds Murph's office. I've only been there once, but I remember the smell of damp concrete and cigarettes. He keeps his main office in the back of a warehouse where he takes care of shipments and traitors... Like me.

I try to keep my mind off of all the things that could go wrong tonight and focus on what happened with Gabriel in the entryway of our house.

His house!

Not ours, his house.

I can still feel the hard length of him pressed against my ass. If only he knew I get aroused just from smelling his cologne in the air. The light but masculine scent of pine and leather.

His words both surprised me and didn't. It's obvious that we have sexual tension between us. But for him to want to know all those things about me? That's somewhat surprising. I'm not even sure I would be able to talk to him about those things. Not only did he want to know about my foster mom but, he wanted to know about my dad and childhood. That would mean telling him about how my foster mom got sick and I had to take care of her. It would mean telling him about all I had to endure from my dad until that night, when he couldn't live without my mom for another minute.

I get pulled from the spiral of memories when the car comes to a stop and both Rick and Gabriel turn around to look at me. Both have this serious and worried look on their face. I might not know how to completely defend myself, but I'm not totally hopeless. I've been working on a lot with Natalie and Elliana. I know now how to shoot, even if my aim isn't the most accurate, and I know a few simple moves to get away from an attacker.

Rick pats Gabriel on the shoulder, a silent conversation bounces between their eyes, and then Gabriel is handing me a small earpiece.

"Put this in first, so we can make sure it's working."

With a small nod, I let him drop it into my waiting palm before slipping it into position in my ear. Once it's firmly in place I fix my hair to cover my ear and look at them both with a questioning expression. Rick pulls out a laptop and starts to load a bunch of different programs before nodding at me. I say a few random words and he nods again, continuing to sort through the programs.

Gabriel looks at me, again with the indifferent mask like this is nothing, "Alright, mic is working. We'll have a communication line open the whole time so we can talk to you. Rick will be working on the cameras in the areas you have to walk through after getting an idea of who's inside. You need to stay away from whoever is in there as much as you can. If they get suspicious of why you're here, just remember to tell them you're giving Murph a surprise visit."

His jaw clenches after the last part. If anyone sees me, I'm supposed to give off the idea that I'm here to seduce Murph. Neither of us are fans of that part apparently.

Running my sweaty palms over my short skirt, I look at Gabriel through my lashes, "Can we have a moment to talk?"

His brows rise slightly before covering it and looking to Rick. Rick nods, telling us we can have five minutes before I need to move. Gabriel rushes from his seat, opening my door, helping me out, and walking with me to the back of the car. He leans against the trunk and shoves his hands in his dark jeans, keeping his eyes on his shoes. I pace in short lines in front of him trying to figure out what to say.

What if something does happen while I'm in there? Will I regret not telling Gabriel how I actually enjoy being around him? Will I regret not telling him I've been wishing he would ask those questions or touch me without hesitation?

Taking a deep breath, I step up to him until my shoes are brushing his, finally getting him to lift his vibrant green eyes.

"My favorite color is dark green. I like mint chip ice-cream. My favorite food is sushi or ramen, I could never decide. My favorite drink is lemonade and my favorite alcohol is either whiskey or vodka depending on the mood. I like any flower scented soap. And my favorite pajamas are anything baggy that doesn't cling to me while I sleep."

I barely am able to get the last breathless word off my tongue before his hands are grabbing my face and pulling me forward. I catch myself on his chest, my fingers curling into the black cotton fabric of his shirt. He doesn't kiss me, only holds me close enough so our noses touch and we breathe in each other's air. His normally bright green eyes begin to darken as they bounce between mine. His brows furrow, like he's trying to piece together everything I just admitted.

He rubs his nose over mine, and groans while squeezing his eyes closed. "This isn't how I wanted to know those things, Shchenok."

Giving him a tiny smile he can't see, I push against the hold he has on my face and gingerly press my lips to his—only enough so they brush as I speak.

"I wanted to tell them to you. We should've been getting to know each other instead of keeping our distance."

His eyes open, and I've yet to see him look so tortured. The feel of his thick fingers sliding back into my hair and pinching it into his fist has my skin tingly with tiny fireworks. I keep my eyes on his as he brushes his mouth over mine ever so gently, causing a whimper to get stuck in my throat.

If I'm risking my life tonight, I might as well risk my heart too.

"Kiss me, Gabriel." He doesn't move, only tightens the hold he has on my hair and I lift on my toes to relieve some of the pressure. "*Please.*"

That's all he needs.

His perfect seductive mouth finally crashes to mine and we both moan at the sensation. I can feel the rush of warmth from my lips, rippling down to my feet, as he ravishes my mouth with harsh attention. I've never felt anything like this, the complete utter heavenly shock going through my body.. and he's only kissing me.

I suck in a heavy breath when his teeth capture my bottom lip and pull on it before his tongue soothes over the sting. It pushes past my lips for a deep taste as his growl vibrates into my mouth. I have his shirt in a death grip that only tightens with each sweep of his tongue and motion of his lips.

A double knock has me jumping back slightly, not toppling over thanks to his fists in my hair. I keep my gaze trained on his mouth and the extra puffiness thanks to the brutal way he just claimed me. When I still don't look at him, he removes one of his fists from my hair and wraps it around my back to pull me flush against him. I snake my arms around his waist and stuff my nose in the warmth of his chest.

He presses a soft kiss on the top of my head, and speaks against my now messy hair, "Thank you.. for telling me those things, moy malen'kiy lepestok."

I nod against him and hold him tighter for a lingering few seconds, then pull away and step back. The tension around his eyes and mouth are less prominent now as he gives me a soft smile and rubs his thumb over my cheek. I lean into the warmth from that one finger and return the smile.

"I guess it's time for me to go in..."

Gabriel's chest moves shakily with a deep breath as he stands straight and nods.

Chapter Twenty Five

Elizabeth

I DO MY BEST TO KEEP my knees from buckling as I strut inside the warehouse side-door with false confidence. It doesn't help my body is still recovering from the drugging make-out session I just had. I shake my head and slap my cheeks lightly, donning my shy but confident mask I normally wear around Murph and his men.

I'm able to make it through the main hallway without colliding into anybody, although I can hear them groan and cheer at whatever game is occupying their time in the main space. When I get two doors away from Murph's office, a thick hand clamps down on my shoulder and spins me around.

I do my best to keep the shock and fear from my face as I look up at Ben. *Of course this dumbass is the one to find me here.*

Giving him the 'I don't give a fuck' smile, I cross my arms to push up my boobs and take a step back, "Hey, what's up Ben?"

He copies my stance and raises a suspicious brow, "What are you doing here, Liz?"

"I came to see Murph."

"Boss isn't here right now."

I shrug and take another step back, "I'm surprising him. I'm assuming he's going to come in tonight?"

He looks me over slowly—taking in the deep V in my shirt, my mini skirt that barely covers past my ass, and my thick-tall heeled boots.

"Surprise visit, huh?" I nod and roll my eyes. "I'm sure he won't be too upset if I let you in looking like that…"

I let him think about it as he continues to eat me with his eyes. My legs tense so I don't start tapping my foot with impatience and nerves. He finally nods and uncrosses his arms.

"Alright, Liz. Go on back to his office. But don't fucking touch anything."

I swallow thickly and nod, turning around and rushing to Murph's office before Ben changes his mind. Once inside, I shut the door and lean against it. With three big breaths slowing my heartrate, I step quickly further into of the small room.

Rick's thick voice flows into my ear, making me jump. "Good job, Liz."

I nod, then remember there's no cameras in here so he can't see me. "Thanks. Hopefully I can get out of here before Murph actually shows up."

There's no response, but I know they both agree. We want to be long gone by the time Murph arrives tonight. Ben will definitely tell him that I'm supposed to be waiting, but I can come up with an excuse for leaving later. Right now, I need to focus on looking for anything the drive could be paired with.

Keeping as quiet as I can, I start looking over the shelves sporadically put around the room. Besides the occasional sketchy document, I don't find anything and move on to the drawers of the desk. I'm able to open every one, which come up useless, except for the middle drawer. I wiggle the handle a little more before looking around for a key. There has to be important things in this one if it's locked.

I look over the messy desk surface for a key, in the cups holding random pens, and again in the other drawers, only to come up empty.

"Guys, I haven't found anything but one of the drawers is locked and I have a good feeling something important is in it."

There's silence for a few seconds before Gabriel's voice comes through, sending a divine tingle up my spine, "Is there a letter opener or knife somewhere?"

Ignoring how bad I want him to keep talking, I look with renewed energy to find one of those two things. After another couple sweeps, I find a small knife underneath a pile of papers.

"I found a small knife. Now what?"

Gabriel's throat clears, "Alright, is it an older desk? Older looking simple lock?"

I nod, squatting down between the chair and desk, "Yeah, looks pretty simple."

"Okay, squeeze the knife between the desk and the drawer, then push the handle upwards to get the drawer to push out, hopefully you'll be able to break it open."

Capturing my bottom lip between my teeth, I put the knife where he said and push with my body weight. With a few wiggles, I'm able to jam the knife in enough for the next step. I hold my breath and use both hands to start pushing upwards on the handle. It barely moves before I breathe out with defeat and sit on my heels.

I groan, "This is a lot harder than you made it sound."

Gabriel's throaty chuckle answers but that's all he gives me.

With another deep breath, I fix my hand position on the handle of the knife and try again. It takes me three more tries before I finally hear a groan then a pop of a lock breaking, just in time to feed my aching lungs with an intake of air. Throwing the knife on the desk, I finish pulling out the drawer and look inside.

My hands start to shake as I see what's been locked away.

Picture after picture of *me*, all looking like they've been taken since I first ran into Gabriel. I flip through the pictures, slowly growing frantic.

Me standing outside Natalie and Rick's wedding venue. Me leaning heavily onto Gabriel as he walks me inside my apartment building. Me talking to Sam when he first drove me. Gabriel and I standing outside my apartment, my eyes giving away the depths of my forbidden feelings for him.

The pictures start to slip from my hands as I get farther.

The ride on Gabriel's bike.

Walking around his backyard.

Me through the gym windows.

He's been keeping tabs on me.

He knows.

I've been so taken aback by what I found I don't realize both Rick and Gabriel are yelling my name through the ear piece.

"Liz, get the fuck out! Now!"

I look up towards the office door, now hearing the steps and muffled voices getting closer. It's too late. I took too long. I'm stuck in here.

My voice comes out weak and breathless, "I'm sorry. I—I can't. He's coming."

Gabriel's voice growls loudly in my ear, "Fucking hide, Elizabeth. *Now.*"

I move fast, pushing all the photos back into the drawer and pushing it back in. I look around the room frantically—there's nowhere for me to go or hide. Every inch is open.

The door handle starts to turn with a light squeak and my inhale gets caught in my throat. Without a second thought I drop to my knees and scurry under the desk, tucking myself into the corner and making myself as small as possible. I cover my mouth with my hand and try to slow my breathing.

The door opens and Murph walks in with someone.

"You said she's waiting in here for me?"

His steps are slow and sure as he comes closer to the desk, and my eyes squeeze closed.

"Yeah, boss. She said she was giving you a surprise visit."

Murph hums, "Well, do you see her in here, Ben?"

Of course, I knew Ben was going to tell him, but I thought we would have more time before Murph showed up. Ben starts to stumble over an explanation until Murph yells at him.

"Shut the fuck up! If she's not in here, she has to be somewhere in the warehouse. Find her before she leaves. I'd like to have a little *chat* with my sunshine."

"Yes, boss."

Ben's thudding steps leave the office, growing quieter the further he gets. I keep my breathing slow as I open my eyes. Murph hasn't moved from where he walked in, but I can hear his solid inhales.

His voice comes out soft, but threatening, "What were you looking for, sunshine?"

The carpet muffles his steps as he moves around the room, possibly looking for anything out of place. They slowly get closer to where I'm hiding and I have to force myself not to whimper from dread. My eyes start to water as memories of my dad come flooding through.

Tears stream down my face as I cry silently. My back starts to sweat from where I'm huddled in the corner. I only tried to show daddy the straight 'A's' on my report card, and he got mad. Again. I thought he would be proud of me, maybe even smile. Instead he stood so fast the chair fell to the ground and he started yelling at me to leave him alone.

"You think good grades are going to bring your mom back? Huh?! I don't give a fuck about your grades you little shit."

I tuck myself further into the corner and put my head between my knees when I hear his belt buckle start to clink loose.

"You don't talk to me unless I say so. You shouldn't even be breathing. You don't deserve to be here after what you did to your mother." I hear the belt snap as he pulls it from his pants, his drunk feet slamming against the tile as he walks closer. "Ten years now I've had to deal with your pathetic existence instead of being able to love my wife. This is your *fault."*

The leather of the belt whistles as it slices through the air, missing me by an inch and slapping the tile loudly instead, making me flinch. I open my eyes, a plea ready on my tongue, when the doorbell echoes through the house. Daddy shoots me a look that withers me further into a ball as he tosses his belt on the table.

"You're lucky I'm too hungry to punish you. Now, fuck off."

I don't hesitate to jump up and sprint to my room, hearing him talking nicely to whoever is delivering his dinner at the door.

My vision clears as Murph's legs appear in front of me. His dress pants wrinkled and sitting too far on top of his cheap leather shoes. Drawers start to slide open around me, as he continues to double check his belongings.

I almost jump as Gabriel's whisper sings in my ear, "Can you talk, Elizabeth?" I say nothing, not risking even a deep breath. "Okay.. Okay.." Gabriel trails off like he's trying to think of a way to get me out, or even to check that I'm okay. He would've heard if something happened, but I have to keep that to myself.

Rick's lethally quiet voice comes in next, "Liz, I need you to stay calm and quiet. I'll be able to let you know when Murph is gone, but not until he leaves the office. You're doing great."

Gabriel speaks quietly, but I hear the desperation and worry loudly, "You're going to be okay, lepestok."

I nod slightly, letting his words ground me further. Murph gets to the middle drawer and gives it a test pull, chuckling deeply when it gives without needing to be unlocked.

"Oh, sunshine. You just had to look in here, didn't you?"

My nails dig into my cheeks as I hold my mouth tighter. His knees bend slowly as he sits in his cracked leather chair. I can now see from his lower stomach down, and my nerves kick higher with the fear he could see me from his position. His fingers flex as his hands hang over the front of his armrests before starting to tap in the air.

"Well, we'll just have to talk about this, won't we?"

My body locks when both his hands rush under the desk, grabbing my arms roughly. My scream comes out pained as he pulls me roughly against the short carpet until I'm on my knees in front of him.

Gabriel says my name so loudly, I almost miss the low chuckles from Murph's chest.

My vision is blurry with unshed tears but I don't miss the crazed smile spreading across Murph's face or the excited gleam in his eyes.

"There you are, sunshine."

Chapter Twenty Six

Elizabeth

MY HANDS SHAKE AS SILENT tears dry to my sweaty skin. In the years I've known Murph, I've yet to see him so unhinged. His smile screams evil intentions as his eyes glaze with what I'm sure is murderous ideas.

"Why did you hide, Liz?"

I shake my head, "I—I wasn't sure who was coming in. I got spooked."

He hums as he leans forward and looks over what I'm wearing. His smile only goes wider as his eyes become hooded.

"I heard you came here for a special little visit. Are you trying to seduce me, Liz?" I open my mouth but he cuts me off, grabbing the back of my neck tightly and pulling me closer until his breath fans over my face. "Or are you looking for something?"

I shake my head as much as I can in his painful hold, "I wasn't looking for anything."

My voice doesn't waver as much as I thought it would and I let it calm my nerves slightly. I can handle this. Fake it till you make it, right? Murph leans closer, tilting his head so his nose touches my neck. All my muscles lock as he takes a deep inhale against my skin.

Gabriel and Rick are hearing this, aren't they?

I tell myself their figuring out a way to get me out as Murph sighs heavily against my clammy skin.

"You've always smelled so good. I wonder if you taste just as good... Should we find out?"

He doesn't wait for me to respond as his tongue flattens against my neck. My eyes clamp shut and I bite my tongue hard enough to draw blood. Sickly spit sticks to me as he drags his tongue up my neck, over my jaw and cheek, finally stopping after licking over my eye. I keep my breathing even as he speaks in my ear.

"So good, so sweet."

When his free hand pulls my hair roughly away from my ear, that's when I realize he's going for the earpiece.

"No!" My voice comes out as a shriek and I try to pull away, but his hand around the back of my neck tightens enough to make me flinch with pain and he pulls away my only hope from my ear.

He throws me back by my neck, my head slamming against the edge of the desk before I can catch myself. I watch with wide blurry eyes and a pounding heart as he gives me another crazed smile, holding the earpiece by his mouth.

"Goodbye, Morozov."

Terror rattles through my bones as he drops the earpiece and crushes it with his heel. Clenching my jaw, I stand quickly and rush Murph in his seat, my hands at the ready to strangle him. I barely move a step before his knockoff shoe makes heavy contact with my stomach, kicking me away.

My back slams into the edge of the desk, pain spreading a fire up my spine and down my legs as my lungs try to get air. I fall on top of the desk, my hands barely catching me before I fall to the floor. Murph's dark laugh bounces off the concrete walls, filling my veins with a much needed fight. My brows set with determination as I look slightly to my left. The knife I used to open the desk sits only a couple inches from my hand.

I don't let all the things that could go wrong take space in my head as I grab the knife tightly and swing around. I was expecting

Murph to still be sitting in the chair, but he's standing behind me, making my aim off. Instead of stabbing him in the neck like I could've, it lands in his side. His roar of pain covers my shocked inhale.

Before I can pull the knife out to try again, one of his hands covers mine with too much force as the other crashes against my throat and squeezes. My air is immediately cut off and my hands instinctively reach for his wrist. He lets me pull the knife from his side, the clang of it dropping to the floor accompanying his animalistic breathing.

His free hand joins the other in the grip slowly crushing my throat. My feet lift slightly off the ground as he pushes up before slamming me down on the desk. My legs kick wildly, my nails clawing at any piece of flesh I can reach on him. He uses his hips to push my legs apart so he can stand between them, giving him a better angle to strangle me.

He no longer looks crazed, he looks explosive. His pupils almost swallow the color of his irises, his lip curled in a snarl.

"You stupid bitch. You really think you could kill me with that tiny knife?"

My lungs start to hurt from lack of air, my attempts towards freedom becoming more frantic as tears run from the corner of my eyes into my hair.

"What? You have something to say for yourself? Maybe I should just kill you now, I'm sure I can find someone else *actually* loyal to help me win the city."

I shake my head, trying desperately to get him to let go, to appease him so I can have just a breath. Darkness starts to close in around my vision, my kicks and clawing slowing down as my heartrate decreases.

I'm going to die here. I'm going to die at the hands of a delusional, abusive man.

His fingers dig deeper and my eyes struggle to stay open. "Then again, what will I do without my sunshine?"

Lifting up my head, he slams me down hard, sharp pain and warmth spreading over the back of my skull as his hands leave my burning throat. Instinct has me curling on my side on the desk and inhaling deeply, sending me into a torturous coughing fit. Slowly, my coughing subsides as my lungs thank me for the much needed oxygen I continue to gulp down.

Murph's chuckle sends my hackles rising but I can do nothing but close my eyes and tuck my knees closer.

"Look at you, sunshine. So beautiful and weak laying there after I let you live. Now, what do I get in return for my generosity? If you were anyone else, I would have kept going until your eyes were empty and your body was nothing more than a waste of space in this office."

My voice is hoarse and soft as I force my words out, "Why didn't.. you kill me.. then?"

His body leans over mine, his hands coming down by my head, "Because, despite my normal habit, I couldn't kill you. At least.. not like that."

My trauma response finally decides to settle over my body, everything going numb as I open my eyes to look at his pale hand. He'll kill me. Maybe not now, maybe not by choking my life away, but he will. Just as my body shows signs of giving up, to let him do whatever he wants, Elliana's voice sweeps through my mind.

"You're not weak. You're no longer stuck in a little girl's body. You can fight back. You can win. Don't let your father win by giving in to evil men. Fight. Back."

I nod to myself and turn my head to look Murph in the eyes. He look so smug, like he just won everything. I won't let him win. I *can't*.

New found adrenaline rushes through my veins as my muscles tense, ready to fight back. With as much force as I can muster, I shove my elbow out and up. The crunch from Murph's nose echoes up my arm as he curses and steps back. I don't give him a moment to collect himself as I launch off the desk, tackling him with the weight of my body. We tumble into the chair, knocking it over and crashing into the ground. I ignore the pain in my ribs as I straddle Murph and use the pointers Nat and Ell gave me to send punch after punch to his face.

I ignore the pain in my hand, ignore the way he tries to block me and throw me off, letting the red rage take over my vision. Blood splatters from Murph's nose and other various places on his face as I alternate between fists. Only when his eyes close and his body goes slack, do I stop.

My heavy breathing is the only sound as I slump on top of him. The adrenaline that saved me starts to crash, every injury pulsing in time with my heart. I let myself look over his unconscious form for only a couple more seconds before forcing my heavy legs to corporate in standing. I find the earpiece smashed a couple feet away, even in worse shape because of our fight.

Now what am I supposed to do?

Chapter Twenty Seven

Gabriel

MY BLOOD HAS TO BE boiling in my veins. I can hear him licking her. I can hear his instigating compliment. My body coils tight when Elizabeth screams. And then...

"Goodbye, Morozov."

My body tenses impossibly further as the crack and static from Elizabeth's earpiece signals loss of contact. I look to Rick as my hands clench on my legs, getting ready for a fight.

"I'm going in for her."

He doesn't have a second to stop me before I'm out of the car and starting to jog towards the warehouse, my body coiled and on edge. I only make it a few feet before Rick grabs my arm and turns me to face him. I step close and growl in his face.

"Are you seriously fucking stopping me from going to get her?"

Rick doesn't back down, he never would. He pushes even closer, his face—I'm sure—a mirror of my own rage.

"There are close to twenty men in there who will see you coming the second you step in. Not only that, but we could make it worse for her if we go inside. We aren't even sure what's happening. She said herself, he's never hurt her."

"That was before she snuck into his office to fucking steal something! You think that crazy motherfucker isn't going to do something to her after that? We promised she'd be protected. *I'm going.*"

I go to turn back around to head inside, but his grip only firms on my arm. This time, I don't turn around. I continue to look at the warehouse door as rage and protectiveness writhes beneath my skin—my chest heaving with tense breaths.

"Gabe, you can't be reckless. You have *one* gun on you. Are you going to risk your own life to save a girl you *hardly know*?"

I turn around then, yelling right in his face, "*Yes!*"

His nostrils flare with a heavy exhale, his word coming out on a frustrated growl, "Why."

It's barely a question.

"How soon did you know Natalie was the one for you?"

His jaw muscle twitches but he says nothing. He knows I have a point. His feelings for Nat were strong from the start. She was *it* for him before they truly knew each other. And that's how it is for me, with Elizabeth.

"She's *it* for me, Rick. Now, let. Me. Go."

His jaw clenches further, but he nods and lets go of my arm. He joins my side as we run towards the warehouse. When we make it halfway, the side door swings open, banging against the brick behind it, and someone stumbles out.

Elizabeth.

My legs are moving faster before it fully registers how she's doing. Her arms hang limply at her sides but her head snaps up when she hears my pounding steps. She only manages two steps before I'm there, pulling her against me and cradling her head to my chest as she collapses. I hold her closely, giving her a chance to recognize that I've got her now, before I scoop her up and jog back to the car. Rick is already sliding into the driver's seat, ready to get us the fuck out of here.

I open the back door and slide in with her, keeping her cradled in my lap as Rick steps on the gas. When we make it out of sight of the warehouse, I gently grab Elizabeth's cheeks and tilt her face up. Relief crashes through me as I look into her eyes. But, it's short-lived when I continue to look her over. There's blood on her shirt, arms, and hands, along with already developing bruises. The knuckles on both of her delicate hands are split and bleeding.

Then there's her throat. My raging fire sparks anew as I see the strangulation marks already darkening her beautifully soft skin.

My chest heaves against her as my arms fight against themselves to not squeeze her closer and hurt her further. I look to Rick in the mirror, and know he sees the pure rage in my eyes as he accelerates even faster.

A soft warm hand rests on my cheek, and I look down at Elizabeth. She looks so fragile in my lap, but so very strong. She fought to save herself. To get out. Even when she was promised she would be protected, and no one was truly there.

She made it out.

Her thumb brushes lightly over my cheek and my body instantly releases some of its tension.

"I'm okay, Gabe. Just minor injuries."

I shake my head, covering her hand gently with my own, "Nothing is minor when it comes to you, Elizabeth."

I try to ignore the pang of guilt at her raspy, forced voice.

"I'll be okay.. You should see the other guy." She gives a weak breathy laugh and minor smile that turns into a pained grimace.

"I have no doubt that you kicked his ass, Shchenok. But, let's not worry about that right now. I want to get you checked out before we talk about anything."

She nods, giving me another small smile, before her eyelids flutter and her head falls onto my chest. Panic seizes me quickly as

I say her name earning no response. I look up at Rick through the mirror.

"Faster."

He nods and continues to weave through traffic to get us to the hospital. I watch Elizabeth's chest rise and fall with solid but slow breaths the rest of the way, keeping her cushioned against me.

It only takes Rick eight minutes to get to the hospital, and I'm out and moving before the car even parks. I hold Elizabeth bridal style and rush through the front doors.

My voice booms in the fairly quiet space, "Get me a room and Dr. Sloane immediately!"

One of the nurses at the front desk sputters before she's on the phone, two more nurses rushing to push a bed from the hallway for Elizabeth to get laid on. When they stop in front of me, I almost refuse to put her down. I lay her on the bed as gently as possible, and step back so they can turn the bed around and wheel her to a private room.

I walk briskly next to them, barely taking my eyes off Elizabeth's still unconscious form. When they finally get her in the room, we only have to wait a few seconds before Dr. Sloane, a doctor on our payroll, walks in ready to check Elizabeth.

"What happened?"

I clear my throat, fidgeting, "We didn't have eyes on her. From what we could gather, she was strangled. Most of the blood isn't hers."

Dr. Sloane nods as she checks Elizabeth's vitals and they get her set up. After looking her over and under certain areas of her clothes, Dr. Sloane decides it's best to do some imaging. When she goes to look in Elizabeth's eyes, her brows furrow slightly and she stuffs her hand between the pillow and the back of Liz's head.

When she pulls her gloved hand away, there's blood coating the blue latex. My heart squeezes painfully as nurses roll Elizabeth out of the room to start imaging and to take a closer look at her head. As I try to follow after them, Dr. Sloane stops me with a hand to my chest and a stern look.

"You need to stay here, Mr. Morozov. We'll keep you updated and bring her back when we're done. Why don't you change your clothes in the meantime."

I try to argue but Rick pulls me away to stay in the room to wait it out.

When the door closes, I look down to realize I have random blood patterns over my pants and shirt, and my heart practically falls from my chest. Rick sits on the bench under the full wall window, watching me pace back and forth around the room as we wait.

How long does it take to do some fucking images?

After thirty minutes of waiting, the door opens and I turn quickly to face it, but disappointment softens my stance as Nat, Dom, and Ell walk in the room. Dom looks to me and nods, walking to join Rick on the bench to—I'm sure—talk over what happened. Nat and Ell come right up to me looking worried and asking questions. I answer them all to the best of my ability.

When they hear about how Rick delayed me from going inside, Elliana looks at him with full disappointment while Natalie walks slowly up to him. We all watch quietly as Rick opens his body to her, looking apologetic but not stopping her from whatever she wants to do.

When she stops between his legs, he gently clasps the back of her thighs. She raises her hand but doesn't move it to make contact in a slap we are all anticipating. Her shoulders slouch and he holds her legs tighter, apologizing with his eyes.

Her voice comes out quiet, but I don't miss the anger and disappointment lacing her words, "Why would you stop him from going in, Rick? We told her she would be protected."

He shakes his head, his voice coming out small, "I couldn't risk losing him, Nat."

He looks around her towards me, silently giving me an apology. I nod but look away. I understand why he wouldn't want me to go in, severely underprepared. It doesn't stop me from being angry with him. I wanted to get to her. If I did, I could've prevented some of her injuries. Prevented her from having to fight for her life like she did.

She didn't deserve to go through that alone, because...

She's not alone anymore.

Chapter Twenty Eight

Elizabeth

MY THROAT VIBRATES with a scream as my eyes open, my muscles tightly coiled and my sheets damp and wrapped around me like I was thrashing. Light filters into the room as the door opens. I shuffle up and cower in the corner of my bed as someone walks in. My eyes are still blurry from my sleeping tears and the person is in shadows from the light behind them. Only when their face comes into view, and I see my foster mom looking worried with watery eyes, do I relax—showing her she can come closer. She doesn't waste a second as she sits on the bed, not minding the wet spot from my sweat, and pulls me into her side. I let myself lean into her soft comfort, wrapping my arm around her thin middle and smelling her usual flowery scent clinging to her nightgown.

Her rough, aged hands smooth down my knotted, wet hair as she rocks us softly side to side. I close my eyes and hold her closer, never imagining I would have such love and comfort from anyone in my life.

"My sweet girl, I'm here now. I've got you."

Her words cause me to start crying again, and she holds me even closer. She starts to hum a song I don't recognize but it slowly lulls me until I'm no longer crying and my eyes are closed with the urge to fall back into sleep.

Her voice comes out soft but raspy, like she's trying not to cry, "What did that man do to you, precious girl. It makes me sick when I hear you crying out every night..."

I shrug, brushing it off like it's not a big deal even though I know it's a problem, "Nothing you need to hear, I promise."

She huffs, moving her hand from my hair to rub my arm that's around her fragile waist, "Well, the only thing he did right in his life is create you. You might not see this now, but you are a strong girl. He made you strong. *Don't forget that. You're living and getting to know a better world. And I'm so grateful that I get to watch you grow even stronger."*

I wake up to a massive pounding in my head, irritating beeps, and a bright light shining across my face. With a silent groan, I lift my hand to cover my face. Pain dances across the back of my hand, and I start to recall what happened.

Getting stuck in Murph's office.

Murph finding me.

Fighting for my life.

Letting adrenaline fuel my punches in order to flee.

Managing to escape without running into anyone while forcing myself to stay conscious.

This time, my groan manages to be vocal, and a strong warm hand covers mine. I jump at the contact, my eyes flying open as I try to pull away and my heart speeds up. I look around the bright room, noticing finally that I'm in the hospital, and look to the person next to me who refuses to let my hand go.

Gabriel sits with a tight worried expression—fear, sadness, silent apology, and relief swimming in the bright grassy fields of his eyes.

I do my best to give him a small smile, no longer resisting his hold on me. I lift my free hand to touch my throat, the soreness irritating. A cup of water comes into view on my opposite side and I look over to find Elliana handing me a plastic tan cup and quickly grab it, draining it of the cold liquid.

Gabriel's deep, tired voice vibrates over my skin, "How are you feeling, lepestok?"

I nod as I hand Elliana the cup back, "Well I'm not dead, so that's a plus."

I give a soft pained laugh, but neither of them join me. They each give me a small smile, then Elliana grabs my attention by lightly touching my shoulder.

"I'm going to give you guys a moment."

She gives me another tight smile before leaving me alone with Gabriel. When the door clicks shut I look over to him with a heavy blink and a slight smile.

He tries to return it but it looks more like a grimace. "I'm so sorry, Elizabeth. We should've gotten in there when we knew Murph found you. I'll never forgive myself for failing to keep my promise. For failing to protect you."

Turning my hand over, I hold his and give him a squeeze, "Gabriel. It's alright. I don't need you risking your safety for me. I obviously handled it and got out alive."

His voice raises, making me jump, "But you almost died! Because we were too slow. Because Rick was busy thinking of the risks. Because I cou—couldn't move quick enough..."

His breathing is shaky, his eyes burdened, and his grip on my hand just short of painful. Giving him another smile, trying my best to show him that there's nothing to apologize for, I sit up with a pained groan and stop him from standing to help me.

"Look at me, Gabriel." I wait for him to get settled back in his seat, and those glowing eyes to reach mine. "I'm *alive*. I appreciate the worry you have for me, I really do but... I think I needed to survive that, *alone*. Deep down, I needed to show myself that I'm no longer a weak child. I can save myself. I can *win*."

His eyes bounce between my own and then he nods, leaning forward and placing a feather light kiss on my bruised knuckles.

"I understand, moy malen'kiy lepestok... Mne ne men'she zhal'.[*]"

Before we can get further into the conversation, the door opens and a medium sized woman with blonde hair enters the room.

She looks me in the eyes with a small smile, "Mrs. Morozov, I'm Dr. Sloane. Nice to see you're finally awake."

My brows shoot towards my hair line before my eyes narrow on the man next to me. "Why did she call me that?"

He clears his throat, a slight blush creeping onto his cheeks as he looks back and forth between me and the doctor. She chuckles loudly, drawing my eyes back to her and saving Gabriel from answering.

"I'm sorry if that offended you in some way, it's just how we put it down so that he could access information without a problem on paper. I would be inclined to tell him anyway, since his boss pays me extra, but just in case something comes up..." She shrugs, giving me a soft smile and stepping closer to the end of the bed.

"Got it, alright."

I shoot Gabriel another glare, refusing to acknowledge how I felt hearing her call me that.

"Now, onto what we found when Mr. Morozov brought you in." I nod for her to continue. "You had a severe concussion, topped with how you spent all your energy, explains why you lost consciousness for a while. There was a slight wound on the back of your head but nothing needing stitches. Your hands are only bruised and slightly split open but will heal in time like nothing happened.

"You did have bruised ribs, but nothing we can really do for that besides pain meds, and thankfully it didn't cause internal bleeding. Your worst injury, besides your head, was your throat. On the outside, there is severe bruising which could take more time than a normal bruise to heal. In general, you could have difficulty with speech—especially louder volumes—with discomfort in swallowing, some swelling, and possible numbness. Can I check for any swelling or numbness?"

I nod and she walks over to the side of the bed, setting her chart on the side table, she reaches over with another small smile before feeling my throat gently. She occasionally asks if I can feel the spots she's touching, and only small places are numb enough that I can barely feel it.

She finally steps back and picks the chart back up, writing while she talks, "Alright, your throat is better than we expected it to be which is a great sign. I'm going to write a script for pain meds that you can pick up on your way out. Besides that, I'm going to request that you spend the next month resting as much as possible to heal, keeping physical activity to the bare minimum. Do you have any questions for me?"

I look over to Gabriel who only raises his brows. I'm not sure why I looked at him like he would need to ask questions for me, but a part of me likes the fact that he's here for support. I look back to Dr. Sloane with a reassuring smile.

"I don't think I have any at this moment."

She nods slightly, "Alright, well in that case, I'll get your discharge paperwork ready so you can get home. Hopefully I don't need to see any of you in here soon."

With one last smile, and a pointed look at Gabriel, she leaves.

Once again alone with Gabriel, I'm not sure how to handle what comes next. Obviously, Murph knows I'm on their side now and I won't be helping him with whatever information he wanted me to steal. Plus he's still alive and now will be plotting against Dom even further, thanks to the unfortunate events from my little visit and the fact that I still have the drive.

"So, what's the plan now?"

I look over to Gabriel as he places his hand next to my leg. "Now, you worry about healing."

My eyes roll, "I meant with Murph. Based off of the recent events, I'd say that I'm not going to be connected to him any further, but he'll be wanting to gain Dom's control of the city even more now... And I might not be safe from him. So, where does that leave u—me..."

Gabriel's eyes darken slightly at the eye roll I knew would get to him, but he's quick to soften his gaze.

"Where do you want it to leave you, Elizabeth?"

I shrug, hiding my eyes by looking towards my blanket covered legs, "I don't want any one of you getting hurt. I might only make things worse by being around."

"How could you being with us make things worse?" His question is quiet, like he's scared by digging too deep I might run away.

"Well.. Murph might look at it like you're taking something of his away and retaliate harder than originally planned."

Gabriel's fingers pinch my chin softly but commandingly as he brings my full face back to his sight. His face is set in determination, and I know whatever he's going to say next he truthfully means.

"You were never his to take or keep. You are a part of this group.. this *family*, just as much as I am. You're with us now. And unless you desire otherwise, it will stay that way. Am I clear?" I nod and his fingers hold my chin slightly tighter as he smirks, "Good. Let's get you home so you can rest in an actual bed, huh?"

Chapter Twenty Nine

Elizabeth

I FALL ASLEEP ON THE ride home after being discharged from the hospital, and only wake up when I feel strong arms lifting me into the air. I'm barely able to crack open my eyes to see Gabriel smiling down on me sweetly as he carries me into the house and up to my room.

Only, when I feel him reach the top of the stairs, he takes a right instead of a left. My eyes struggle to stay open as I look up at him with confusion.

"Where are you taking me? My room is the other way."

He shushes me softly, "Just go to sleep, Shchenok. We can talk more after you rest for a bit."

I want to argue, to tell him that I just want to be in my bed. But, darkness calls me just as a door opens and the familiar scent of Gabriel's cologne surrounds my senses.

When I wake up again, there's daylight streaming through the window, warming my body beneath the silk sheets.

Wait... Silk sheets?

I shift onto my side, the one without bruised ribs, and try to open my eyes. This time, it's less of a struggle to get my eyelids to cooperate. When I manage to get them mostly open, I look around without moving my head.

There's dark wood flooring, dark green walls, and gold accents around the room. I'm covered in black silk sheets on a massive bed that smells like Gabriel. *Am I sleeping in Gabriel's bed?* I try to sit up but a sharp pain in my side has me freezing. With a few calming breaths, I'm able to fully sit up enough to lean back against the pile of pillows blocking off the headboard. There's no sign of Gabriel being in the room, and the bathroom light is off, meaning Gabriel left me in here by myself.

I'm not sure why I'm in here instead of my own room, but I guess the only way to find that out is to ask. As I start to uncover my legs, another realization has me freezing. I'm in a pair of boxers and a baggy white shirt. Both of which are not mine. My body heats with a mixture of anger for being changed while I was dead to the world, and arousal at the fact that Gabriel had to have changed me into *his* clothes.

I fist a handful of the white shirt and bring it close to my nose. Closing my eyes, I inhale a mix of pine, leather, and something else than can only be described as Gabriel. With a soft smile lifting the corners of my mouth, I drop the fabric and start to stand from the bed. I'm not sure when the last time I ate was, and my stomach is reminding me of that.

Before my feet can fully touch the ground, the bedroom door opens.

"What do you think you're doing, Elizabeth?"

Gabriel strides into the room, looking like a God with only a pair of black sweats on and freshly washed hair that sits perfectly tousled. His bulging arm muscles and sculpted abs are on display for my viewing pleasure, but I attempt to keep my eyes firmly on his face.

I clear my throat and answer in a strained voice, "I'm hungry. And I need to pee."

The mention of me peeing doesn't stop his sure steps towards where I'm trying to stand. He stops in front of me but doesn't crouch or move to help, only staring at me like I did something to aggravate him.

"You're supposed to be resting. If you wanted food you could have called or texted me, I made sure to leave your phone on the side table."

I look to the side, and sure enough, my phone sits there with a glass of water and one of the pain meds I was prescribed. Looking back up to him, I give him a shy smile.

"I still need to pee, Gabe."

Without another word, he puts his strong hands underneath my arms, and lifts me up into a standing position carefully. He gestures towards where his bathroom is, and I test out walking. There isn't too much pain, besides for some soreness in my thighs and an ache in my side. I make sure to walk slowly and carefully, not exerting myself like the doctor asked. When I move to shut the bathroom door behind me, Gabriel's hand holds the edge.

My brows push together as I look to him, "I'd like privacy."

He shrugs and smirks, "Too bad. I won't look if it makes you feel better, but you're not shutting this door."

Suppressing the urge to roll my eyes, I go with giving him the middle finger over my shoulder as I walk to the toilet. His quiet chuckle is barely heard over the dull pounding in my head, but it makes me smile anyway. When I'm done and have washed my hands, Gabriel steps into the bathroom and starts to lift me up. I stop him with a swat to the arm.

"What do you think you're doing?"

He looks at me like I've gone crazy or stupid, "Carrying you back to bed. You shouldn't push yourself more than necessary."

This time, I can't help the dramatic eyeroll. "It's not like I'm recovering from major surgery, and this isn't the first time I've had to function with body aches and bruises. I'm fine, nurse Gabriel. I can walk."

When I go to step around him, he blocks me again, backing me up towards the sink.

"I think I just saw an eyeroll, Shchenok. Or am I mistaken?"

My swallow gets caught in my sore throat as I shrug. His head tilts to the side as he takes the final step towards me, my back hitting the counter and his arms coming out to block any exit. He leans close and looks over my face with indifference.

His voice comes out deceptively soft, "Do you not remember what I said about rolling your eyes at me, Elizabeth?"

My breathing starts to pick up as I watch his lips. When he notices me staring, that irritating confident smirk lifts a side of his mouth. Clenching my jaw, I look up to his eyes only to see that's also a mistake. The bright green of his eyes is nonexistent. They look like a field right before a storm. Dark, wanting, and hungry.

"You're lucky you're recovering from injuries. The next time I see you roll your eyes at me when you're healed, I won't hesitate to bend you over the closest piece of furniture and spank that delicious ass raw."

He leans closer, running his nose along my bruised throat and taking a deep inhale—a deep growl vibrating against me on his exhale. I can feel his cheeks tighten with a smile as I close my eyes and picture his words.

"Or maybe... I'll just bend you over and fuck your tight pussy so hard you'll be too sore to sit, even as you beg me for more."

A whimper I have no choice but to let escape covers what little space is between us. His dark chuckle runs over my chilled flesh, goosebumps sprouting along my arms from the promise in that one noise.

He leans away just enough to look in my eyes, his face suddenly serious and devoid of any signs of the promise he just made. I take that as my que to follow orders, and lift my arms around his neck so that he can carry me back to bed. He lifts me up by the backs of my thighs carefully, wrapping my legs around him, and smirking like he just won the game. I duck my head to lay it on his shoulder, hiding the blush heating my cheeks from the position he's carrying me. *If I felt better, I wonder if he would take advantage of my open legs wrapping around his trim torso.* He looks only at me as he walks us out of the bathroom and to the bed, setting me down gently.

When I get tucked back in, he cages my body with his arms and leans over me. "Are you going to stay right here and continue being my good girl, Elizabeth?" I nod, earning a satisfied smile I want to lick from his lips. "I'll go get you something to eat."

With a soft kiss to the tip of my nose, he leaves me trying to get a good glimpse at the unknown tattoo peaking up on his hip from the band of his pants as he walks out.

Chapter Thirty

Gabriel

I DECIDE TO MAKE ELIZABETH an omelet with mushrooms, onions, tomatoes, and cheese paired with some yogurt and a glass of lemonade. As I finish setting everything on the tray, the door leading to the garage, almost silently, opens.

My gun is out from its hiding space by the fridge and pointed towards the entryway before the person takes two steps inside. As soon as they cross the threshold, my gun is on their temple.

Copper hair, 5'5", calm blue eyes.

I drop my gun on a heavy exhale, "Shit, Nat. What the fuck are you doing here? I almost shot you."

She shrugs and keeps walking into the kitchen, giving me an amused smile as she sits at the island, "You didn't though. I came to check on you guys, see how Liz is doing since I didn't get to see her before she left the hospital."

I tuck my gun back in its hiding place and run a heavy hand through my hair, "She seems to be doing okay. Hurting, obviously, but she was insistent on walking to and from the bathroom on her own."

Nat's light laugh has my jaw clenching as I grab the tray with Elizabeth's food.

"Well, she's not totally broken, Gabe. She can handle a trip or two to the bathroom on her own." When I don't answer and continue to fiddle with the fork on the tray, she sighs. "Do you blame yourself for her injuries?"

"Of course I do. How could I not?" I look up at her with pinched brows and tight shoulders.

She gives me a soft smile, "Does *she* blame you?"

Taking a deep breath, I shake my head. She said she needed to do that, escape, on her own. She had to prove something to herself. But, that doesn't make me feel any less sorry for failing to protect her like we promised. I *promised* she would be okay. She might be alive.. but she's hurt.

"If she doesn't blame you, Gabe, then you can't hold it against yourself for too long. It's obvious you really care about her, so just show her that. Help her while she heals but, don't be overbearing. Let her see that despite what happened, you're there for her."

I nod, "Yeah.. alright. Thanks, Nat."

I grab the tray of food and flick my head for her to follow me. She might as well talk to Elizabeth if she's here. I'm sure she wouldn't mind the company. When I open my bedroom door, Elizabeth is exactly where I left her and I give a sigh of relief. She could be in worse shape, but I wouldn't like seeing her even slightly hurt. She didn't deserve what she went through, but I know Nat is right. I can't keep blaming myself, I need to take care of her.

Elizabeth looks up and a full smile pushes her puffy cheeks out, "Natalie! What are you doing here?"

Nat walks past me and slides into the bed beside Elizabeth like this isn't *my* room. "I wanted to come check in with you. See how you were doing since you got home."

They give each other a light hug before I set the tray in the open space next to Elizabeth's legs. I give her a sheepish smile, my cheeks growing irritatingly warmer.

"I made you an omelet, but I can make you something else if you'd like."

Her smile softens on me but isn't any less bright as she takes my hand in hers, "It looks really good, and I'm starving, so thank you."

I nod in acknowledgment with a warm smile, give Natalie a warning look, and take my leave so they can have some alone time after grabbing a fresh shirt. My chest tightens as I close the door and I rub a fist over the center while I head down to my office.

With how I grew up, lost my mom, and was homeless for a short time before I found my way into Rick and Natalie's lives, I didn't think I would ever be in the position I am now. Lusting and caring after a woman who carries burdens on her shoulders but doesn't let it take her down. I might not know all of what's happened in Elizabeth's life, but I know it wasn't good for a very long time. Hopefully, I'll be able to show her how good life could be... With me.

Because if there's one thing for certain, I'm not going to let her go. She's mine now. I'll die before someone takes her from me, and even then, I'll still hold her heart and soul in my decaying hands.

I sit in my office chair with a heavy sigh, rubbing my eyes as I lean back. I should try to get some work done with Natalie here, but I can't seem to focus on anything. My mind is a mixture of worries and memories I don't want. I let my arm drop and lean further back in my chair, keeping my eyes closed and my face turned up to the ceiling.

I miss you, mom.

I think back to the happiest times we had before she died. Her coming home with a rare takeout dinner. No signs of drug use, only a bright smile with clear brown eyes. When she finally decided to get clean, I still remember the exact moment my chest lightened. She sat me down on the couch for a serious talk, holding my hands in hers, and her eyes looking apologetic, determined, and sad.

"I'm so sorry, my baby. I haven't been able to be strong enough for you, but I'm going to do better. Be better. Because you deserve the world, little prince."

I nod, a little confused as tears threaten to build. "You've always been strong to me, mom. Especially when father was still here. You're the strongest woman I know."

Her singular laugh comes out choked as the first tear slides down her plump face. One of her hands raises, cradling my face and providing warmth to my cold cheek.

"What did I do in my life to deserve such a good son?"

I force my lips to turn up in a small smile as I shrug, earning another choked laugh from my mom. She lets go of my cheek and pats my hands before standing.

"I'm going to be the mom you deserve, little prince. No more hiding away in pills. I'm not going to run away from the hard things any longer. Afterall, I need to be able to remember the big moments in your life."

I scoff a laugh, "I don't think there will be any big moments, mom."

Her lips turn up in a sad smile, "You'll have plenty of big moments, Gabriel. Someone like you can't avoid them."

My deep exhale is the only sound in the room. I think about my mom often, and how her life was taken too soon. She didn't deserve to be used like that. To be killed like that. My mom was a great woman. Even in her addiction, she never stopped showing how big her heart was.

I know why she started using. My father. The asshole that left her for a young mistress and after a time refused to give my mom any child support. He didn't deserve the time he got with my mom. He definitely didn't deserve her love, even after he hit us.. even after he left. I haven't heard from or seen the man since he stopped giving my mom money, and I couldn't care less. He could be dead somewhere and—not only would I not know—I wouldn't care.

I'm glad he left. And I'm glad my mom was able to eventually realize that she could be happier and do better without him in our lives. Even if I hate him, I still have to remind myself that I'm nothing like him. He was abusive and heartless, not caring about his wife or son. I vowed after the first time he hit me, I would never become anything close to the man he is.

I'm my mother's son.

It's been three hours of Nat hanging out with Elizabeth and I've stayed in my office the whole time. I've done a few different tasks I've been putting off for work and informed Rick that I would be working from home while Elizabeth recovers, which wasn't a surprise for him in the least. Our little argument outside of Murph's warehouse made it pretty clear to him that I would do a lot for my little petal. Including risking my life.

There's a light knock on the door before it opens and Natalie strides in with her usual smile. I lean back in my chair and set my glasses on my desk, watching her sit comfortably in the chair in front of me.

The chair Elizabeth got wet when she came in that one morning.

I blink rapidly to clear my mind before I get hard in front of her. Aimlessly looking through documents on my computer, I direct my question to her.

"How's she doing?"

"Why don't you go up and check on her? She looked to the door a couple times expecting you to come back in."

After a few moments, I shake my head, finally turning and giving her my full attention, "I didn't want to interrupt your time with her. She needs her friends and the company while she heals."

She nods smally with a smile, "She also needs *you*, Gabe. You're her safe space right now. You're the savior in her life at the moment, not me or anyone else in this family."

"I'm no savior, Nat. We both know that."

Her smile gentles as she stands to leave, "You are to her."

With a blown kiss and a small wave, she leaves my office. I blow out a heavy breath and tilt my head back against my chair. I'm no savior, but I know damn well I would do whatever it took to protect Elizabeth. My hands clench and unclench before I get the courage to go back in my room. According to Natalie, I'm Elizabeth's safe space. So I need to continue to be that, even if it'll be hard.

I don't bother to knock before opening the door. *It is my room.* When I step inside I find the bed empty. My heart picks up speed as I look over the space, finding the bathroom door cracked with the light on. Taking a deep breath to calm my nerves, I walk on silent feet to where I assume Elizabeth is.

Her elbow is all I see before I push the door open enough to lean on the frame. I cross my arms over my chest as I look her over. Her thick tanned legs lead up to where I know my boxers are resting against her plump ass, and my shirt flows over her torso. Or it would if it was down.

She stands at an angle, my shirt lifted up on one side as she looks over her bruised ribs. Her brows are scrunched together as she gingerly pokes around, testing out the area. I fist my hands under my arms so I don't reach out and cover her smooth, tempting skin. I remind myself she's recovering from her injuries and is too delicate to play with right now, but that doesn't stop my dick from starting to harden behind my pants.

When her gorgeous eyes lift to look at herself in the mirror, they widen as she finally notices me behind her. The hand holding up the shirt tightens in the fabric as her free one clutches the counter like she would fall over without the support. My eyes drift over her body once more, now that she's watching, and I take my time. I admire every inch of her body, noticing her breathing growing heavy with each pass of my gaze. She starts to lower the shirt, like she's trying to hide behind the fabric.

"Don't."

Her hand instantly stops its descent at my rough voice. Her chest and stomach move with shaky deep breaths as I bring my eyes back up to meet hers. I drop my arms and push off the doorframe, walking calmy and slowly towards her even though my muscles are coiled tight. Our eyes stay locked as I get closer, the air around us becoming dense and charged.

"Turn around." She starts to lower the shirt as she turns but something on my face shows her to keep it up.

When she finally faces me, I can see the blush on her cheeks and the dilation of her pupils. My lips twitch when I catch her lips slightly parted as she stares at mine. But, the joy from that is short lived when I look down to the bruise on her ribs. It's worse than when we left the hospital, purple in color. I know what she's feeling beneath her flawless skin. As I meet her gaze again, whatever is in my eyes has her leaning in.

I step closer until her heaving chest barely brushes against my shirt. I crook my pointer finger and place it under her chin, tipping it up until I can see her full face from my height. Her lashes flutter as her lips part even further.

"Gabe..." Her voice is strained but breathless, causing my dick to jump.

My jaw clenches and I hold her gaze as I lightly run my finger down over her bruised throat to the collar of her shirt.

"How are you feeling, Shchenok?"

Her shoulders lift in a half-ass shrug and I hum, leaning back enough to see she still holds up the side of the shirt, showing off the bruising on her side. I take a step back and hold the scrunched shirt in my own hand, brushing hers away in the process so she can relax her arm. Taking a deep calming breath, I bend down until I'm on one knee and head-on with her bruise.

Rage threatens to take hold as I get a closer look at her side. *That motherfucker better enjoy the time he has left.*

I lean my face forward until my breath fans across her heated skin, and I look up. Elizabeth's gorgeous hazel eyes are still locked on me, silently urging me to do whatever I was thinking. Her small hand lifts shakily and her slender fingers thread into the hair on the back of my head, gently pushing my face until my lips are pressed delicately on the bruise. My eyes close as a deep sigh leaves my nose. Her fingers tighten slightly in my brown strands as I press gentle kisses all over the area, not leaving an inch untouched. By the time I finish and look up at her, she's holding my hair so tightly there's a sting in my scalp and her eyes are closed with her face pointed down at me.

Pulling away from her side, I gather her hands in mine, and place the same soft kisses over her split knuckles before standing back to my full height. Her eyes remain closed and her breathing remains quick as I glide my fingers up her arms, over her shoulders, until I hold her jaw. Tipping her head back, I bend forward and repeat the attention from my lips over the bruising on her neck. She grants me with a whimper and a breathless rush of my name.

When I'm done, her eyes open to show the unshed tears lining her bottom lashes making the green show more than the brown in her irises. My lips tip up into a small smile as I kiss the tip of her nose.

"Does a bath sound good before I make some food?"

I hear her breathing pause before she nods in my hands smally, causing my smile to grow just a little more.

Time to take care of my girl.

Chapter Thirty One

Elizabeth

I WAS SURPRISED WHEN Gabriel showed up in the entry to the bathroom. I was embarrassed to have my bruising on display like that, but when I saw the fire in his eyes and the set of his jaw, I knew I shouldn't be. My knees had to lock in place while he showered my injuries in the most gentle kisses, so that I didn't collapse on top of him.

The way my body reacts to him is something I've never experienced. Even with the pain I'm feeling, all I could focus on was his mouth on my body as I tried not to beg him for more. The doctor said no intense physical activity for a month, and I can only assume anything sexual with Gabriel would be intense. I almost didn't want to remove my hand from his hair when he grabbed it. His perfect brown strands are as soft as they look, if not softer.

His smile increases my heart rate as his green eyes shine like freshly mowed summer grass. He gives me another gentle kiss on the tip of my nose then lets my face go. A silent plea for him to keep touching me echoes in my mind as I watch his strong body walk to the tub in his bathroom to start filling it up. My feet stay planted while he throws some soap and bath salts into the steaming water slowly filling the white porcelain. When it's full to his liking, he walks back over to me with masked eyes. I give him a shy smile which he returns with a slight caress down my cheek.

"Let me know if you need anything."

He turns to leave causing my eyebrows to crease. I don't think about the consequences of my actions as I reach out and grab his shirt before he gets too far. He looks over his shoulder with a questioning expression, and I let go of his shirt and avert my eyes.

After a beat of silence and him turning around to face me, I finally get the courage to ask my question. *Even though I lack the courage to look at him as I do.*

"Will you.. stay in here with me?"

I watch in my peripheral as his body tightens then relaxes with a heavy breath.

"If that's what you wish, moy malen'kiy lepestok."

I nod and turn to walk to the tub. I stay facing the water as my shaky hands move to take my shirt off. When it lifts to just below my chest, a pain radiates down my side causing my breath to catch and my movements to stop. Before I can start trying again, I feel Gabriel step up to my back, placing a strong calloused hand on my arm.

"I'll get it."

I nod and slowly lower my hands so the shirt falls back to my thighs. I wait for him to lift my arms or start to lift the shirt, but I don't expect to feel cold steel pass on my leg causing my lungs to freeze. The ripping of the fabric is the only sound in the space as Gabriel slices up the shirt, staying a good distance from my skin. As soon as he cuts through the collar, the shirt slides off my arms to pool in front of my feet. I look down to see my nipples are hard and my breasts shake with my long inhale. Without having to ask, his thumbs slide into the band of the boxers, and he guides those down my legs, lifting each of my feet by my ankles so I can step out.

When I start to turn to face him, his hand lands on my shoulder and stops me. "Get in."

I obey immediately, using his hand as a stabilizer as I step into the slightly below scorching water that smells of citrus and roses. His hand stays in mine as I lower myself slowly deeper until my butt is firmly planted and I'm rested against the back of the tub with my head leaning on the edge. I look from beneath my lashes to where he stands, seeing he's turned his head towards the opposite side of the bathroom from where I'm sitting.

My heart clenches at seeing him trying to respect me by keeping his eyes averted.. but, it makes me realize I *want* his eyes on me. I want to see how his eyes change as they take in my naked body slumped in the mostly clear water. I clear my throat and shift my legs, causing the water to slosh against the sides slightly.

"Gabe..." He grunts his acknowledgement but doesn't turn to look at me. "You.. you can look at me. I didn't ask you to stay so you could stand there and look at the wall the whole time."

His broad chest moves with a deep breath and his hands form tight fists before finally turning his body and face to look at me. When his eyes stay on mine, his face tense and jaw locked, I give him an encouraging small smile and nod my head. He picks up on my que that it's okay to look, and I watch with eagerness and nerves as the muscle in his jaw ticks and his eyes slowly track down from my face.

With each inch his eyes move down, the ticking in his jaw increases and the green of his eyes grows darker, into my favorite color. The water laps against my breasts with my heavy breathing, waiting for him to move or say something. When he finally gets to the space between my legs, his nostrils flare and his pupils grow even bigger. My thighs push together as his hands clench and he brings those deep green eyes back to mine. I swallow thickly waiting for something, anything.

He does nothing.

His jaw ticks a few more times before he smirks and seems to force his body to relax. "You're astonishingly beautiful, Elizabeth. Every inch of you. Yesli by ya mog dobit'sya svoyego pryamo seychas, ty by krichal i prosil poshchady.[*]"

My brows twitch to show my confusion, a war inside me on if I should ask what he said. But, there's a dark part of me that likes knowing he's talking dirty to me in Russian. His smirk deepens as he walks to crouch behind me and the tub. His arms drape over the edges just like that one night, and he swipes my half wet hair over my shoulder so his nose can press against my skin. He takes a deep inhale over my pulse before groaning and laying his forehead against my temple.

His voice comes out as a whisper, but it vibrates against my ear, "You have no idea what you do to me, Shchenok."

I match his whisper, "Why don't you tell me?"

His dark chuckle reverberates throughout my body, causing goosebumps to pop up despite the warm water cradling me. He doesn't answer me as his hands dip down into the water. His thick fingers swish the water around my hips, brushing occasionally against my sensitive skin. He rubs his chin down my neck and over my shoulder, coming back slowly to rub his nose below my jaw.

"How're you feeling, Shchenok?"

I nod shakily, "G—good."

He hums deeply, "How's that pretty pussy feeling?" A whimper tickles my throat as I give another shaky nod. "That's not an answer, Elizabeth. How's it feeling?"

My eyes close with his dark voice. I take a deep inhale, unsure of how to answer his question. I'm needy, I'm turned on, I'm wanting him to control my body like he took control of my life. Opening my heavy lids, I watch his fingers brush against me as I answer softly.

"Needy."

I don't notice he moved his face until I feel his teeth wrap around my shoulder and bite down. My gasp almost blocks out his tortured groan as he bites just a little harder, radiating a delicious sting over the area. His teeth scrape against my shoulder as he pulls off, making my breathing go shallow and my legs to push tightly together. The cool air of the room sets my body more on edge as it goes against the warmth I'm cocooned in, in the tub.

His hands finally hold my hips, his fingers slightly digging into my flesh making the extra fat I have there bubble up around them. My lungs freeze as his warm, soft tongue slides up the side of my neck and flicks off the edge of my jaw, before his teeth playfully nip it.

"Do you need something to relax, moy malen'kiy lepestok?"

I nod but when he doesn't continue, I realize he's waiting for me to vocalize my request. "I do. Please.. Gabriel.. *Please* touch—"

My words cut off on a gasp when his hands splash the water to fit my heavy breasts in his palms. My head falls back to the edge of the tub as my eyes fall closed. His strong fingers massage what they can grab, some remaining out of his grip.

His next words come out on a growl as his fingers pinch my peaked nipples, "I won't make you beg too much yet, baby. But, I love hearing it anyway."

A breathless moan pushes from between my lips as he pinches my nipples harder and pulls them outwards until they pop from his hold, my back arching with the release. A whimper is my only indicator that I want his hands back on me as they fall back near my hips. I don't need to wait long before my silent request is fulfilled and one of his big hands spans across my lower stomach, and the other holds above my knee tightly.

I go to move his hand from my tummy pouch, one of the spots I'm most self-conscious about, but he holds onto the fat that's there tighter, refusing to let go.

"I will touch, hold, and play with what I want, Elizabeth. You asked for this, there's no turning back now."

After a moment of hesitation, I let my hands drift back to my sides. He places a kiss below my ear, then let's his lips brush against it as he speak again.

"Such a good girl for me. I think you deserve a little treat."

My swallow gets stuck in my throat as he uses the hand on my knee to pull my legs open until they rest of the sides of the tub. So slowly, he slides his hand down from my knee until it hovers barely above my pussy, the heat from his palm and the water tortuous. My hips push forward trying to get his touch on me, but he keeps himself at the same distance with a dark chuckle.

"So eager, moy malen'kiy lepestok."

I sit back and try to relax, waiting for him to touch me and not show how needy I am to finally feel him against me. Closing my eyes tighter, I wait patiently. When his hand finally covers the last remaining space between us to cup me, I can't stop the moan that fills the otherwise quiet space. He pulls up until his fingers can reach my entrance and they start to tease the area as his other hand tenses against my stomach.

His voice comes out breathless and almost as needy as I feel, "So fucking wet.."

I nod at his statement and push my legs harder against the sides of the tub so I don't trap his hand down there. He sticks in the tip of his finger but no more, a suffering weak whimper tightening my throat. He shushes me softly as he removes his finger and moves it to my throbbing clit. He presses down, hard, and my legs start to shake making the water ripple around me. As he lets up on the pressure, he starts to rub in slow lazy circles. I only last a few seconds before my moan escapes and my hips start to pulse forward.

Somehow, he manages to push through the water to slap my clit and my eyes spring open with a sharp inhale and he chuckles when I unconsciously chase for more. He continues to torture me with slow strokes, then grants me with a few hard and fast ones before slowing down again. I'm breathing heavier, his hand on my stomach lowering to hold my hips back, and his lips start giving kisses up and down my neck. My whole body is on edge, he's barely touched me and I feel like I could explode at any moment.

Without any warning or signs, two of his thick fingers plunge into me making me cry out and my chest to push up as my head flings backwards. My fingers don't match the girth of his, and I can tell my walls see the difference as they pulse against him with slight discomfort. He isn't moving his fingers, and is no longer rubbing delicious circles around my clit. His thick short breaths rush from his nose, brushing over the pebbled skin of my neck.

"Fuck... YA ne ozhidal, chto ty budesh' takim napryazhennym. Mne ne terpitsya pogruzit'sya v etu shelkovistuyu pizdu.[*]"

His unknown words cause shivers to roll down my body and unintelligible sounds to move my tongue. I don't know what I'm saying or how loud it is as he pulls his fingers from me slowly with a moan of his own. Again with no warning, he pushes them back in swiftly and my back arches once more. His thumb presses firmly against my clit and he begins to wave his fingers in a come hither motion, not stopping me as my hips move with him. He's playing with my pussy like he knows it, like it's his. And I can't argue that after this, it might be. Pinpricks light my skin in a delicious fire as my lungs cease function and my muscles start to lock.

I don't even realize what's happening until my body twitches, I can't breathe, and fireworks go off from my head to my toes.

"That's it baby, let it take you. Fuck, you get so tight when you come."

Gabriel's words increase the intensity of my orgasm until it slowly starts to subside. His fingers don't stop, but they slow to help coax me down from my unexpected high and I finally get air into my lungs. His calloused fingers brush lightly over my stomach, helping to relax my muscles until I'm a heap of bones and muscle in the now lukewarm water of my bath.

He gives me three kisses along my neck before biting my ear and pulling his hand away from my sensitive pussy.

"You did so good, lepestok. Looked so pretty as you came around my fingers. I can't wait to see what you look like coming all over my cock."

My eyes open heavily with a silent hum of agreement. My clit pulses in time with my heart, my walls clenching around nothing like it's already missing him filling it. I can't move, can't do anything as I watch his hands and arms pull away from me and out of the water before he stands and walks away from the tub. My nerves start to spike as he moves closer to the door, my legs closing to bring my knees to my chest. Wrapping my arms around my legs, I lay my cheek on them and look to the wall to my left.

He didn't even hesitate to leave. To pull away from me.

Despite his last words, a part of my heart hurts at the fact that he didn't hold me longer.. didn't *actually* kiss me or look in my eyes as he spoke. For all I know, he didn't like what he did or how I felt under his hands. But, then I think of his moans and groans, the way he squeezed me and held me down like he wanted to get in the tub with me, how he didn't stop kissing my neck and how heavy his breathing was. What he said after...

He definitely liked it.

But then, why did he leave when it was over?

Chapter Thirty Two

Gabriel

I STEP OUT OF THE BATHROOM, leaving Elizabeth in the tub, as I try to get ahold of myself. I'm hard as stone behind my pants, my heavy breathing the only sound in my bedroom as I rake my wet hands through my hair. I actually got to touch her, look at her, watch her come apart in my arms...

The feel of her tight little pussy around my fingers almost felt like heaven, and my body shivers as I imagine doing it again. I wasn't lying when I said I wanted to feel it wrapped around my cock. I already know she'll be my undoing. There was a slight hesitation from me when I felt how tight she was. I almost thought she might be a virgin, but she didn't cry out in pain or tell me to stop. She definitely enjoyed what we did, now I just have to hope she doesn't regret it—because I'm already addicted.

With one more calming breath, and an adjustment of my dick so it isn't tenting my pants, I grab her some new clothes of mine, her pain med and water, and walk back into the bathroom.

She's wrapped around her legs and looking to the wall, breathing slowly and deeply. The way she's curled around herself immediately puts me on edge. Did I hurt her? Is this her regretting asking me to touch her? I step closer on silent feet and squat down until we're on the same level. Setting the clothes on my thigh, I reach out and run my hand softly down her smooth back. Her catching breath is the only reason I know she didn't hear me come in.

"Elizabeth.. look at me."

She clutches her legs tighter before turning her head, and laying her cheek back on her knee. Her eyes are half closed, looking like she could fall asleep any minute, and her lips are pulled slightly into a frown. Giving her a gentle smile, I hold out the pain med and water so she can take it. I'm not sure how she's feeling with her injuries right now, but I saw how locked her body was right before release hit her. I don't want her to get any further aches because of that tension. She looks from the pill to me and back again before taking it and slipping it between her lips, swallowing it with two big gulps of water.

I take the glass back and set it on the floor. "Are you ready to get out? I got fresh clothes for you."

Her eyes sag as she lightly shakes her head. My chest deflates at her expression, hoping her closing herself off is from something other than what we did. Putting my arms on the lip of the tub, I rest my chin on them and give her another small smile. She doesn't return it but doesn't break eye contact either, which lightens my shoulders.

"Why did you walk out so quick?" Her words come out softly, like she was second guessing her question as she spoke.

My brows crease as I look over her face. *That's why she's upset? Because I walked out?* Lifting my head, my arm moves out so I can pet her semi-wet hair.

"I only wanted to get you your pain med in case your aches got more intense, and some new clothes. That's all, lepestok. I'm sorry if that made you upset." I give her one final stroke over her hair before standing.

She watches me with curious big eyes as I set her clothes on the counter before stepping into the tub with her. Her back snaps straight as her eyes grow wider.

"Gabe, what are you doing?"

I shrug and bend down, sloshing water onto the floor, and grab her arms before she can move away to drag her into my lap. Shifting her sideways, I cradle her head in the crook of my neck and wrap my arm around her chilled torso. She sits tense at first, before relaxing into me with a sigh. I rub my thumb up and down her back, keeping her tightly pressed against me as I kiss her hair. We say nothing to each other, just enjoying the moment where I can freely hold her in my arms, feeling her bare skin.

When I feel her begin to shiver, the water now cold and my clothes soaked through, I switch the position of my arms in order to carry her and stand. She clutches my wet shirt tightly when I lift her from the water and step onto the cold tile. Without letting her down, I grab a fresh towel from the shelf by the door and sit on the toilet lid to wrap her up. With the towel nicely wrapped around her and her shivering subsiding, I gently slide her off until she's standing and faced towards me.

She keeps her eyes down as I begin to dry her, making sure not a single drop of water remains. As soon as she's dry to my satisfaction, I put the towel on the counter and grab the fresh clothes I got for her. Before I can turn fully back, I notice she's already trying to cover parts of her body with her arms. My lips tilt downwards and I drop the clothes back down to pull her between my legs by the backs of her juicy thighs. She keeps her eyes downcast and tightens her arms around herself.

Letting out a deep breath, I squeeze her thighs, "Look at me, Elizabeth." She starts to shake her head but I cut off her movement with a deep command in my tone, "Now."

Her muscles lock under my hands but I ignore it as her hazel eyes peek through her lashes to meet my gaze. I want to give her a reassuring smile, something softer than the current irritated look on my face, but I can't. I have no idea how she can't see how stunning she is. How every inch of her body is something to be cherished and worshipped. Pinching her chin between my thumb and forefinger so she can't look away, I take my time looking her over, trying not to get even more irritated with the bruising on her perfect skin.

When I'm done with my assessment I keep her doubtful gaze hostage as I speak.

"You, Elizabeth Greene, are a woman who should be proud of her body. I've never met a woman I've wanted or craved more in my life.. that I've wanted to prove to the world I deserve. You are imperfectly perfect, and I would walk through hell and back in order to prove just how gorgeous you are. There's not a single thing I would want you to change about yourself, inside *or* out. So stop hiding, especially from me."

Unshed tears line her bottom lashes until a single one falls down her cheek. I wipe it with the pad of my thumb as I let go of her chin and sit back, waiting for her to lower her arms and accept herself. It's slow, but she lets her arms drift to her sides. I don't want her trying to cover back up, so I keep my gaze locked on her face.

Giving her a satisfied gentle smile, I grab the clothes again and start to dress her. She gives a little grunt of pain at having to lift her arm all the way up on the side of her bruising, but shows no other signs of discomfort. Once she's covered in another one of my shirts and a pair of boxers, I point to the toothbrush I grabbed from her bathroom earlier. She follows the silent request, but keeps her gaze averted until she's done and ready to go back to bed. I let her walk back into the bedroom on her own, even though my arms are tense with the want to carry her there. I stay a foot from the edge of the bed as she climbs in, pulls the blankets to her shoulders, and lies on her back.

I turn to go to my dresser, wanting to get out my drenched clothing, but I stop and look over my shoulder when I hear the sheets rustling. Elizabeth is sitting up, looking at me with her face tilted down and her fingers fidgeting nervously.

"What is it, Elizabeth? Do you need something?"

She shakes her head, then nods, taking a deep breath before her lips part to speak.

"Are you not going to be staying in here?"

I give her a full smile as I chuckle, "I'm just changing my clothes and making us some food, then I'll be back to hang-out with you for a little bit. Okay?"

She gives me a small smile, nodding as she leans back to get comfortable against my pillows. I stand and watch her for a few more seconds. Memorizing the way she looks swallowed by my sheets and California-king bed. My chest becomes heavy as I finish grabbing my new clothes and I rub it with a fist as I walk out of the room I don't really want to leave.

TWO WEEKS LATER

I wake with a groan and groggy mind to the loud chime of my doorbell. My eyes stay closed as I roll out of bed and walk to the bedroom door, only to knock my knee into the corner of a dresser. With a whispered 'fuck' I open my eyes halfway and finish my trek.

I've been sleeping in the guestroom since Elizabeth has been sleeping in mine. There's been more than one night over the last two weeks where I've almost stayed by her side. But, I haven't brought myself to do it. She's still closed off about certain aspects about herself, no matter how gently I try to ask for information. I sit with her every day when I can take a break from work, and we binge watch different shows or movies and make mindless but pleasing conversation.

She hasn't asked me to touch her again, so I haven't. I told her I wouldn't unless she asked and I'm sticking to that. *For the most part.* Until she wants to fully admit that she's mine, I'm only touching her if she verbally asks me to. Besides a nose kiss or holding her hand here and there. But since that bath two weeks ago, she hasn't said anything. I occasionally see that wanting look in her eyes, or the way she watches me when I cook or when we sit in bed and she thinks I can't see her.

I want to be close to her, to touch her, hear her heart against my ear, feel her breath against my lips.. I *need* it..

The doorbell rings another time right as I step off the stairs.

With an irritation in my tone, I talk loud enough they can hear me, "I'm fucking coming, calm down."

They've probably woken Elizabeth up by now.

I swing the door open with a scowl and look slightly down to see a terrified looking delivery guy, holding a small box. I try to lessen the irritation on my face but it obviously doesn't work when he swallows thickly and drops my gaze.

"Sorry for the disturbance sir, I'm just dropping this package off. I need a signature."

My brows crease as I let go of the door. I didn't order anything, and I don't think Elizabeth did either..

"Who's it from?"

This guy isn't with the usual delivery companies, so it has to be from another family in the mafia. I just don't know who or how they got my address.

"I—I'm not sure. There's no return label, sir."

I nod and reach for whatever I need to sign to get him to leave. He hands me a small tablet with an attached pen and I scribble my name before yanking the box from his shaky hands. I barely toss him a glance as I go to shut door, uttering a quick thank you.

I look over the box as soon as the door is locked, seeing there really isn't a return address. There's actually no label at all. Being a little more careful with it, I carry it to the kitchen and set it on the island to cut the tape. I'm careful with the knife as I slice, not wanting to poke whatever is possibly inside.

With the tape cut, I carefully open the flaps until I look down into the box. There's another small box, but this one is a black fabric one, tied with a darker black bow. I'm not sure what it is, but it looks like either a hit marker or a threat. I run back up to the guestroom, grab my phone, and run back to the kitchen as I call Dominic. He'll want to know that I just got a mystery package directly to my house.

"Hello."

I roll my eyes at his blunt tone as I stand in front of the box. "Nice to know you also sound like an asshole in the morning, Dom."

I hear his quiet chuckle and sheets rustling, "Why are you calling me so early on a Saturday, Gabe?"

I totally forgot it was Saturday.. That makes this delivery even more questionable.

"I just got a discreet package delivered to my house."

There's a tense silence before I hear him moving, "What's in it?"

I shrug as I look into the box again, "Just another box, except this one is made of black fabric and tied with a bow."

He hums, but says nothing as he still moves around. I wait patiently, eyeing the box but not wanting to touch it.

"I'll be at your house in ten."

He hangs up, not even waiting for my response. I don't need him coming to check it out, I just wanted to notify him. But, after everything he and Rick have had to go through over the last few years, it makes sense that this package might put him on edge.

I decide to start making some breakfast while I wait for him, hoping Elizabeth didn't wake up from the doorbell.

Chapter Thirty Three

Gabriel

TEN MINUTES ON THE dot, Dominic strides through my garage door like he owns the place. I shake my head, placing the finished pancakes on the stack already on a plate and lean against the counter as he strolls into the kitchen, eyes already on the box on the island. He stops in front of it, looking in to see I still haven't touched the smaller box inside. He looks to me with intense eyes and a smirk.

"Look at you, waiting for me to get here to open it. How responsible."

I scoff, "Whatever Dom, we opening this thing or not? If I get poisoned or something at least you're here to do something about it."

He gives a soft chuckle, motioning with his head for me to join his side. Together we look into the box and I take a deep breath before carefully pulling out the black one. I set it gently on the counter and start to pull on the bow until it falls around the box. With a thick swallow I lift the lid off the box and Dom and I both lean closer. Nothing dangerous. No trick or hidden explosive. Just a note on a small stack of what looks like papers. Dom picks up the note and reads it out loud.

"You have something of mine. I will take it back."

He looks to me with tension lining his face, I'm sure matching my own, and I pick up the stack under the note. It's not papers, it's pictures—all the size of a miniature polaroid. The first one is slightly blurry, like it was taken quickly at a distance. I bring it closer to my face before being able to make out what it is. I hand it to Dom with an irritated huff.

"It's all of us sitting at the table at Rick's wedding."

I look closely at the next one, seeing it's when we were moving Elizabeth out of her apartment.

So far, they both have Dominic in them. Is it because of him? They want the city or territory back?

But then I look at the next one and my breathing cuts short. Dom hears it and leans closer to look at the picture I'm holding, feeling him go tense when he notices what it's of. I can't take my eyes off of it, feeling rage building in a slow fire throughout me. It's wanting to consume everything in my presence, leave no inch untouched. I want to hurt all the men that have been helping watch my house.

My vision starts to redden around the edges as I look at the clear picture of Elizabeth.

She's walking around the perimeter of the small forest surrounding the house, looking as though she was weaving in and out of the trees with a serene smile on her lips. I throw the picture down and look at the next one. This one is through the window of the gym as she runs on the treadmill. The next is of her through her bedroom window as she gets ready to lay in bed.

Dom is stiff and breathing heavily next to me as he sees what I'm seeing. Elizabeth is what is wanted back. And I have a very strong feeling of who wants her.

Dominic is the first to speak, his voice low and angry, "How the fuck did they get so close to your house?"

My tone matches his as I crush the pictures in my fist, "Some of the men guarding are obviously not doing a very good job."

"I guess we'll have to have a little chat with them and fix that."

"Fix what?"

Elizabeth's curious soft voice shocks us both and we turn around with wide eyes to see her standing in the doorway wearing sweatpants and a tank top. I keep the pictures in my fist behind my back and try to give her a small smile.

"Oh nothing, just some stupid stuff at work. People skipping important details, nothing to worry about."

Her eyes are slightly skeptical but she nods and gives Dom a shy smile, "Hey, Dominic. You're here early for a Saturday. This little stupid thing must be important."

I look at Dom to see he's fully relaxed with his usual indifferent mask firmly in place, not returning her smile but keeping a light friendly tone as he speaks, "I get unnecessarily worked up about stupid things. Elliana hates it."

Elizabeth hums as she nods then tries to peer over my shoulder. I tense until her eyes light and she speed walks behind me to the pancakes I totally forgot about.

"You made pancakes! Ugh, thank god, I'm starving."

I turn to face her, sliding the crushed pictures into Dom's hand so he can hide them as I move the black box into the bigger one. I'm quick to clear the space on the island and hand Dom the useless boxes so he can leave with them. I don't want to scare Elizabeth or put her on edge. She feels safe here, and I don't want her feeling otherwise. I'll get new men to guard the grounds that don't want to lose fingers over being neglectful of their duties.

Dominic starts to head back to the garage, stopping in the doorway and giving Elizabeth a small smile, "Have a good day, Elizabeth." He looks to me, eyes all business, "When you're ready for that meeting or anything else you need help with, let me know."

I give him a nod and look back to my little petal as she piles four pancakes onto a plate with a serene smile. When I hear the garage closing, I still can't manage to move. I just watch as Elizabeth pours way too much syrup on her pancakes, grabs a fork, and moves to sit at the island. She completely ignores my presence as she stuffs a big bite between her perfect pink lips, her cheeks puffing out while she chews. Only when she goes to take another bite does she look at me with wide eyes, the fork still in her mouth.

Her words come out muffled around the bite on her fork, "Whu?"

I finally snap out of my daze of memorizing the moment and chuckle, moving to grab my own plate of food. "Nothing, just didn't think someone so small could take such big bites."

She laughs with a mouthful and I look over my shoulder to watch, my smile growing at seeing her cheeks puffy and pink as her hand covers her full mouth. After she swallows she looks at me with a roll of her eyes, seemingly unaware that she did so.

"I'm a big girl, I take big girl bites. Don't hate on my eating. I told you I was starving."

I groan as I watch her lick syrup from the corner of her mouth, making her eyes widen and flash with desire. With my food forgotten, I take slow and calculated steps towards her as my dick starts to swell.

"Did you notice what you did, Shchenok?" She shakes her head with her eyes still wide. I grin hungrily as I step behind her and lean so my lips are near her ear. "You rolled your eyes at me."

She has a sharp intake of breath before whispering softly, "I didn't know I did..."

I hum and look down to see her nipples poking against her thin tank top. My hips grind forward against the back of her chair, just to feel something.

"What do you think we should do about that, Elizabeth?"

Her chest begins to move heavier, her fork clenched tightly in her fist on the counter while her other hand lays flat on the other side of her plate. She doesn't answer me but I see the way her legs push closer together and her hips shimmy slightly in her seat. I give her ear a soft kiss and watch with adoration as a slight shiver racks her body. I move lower to press another one under her jaw, still watching as her chest stops moving and she holds her breath.

Without warning I bite into the curve of her neck, trapping her body in with my arms as her head falls the side and her fork clatters and sticks to the counter. Goosebumps start to sprout up her arms and I bite slightly harder before licking the same spot and pulling away. She doesn't give me the chance to pull my arms away. She grabs ahold of my wrists tightly, her chest moving quickly to accompany her heavy breaths through her nose. Intrigued by what she's going to do, I let her lead my hands away from the counter. My whole body hangs on a delicious edge as she places my hands atop her tits, her nipples poking into my palms.

I take the opportunity she's giving me and squeeze them, trying to get all of them to fit into my hands even though I know they won't. A breathless moan leaves us at the same time as I begin to kneed them. I'm soft at first but notice her shifting, like she wants more, and close my hands tighter. This time, her moan isn't soft, it's loud and bounces off the kitchen walls.

She makes me lose control. She makes me lose sight of what I'm trying to achieve with her. Of what I want her to see in me.

Gripping under her arms, I pull her out of her seat, kicking the chair away, and gently throw her on top of the counter on her back. Her arm knocks against her plate and I push it away, sending it crashing to the floor. She gasps and lifts her head to look at the mess I made.

"Gabe you—"

I cover her mouth with my hand, my fingers digging into her puffy cheeks as I push her head back down. When her Fall eyes look to me, her pupils dilate and a growl bangs in my chest.

"I only want to hear my name or you begging for more. If it's neither, keep it in that pretty head of yours."

I wasn't asking but she nods anyway, so I release her mouth. She starts to breathe heavily through her open lips, watching as I reach towards the bottom of her shirt. When I grip the flimsy material, getting ready to rip it off of her, she says my name again and I look up, quirking my brow. She bites her bottom lip but doesn't say anything else and I lean over her tense body so our lips are lined up. I give her plump bottom lip a playful nip, keeping our gazes locked.

"You said you were starving. Well, so am I."

I hold her shirt tighter as I finally give in and crash my lips to hers. I can feel her whimper throughout my body, causing it to shiver in anticipation. I open my mouth and stick out my tongue, tracing her lips. Her mouth parts on a sharp inhale and I take the opportunity to stick my tongue inside for a taste.

She doesn't stop me as I swipe my tongue over hers. She's shaking beneath me, her arms raising and her fingers falling into my hair. I groan into her mouth, and she copies. Her tongue dances with mine in the most perfect way. She tastes like sweet syrup, making me want to lick all the sugar from every inch. I continue to kiss her and plunder her mouth as I lift my torso and rip her tank top with ease until it's a scrap of fabric hanging from her shoulders. With her shirt gone, I lay back on top of her as she moans, only to be disappointed when my own shirt is in the way from actual contact.

I shove my hands beneath her, one under her ass so I can grind against her covered pussy, and the other under her head so I can grip her soft, brown hair. I grip one side of her ass tightly as her hips begin to match my motion, my hand not able to cover her full cheek.

With one last lick and lock of our lips, I lay my forehead on hers to look down at her puffy mouth with satisfaction. She pulls my hair tighter with a mix of a whimper and a moan. I look into her lust drunk eyes with a smirk.

"Look at you being so needy to feel my cock, Shchenok. You're beautiful when you beg silently. But, I want to hear it. *Beg me.*"

She licks her lips as she looks to mine, "Gabriel, please. Please, please, *please*."

I hum and give her a lick from her chin to the tip of her nose, "Please what, baby?"

Her head moves side to side as her eyes close briefly before meeting mine again.

"Please, do something, anything. I want to come…"

I grind harder against her, pinning her hips with mine so there's no more movement to keep her going and she grants me with a frustrated moan. I lift my head and pull her hair a little harder so her chin is angled upwards.

"You want to come, or you want *me* to make you come baby?"

She tries to move her hips again but I press down harder. Her eyes flare with anger that brings out the desperation also swimming in her hazel eyes.

"I want.. I want you to make me come, Gabe. *Please.*"

I give her one thrust, watching her eyes roll back as they close. "I don't think I will yet." I pull away until no inch of my body is touching hers, watching as she melts with frustration against the counter as I smile. "You haven't earned it yet. We still have to deal with that eye roll you gave me a minute ago."

Her eyes flash open as she looks to me, shivers starting to wrack her body. I ignore the throbbing of my dick and move back another step, motioning for her to stand. She sits up slowly, jumping off the counter easily, and looks up to with hooded but bright eyes. I give her another hungry smile as I make a twirling motion with my finger.

"Turn around."

She does without hesitation. With her facing the counter, I pull the remaining fabric of her shirt off and throw it over my shoulder. My hands are shaking slightly as I lift them, but I ignore it as I run gentle, teasing fingers across her smooth back. She shivers again as I trace her spine from bottom to top. I let her feel my fingers sliding into her hair before grabbing a handful and pushing her forward slowly until she starts to lean over. She lets out a small moan when her perfect tits press against the cold hard surface of the counter.

I let go of her hair to trail my fingers down over her back until they slip beneath the band of her pants. I don't move them as I grip the material and lean over to speak in her ear, pressing my dick into her ass so she feels just how hard she makes me.

"What did I say would happen if you rolled your eyes, Elizabeth?"

She breathes in quick pants and pushes her ass back further before answering, "That you would spank me raw."

I smile against her ear and grind into her once more, "That's right baby."

She whimpers as I pull away, leaving her to grow cold against the hard surface beneath her, and pull her pants down until they drop to her ankles. I rub my hand over both sides of her plump ass as I look over just how wet she is. Her thighs and pussy shine under the kitchen light with her arousal. My smile only grows at the sight of her so ready and needy, my cock jumping with eagerness to plunge into her. The only thing swirling through my mind is a dark voice repeating '*mine*'.

I rub over one side of her ass, getting it nice and warm, my voice coming out dark as I speak, "What are you getting spanked for?"

Her voice is soft and needy, "Rolling my eyes."

"Good girl." I take a deep breath, keeping my hand still as my other presses down in the middle of her back. "You're getting ten. Your safe word is red."

I don't let her respond before delivering the first spank, her entire ass rippling with the impact.

Chapter Thirty Four

Elizabeth

SAFE WORD IS RED.

My lungs don't know how to function as the first slap of his hand lands on my ass. It's a painful sting, even though I doubt he put his full strength behind it. My eyes start to water from the pain but a moan joins into the confusion as the spot grows warm as he rubs over it, soothing it slightly. I've never been so confused on my physical feelings. It hurt, but I also liked it, especially when he started to rub over the spot.

I mark the first one in my head and flatten my palms next to my head in preparation for the next one. It comes when I least expect it, and in a different spot than the first one. The process starts all over again—first a sting, then pain, then heat as it calms.

By the fifth one, I sound like I'm hyperventilating and I can feel arousal dripping down my thighs. Gabriel starts to rub the opposite cheek, getting that one ready for his heavy palm and I whimper as something brushes against the sensitive skin of the freshly spanked side.

His voice comes out rough and tense, "How many left, Shchenok?"

I try to swallow and calm my breathing enough to answer, realizing my eyes are closed and tears are trapped behind my lids, "Five."

He gives the middle of my back a soft kiss, causing me to arch towards him, and he speaks softly against my sensitive flesh, "Ideal'nyy malen'kiy lepestok.[*]"

I hold my breath as I wait for the first connection of his hand, and when it lands my moan comes out like a cry. I'm sensitive everywhere, and the reverberation through my ass has the other side accompanying the sweet torture.

He moves to different areas with each slap, until all five spanks have covered the entirety of my ass cheek, then he gently rubs over both sides.

"Such a good girl, Elizabeth. The sight of your ass now that I've marked it could send me to my grave early. I think I might've just found my new favorite way to get you to listen."

I whimper and squeeze my eyes closed, finally able to relax my body against the hard counter. But, just as my body is subsiding from its shaking, Gabriel's strong hands spread my ass and some of my thigh fat apart as his body heat covers the back of my legs. My entire body locks and my eyes fling open when I feel his breath between my legs.

"Now, you deserve to come, lepestok."

That's the only warning I receive before his hot mouth is on me, his tongue spearing into me to lick up every drop of my arousal. My eyes roll to the back of my head as I spread my legs wider. He growls at my invitation, and holds my abused ass harder as he consumes me. I never thought this would be something I could die for, but it definitely is. Heat slowly starts to crawl from my toes to my head, little prickles igniting in my belly.

I moan his name loudly, trying to reach back to grab him but unable to reach. He must feel or see me reaching for him because he lets go of my ass, running his tongue lightly and slowly over my clit, and gathers my wrists so they're together and under me in one of his big hands. When he's adjusted me to his liking, he sucks harshly against my clit, giving it a little nip before licking it roughly and quickly. I barely have a chance to adjust before I'm bucking back into him and the euphoria of an orgasm is on the horizon. Soft, pleading words escape me but I have no idea what I'm saying. With one last nip on my clit, he sucks harshly, and I'm seeing stars. I cum hard, now thankful he's holding my wrists hostage as my body is locked tight and spasming. When I start coming down, he eases his suction and slows down the roll of his tongue.

As I start to melt against the counter and into him, he leaves my sensitive clit alone to lick my entrance, thighs, and part of my ass clean. It's the most enjoyable feeling as it keeps me grounded from the aftershocks of my orgasm. He gives a final flick to my clit when he's done and stands behind me, letting go of my wrists. I bring my heavy arms up to help me stand and I turn around almost drunkenly. My eyelids are heavy, my muscles lacking the energy to properly function. When I look up to meet his gaze, I can't help my fresh arousal at seeing the fiery green of his irises. He looks over my naked body, and I realize I don't even have the temptation to hide myself from his eyes. He makes me feel beautiful and wanted. He makes me feel craved.. like a unique jewel—a source of water in a barren desert.

I let myself see the glaze of his eyes as he looks over every bare inch of me. I make myself believe that he truly does see me as he says.

I look him over while he's preoccupied with his own view. His shirt and pants cover most of him but I notice the bulge of his muscles straining the fabric of his shirt. I stare at the veins crawling along his forearms to his thick hands. Then, I catch on the big bulge in his pants. I've yet to fully see his cock, and I badly want to. My fingers twitch with the urge to pull his pants down until his dick is free and in front of me so I can admire it.

Why can't I do that? He's gotten to see and taste me, it's only fair.

The thought that I could potentially have him against my tongue makes my mouth water, but my nerves also start to act up. The one guy I slept with barely went down on me, and I *definitely* didn't offer to do it for him. Gabriel would be the first guy to have that part of me.. and that kind of excites me.

Without letting my slack muscles slow me down, I sink to my knees and swiftly pull down Gabriel's pants until they rest at his knees. He's too slow at stopping my hands, and I see the muscles in his thighs tense as his cock bobs in front of me. I lick my lips as I look him over.

He's big.

I've only ever seen one dick in person, and it definitely didn't look like this. Gabriel isn't only long, but he's thick. There's a bead of precum at his tip, and I don't stop myself from leaning forward and tentatively licking it off with the tip of my tongue.

Gabriel's curse comes off on a growl before his hand finds its way in my hair and holds on tightly. I look up at him through my lashes with a winning, sweet smile.

"You got to taste, I think it's only fair."

Another growl vibrates from his chest which heaves with deep breaths. He looks on the brink of losing all control and a big part of me wants him to. I want him to break me only to put me back together again after. He looks over my face like he can't believe I'm offering this, like I'm offering him something no one has before. I'm not sure who he's been with before or all the things they done—because he's obviously pretty experienced—but I know I'm giving him a part of myself that I would only trust in his hands. Not only a piece of my body, but also a piece of my heart.

I just hope he doesn't destroy it.

He smirks that irritatingly hot one he normally does and uses his free hand to pump himself right in front of my face, capturing my attention by the action.

"You want me to fuck your pretty little mouth, baby?"

I nod and lick my lips as I look up at him again, "Very much."

He groans as his smirk grows wild, "Have you sucked a cock like mine before, Elizabeth?"

I look back to his hand pumping up and down as I speak shyly, "I've never done it before in general."

His hand stops mid-pump and I look back up to his face. He has a mixture of shock and great pleasure twisting his features and I'm not sure what to make of it. Would he even want someone inexperienced like me to give this a try? He looks pretty big and thick, and I'm not even sure how much of him I'll be able to take. I know the gist of what to do, but I'm not sure how pleasing it'll be for him.

I begin to pull away from him as he stays silent, but he doesn't let me get far as his hand tightens in my hair and pushes me until my lips are grazing against his leaking tip.

His voice is rough and on edge, like he's holding himself back, "Let's see how much you can take, Elizabeth. Show me how good of a slut you can be for me."

My lips open as I look to his big hand at his base, holding it steady for me. I hold my mouth as wide open as I can manage, my tongue covering my bottom teeth. My nostrils flare with each of my heavy breaths but I slide my hands to his thighs and squeeze, letting him know I'm ready.

So slowly, he slides his thickness over my tongue and into my mouth. My lips stretch to accommodate his girth, but my eyes close on a moan as his flavor washes over my tastebuds. I didn't think I would enjoy the taste so much, but I do. He pushes in slowly until I feel him bump the back of my throat and I gag. When I open my eyes and look at how much I've taken, I'm about half way down. I whimper around him, swiping my tongue left and right in order to taste more.

I look up at him to find he's staring at me with deep green eyes and a tense jaw, his entire body is locked, strained with whatever little control he has left. He lets me pull back until just his tip is between my suctioned lips. I circle my tongue on a moan, tasting more of his sweet and salty precum. He lets me take a few bobs of my own, and I keep my cheeks hollowed and my tongue flat on the bottom side of his cock, feeling the random veins under the skin roll over my tongue.

His thighs tense impossibly further under my palms, then he snaps. Both his hands are in my hair tightly and I look up to him with every ounce of trust I have to offer. He swallows thickly, his jaw feathering twice, before he takes a deep breath.

"Tap my thigh if it's too much. Otherwise I'm not stopping until you swallow every last drop of my come."

I blink and flick my tongue over the slit in his tip in confirmation that I understand. That's his last string of restraint snapped. His fingers curl into his fist in my hair, and his hips start to thrust fast. My eyes start to water because of his speed and girth, my mouth still only getting halfway. I breathe through my nose as much as I can, but realize it makes it worse when he hits the back of my throat and I have to try not to gag around him.

The first tear slides down my cheek, and when he notices it, he smiles viciously. I moan at the smile, but it comes out strangled around the size of him. My fingers clutch his thick muscular thighs tighter as he speeds up and starts to go even deeper, actually slipping slightly into my throat from my flattened tongue. I'm almost at the base of him with how deep he's pushing into my mouth and I feel my own arousal starting to slide down my thigh again.

He speaks in heavy breaths but doesn't attempt to slow his pace, "Fuck, so good at choking on me. Ty vyglyadish' takoy krasivoy, kogda plachesh' vozle moyego chlena.[*]"

I moan at his words and watch as his eyes roll at the feel of it around him. Within seconds he's thrusting harder but shorter, his body locking under my hands, and then I feel him jerking against my tongue. Warm spirts of cum start to coat my tongue and I swallow greedily. He's the perfect mixture of sweet and salty and I could survive off the taste of it. He slows and softens his thrusts as he comes, and I take over dragging my mouth and tongue over him to get every drop I can. When I don't feel or taste any more, I look up at him and pull off with one last lick.

His eyes are hooded and his chest heaves with deep heavy breaths as he removes his fingers from my now tangled hair. I give him a soft satisfied smile and close my eyes when his palms cup my cheeks, his thumbs clearing off the tears from my face.

"Such a good girl for me, moya lyubov'.[*] Ty dlya menya takoy osobennyy.[*]"

When I open my eyes to give him another smile, my eyes catch on the tattoo down the side of his thigh, leading to his hip. *How did I not see that earlier?*

Chapter Thirty Five

Elizabeth

I RUN MY FINGERS OVER the artwork covering part of his thigh, leading towards his hip. It's a cherry blossom tree, some flowers floating off of the branches and growing bigger the closer they come to his hip. It's beautiful, reminding me of the way my room is decorated. It makes me wonder why he likes this tree and flower, why it's obviously important to him.

When I notice how stiff he is under my exploring fingers, I quickly pull back and look to my legs as I sit back on my heels.

"I'm sorry..."

His voice comes out stiff and not like how he would normally talk to me, "Why are you apologizing?"

I shrug smally, keeping my eyes down, "I just.. I didn't notice the tattoo before and it's so pretty, I couldn't help but take a closer look. You obviously didn't like that, so I'm sorry."

He says nothing. He doesn't move. So I finally look up at him.

The muscle in his jaw is pulsing, and his brows are slightly creased like he's confused and trying to solve a difficult problem. His green eyes swim with so many emotions, I'm not sure what he's actually feeling. I want to know what he's thinking, if I overstepped or made him uncomfortable with my intrigue in the hidden ink. When he still says nothing, and continues to look over my face, I stand quickly. My legs wobble slightly but I don't let it stop me as I pull up my sweatpants and move to leave with fast feet. I only make it a couple steps before a soft but demanding grip is wrapped around my bicep and I'm pulled back into a solid chest.

Something feels intimate about the way my bare back lays against Gabriel, even if he still has a shirt on, but I shove that feeling aside when I feel his lips near my ear.

"Where do you think you're going, Elizabeth?"

I take a deep breath to keep control of my irritation and hold still, "To my room."

The shake of his head moves a few strands of my wild hair, his hand tightening around my arm before he lets me go. He might not be holding onto my arm anymore, but I feel like he's still crushing me into him. The energy around him pulling me in so I likely never escape. His deep calm breaths move his chest against me, and I close my eyes to take in the moment.

He hasn't been sleeping in his room since I've been in there, and this is the first time he's touched me sexually since the bathtub. I crave the feel of his arms around me at night, for his mouth to be on my skin, his words to be flowing like the perfect melody through my ears.

There's something about those feelings that clenches my heart, but I choose to ignore that. It can't be what I suspect it is.

I keep my eyes closed and my legs in place. He doesn't move either. We stay in suspended silence, waiting for someone to make the first move. Who will pull away from the other...

The answer sends a pang through my chest when cool air suddenly meets my back. I swallow the plea for him to stay.. to talk to me. I open my eyes with a deep breath, and walk out of the kitchen without looking back. He might not be ready to talk about what his tattoo means to him, but he could've said something instead of letting me go.

He let me go...

It's been a week since the kitchen incident. A week of radio silence from Gabriel. He shut me out, *again.* I can't blame him, it's not like I've searched him out or opened up myself. After I walked away from him a week ago, I moved back into my designated room. The one matching the tattoo he seems to be protective about.

Each night, I've waited for him to come in. If not to talk about what happened, then to at least check in with me. But, no. I'm left alone every single moment of the day. I don't even see him around the house now. He's either in his office or in his room. I feel like this new awkward distance between us is my fault, but then I have to remind myself that he's the one who freaked out. He's the one who let *me* go.

With the sun shining through my windows, giving my room a beautiful orange film over the pink flowers dotting my walls, I decide that today I will make myself get back to something normal. I no longer have a job, so I have nothing to occupy my days. My body is pretty much healed, except for the random pain in my side. Forcing a smile to my face, I send Elliana and Natalie a text in our group chat asking what they're doing today.

Even though they check in with me either by text or a phone call, I haven't actually gotten to hang out with them. At first it was because I had to be resting, but this last week has been because I'm too nervous to ask Gabriel if I can leave or have them over. I have no idea what he does during the day, but I never want to interrupt him. Just the other day I heard him yelling angrily at someone from his office as I headed to the kitchen. It was a little scary, but also really hot. Something about that angry voice of his set my nerves firing and an ache forming in my core.

Just as I slip out of bed, my phone dings and I look at it with a genuine smile.

Natalie was the first to answer.

I have to be at the bookstore for a few hours, but I'm free after that.

Elliana texts almost immediately after.

Girls brunch?!?!

I laugh lightly as I type out an excited yes and walk to my bathroom. Already, the day seems to be going in a good way compared to the previous ones. Both Natalie and Elliana have quickly become my good friends. They might be older than me by a decent amount of years, but they don't treat me like I'm some annoying younger sister leaching to them. They treat me like an equal, like I've always been their friend.. like I really am a part of their weird little family.

We agree to have brunch at eleven thirty, which gives me about four hours to fill. Elliana says she'll be coming to get me around eleven since Gabriel still won't let me leave on my own. *Which seems totally reasonable after the warehouse incident.* I decide I'm going to try the gym—see how much my body was really effected by my injuries. I feel almost one hundred percent now, and I'm hoping I can get back into training with the girls soon.

I brush my teeth, throw my hair in a messy bun atop my head, and put on some leggings and a tank top. I look over myself in the mirror and notice a few different things. One, even though I've been recovering from injuries, I look glowing and healthy. Two, my clothes seem to be fitting just a little tighter, laying against my curves a bit more. And three, I don't see any bruises. With a small smile, I nod to myself and grab my headphones and phone before heading to the gym down the hall. *I can't wait to feel the mental blankness I fall into when I'm on the treadmill.*

I open the door to the gym slowly, peaking my head in to make sure Gabriel isn't in here. When it looks clear, I slip in and walk over to the treadmill. A thrill runs through my muscles, and I'm surprised by how much I'm excited to get back into training my body. I never imagined I would miss working myself until I feel like a limp noodle.

After about fifteen minutes of running, with my music blasting in my ears, I slow to a jog before turning it off and heading to the water jug. I didn't stop smiling the entire time, like my lips didn't care that I was sweating my ass off and breathing somewhat heavily. I chug about three cups of water and then head to the mats to stretch. My body isn't aching like I was afraid of with my almost healed injuries. My side doesn't feel any pain, my legs feel strong, and it didn't hurt when I was gulping air into my lungs.

I let my smile—that seems almost natural at this point—stay on my face as I start my stretches. I keep the music playing in my headphones, letting the melodies help relax my tense muscles. My eyes are focused on my fingers reaching towards my sneaker covered toes, but there's a feeling like eyes are on me. I keep my movements relaxed as I sit back up and get on my knees for a "stretch". That feeling of being watched intensifies, a heavy presence closing in on me. My hands flex as I stretch my arms over my head. In my peripheral someone reaches towards me. I let the things Elliana and Natalie taught me run free, grabbing the wrist I now see and reaching my other arm up without looking to grab their neck. I stand swiftly as I use their forward movement to throw them to the ground, placing my knee on their chest and twisting their wrist as soon as their back hits the mat.

My breathing is heavy, my body tight and ready to defend myself, but when I look at the face below me, my cheeks heat and I move away quickly. I pull my headphones down until their around my neck and cover my mouth with wide eyes. My head is shaking like I can't believe that I did that, but also because of who I was able to the take to the floor.

Gabriel is looking at me with shock written all over him. Then he starts laughing. His shoulders shake with how hard the laughter is as I stand in shock. His eyes are crinkled in the corners, his mouth spread into a wide grin showing his beautiful teeth. The laugh is so free, so natural, so mesmerizing. I lower my hand from my mouth and try to speak over his laughter that's doing things to my body I don't want to focus on.

"I'm so sorry. I didn't know it was you, I just reacted."

He sits up slowly, shaking his head and quieting his laughter. When he seems to have composed himself, he looks up to me with shining eyes and a big smile. His words still come out with a hint of laughter behind them.

"Don't apologizing, lepestok. That was actually impressive, good job."

My cheeks heat even further as I smile smally, "Thank you..."

He shakes his head again as he stands, crossing his arms over his chest to showcase his muscles, suddenly serious. "What are you doing in here? You're supposed to wait a month before serious physical activity."

I resist the urge to roll my eyes, propping my hands on my hips instead, "I feel good. Great even. I ran for a little bit and don't feel anything wrong. I'm fine."

He doesn't move, just keeps looking at me with that serious expression I assume he gives to his employees and guards. When he still doesn't say anything I sigh and throw my arms out in exasperation, deciding it's better if I just leave. He obviously came in here to workout based off his light shirt and workout shorts. When I turn to leave, he grabs my wrist and keeps me in place. He doesn't pull me closer and I don't look at him. I'm still upset with him for letting me leave the other day instead of talking to me. I pull my wrist out of his grasp, not surprised that he lets me, but keep my back to him.

After a few heavy seconds of silence, he speaks softly, "Why don't we spar a little? Show me what you've learned so far..."

He leaves it open, like he's expecting me to say no and walk away. But the idea of putting him on his ass again and hitting him as much as possible is too pleasing. I turn around with a savage smile, watching with even more excitement as his eyes flare.

"Alright. Let's do it."

He gives me that cocky smirk and steps back until we're in the middle of the mats. I follow him to the middle and look around, raising my brows when he just watches me and waits.

"Are we not going to use pads or anything?"

He shakes his head, looking down at me with fire in his eyes, "Nah, I want to see if you know what you're doing without pads or gloves. Show me what you got, Shchenok."

Closing my eyes, I take a deep breath and then open them to get into my fighting stance. He looks it over like an instructor, not lingering over the parts of my body I know he enjoys.

"Good. Now, come at me."

I walk close instead of charge, watching as he doesn't raise his arms to block himself and stands perfectly still. When I'm close enough to reach out and punch him, I do. I aim a punch to his ribs, but it doesn't land when he quickly reaches out and pushes my arm, using my momentum against me. I start to fall forward but catch myself and step back to get back into my stance. I sneer at him and start to throw different punches.

None of them land.

He either blocks them or moves out of the way. I start to grow angrier that I can't seem to get a hit in. I remind myself that Elliana said I need to keep calm, to keep my breathing in check and not let my head wander off. So I take a step back, and pause to control myself. Gabriel finally looks like he's ready for a fight, to defend himself. I think back over how he controlled his movements while I was throwing useless fists. I think over which side is more dominant—how he moved to block and duck from me.

I let a little smirk lift the corner of my lips, finally grounding myself. Then I go after him. He's fast, and strong, but I start to notice areas that are open on his body. When he blocks my next hit, I aim a swift fist to the open area of his stomach and actually land a blow. I step back quickly as he grunts and looks to me with wide eyes.

He chuckles and stands straight, "Damn, you actually got me."

I smile broader, "And I'm about to do it again."

I hold back the strength of my hits since I'm not wearing gloves, but I send punch after punch towards him, landing about half. Each time I get him, his eyes gleam with what might be pride and it lightens my body unexpectedly.

The last punch I send, catches him in the side of his jaw and I step back to put space between us and rest my hands on my hips while I try to calm my breathing. I smile brightly as he rubs his jaw and looks me over.

My clothes are sticking to my sweaty skin, strands of my hair are falling out of my bun and over my face, and my lungs are fighting to get enough oxygen to relax. I've never felt better.

A laugh starts to bubble up my throat, and I can't stop as I start to laugh uncontrollably. My body bends forward, my knees catching my hands as my lungs wheeze with my deep laughter. When I look up to Gabriel, his eyes are wide and his body is locked like he's preparing to run from a crazed animal. It only makes me laugh harder. My eyes are watering by the time I'm able to get my laughter under control as I stand straight and rest my forearms atop my head.

I look over to Gabriel and see a calmness over his features, his lips turned up in the tiniest smile. I sober instantly and clear my throat, cutting off eye contact.

"Why are you looking at me like that?"

I keep my eyes off him even as he starts to talk in a deep, mesmerized tone.

"Your laugh is beautiful."

Chapter Thirty Six

Gabriel

I WATCH HER SHUFFLE on her feet, like she's uncomfortable with my compliment. My smile spreads without permission, and I take the moment to look over her face while she's not watching. There's sweat lining her hairline, her face flushed from the activity we've been doing, and her eyes are glazed as if she truly enjoys what she was able to accomplish this morning.

She's completely stunning.

But then I think about what her face looked like that morning in the kitchen. She looked disappointed and sad. *I disappointed her.* The reaction I had towards her looking over my tattoo was uncontrollable. The only people who know the meaning behind my tattoo are Rick and Natalie, since they came with me to get it. It was an emotional experience for me, a vulnerable moment. I forgot I had it because I was too consumed by her on her knees for me.

I quickly move away from that image before I get inappropriately hard.

I've been avoiding her since that morning. I don't know why, so I don't try to think too hard on the exact reason I've been hiding from her like a fucking coward. I've also been busy working with Dom and Rick to try to figure out what we can do to take Murph out of our fucking lives. He's a pain in the ass and a danger to the woman in my life I would do anything for. He needs to go, and *soon*.

Elizabeth finally looks to me, with a silent question in her eyes I don't know how to read. She clears her throat and lowers her arms to point over her shoulder. She can barely look at me as she talks.

"I'm going to go clean up. I'm going to brunch with Elliana and Natalie later."

I nod and rub the back of my neck, "Okay..."

She nods back, hesitating as she starts to walk backwards before finally turning to walk out. I watch her leave. *Again.* Then something snaps in my chest. How many times am I going to let her go before I can finally open up to her? She needs to see that I'm able to talk to her, to tell her what I'm feeling. *And not just when I want to fuck her to sleep.*

Before I know it, I'm opening the door and walking down the hall. Her bedroom door closes softly but I don't let it stop me as I get closer and swing it open. She's already walking into the bathroom but she stops and looks to me with her wide hazel eyes when the door bounces off the wall. I stay in the doorway, but start to vomit words towards her like she asked me to explain everything about me in five seconds.

"The tattoo is for my mom. She was murdered when I was about seventeen. She loved cherry blossoms and had different decorations of it all around the house. She's a sensitive subject for me, that's why I freaked out when you started touching it. I was scared to open up about her and my bloody past. But you don't deserve that. You deserve me being honest and open with you. And I want to be. It's just a little terrifying because I don't know what the fuck I'm doing. I don't do relationships. I've never dated a woman longer than a month and I wouldn't count that as dating since I rarely saw them outside of the bedroom.

"But, I want that with you.. A relationship, I mean. I want to talk to you about my bad days, when I come home to you at night. I want to open up to you about my shitty past and how that fucked up my head. I just... I want *you*, Elizabeth. And I'm sorry that I haven't been able to be what you need. I—"

She cuts me off by jumping into my arms. I grab her without thinking, wrapping my arms around her waist and squeezing her into me. Her eyes are glossy, her lips tipped in a sad smile.

"It's okay, Gabriel. I figured your tattoo was a sensitive subject, I wasn't going to pry. But thank you for willing to be open with me. You've been what I needed.. Even when you ignored me."

She gives me a bigger smile before pushing her lips softly against mine. I keep my eyes open and wide, not believing that she so easily forgave me for being such an ass. When she pulls back and open her eyes, I decide that wasn't enough. I need more. I slide my hand into her hair that she pulled out of her messy bun and hold tightly, pulling her face back towards mine. My eyes stay locked on hers as I speak against her lips, wanting to drown in the brown and green of her irises.

"You are one of a kind, moya lyubov'. YA iskrenne veryu, chto ty sozdana dlya menya.[*] I would do anything for you, I hope you know that."

Then I close the short distance between us, and devour her.

She moans into my mouth, the sound vibrating on my tongue and causing my arms to lock tighter around her. I want her so badly, in any way that I can have her, and that's frightening. But, I choose to ignore that and allow myself to sink into the kiss. I don't stop or slow until we're panting against each other, her legs wrapped around my waist to hold me close to her. Only then, do I slow down, keeping it light and affectionate. Her delicate fingers cling to my shirt, like I might slip away if she isn't holding tight enough.

With a final, soft kiss, I pull away and lower her back to the ground. I pull my hand from her hair and cradle her cheek. She leans into my palm with a pleased smile, making my lips copy hers. I rest our foreheads together and just breathe with her. When my heart has calmed, I give her slightly salty forehead a peck and reluctantly let her go.

She looks to me with sad crinkled eyes, almost as though this is the last time we'll be this close. I give her a reassuring smirk and gesture to the bathroom.

"We'll sit down and talk when you're back from your brunch. Alright, moy malen'kiy lepestok?"

She nods, and watches me as I leave. When I close her bedroom door, I lean against it and listen until I hear her shower starting. I walk away from her room, a heaviness settling in me that I'm not sure how to interpret. I scrub a hand over my face as I make my way to my office. I was going to work out before I saw Elizabeth in there, but now I think I'll get to work and give Dominic a call. Maybe we can have a meeting while Ell is out with Elizabeth.

We need to come up with a final plan, and fast, because I have a sinking feeling that this time with no sign of Murph is going to come to a close soon.

As I settle into my office chair, I pull out my phone and call Dominic.

He answers like he does for everyone but his wife, "Hello."

I laugh lightly and lean back in my chair, "Don't you sound charming this morning."

He grunts, "I have to give up a child free morning with my wife so she can go eat breakfast and drink before noon with yours."

My answering smile to him calling Elizabeth my wife is unexpected and I smother it before replying.

"Well, I think that gives us a good time to sit down and discuss our plans with Murph. I don't like that he's been silent for a whole week."

"I don't like it either. Elliana should be getting Elizabeth around eleven, so be at my house by eleven thirty. I'll let Rick know in case he wants to join us."

I nod, "Sounds good."

I hang up without a goodbye, since he would've done that anyway, and toss my phone on my desk to run my fingers through my hair. A deep sigh leaves me as I look to the ceiling. My mind starts to wander off to different thoughts that I don't want to entertain, but do it anyway.

When we finally end Murph and his stupid little club, Elizabeth will be free to go about her life. I'd like to think that she would stay here with me, and choose to stay a part of this family. I'm not sure what she will want to do since we haven't talked about it, but I'm going to have to ask her eventually. When she's able to finally get her life back, I need to know if I'm going to be living in bliss or if I'm going to be mending a broken soul.

My office door is open so I can see whenever Elizabeth leaves, and just as I start to get focused in a new program Rick and I are building I hear her coming down the stairs.

"Elizabeth, come here a moment."

Her steps falter, but then get louder as she comes closer. She peaks her head in but doesn't step inside as she gives me a puzzled look. I lift a hand and motion for her to come inside, which she does but still stands too far away. Before I tell her to get that sweet ass over here, I look over her outfit choice for her girls outing.

She's wearing a mid-thigh dark green skirt that flares off of her wide hips, and a tucked in black tank top with thick straps and a V deep enough to show a teasing amount of cleavage. My dick decides it likes the outfit, so I lean back in my seat and run my fingers over my lips that are tilted in a smirk.

"Come here, Shchenok."

I see her throat move with a thick swallow before she walks tentatively around the desk. I swirl my chair so when she stops, she's standing right in front of me. She doesn't say anything but I can see her heavy breathing and the erratic pulse in her neck. Lowering my hand, I look into her eyes that are glossed with anticipation and tilt my head.

"Are you wearing panties, Elizabeth?"

She swallows again before she nods, like she wasn't sure what the correct answer would be. For some reason, that pleases me. I wouldn't mind if she wasn't, as long as I'm with her so I can slip my hand between her thighs to tease her.

I give her a nod, holding her gaze as I smile bigger, more vicious.

"Are you going to think of me while you're at your little brunch?"

Her shoulder lifts with a half shrug, "I don't know..."

I hum and lean forward, pulling her between my legs so I can run light fingers over her thick thighs. "Should I make sure that you do?"

Without letting her answer, I grab her hips and pull down until she's on her knees at my feet. I run a hand over her nicely brushed hair before reaching to my shorts and pulling them down just enough so my dick is free. I'm already hard—how could I not be with her in that outfit? I watch her pupils dilate as her gaze focuses on what's now being stroked with my hand. I've thought about her hot little mouth since the kitchen, fucking my fist every night to the image of her choking around me.

I tilt my cock until the leaking tip is towards my little petal, and groan as her tongue peaks out to moisten her lips. With my free hand, I reach out and pet her hair affectionately. I could cum just from her eyes focused on my hand pumping up and down my cock. But, I'd rather feel her lips wrapped around me instead. I stop pumping and remove my hand to let it hang over the arm of my chair. I pinch her chin with the hand that was stroking her hair, forcing her to look at me. Giving her a cocky smirk, I gesture with my head to my cock that's jumping against my shirt covered stomach.

"Suck."

She doesn't even hesitate to reach a hand forward and lean in, causing me to move my hand from her chin quickly. I put my hand lightly on the back of her head as her tongue runs circles around my tip. I flex my legs to resist shoving myself into her mouth. I don't have to wait long though before her lips close around me and start to glide down. My hand only serves as extra weight on her head as I watch inch after inch of my cock disappear inside her mouth.

When she gets a little over half way, she gags, her throat contracting around my tip and sending a delicious sensation up my spine.

"Fuck, baby. That's it, choke on it. Let's see if you'll cry for me again."

Wrapping her hair around my fist, I hold her head in place as I lift my hips off my chair to fuck her perfect mouth. Her moan vibrates up my cock and into my stomach, only making me thrust harder. I start speaking roughly in Russian even though I have no idea what I'm saying. Her hands slip beneath my shorts to grasp my thighs, her nails biting into my skin and adding even more sensation.

Right as I'm about to cum, I pull her off me with a wet pop watching as a string of drool links her bottom lip to my tip. I use my free hand to pump myself quickly. My voice comes out rough and tortured as I look into her hooded eyes.

"Tongue out."

She doesn't hesitate to stick her tongue out, her gaze moving to the cum that's now shooting out. I watch each shot end in a different spot and get a sick sense of pleasure when it ends up outside of her mouth and on her glowing skin. My hand slows as the zing up my spine disappears. When I'm empty and growing soft, I keep the hair from her face and put my cock away. Her tongue slinks back into her mouth and I can't pull my eyes away from her throat as it bobs with her swallow.

A growl slithers up from deep within me as I rub my thumb roughly over her lips, smearing in the cum that landed there.

"Such a pretty little slut. You did good, moy malen'kiy lepestok."

She hums, her smile small as she closes her eyes.

I look over her face to see some cum outside her lips, almost on her cheeks. I continue to hold her hair back and use my free hand to do what I'm hoping she'll keep thinking about while she's away.

I use my thumb, and spread my cum over each of her cheeks, rubbing it in until there's no sign of it being there. My smile is nothing but territorial and satisfied as I finally let go of her hair and massage her scalp as I lean forward to give her a quick kiss that she returns with a soft sigh.

When she opens her eyes, I give her a soft smile and lean back in my chair.

"Better get going, Elizabeth. Elliana is waiting."

Her cheeks immediately go pink and my smile widens. She glares at me as she stands, trying to come off like she isn't turned on as fuck right now.

"I'm telling her you're the one to blame for me taking so long to get out of the house."

I chuckle as I turn back to my desk and look to my computer, "Please do. Although, I'm sure she'll want details as to why."

She says nothing but I can see her body locking in my peripheral. I chuckle again, giving her a quick glance, before focusing on my screen again. Her shoes barely make a sound as she stomps out of my office, giving me one final glare before leaving.

Her glares mean nothing to me when I know she's drenching her panties right now with what I did to her. I also know that we're going to have an eventful afternoon once she gets back.

Chapter Thirty Seven

Elizabeth

I SLIDE INTO THE PASSENGER seat of Elliana's car with heated cheeks—Gabriel's scent flowing into my nostrils which each inhale—and soaking underwear.. but I try not to let that show as I give her a bright smile.

"Oh man, am I ready for girls time."

She chuckles lightly as she looks me over, "Yeah, I can see that. How's Gabriel doing this morning?"

My cheeks heat impossibly further as I look out the window, "Oh you know.. same ol', same ol'."

I clear my throat when she starts to laugh louder, finally pulling out of the driveway. When her laughter starts to quiet down I shoot her a quick glance, and see she's still smiling wildly. I roll my eyes and throw my hands up with a dramatic sigh.

"Alright, what?"

She chuckles again and shakes her head, "Oh, nothing. Though, it's about damn time you fucking got some."

My eyes widen, though my words come out on a harsh laugh, "We haven't had sex!"

She gives me major side eye before looking back to the road, "No one said anything about sex. There's plenty of other... Fun activities."

I smother my face with my hands, embarrassment heating my body even though I start laughing. I decide to fill her in with minimal details about how close Gabriel and I have gotten, 'bedroom' wise. She doesn't stop smiling and teasing me all the way to the restaurant, and I let her. I've always wanted a friendship like this. Someone to talk to about the guys in our life, things going wrong or right, or just giving each other shit about stupid things. My heart feels full as we get out of the car and walk inside to see Natalie already sitting at a table with three bright pink drinks waiting.

Before I even get fully settled into my seat, Elliana is leaning towards Natalie over the table with a wicked smile.

"Guess what news Liz has to share..."

Natalie looks to me with high brows and a slow building smile. I roll my eyes and run a hand through my hair. Of course I'm going to have to talk about this again. I'm not used to talking about sexual things with friends. I feel awkward and I'm not even sure how much detail to give.

When I continue to say nothing, Natalie laughs and pushes a drink towards me. I gulp it down until it's half gone before I realize it's alcohol and make a face when I finally draw in a breath. Natalie and Elliana sit patiently, waiting for me to be ready to share for the group.

"Okay... Gabriel and I might have started doing some *stuff*."

Natalie raises a single brow, "What kind of stuff?"

I groan and roll my hand around, "You know, bedroom stuff."

I can see her trying not to laugh, and I'm not sure if it's at me or because it's a little funny that I'm so shy about the subject.

"Liz, I'm going to need more details. And not because I don't know what you mean, but because I think it would be good to talk about it. Also because I'm curious as fuck."

This time, we all laugh and I melt into my seat a little more, feeling the alcohol warming my empty stomach. So, I decide to tell them—in a quiet voice—what happened during my bath, and what happened in the kitchen. But, I leave out what happened in the office since I don't want them to think I'm gross or weird because I have cum on my face like lotion.

Natalie is the first to speak when I'm done, "I knew that kid was a little freak. I'm not surprised, though I *am* surprised it took him so long to do something."

I choke on the last sip of my drink before I set it down and Elliana giggles at my side. She gives me a few pats on the back as she speaks.

"How do you feel about your experiences so far?"

I shrug and give her a small smile, "I mean.. I like it..."

They both look at each other and Natalie tilts her head at me. "But?"

I sigh, twisting around my empty glass, "But, every time we've done something he ends up pretty much ignoring me afterwards. I'm afraid that if I embrace it and fully give in that this might be a repeat thing. I can't handle giving myself over, for him to only leave me alone once he gets whatever he wants from me."

They let me sit in silence as I think over my next thought. He said he wanted me this morning. Like an actual relationship. But how am I supposed to say yes to that when I don't know if he's going to keep shutting down. He wants to talk to me and communicate, I know that, but he also isn't used to doing that. He's allowed to have trial and error with this new situation. There's still that 'but' at the back of my mind though.

"I just... He said he doesn't normally do relationships. How do I know if giving in is going to turn out good instead of blowing up in my face and hurting my heart in the process?"

Both of the girls give me sympathetic smiles, each grabbing one of my hands to hold. Elliana is the first to draw my attention with soft words.

"You don't, Liz. We don't know if the person we give our heart to is going to crush it or cradle it, but that's the whole point of a relationship. To see what they do with what you give them. You don't need to give him your full heart right now, but at least try it.. give him something."

Natalie nods as she picks up where Elliana left off, "She's right. Rick crushed a tiny part of me when we first met. I didn't want to give him another chance, but I eventually realized that I couldn't *not*. Something about being around him just felt so right, so I had to take another leap and hoped that time he caught me.. and he did."

They both give me another encouraging smile and I nod, giving them a bright one in return. From there, we order our food and more drinks. They both tell me different sex stories from their relationships, and I have to hide my blush. They're so open about everything, like they don't care about talking about it since they are living happily with someone they love. And I'm happy for them...

I just don't know if I'll have the same ending.

GABRIEL

I take my bike over to Dominic's house, needing to feel the calmness from the speed and air around me. There's two things that relieve my stress. Riding my motorcycle, and killing. Well, also sex. So three things.

When I get to Dom's, he's already waiting on his front steps for me. I leave my helmet on my seat and walk up to him with a nod. He only nods back and leads me into the house and to the kitchen. Rick is already in there, pouring whiskey into three glasses. He doesn't look up even though he talks directly to me.

"How's your girl doing?"

I huff a breath out as I sit down at the counter, reaching for one of the drinks, "A lot better. She even worked out a little this morning before going to brunch. I had her spar with me too."

He finally looks to me as he takes a sip of his whiskey. Dom sits next to me, draining half his glass in one go. Rick sets his glass down with a quiet clink and rests his forearms on the counter, looking at me with a silent apology in his eyes.

"Good..."

I know he wants to apologize again for holding me back but I just give him a nod and move on to the more important topic right now.

"So, have we seen anything from Murph yet?"

Dom shakes his head, "No. He hasn't been seen at any of his usual spots and hasn't been communicating with anyone from what we gathered. Obviously, he's talking to someone since his men are still fully functioning. But, we don't know how since Rick hasn't been able to find anything from the devices he was able to get into."

I hum and take a big gulp from my glass. Right as I swallow I think of something that I want to slap myself for not thinking of before.

"What if we ask Elizabeth to try to look?" Both Dom and Rick look to me with equal confusion and intrigue, so I elaborate, "She was his tech person. She might know something we don't or be able to get into something of his we haven't thought to check."

Rick shrugs as he straightens, "It's worth a shot."

When they found out that Elizabeth was also into cyber shit like Rick and I are, they were shocked to say the least. Not because she's a woman, but because of how disastrous her life has seemed to be since childhood. I want to ask her why she chose that to get into, and how she learned how to do everything she knows. She didn't go to college—shit, neither did I—but I at least had Rick to learn from. I want to know how she's so... *Good.*

We all decide to start making a plan on how to draw Murph out. He needs to be taken care of. With him in hiding, it puts me more on edge where Elizabeth is concerned. I barely wanted to let her go to brunch with the girls. We have no idea when he'll decide to pop up, or what he'll do.

In the middle of us brainstorming ideas, Dominic's phone pings with a text which he looks at immediately. Whenever his daughter or Elliana aren't around, he's more vigilant about his notifications.

My chest squeezes when his body stills and the muscle in his jaw starts to feather. Rick notices it too, leaning forward with that scary-serious look of his and asks what's wrong. Dom looks to him before looking to me.

"Do you know what Elizabeth found in Murph's office?"

My brows crease, "I thought she didn't find anything. She never said she did."

His nostrils flare as he breathes deeply, Rick looking just as confused as me. Dom downs the rest of his glass before he elaborates, and I try not to let my irritation show that he's taking his time.

"She found photos of herself in Murph's desk. Which means he was keeping tabs on her before we knew, and before he even thought of sending us the photos you got."

He looks in my eyes, letting that sink in. Elizabeth found pictures proving she was never fooling Murph, and didn't mention it to anyone. Granted, she went through a traumatic experience but, she's been acting like herself for almost two weeks. Yet, she still never mentioned it. Obviously she didn't forget because she just told the girls about it at brunch, hence Elliana's text to Dominic.

"Are we sure she isn't working with him against us?"

My eyes dart to Dom, who looks serious after asking that stupid fucking question. My molars grind so I don't lose my shit and punch him in the face.

"You mean the guy that tried to fucking kill her? I'm pretty sure, Dom."

He blows out a breath, his eyes softening slightly, "I'm sorry. We just need to check all the boxes. If she isn't trying to help him, then why not tell us about what she found? Not only is it a sign of his total obsession with her, but it puts us all at risk now that we've kept her."

"*We* haven't kept her. *I've* kept her. Am going to *continue* keeping her." When he raises his brow, I blow out a heavy breath and speak quieter, "But I understand your point."

I push my half empty glass away from me, looking to Rick when he clears his throat.

"I think it's time you have a serious talk with your woman, brother."

I nod and stand to leave, my words coming out dark as I walk away, "I plan on it."

Chapter Thirty Eight

Elizabeth

ELLIANA DROPS ME BACK off at Gabriel's house and I don't notice until I'm walking to the door that I actually got a decent buzz while I was out. I giggle to myself as I walk inside and look towards Gabriel's office. The doors are closed and the lights are off, so he's probably not in there. With the confidence boost from the alcohol and my arousal still pretty high from what he did to me in his office, I have a greedy urge to find him and see if he'll do more things to me.

I like the way he controls my body. There's something so comforting about being able to let go like that, knowing he's there to catch me even while he demands dirty things from me.

After making a round about the house, I realize that he isn't even here. My shoulders slump slightly with my disappointment as I walk back to the kitchen to get some water. I decide I'm going to take a walk around the tiny forest surrounding the house, so I grab a water bottle, take a few gulps, and leave it on the counter. I walk out with a slight smile through the side door in the garage, noticing Gabriel's bike missing.

Damn, I almost forgot how much I enjoyed the ride he took me on.

Making a mental note to ask him for another ride when he gets home, I let the sun warm my skin as I walk closer to the tree line. I haven't admitted to Gabriel yet, but I love his house and the surrounding forest. It's like I'm living in the middle of nowhere except I know the city is close by. It's a little escape without being away from important things like grocery stores and friends.

I'm right at the tree line, stepping between two thick trunks when I hear the rev from Gabriel's bike as it comes down the driveway. I turn around with a smile, watching as he stops his bike, but then I notice how quickly he's stopping and turning it off. From here, I can feel how angry he is. His energy has always been strong to me, and right now? He's practically fuming. He's a decent distance away, but that doesn't stop him when he hops off his bike and turns his head right to me. My lungs freeze as my muscles lock. I might not be able to see his face, but I can see how quick and heavy he's breathing. I take a small step back, triggering him to turn his full body towards me. I take another step, getting ready to ignore him and disappear into the forest.

"Elizabeth!"

Despite the distance, his voice is loud, thundering through me in warning. My heart starts to speed as he starts marching closer. Without a second thought, I turn and run. My pulse is racing, my stomach is in my throat, and arousal starts to gather in my underwear. Who knew being scared could be such a turn on?

I take a quick look behind me to see if he stopped and decided to go back inside.

Nope. He's chasing after me.

My heart jumps even more when I see his black helmet still on, hiding me from the anger that's sure to be twisting his features. He's catching up to me and quick, so I do the only thing I can think of.

I run faster.

I might not have been using the treadmill for a couple weeks, but my muscles remember how to push me forward with max speed. I try to control my breathing as much as I can with how fast my pulse is as I weave through trees to get away. Only when my lungs start to squeeze and my thighs burn do I slow down. That's when I notice, I don't hear him behind me anymore.

I get down to a jog before stopping completely, breathing deeply through my nose so I can listen. There's no pounding of feet, no heavy breathing, no twigs snapping. *Did he give up and turn around?* I turn in a circle, looking around me in case he's nearby. He's not there. I can barely make out the outline of the house through the trees, and there's no sign of Gabriel or his helmet.

Something snaps to my left, and my head follows suit. Still nothing. Again, something crunches to my right. This time my whole body turns to face the noise, still not catching sight of a thing. My breathing increases again, a warmth gathering in my stomach.

"Where do you think you're running to, Shchenok?"

His voice is deep, and close by, though I still can't see him. *I might not be able to see him, but he can definitely see me.* I don't answer as I continue to look around.

Leaves crunch to my right, but when he speaks again I can't tell from which direction.

"Are you running from me, Elizabeth?"

I nod, my confirmation coming out soft and breathless. I hear his dark promising hum on my left and spin that way. Still no one. My hands clench at my sides as I continue to turn in a circle. A deep chuckle bounces off trees from my right and I stop moving, keeping my eyes on the spot I thought I heard it. My swallow gets stuck in my throat when I feel fingers brush lightly over my hair. After a seconds pause, I spin to look behind me only to find the space empty.

"Do you think I can't catch you again? I promise you, *I will*."

My throat closes around a whimper and I clear it, twisting so I can face where I know the house is outside the trees. "Will you?"

"Always." This time, his voice is so close I can practically feel it.

I don't look, allowing the shiver his words give me, but keeping my sight focused on the path ahead. I can get away, I just have to be quick. This time, when I feel his fingers brush over my hair, I ignore it. Then I feel something hard against the back of my head and my body locks before realizing it's his helmet. He nuzzles it against my hair, the growl he gives sounding deeper from inside it.

I barely recognize his voice when he speaks, the tone a mixture of rage and need.

"Better run fast."

Not hesitating like the first time we played this, I take off. Dirt shifts beneath my shoes as I push my legs as fast as they'll go. I'm not sure if I'll be able to outrun him, and I also know I don't entirely want to. I want him to catch me. I want to see what he'll do when he has me.

I don't hear him behind me, but I don't risk slowing down to look. I race towards the garage door, almost slipping as I go through the doorway. Running through the small eating area, kitchen, and dining room, I think I might have lost him. *I'm wrong.* I skid to a stop when I see Gabriel standing next to the stairs, his head tilted to the side and his chest moving quickly.

"Gotta do better than that, Shchenok."

I charge forward, staying out of his reach as I run up the stairs, taking two at a time. As I get to the top, I grab the banister and use it to swing right. I'm not sure why I head for his bedroom, but I do. Just as I get to his door, I hear his heavy steps echo down the hallway. I slide in, slamming the door behind me, and lock it. I'm safely in his room, he didn't catch me, I think I've won.

Until I hear his dark chuckle on the other side of the wood. I step back slowly until my legs hit the bed. There's not a moment for me to hide before the door busts in, splintering the wood on the frame. The door bounces off the wall and he catches it with a flat hand.

Neither of us move, each of our breaths heavy and the only sound in the room.

"We need to talk, Shchenok."

I move to take a step back but fall against the bed instead. When he starts to move forward, I frantically crawl backwards up the bed. Right before I reach the pillows, he's at the foot of the bed and grabbing my ankle, pulling down until my knees bend over the edge. He grabs my wrists tightly, holding them above my head, and pinning me down with his body. I can feel his erection pressing on my stomach and I bite my lip to hold back my moan.

His tinted visor hides his eyes so all I'm able to see is my flushed face and wild hair. His hum vibrates against me and I close my eyes as he leans his head forward. He nuzzles his black helmet against me, like he's hoping he can feel it.

"Not being a very good girl running from me, Elizabeth."

My voice comes out rough and breathless, "You told me to."

His chuckle is deep as he lifts his helmet covered face from mine, "Not the first time."

I keep my eyes closed and slow my breathing, even if my body refuses to relax. The warmth of his body leaves mine, but his hands still hold my wrists. I listen intently as he moves around me, pulling my wrists together and holding them with one hand. He gives my arms a slight pull, my body sliding further onto the bed, and my eyes pop open to look at him. I might not be able to see it, but I know he has that hungry smile twisting his lips. I can feel his eyes moving over my tense body, and my thighs push together with the heat his invisible gaze gives.

With one big pull, he slides me from the bottom of the bed to the top and my lips open with a shocked inhale. He doesn't say anything as he swings a leg over my chest until he's straddling me. I'm not sure what to do other than stare at his dick that looks like it's in pain as it stretches out his jeans. Only when I see his hands drop to his thighs do I realize that my arms are still raised above me, and now something else holds them in place.

When I look up, I see two thick leather bands wrapped around my wrists, linking together with a strap that moves behind the headboard. My face swings to him when a heavy finger starts sliding down my neck and over my collarbones.

"I think I like you like this, Shchenok."

A whimper slips from me without permission, only making him chuckle in response. I swallow thickly as he slides down my body until his fingers link in the waistband on my skirt. He teases the skin on my lower stomach before grabbing the dark green material and pulling it from my waist, tossing it to the side.

His helmet tilts up, showing he's looking at me, as he grabs the flimsy fabric of my underwear and ripping it from me. When the cool air slides over my sensitive clit I have to bite my lip so I don't moan. The feel of his jeans rubbing against the inside of my thighs as he spreads my legs has my pussy pulsing around nothing, silently begging to be filled. When I'm spread to his satisfaction and he can see how much I've enjoyed our little game, I'm granted with a deep, dark moan that I feel over every inch of my skin.

My breath catches when he shifts backwards so he can lay on his stomach, my legs draped over his shoulders and pressing into his helmet. I'm caught off guard and confused as I watch him lean forward until his visor is pressed against my pussy, my breath rushing into my lungs on a loud intake. He groans into his helmet, pushing against me even harder. I can feel my lips and arousal spreading out against the black shield closing me off from his hypnotic green eyes.

"You're going to grind against my perfect window until you come, while I enjoy the show. Understood?"

It takes a few seconds for me to understand what he's asking. When I do, I give a tentative tilt of my hips only to feel a beautiful zing rippling down my legs. I'm so sensitive and turned on, I doubt this will last long. I don't let the fact that he's staring *directly* at my vagina have effect over me or my mind as I keep rotating my hips against him like he asked. My arms give a tentative pull against my restraints only to receive a subtle sting.

I want to touch him, to feel his lips against me, to have his eyes on mine as he licks me. I continue to roll my hips against his visor while wild pleas fly from my mouth almost silently.

"That's it baby.. fuck, just look at how wet you are for me."

I nod my head as I push harder, a delicious pressure starting to grow. This might be the most depraved thing I've done in my life, and I couldn't love it any more than I already do. When I get close to cliff jumping from my orgasm, Gabriel growls lowly, his fingers reaching up and digging into the fat of my thighs.

"That's it, lepestok. Fucking come for me. Let me see my pretty pussy come."

Shock waves hit my body with no remorse. My legs tighten around his helmet, the curves biting into my skin. My chest reaches for the ceiling like a string is pulling it up as my eyes shut only to see stars igniting in the darkness behind my lids.

As my hips stop moving, he starts to roll his head against me to drain out every last shiver my body has left. Only when I start to go lax, and my legs start to slip from his shoulders, does he remove himself from between my legs.

His voice, suddenly free from the air of his helmet, sticks to my skin with its hunger, "Such a pretty girl. Vy sovershenny dlya menya, moy malen'kiy lepestok.[*]"

I can't bring myself to have the energy to open my eyes, but I try my best to hear what he's doing. All I can get is a rustle of clothing and soft footsteps. My eyes stay closed, my mind barely registering my hands are still bound, as the bed dips between my legs.

His heat covers my chest, but he doesn't lean fully down and I whimper in a plea to feel him on top of me. His chuckle is against my mouth, and I lift my head to find his soft plump lips. He barely lets me brush my lips against his, and when I whimper again he shushes me quietly so I lay fully back down. As I'm flat on my back, he roughly pulls my shirt up until my breasts meet the chilled air. His rough calloused hand takes turns kneading each side, tweaking my sensitive nipples, and forcing my lungs to forget how to function.

He shifts upwards, and I feel his bare cock cover me between my legs. My eyes pop open, immediately finding his dark, glowing green irises. New found energy ignites throughout my body, but I keep myself perfectly still. He gives me a devilish smirk, giving a teasing thrust between my folds, causing my air to cut short on its way into my lungs. Only when I keep my eyes on his, does he lean down for a kiss. It's a quick brush of his tongue and locking of our lips before he pulls away to speak into my eager mouth.

"You ready for me, Shchenok?"

Chapter Thirty Nine

Elizabeth

"YE—"

My reply cuts off on a gasp as he shifts and quickly thrusts into me. He bottoms out but doesn't move again, letting me adjust to the unexpected intrusion. His bare, broad chest heaves with his deep breaths, and I look down to see his abs flexing and his hips flush with mine.

"Look at me."

Without hesitation, my eyes reach for his. I'm granted with blown pupils and dark green irises. His name rushes off my tongue in a rough whisper and he smirks down at me. I lift my head for another kiss, and this time he lets me have it. He devours my mouth, causing a deep moan to vibrate up from my chest. A groan echoes back at me as Gabriel grinds forward. My legs spread wider and my back arches with how deep he's able to reach. It's been four years with nothing but my fingers, and it feels like I'm losing my virginity all over again.

Gabriel gives a nip to my bottom lip before pulling away to speak against my open mouth.

"You okay, moya lyubov'?" I nod, keeping my eyes closed and focusing on how much I want him to move to ease the sting between my legs. "Good. What's your safe word?"

I squeeze my eyes tighter as I try to remember. When I get it, I lift my heavy lids to look at his tense features.

"R—red."

The growl he gives glides over my skin. "Good girl."

No other warning. No other words.

He pulls out, pauses for barely a second, and starts to thrust into me with no remorse. My cries and moans only grow louder when he leans farther up and captures my throat in his thick hand. My eyes open to watch him piston in and out, his abs flexing which each push forward, and his fingers tightening around the sides of my throat. Veins snake from his hand all the way to his bicep, and I moan his name at the beauty of it.

"Fucking perfection, Elizabeth... Shit..."

My toes begin to curl as warmth starts gathering in my belly. I didn't think it would be possible to cum without any stimulation to my clit. I was wrong. He keeps hitting a spot deep within me, sending pleasure zipping throughout my whole body. Before I can process exactly what he's doing—his teeth capture my peaked nipple, and my back curves with the first spark of my orgasm.

He doesn't slow or relent as the sensation rolls over me in thick, crushing waves. When it starts to dial back and my hips squirm to get away, he pulls out and grips my hips harshly. My world spins as he flips me to my stomach quickly. He closes my legs and pushes between my thick thighs, only to plunge back in. I cry out his name, pulling against the cuffs still holding my wrists, and he chuckles darkly against my ear.

"You think we're done, baby? Not even fucking close."

I make a sound between a cry and a moan as he picks up his pace again, leaning back on his knees so the cold air chills my damp back.

"Gabe... I—I can't. It's too m—much."

A harsh smack lands on my ass, making me cry out as a tear slips down my cheek.

"It's not nearly enough, Shchenok. You feel way too good not to make this last."

He slaps my ass again and growls loudly before squeezing it in his hands with rough fingers.

"Come on, baby. Let me feel you come around my cock again. Give me one more."

My head is shaking as I shove it into his silk sheets. My body feels like it's on fire and my skin is starting to get too sensitive. I can barely focus on anything besides the feel of his cock moving too quickly and his rough voice speaking in Russian. The sound of our bodies slapping together is pure music. I didn't think sex could be like this. Rough, carnal, and euphoric.

"Fuck... Elizabeth, you better fucking come for me again." One of his hands squeezes beneath my hips, his fingers finding my clit and pinching it harshly. "Now, baby."

My body doesn't have a choice but to listen to him. My muscles lock and my lungs stop working as another orgasm crashes into me. An increasing wetness leaks from between my thighs and onto the bed, but I barely notice it as I repeat Gabriel's name like a mantra. He gives me three more harsh thrusts before he groans my name and his cock pulses inside me.

I become jello beneath him as my orgasm calms and he slows his strokes until he stops completely. His heavy breathing rushes out against my shoulder as he leans forward. He rests his sweaty chest against my back and I hum with pleasure. He uses his rough fingers to wipe tears from the side of my face as he gives soft kisses to the sensitive skin of my shoulder.

"You did amazing, moya lyubov'. You feel so good wrapped around my cock. Such a good girl, I'm so proud of you."

I hum again as he pulls out and kisses softly down my back, kneading my muscles as he goes. He moves from over me, and I open my heavy eyes to watch him release my wrists. He massages the sensitive skin from when I was pulling against the restraints, giving more kisses there. When he finally looks to me, I see nothing but pleasure and happiness shining on his beautiful face. I give him my own satisfied smile as my eyes fall closed once more.

"Come on, moya lyubov', let's get you cleaned up and comfortable."

He scoops me up from the bed with strong arms, and I melt into his chest with a smile still tilting my lips. He carries me into the bathroom, setting me on the toilet to start to shower. My eyes are still heavy and my body so relaxed that I have to lean on my knees so I don't slip from the toilet. Gabriel's thick fingers pinch my chin and tilt my face up, and I finally open my eyes again.

He's giving me a soft smile, tilting his head towards to the shower, "Come on, baby."

I nod and use his arm to help myself stand up. Once I step in, my eyes finally find the strength to remain open as more energy floods my system as I watch him step in with me. He gives me that cocky smirk with a wink, grabbing my hips and leading me into the warm spray of water. I keep my eyes on his utterly content face as he tilts my head back to get my hair wet.

I want to ask him why he was mad when he got home, but I don't want to ruin the moment so I push it to the side for later.

When my hair is fully wet, he pulls me from beneath the water to drag a soapy cloth over my relaxed body. I hum as he brushes the cloth over my sensitive nipples, and he smirks in response but doesn't linger there. I might've just cum three times in the last who knows how long, but I can't wait to feel him inside me again. It felt like we fit perfectly, and I'm already craving more.

When he stays standing and goes to wash between my legs, he pauses, his body suddenly tensing. I touch his arm softly with furrowed brows.

"Gabe.. you okay?"

He pulls the cloth completely from between my legs and I notice the slight amount of blood soaking into the white fabric. His tight body shows signs that he's freaking out so I cup his face and tilt it up so he's looking at me instead of the cloth. His eyes are glossy and dark, his jaw tense against my fingers. I give him a gentle smile and lean up until our foreheads rest together.

"Hey, I'm okay. I promise. You didn't hurt me. I loved every moment."

He swallows thickly and closes his eyes briefly before meeting my gaze again. "Were you... A virgin? Fuck, I wouldn't have been so rough Elizabeth, you should've said something."

A light laugh tickles my throat but I swallow it, giving him a nose kiss like he usually does for me.

"No, I wasn't a virgin, Gabriel. But..."

He pulls his face further from my grasp but steps closer, wrapping a strong arm around my soapy middle. "But, what?"

I shrug, sinking into his wet hold, "I've only had sex once, and that was four years ago."

He freezes against me, and I can't quite place how he's feeling. There's different emotions swimming in his green gaze—his jaw tense, his breathing slow and deep. Before I can finish my intake of breath, my back is against the cold tile of the shower and Gabriel is smashing his hard body against me. His arm tightens around my waist, his face leaning closer until his lips brush mine as he growls deeply, the sound reverberating through my chest.

"*Mine.*"

My eyes flare seconds before his lips crash to mine, consuming me in a possessive kiss I feel all the way to my toes. I whimper against his relentless, rough affection and wind my arms around his neck. His hips twitch against my stomach, and I notice then that he's hard again.

He leans down further, leaving my mouth to bite and kiss his way down my neck. My breathing is quick through my open mouth, my eyes closed to focus on the feel of his lips against me.

"G—gabe.."

He hums, biting against my quick pulse causing a pleasurable ripple to roll down my spine. I want more. I want him again. Now that I've had him, I don't think I can go a day without. Not just the sensation of him completely filling me, but also the way he takes care of me afterwards. I want it all, every day.

I open my eyes to find his when one of his hands comes between us to play with my heavy breasts and peaked nipples. He's focused intently on the way his hand isn't able to fit my full breast, his eyes burning with my favorite color. One of my hands snakes its way into his wet hair, holding tightly—the other moving to his face so my thumb can trace the perfection of his lips. He smiles under my finger, looking down into my eyes with newfound hunger.

His hand moves from my chest to between my thighs, gently playing with me as his face nuzzles my neck.

"How's this pretty pussy feeling, lepestok?"

I close my eyes, rubbing my head against his as I whisper my answer, "I think it misses you already."

His chuckle is deep and playful against my wet flesh. "Is that right?"

I nod, biting my lip in anticipation for what might come next.

I'm not left wondering for long. He turns us so my back is against his broad chest, his back taking the brunt of the spraying water. His legs push mine farther apart as his hand slides down my still soapy body to glide between my legs.

"I'll just have to take care of my girl in here then. I don't want to leave it feeling lonely."

His hand leaves me only for a second before his wet fingers slap against my clit, causing my knees to buckle. He catches me easily with a strong arm around my waist and a thrilling dark laugh. I lean back against him, my hands holding onto his thick arm to help myself from collapsing. He slaps between my legs again, and a crying whimper scrapes from my throat to bounce off the shower tiles. One more has me panting, my nails digging into his tan skin, and mumbled words rolling from my tongue.

Removing his big hand from between my trembling thighs, he closes it around the front of my neck and pulls down until I'm bent forward—my ass pressing into his hard impressive length. He takes the arm from my waist, and rubs over my ass with a deep satisfied groan.

"I'm going to love breaking you, moy malen'kiy lepestok."

Chapter Forty

Gabriel

HER WHIMPER IS LIKE music to my ears as I look over her wet trembling body, rubbing her fat ass with an eager hand. *Goddamn, she's so fucking perfect.* I give her ass a test slap, groaning when it ripples all the way to the opposite side. Death could take me now, and I would have no complaints if this was what I had before me as I went.

When I was washing her, and saw the blood between her legs, I started to panic. I was sort of rough with her, wanting to take out some of my frustration. I thought she was actually a virgin when I saw the red melting into the white of the cloth, but then she told me the truth. She hasn't had sex in *four years.* Not only that, but she's only done it one other time. The need to officially claim her as mine was something I couldn't ignore after that. The only man that's going to be between her legs from now on is *me.*

If anyone else tries, they're going to see nothing but my smile as I slit their throats.

Her round, perfect ass sways from side to side against my hard cock, and I can't stop the smile that spread my lips at her eagerness. I tighten my fingers around her throat as I line myself up. I tell myself to take it slower and easier this time—but when I slide in until I'm flush with her ass, I know I won't.

She feels like a drug, and I won't deny that I'm addicted.

I realize I'm not moving when her sweet, shaky voice echoes off the walls, "Gabriel.. please.."

Gripping her ass in a tight grasp, I pull her up by her throat until she's arched perfectly and I can whisper in her ear.

"Don't worry baby, I've got you."

With need heating every vein in my body, I drive into her without letting up. With each thrust forward, the wet slap of our bodies bounces into the humid air. My eyes just about roll back into my head at the sight of her ass moving, the ripple it has every time it bounces off my stomach.

A breathless curse leaves my lips as I hold her throat tighter, cutting off her air flow. Her walls pulse around me, and I know she's getting close to another orgasm. Her small delicate hands slam against the tile of the shower, holding herself up so she doesn't fall. After another couple seconds, I loosen my grip around her dainty throat and let her gulp in a few breaths.

"Gabe.. I'm going to.. I want to come.."

Her quiet pleas only send me slamming into her harder, making sure to hit the spot I know now makes her eyes roll. *She's close, and so am I.* Cutting off her air again, I dig my fingers into the soft flesh of her hip, and tilt her head more so I can watch her back arche further.

My words come out rough and animalistic, "Come for me, Shchenok. You don't come, you don't breathe."

Her fingers dig into the wall as her sweet little pussy convulses around me. I feel her jaw press into my hand as her mouth opens just as her legs give out and I see her eyes starting to fall closed as her arms fall from the wall. I let go of her hip, wrapping my arm around her middle to keep her standing as her orgasm slows.

"Where the fuck do you think you're going, Shchenok?"

I let go of her throat to cross my arm over her chest so she remains standing. I know she was starting to black out as she came, and there's a dark part of me that thoroughly enjoys that. With a few more slams forward, I feel warmth tingle up my spine.

"Goddamn, Elizabeth..."

My eyes close as I cum, and I thrust more softly—more shallow. Her pussy practically sucks all the remaining cum up that I have left, leaving my body weak and satisfied. When my cock twitches with the last spirt, I pull out and hold her soft body against my chest.

She hums with a smile on her perfect lips as she tilts her head back to lay it just below my shoulder. I tighten my arms around her, stuffing my face into the crook of her neck and give her soft kisses with a smile.

"You did so good, taking my cum like my perfect little slut.. My good fucking girl." She hums again, lifting a heavy arm to wrap back around my neck. "Amazing, moy malen'kiy lepestok."

With a final kiss to her jaw, I relax my tight hold against her to put her back in the water to finish cleaning her off. Once she's nice and clean, I lean her against the wall to quickly wash myself. I need to get her hydrated with some food in her stomach before we talk.

Despite our little escapades, I haven't forgotten why I came home angry. And I doubt she's forgotten the anger I had either.

Moving quickly, I wrap a towel around my waist before putting one around her shoulders and carrying her from the bathroom. I set her on the edge of the bed, smiling at the glowing, satisfied look on her gorgeous face. If she thinks she can leave after this, she's gravely mistaken.

Grabbing two of my shirts, a pair of boxers, and some sweatpants, I walk back to my tired little petal. She gives me a soft smile as I finish drying her off, and I return it. Surprisingly, she lets me dress her with no complaints and my heart gives an extra heavy thump. Once she's dressed, and sitting again, I quickly throw on my own clothes. When I look back to her, she's no longer looking at me but to the decent size wet spot darkening my black sheets. I swallow my laugh at her wide eyes and tight shoulders, walking over to squat down in front of her.

"What's that look for, lepestok?"

She doesn't meet my eyes as she shakes her head smally and talks in a horrified whisper, "Is that pee? Did I fucking pee in your bed?"

Then she swings her wide frantic eyes to mine, and I bite my lip not to burst out laughing. Her hands come up to cover her face, her elbows falling to her bent knees. I clear my throat so I don't laugh, because I know that won't help her misplaced embarrassment.

"Oh my god, I can't believe I fucking *peed..* that's so embarrassing!"

Now, I do let out a soft chuckle. Her head lifts up with impressive speed as she sends a glare my way. I give her a bright smile in return, running a gentle finger over her freckles and down her cheek.

"You didn't pee, Elizabeth."

She throws an arm towards the spot on the bed, her hazel eyes bright and burning, "Then what the fuck is that?!"

I clear my throat again, lowering her arm gently back to her lap, "You squirted."

Her brows crease for a few seconds before smoothing out and inching up her forehead. "Oh..."

I give her a single nod, leaning forward to give a soft kiss to her nose then to her soft lips. When I lean back, her embarrassment is less, but not totally gone. Giving her a reassuring smile, I grab her hand and pull her to stand.

"Come on, lepestok. Let's go get some food before we talk."

Her eyes tilt slightly down at the reminder of our much needed chat, but she doesn't remove herself from my grasp as we make our way downstairs.

After making us each a grilled cheese and sitting down at the smaller dinner table, I let her eat half before finally bringing about the topic we need to discuss.

I watch her fiddle with the remainder of her food as I start talking, "So, Dominic was informed that you found something in Murph's office that could've been useful information. Do you want to tell me what it was?"

Her eyes find mine, betrayal lighting them before dying and an apology taking its place.

"In the locked drawer of his desk were pictures of me, starting from when I went to Rick and Natalie's wedding." I open my mouth to ask another question, but she continues quickly, "I honestly hadn't thought about them until this morning when Natalie and Elliana were telling me how Murph has gone into hiding... I was planning on telling you when I got home, but I told them about it in the moment.. I'm sorry."

My muscles that I didn't notice were tense, relax. I know her mind probably blew that piece of information to the side while it processed the unfortunate events that took place after she found them. I don't blame her for not saying anything, it's completely understandable that she didn't remember them until now.

I give her soft smile, and reach across the table to hold her slender hand, "It's okay, Elizabeth. I might've been upset in the moment, but I understand why you didn't mention it before. You went through something traumatic, and that's not something you need to ever apologize for. Because it wasn't your fault."

Chapter Forty One

Elizabeth

IT WASN'T MY FAULT.

I don't know why it took me until he said it for it to sink in. It wasn't my fault that Murph tried to kill me. And, it wasn't my fault when my father abused me either. For some reason, it's easier to forget about it and come up with excuses for the actions. But now, I understand that I don't need to do that. I don't need to hide those things because it doesn't reflect badly on me. It reflects badly on *them.*

I give Gabriel a tentative smile, "Thank you..."

He nods softly, giving my knuckles a caress before letting my hand go to grab his food. I watch him take a big bite as I think. Obviously Elliana told Dominic about what I said and that's how he found out. But, why was what I found useful information? How could it have helped us in any way? We knew that he was aware that I had been around them and was continuing to be around them. So how were those pictures something that could've helped?

Only one way to find out.

"Gabe.." He looks up from his plate with a lifted brow and I swallow thickly before asking, "Why could those pictures have been useful information?"

He pauses chewing, looking over my features with tense shoulders. When he finishes chewing, his throat bobbing with a slow swallow, he leans back in his chair and crosses his arms.

"Murph sent me a little package a couple weeks after he found you in his office. it contained some pictures of you with a note."

My anger starts to bubble in my veins, but I hold it in, copying the way he's sitting.

"What did the note say?"

His jaw ticks once. "That we have something of his, and he's going to take it back."

The anger at not knowing about this evaporates, getting replaced with dread and anxiety. My arms tighten across my chest and I look down to my plate. I'm not Murph's, and he has no rights to me. But he's a crazy motherfucker, always thought I belonged to him in some way, so it's not surprising he's pissed off that I'm now staying within Gabriel's little family. Now I know why Gabriel and the guys have been having so many meetings, their trying to find where Murph is to finally finish this.

That only makes me more nervous because we *don't* know where he is. If they haven't been able to find him a month later, who knows when we will. As my thoughts start to spiral, Gabriel clears his throat to gain my attention back, so I look to him with the blankest face I can muster.

"I had the idea this morning, that since we haven't been able to find Murph.. Maybe you could."

My brows crease as I lean forward to rest my arms against the table. "How would I be able to find him if you guys haven't?"

"You know him better than we do. You know the places he would go, devices he would use, and ways he would be able to keep his men working without being seen..."

He leaves it open like he could be wrong but doesn't want to be. I swallow thickly, biting my lip to think it over. Granted, I've been working for Murph for a few years, but I don't know everything about how he operates. As far as I know—he has the one warehouse, the diner, an apartment in the city, and a house outside of the city limits. I usually was the one do work on any devices, but considering he outsourced for the flash drive he tried to get me to use, who knows what other devices he has that I don't know about.

Gabriel sits quietly, letting me think. My knee starts to bounce as my anxiety rises. I don't think I would really be much help. *But I can try, right?* Taking a deep calming breath, I finally look back to Gabriel with newfound strength.

"Where have you guys looked so far?"

His lips twitch before he answers, "We've had eyes on his apartment, warehouse, and diner. There's been no sign of him."

"You haven't been watching his house?"

Now Gabriel is the one who's confused, "What house?"

I raise my brows and sit straight in my seat, "The house he has outside of town. I don't know if he has it under his name, but he definitely owns it."

His hand lifts so his fingers can pinch the bridge of his nose as he sighs out a curse. When he moves his hand, he looks ready to give orders.

"I need to know about the house and whatever else you can think of."

I nod and shrug, "Sure. Can I use your computer?"

His brows pinch slightly before he nods and stands to lead me to his office.

If you would've told me three months ago that I would spend an entire afternoon getting fucked to within an inch of my life only to then be hacking into shit to find a man that tried to kill me, I would've told you that you were fucking crazy. *Oh, how my life has changed.*

Gabriel sits down at his desk first, logging in to his computer and getting his monitors ready to go for me. When he moves away, I take his place in the comfortable chair and take a deep breath. I can do this, I just need to think about what I've learned over the past few years with Murph. Looking through all the different resources on Gabriel's computer, I have to hide my excitement. I've never had so much at my fingertips. I can *definitely* work with this.

Within a couple of short minutes—I have all the records pulled up on Murph's house, the cameras on each of his properties up with live feed, the two phones I know Murph uses are screensharing, and his office computer logged into and waiting on the second monitor.

When I look over my shoulder to smile at Gabriel, I have to bite my lip so I don't laugh at his wide eyes and frozen form. He doesn't move as I continue to look at him, so I clear my throat, brightening my smile again when his eyes reach mine.

He blinks quickly, looking back to the screens as he pulls out his phone, "Good shit, lepestok. I'm going to give Rick a call to see if he'll come over to help look through everything."

I nod and watch him walk out of the office with his phone to his ear as Russian flows heavily from his tongue.

Twenty five minutes go by of me sitting alone in Gabriel's office, waiting for Rick to get here. I've been sorting through stuff while I wait, so I can get at least *some* of the stuff done. His emails are just the usual shady business shit, nothing out of the ordinary, and most of his texts on both phones are just the normal orders he gives out to his men—or to women he's sleeping with that I could've gone without seeing.

When I go to start looking over any documents for his house, Gabriel and Rick come into the room. Rick gives me a friendly smile as he walks around to my side of the desk.

"Hey, Liz. I heard you got some new stuff for us to look into."

I nod as I stand, returning his smile, "Yeah, hopefully you guys are able to find something helpful. I looked through some of the stuff while I waited but didn't find anything we didn't already know."

He takes a seat in the chair, looking through what I was already able to pull up. After a few moments of him looking quickly through different programs, he turns to me with high brows and an impressed expression.

"Damn, Liz. You want to take over Gabe's job?"

I laugh as Gabriel rolls his eyes and flips Rick off. Rick laughs and gives Gabriel the middle finger right back before getting down to business. I feel awkward just standing over Rick's shoulder, but I feel like more eyes on the stuff will work better. He finds the same results I did with most things before moving on to the security cameras on the various properties. He looks through them all fairly quickly. Nothing is out of the norm. When he's about to move out of the box with the only camera on the property for Murph's house, I stop him with a hand on his shoulder.

He looks up to me with a silent question on his face and I point to the bottom right corner where you can barely make out the edge of a red vehicle.

"Is it me, or is that Murph's car color?"

Rick and Gabriel both lean closer until they see it, both giving me a proud smile causing a blush to heat my cheeks. I almost stop Rick when it seems like he's about to leave the screen but don't when he does something else. He bring up a separate box that's full of code, typing quickly while looking totally relaxed. Within a minute, the camera starts moving on the video feed, tilting down to get a better view of the semi-hidden vehicle.

My brows rise as I speak with soft excitement, "You have to teach me how you just did that."

Rick chuckles deeply, keeping his eyes on the screen, "I'm down to teach you new things, kid. You're already pretty advanced so I'm sure you'd get new things pretty quick."

I laugh softly, now more intrigued by everything Rick is capable of doing. It's no wonder he's the right hand to Dominic and the head of his tech company, dude is seriously talented. I'm too busy looking over everything Rick is doing to notice Gabriel moving closer to me. His thick fingers slide softly into my hand, interlocking mine with his. My cheeks grow warmer as I look at him out of the corner of my eye.

He's already looking to me with the softest look I've seen on his face since I've known him. He squeezes my hand, trying to portray something in the action, then leans over to place a gentle kiss on my forehead. I squeeze his hand in return, melting into the carpet beneath my feet.

I've only known him for around two months, and I already don't think I could ever want to leave his side. There's something that feels so right, deep in my soul, when I'm around him. He makes me feel things I've never gotten to experience before while treating me both like his personal slut and most cherished possession. *I love it.*

I don't have the opportunity to get further into that train of thought before Rick clears his throat and starts to talk in full business mode.

"Murph is definitely at the house outside of the city. If it wasn't for you, Liz, we wouldn't have known he had it. When we dove into his properties, this one didn't show up because there's actually no records of it even existing." He gives me a proud smile over his shoulder before continuing to talk to the screen, "We can assume he's going to keep hiding there until he makes his next move. Since we have no idea what that is or when it will be, we need to make a plan to act before he does. I'll have Dominic meet with us, Gabe, and we'll come up with a plan."

He closes out of all the programs, after making sure he can keep access to Murph's house camera, and stands from the chair with a satisfied smile. He looks to Gabriel but says nothing, and I take that as my sign to let them have a chat. I lift on my toes, placing a kiss against Gabriel's cheek before pulling my hand from his to leave. I only make it two steps before he grabs my wrist and twists me back around until I bump into his muscular chest with wide eyes.

I look at him from beneath my lashes as he pets my hair with a small smile and bright eyes.

"I'll only be a minute and then we can keep watching our show. Go wait in our room."

He gives me a deep kiss, causing my heart to flutter, then let's go—giving my ass a playful swat as I walk away. I can't help the huge smile twisting my lips as I make my way up the stairs. *Our show.. Our room..* I didn't think he would make something so small like a TV show be something that was ours. That's also the first time he referenced his room as 'ours', and it's a little nerve racking.. But, I really like it... *I really like* him...

With a little giggle and a big smile, I practically skip into 'our' room to get our show ready on the tv.

Chapter Forty Two

Gabriel

I WATCH ELIZABETH LEAVE, not able to tear my eyes from her until the door closes. When I look back to Rick he's giving me a smug look that I want to smack off his face. *Dick.*

He chuckles at the look I give him before patting me on the back. "You guys share a room now, huh?"

I shrug, feigning nonchalance, "It's a new thing."

"So, you guys finally get over all the childish shit?"

"Yes, asshole. She wasn't even really doing anything wrong. I've been the one that kept pushing her away because I was scared. But I'm not now... Much."

His smile is like one you would get from a proud sibling. "I'm happy for you, Gabe. Really."

I give him a small smile and pull him in by his neck to rest our foreheads together, "Thanks, brother."

He squeezes my neck before letting go, ready to move on to business.

"I'll update Dominic on my way home and we'll all come up with a time to get together tomorrow to make a plan. We're going to have to act soon since we don't know what Murph is planning. You need to be careful with Elizabeth going anywhere. We don't know if he plans on trying to snatch her or attack us. Just be careful."

I nod, "Alright. Call me in the morning when you guys are ready to meet up."

He gives me a tight hug before walking out. I make sure to shut down and lock my computer before making my way up to my little petal. With everything finally coming to a close and Elizabeth and I getting closer, there's a lightness to my chest I haven't felt in a while.

I open the door to the bedroom and lean against the frame to watch Elizabeth with a smile. She's changing the sheets on my huge bed all by herself, and I've never seen anything cuter. Her slender arms are trying to pull the final corner of the sheet on while her lip is captured between her teeth. I walk over as she struggles to lift the bed and pull the sheet tight, giving her a playful bump with my hip to get her out of the way. She giggles lightly and my smile grows at the sound. When I first met her, I wasn't sure I would ever get to hear such a carefree sound from her.

When I get the bottom sheet settled, I work with her in a comfortable silence to put the top sheet and pillows back on. When it's all done, I jump on the bed, grabbing her arms and pulling her down with me. She laughs loudly as she bounces, and my heart squeezes. Grabbing her around the waist, I pull her against me until she's practically crushed between my chest and my arms—planting a kiss to her soft, long wild hair.

My voice comes out soft, almost guarded, against her head, "Just a little while longer, lepestok, and you won't have to worry about Murph anymore."

She nods against my chest, her voice coming out just as guarded as mine, "But I'll still have you..."

I hear the hope there, and I don't waste a second to ease her mind.

"You'll always have me, Elizabeth."

I feel her smile against me as she snuggles closer. Giving her one more kiss on her hair, I lean over and grab the remote to start our show.

After one episode plays, Elizabeth starts to fidget against me—seeming to not be able to lie still. When the second one is almost over, I can't ignore the tension in her muscles and the way she is slightly pulled away from me. I look to her when the third episode is loading and see her chewing on her lip, her eyes on her hand that's laying tensely on top of my stomach.

I don't want to continue this whole, bottle your feelings up shit, with her. When I told her that I wanted to communicate and be honest about my feelings, I hoped she knew that I wanted her to do the same. Obviously, something is eating at her. I'm not sure where her mind is at, but I sure plan to find out.

Turning off our show, I grab her chin and tilt her face up until those gorgeous hazel eyes are on me. I give her a small smile and pinch her chin lightly.

"Where'd you go, moya lyubov'?"

She returns the smile, pulling her face from my grasp and sitting up. I copy her movement, sitting up and leaning back against my pillows. I wait patiently as she gathers her thoughts, her eyes bouncing around like she's looking at a variety of words in the air.

Her eyes stay on her lap as she talks smally in a way I haven't heard from her, "I want to talk to you about my dad.."

My brows start to rise, but I force my face into neutrality when she looks up at me.

"Okay. I'm all ears."

Her eyes bounce between my own, her mouth opening and closing like she isn't sure how to start. It takes her a couple minutes, but she finally gets there.

"My mom killed herself before I was one. I'm not exactly sure when. I do know that she had really bad post-partum depression, and that's why she took her life." She takes a deep breath before continuing, "My dad always blamed me for that. He would say I was the reason he couldn't be happy anymore, and I was the reason my mom was gone, why his wife was gone... When I was around five years old, he started to take out his anger and depression on me. He would yell, hit me, or throw me around for no reason. Granted, if he had a reason it wouldn't even be valid, but you get my point.

"He would use his hands, belt, shoes, pretty much anything until I was crying or passed out from the pain. He would take me to the hospital occasionally if my teachers noticed anything, but he would pay the doctors off so nothing showed in my record. Except one time.. He found me hiding in my closet and threw me across the room. I hit the wall before the floor and landed on my wrist causing it to sprain. That was the only time the doctor wouldn't take the bribe. Once I got older, he stopped *physically* abusing me. I think it was partly because I got too big but also because I started to look more like my mother."

Her voice starts shaking as well as her hands, so I scoot closer to her and hold her hands in mine, rubbing soothing circles in her palm. She gives me a watery smile before looking away to finish her tragic story.

"When I was seventeen, I got home from school to find him sitting on the floor of their room with her picture and a gun. At first, he pointed it at me, again blaming me as he cried... But, he couldn't pull the trigger. My eyes were closed when he shot himself in the head. I was willing to die in that moment if it meant getting away from him, but he took himself instead. Again, I think it's because—to him—it looked like he would've been shooting *her*. A couple days later I ended up on my foster moms doorstep with two boxes, a suitcase, and a shit load of trauma. She took me in with a smile on her lips and tears in her eyes.

"Soon, I found out that her husband had passed away while they were waiting to take in a foster child. She wasn't able to have children, so this was the next best thing for them.. helping children in need."

She smiles fondly as she talks about her foster mother, and I already know that she was the closest thing to a parent that Elizabeth ever had. My heart hurts for her, I might've also had an abusive father, but at least I had my mother to love me. Without her, I would've been far worse off in life. Possibly even dead by now. I snap back to the moment as Elizabeth continues with love in her soft voice.

"She became very important to me really quick. She was warm and loving, always there for me when I needed her. She gave me the affection I grew up without, and I will always love her for that. But, when I was eighteen, only a year after I started living in her house, she told me she was sick..." She takes another deep breath, tears starting to glaze her eyes. "She had known for a while, but didn't want to burden me with the trouble. She didn't think I would grow so attached to her like she was to me, so she wanted to keep it to herself. But then I started to love her, and didn't leave after I was eighteen, so she finally told me.

"After that, I was the one that started taking care of her. She grew rapidly worse, and there was nothing I could do to keep her with me. My heart was shriveling all over again... And then one day, I woke up next to her in her bed, like I had been doing for months..." Her next words come out on a broken sob, "And she was gone."

I pull her against me, smashing her into my chest and doing what I can to show her the affection she deserves in this moment. Stroking her hair, I give kiss after soft kiss, letting her cry against me as she relives losing her only real mother. My heart breaks with her, and I close my eyes tightly to suppress the tears stinging my eyes. Her crying slowly stops, but I don't hold her any less fiercely.

I start to rock us both, pouring all the love I have in my body into her—hoping she can feel how appreciated, loved, and strong she is. Her fingers are curled tightly in my shirt, her nose taking deep inhales against the fabric.

When I look down, I see her eyes closed and tears drying on her pink cheeks. I look over the freckles dotting her nose, her thick black lashes fanning over her cheekbones, and her plump bottom lip barely touching her top one.

As I kiss her forehead and she doesn't move, I realize she's fast asleep and I smile into her hair. When I speak, I speak lowly so I don't wake her. My voice comes out rough from the tears I held back at her story.

"You are so strong, Elizabeth. Maybe the strongest woman I know.. Just like my mother. She would love you, if she was still with us... YA lyublyu tebya, moy sladkiy lepestok.[*]"

Chapter Forty Three

Elizabeth

I REMEMBER FALLING asleep after I cried—after telling Gabriel about my dad and foster mom. Now I'm awake in the middle of the night. I'm in the same spot as when I fell asleep, meaning he hasn't moved the whole time. I lift my head slowly so I don't wake him, to look at his sleeping face. I'm not disappointed when I see the way his dark lashes lay over his cheek bones, his jawline perfectly cut and shining in the moonlight coming in through the window. I smile as I listen to his light breathing that's steady in his sleep.

My eyes stay on his plump lips that are slightly parted, now remembering that he was talking to me before I was completely lost to the abyss. *Even if I'm not sure what he said.* With a small smile on my lips, I lean up enough to plant a soft kiss on his lips. He groans as his mouth chases mine, even in sleep.

This is the first time we've slept next to each other, and I know now why people enjoy this. There's a deep sense of comfort at being in his arms when I'm vulnerable to the world around me as I drift in darkness. I don't think I could find a better feeling that gives me such warmth. Just as I go to remove my eyes from his perfect face to fall back into nothingness, I hear something coming from outside. My ears perk up as I hold my breath to listen closely.

It happens again, but I can't tell what I'm hearing. I'm not sure if I should wake Gabriel up to check on it, or just look on my own.

It's not coming from inside the house, but it's close outside. I decide to just look on my own, slipping from his hold slowly so he doesn't wake.

When my bare feet touch the cold wood of the floor, I tiptoe to the open bedroom door and close it behind me. I keep light but quick feet as I make my way to the kitchen where I know Gabriel has a gun stashed. My aim wasn't perfect the last time I practiced, but it wasn't bad enough to totally miss. I make my way to the front door, looking out of the misted windows there.

Breathing quietly, I keep my body hidden as I look, waiting for something to move. I start to think my ears were mistaken, but then a dark figure moves from the side of the porch and heads towards the front door. My lungs freeze as I watch them stand in front of the door, bend forward, then step back. I hold the gun tightly in my hands as I move to open the door as they start to walk away on quiet feet. This person isn't one of Dominic's men that normally guard the property, because they never come to the door.

Keeping the gun in one hand, I unlock the door, clasp the doorknob with a clammy palm, and take a final deep breath. I swing open the door quickly, aiming the gun at where I know the person will be standing. My finger is on the trigger, ready to pull it, when the person spins around with wide eyes.

My hands start to sweat as confusion rolls around in my head. My voice comes out soft, and suspecting.

"Sammy?"

I see his chest still, like he's holding his breath to see if I'll shoot him or not. There's panic in his eyes as an unsettling feeling tilts my stomach. I risk taking my eyes off of him for a second to see what was put in front of the door. Gabriel told me about the black box Murph had delivered with the threat to take me back.

And that's exactly what this box looks like. It's black with a black bow, sitting as tall as a soda can.

I hear Sammy move and look back up, clutching the gun tighter in my hands. He turned to face me, and he seems to look panicked.. but there's something off about the glint in his eyes. My face sets in determination as I keep my aim locked on his chest.

"What the fuck?"

He starts to shake his head, holding up his hands, "I was on duty and noticed the box there. I was only looking at what it was. I swear, Elizabeth."

My brows furrow as I replay what I saw from the window. No, he definitely was putting it down. Not just looking at what was already there. If this is what I think it is, Sam is a traitor and working for Murph.

I give one shake of my head, planting my feet firmly against the marble flooring, "No, you put it there. I watched you do it."

His panic lasts one more second before it melts and he starts to smile. He lowers his hands to put them in his pockets, the glint in his eyes now making sense.

"Who do you think Gabriel will believe about this? His temporary toy? Or one of his best friends?"

My breathing starts to rush quickly from my nose. I want to believe that Gabriel would see who was lying in this situation. I try not to think about how Sam called me a *toy* as I try to portray like I'm not second guessing my next choice.

I give him a smirk and raise the gun to point at his head, "I think he'll choose his *toy*. Should we test the theory?"

He chuckles even as his eyes start to spark with fear, "You won't shoot me, Elizabeth."

I cock my head to the side, relaxing my face into the perfect innocent expression, "I won't?"

His jaw locks as he looks over the way I'm holding the gun. I'm not shaking, my stance is ready for the recoil, and my finger lays gently on the trigger. I right my head with another smirk.

"You're the one that called me a fox, remember? Let's see how nasty my bite is."

I don't hesitate as I move the gun to aim at his side so he won't die, and pull the trigger. My body rocks slightly with the recoil, but my legs and arms stay solid. Sam falls to the ground with a grunting cry, his hand moving to cover his side.

His next words come out on a roar of pain, "You fucking bitch!"

I lower the gun enough to stay trained on him as he lays on the floor.

"Say another word and my next shot won't just be a wound."

My grip on the gun tightens so he doesn't see the shaking in my hands. I know Gabriel woke up with my shot, I only have to wait till he comes down the stairs. I don't have to wait long before I hear his panicked voice yelling my name. I yell back at him where I am, not totally able to hide the shaking in my voice.

His feet pound against the stairs as he makes his way quickly to where I'm standing. As soon as he's by my side, he ignores the bleeding man on the porch and starts to look me over with wide, worried eyes. I give him a brief smile before motioning with the gun to Sam.

"I'm fine. We have a problem."

He finally takes his eyes off me to notice Sam. Gabriel's body locks before he moves to step towards him. I stop him with a hand to his arm, and he looks at me with furrowed questioning brows. I tilt my head to the box still sitting at the foot of the door, keeping my eyes on him to gauge his reaction as I try to keep myself put together.

"He was dropping that off, Gabe. It looks like the one you told me about."

Gabe bends down, grabbing the box from the ground, and opens it. I move my sight back to Sam to see him really starting to panic as anger starts pouring off of Gabriel in waves. He throws the box inside, his sight now locked on the traitor bleeding on his porch. His strong and steady hand reaches out and takes the gun from me. Using his free hand, he places it against my stomach and starts to push me further into the house.

"Go inside, Elizabeth."

I hold his hand against my stomach, shaking my head, and looking at his tense profile, "I want to help.."

He takes his eyes from Sam to look at me. His gaze immediately softens once it reaches my face. He looks me over quickly before nodding once and looking back to Sam.

"Get my phone and call Dom and Rick. Tell them what happened and to come over immediately."

Giving his hand a quick squeeze, I let go and run to get his phone from his room. I sit on the bed, still ignoring the shaking that's uncontrollable in my muscles, and call Dominic first. He answers after three rings with a gruff hello.

"Dominic, it's Elizabeth. Long story short, Sam is working with Murph. I shot him on the porch and Gabriel needs you and Rick to come over."

There's barely a second between my last word and his first, "I'll call Rick. We'll be there in ten."

He hangs up without another word and I pull the phone from my ear. Shock starts to slither in to cage me in my sitting position on the bed.

I just shot a man.

I notice my breathing and how erratic it is. I can't go into shock right now. I told Gabriel I wanted to help, and he won't let me if I'm reacting this way. Closing my eyes, I focus on slowing my breathing and calming my body. With each deep breath, I concentrate on the scent of pine and leather, letting it help settle me. It's takes a couple minutes, but I'm finally calm enough that my shaking isn't as prominent and my breathing is under control.

Keeping Gabriel's phone, I rush my way back downstairs to see that neither Gabriel or Sam have moved. I can't see Gabriel's face, but I can see the utter panic on Sam's as he tries to talk Gabe out of whatever is going to happen next. I keep my steps light as I walk closer, but stop when I get to the box that was thrown inside. It's sitting on its side, the contents spilling out onto the marble flooring. I squat down to look over what was inside without touching it. There's more pictures of me. There's also another note. I flip over the thin white paper to read the chicken scratch on the other side.

'She's mine. But, I'm willing to negotiate.'

I squeeze my eyes closed against the idiotic delusion that this man has. He left a phone number I don't recognize below his words. I look up to Gabriel and the way he towers over Sam. His back stretches the cotton fabric of his shirt, his muscles tight with how hard he's holding his gun. I think of the pure panic on his face when he thought I was hurt. I think about Dominic, Rick, and the girls. How Murph seems like he'll do anything to get to me.

What if they get hurt because of me?

Taking a deep breath, I put the number he wrote down into Gabriel's phone, setting the note back how it was, and walking on quiet feet to the back door. I keep my sight on Gabriel as I slip out, sighing with relief when he doesn't hear me close the door. Hitting the green call button, I walk quickly to the tree line around the house. Murph answers before I can make it between the trees.

"Morozov, I didn't think I would be hearing from you so soon. Did you find my delivery man? I'm sure that was a shock for you, considering he was a friend of yours."

He sounds so smug I wish I could punch him through the phone. I answer when I make it past the first tree.

"It's not Gabriel."

There's silence for a few seconds before Murph chuckles. "Oh, my sunshine. I definitely didn't expect this. To what do I owe the pleasure?"

I roll my eyes, my anger replacing the remaining panic in my veins, "Cut the shit, Murph. What is it going to take to get you to leave Dominic and the Morozov's alone? To leave the city like you were never here?"

He hums annoyingly, "Leave the city that I should be running? I don't think I can do that."

An aggravated breath rushes from my nose as I think. He wants *me*, right? Could I get him to leave if I go with him willingly? It's not what I want to do.. I don't want to leave Gabriel. But if it's between Gabriel being alive, and me staying with him? I would rather he be alive.

"Alright. What would you say to leaving, never coming back here or bothering them again, if I come with you."

He says nothing. There's silence for so long I have to check the screen to make sure the call is still going. He probably knows that Dominic will win this fight, even with casualties. The offer I'm making *ensures* he stays alive.

His voice finally comes in with masked emotions, "You'll come willingly? And stay?"

My answer cracks a small part of my heart, "Yes."

He hums, "Dominic won't come for me after we leave?"

"No."

"I want to hear it from him. And Gabriel. Two days, my house outside the city, nine pm."

He doesn't wait for me to answer before he hangs up. My eyes close as I fall to the ground. I lean my shoulder against a tree as I breathe deeply. My heart is breaking for what I'm going to do. The plan strings itself together quickly in my mind as I control my breathing. When I open my eyes, I use the last amount of strength I have left in me to stand and walk back inside the house.

Everything will be okay.

When I get back in the house, doing my best to hide all my inner turmoil, I find Dominic talking to Gabriel by the stairs as Rick throws a tied up Sam into the back of a black SUV. Walking slowly, I make my way past Gabriel and Dom to where Rick is closing the trunk on Sam who's yelling through his makeshift gag. As Rick turns to face me, his eyes widen before he schools his features and gives me a tentative smile. I don't return it.

I step closer to speak softly, "I need to talk to you."

He shoulders stiffen as he looks to where Gabriel and Dominic are talking inside. Looking back to me, seeming vicious and seriously scary, he nods and leads me further down the driveway to lean against a different car. He says nothing as he waits for me to talk. I shuffle on my feet for a few moments, thinking over how this is going to go—how I'm going to explain my plan. Finally, I look to him and square my shoulders.

"You would anything to keep Gabriel safe, correct?"

His brows pinch slightly as he nods, "Of course."

I nod back, crossing my arms over my chest, "Good. I have a plan."

It takes Rick a little convincing to agree with my idea before we start to iron out the details. By the time we're done and walking back to the front door, Dominic and Gabriel are walking out. Rick speaks to them first. We both agreed that coming from him, they would actually listen.

He tells them about my call to Murph, which Gabriel is not happy about, before going into a plan. I'm going to go with Dominic and Gabriel to meet Murph at his house in two days. Showing Murph that they're willing to let him go free, and me with him. But, Rick is going to be sneaking in and getting into a good hiding space.

Before Murph has a chance to actually take me, or go back on his word of not harming anyone, Rick is going to shoot him from his hiding spot.

When he's is done explaining, Gabriel grabs my arm and pulls me from Rick's side to his.

"Absolutely not. I'm not putting Elizabeth in that situation."

Rick looks to him with intense features, "Even if we'll finally get rid of that shit bag for good? She'll be fine with you and Dominic. Or do you not trust us to keep her safe?"

I swallow thickly as Rick looks at me quickly before gluing his sight back to Gabriel. I look up to watch Gabriel's jaw clench tightly, the muscle there bulging. Dominic says nothing, looking between Rick and I with his arms crossed over his chest. He knows we were coming up with this while he talked with Gabriel.

Looking away from him, I lay a gentle hand on Gabriel's cheek and pull his face towards mine. I lean up on my tiptoes and gingerly press my lips to his, feeling his shaking exhale through his nose. I give him a slight smile as my thumb strokes his cheek.

"It'll be okay, Gabe. We need to finish this, and this is the way to do it."

Dominic asks the next question, "He has men who won't like that's he's dead and will retaliate. How is that going to solve anything?"

Rick smirks at Dominic, copying his stance, "Because half his men are going to run away shitting their pants when they don't have their boss to hide behind. We can handle the rest."

Dominic's jaw twitches as he thinks. My attention gets drawn back to Gabriel as he turns his body to me and wraps me in his strong arms, "Are you sure about this? Your life could be at risk if you're there."

I smile to hide the burning behind my eyes, "I'm not worried. I trust you guys."

He bright green eyes move back and forth between mine. When he sees whatever he was looking for, he nods slightly. He looks back to Rick with tight shoulders, keeping his arms around me as he speaks—the timber of his voice vibrating into me.

"Okay. Let's solidify details tomorrow.. or later today I guess, since it's almost three in the morning."

Rick gives Gabriel a loving, slight smile and nods. Both him and Dom give Gabriel a pat on his shoulder as they head to their cars, taking Sam with them to do whatever they're going to do with him. I can already bet that Rick and Dominic are going to be going over the details for meeting Murph before coming back over later.

Gabriel continues to hold me tightly as we watch their taillights disappear down the driveway before they're gone. When he still doesn't move, I pull back slightly to look up at him.

"Come on.. Let's go back inside, love."

He looks at me then, pausing for a few seconds before holding my hand and leading me back to our room.

Chapter Forty Four

Gabriel

I WALK ELIZABETH BACK to our room while I try not to let my thoughts spiral. The pure terror I felt when I woke up to a gun shot with Elizabeth gone from the bed, was like nothing I've ever felt. My heart has never beat so loud or quickly. Then I heard her voice and could barely think as I barreled towards her. She was safe. But, there was the fucking shitbag Sam bleeding at her feet. *I still can't believe he was a traitor.*

When Rick talked about the plan, that terror was slowly sinking back into my muscles. I don't want to put Elizabeth at risk. Yes, there's a huge advantage to doing this plan. But if something happens to her during it... I don't know what I would do..

Elizabeth pulls me from my thoughts when she tugs me onto the bed. She lays on her back, and I don't hesitate to lay over her—wrapping my arms around her and laying my head over her heart. She wraps her arms around my shoulders in return, her slender fingers gliding into my hair to scratch my scalp. I close my eyes, breathing her in and listening to the soft beat of her heart.

My words come out broken and soft as I whisper them against her, "Please don't leave."

Her fingers freeze for a fraction of a second before continuing, her other arm tightening around me, "How could I leave you? You hold me too tight."

She laughs lightly, her stomach and chest bouncing me slightly and I realize how tightly I am, in fact, holding her. I loosen my arms around her and lift my head with a smile. Her hazel eyes are bright, looking more brown than green, and her smile puffs out her cheeks. I take the moment to memorize the way her freckles thin as they get further from her nose, the way her pupils dilate as she stares at me, and how her heart feels pumping beneath me.

I crawl up her body until our faces are level so I can nuzzle my nose against hers. Her eyes close, and I take the chance to place soft, slow kisses against her mouth. She melts beneath me, a quiet but pleased hum vibrating her throat as I slip my tongue into her mouth.

The kisses go from slow and affectionate, to fast and hungry. Our hands claw at each other's clothes until she's completely bare beneath me, our bodies colliding together. My hands shake as I hold her arms above her head, spreading her thick legs with mine until my cock nestles against her already wet pussy. I lick and bite from her mouth down to her chest, letting go of her arms to grab handfuls of her tits. Her hands are curled into the pillow behind her when I look up, my mouth tilting into a smirk when I see her eyes focused intently on the way I suck her peaked nipple. I give it a few more licks, a quick bite, and one last suck before copying the attention on her other one.

Her back bows as my name flies breathlessly from her perfect mouth. I hum against her heated skin as I continue to lick and nip my way to her hips, biting the tummy pouch she hates so much. My hands grip her thighs tightly, enjoying the way they look digging into them, before lowering my face to lick from her entrance to her clit. When her teeth capture her bottom lip in an attempt to stay quiet, I decide that's not okay. I nip at her clit before sucking harshly, groaning at the scream that tears from her throat.

I close my eyes as I enjoy the taste of her perfect pussy, moaning against her soaked flesh as I stuff two thick fingers inside her. I work hard and fast to get the satisfaction of her cumming on my face. It only takes a couple minutes before she cries out my name, her thighs crushing my head, and her walls convulsing around my fingers. As she starts to come down, I withdraw my fingers and give her clit a final lick before crawling my way back up her body.

Her eyes are glazed and heavy lidded, her lips parted with panting breaths, and her fingers still clutching the pillow behind her.

"Such a good fucking girl, Shchenok."

She smiles and closes her eyes, putting her heavy arms around my neck and pulling me down for a kiss. I moan into her mouth as I slip my tongue inside. When she starts to suck off her taste from my tongue, my hips grind forward—letting my cock slip between her folds. She moans with me, raising her hips to get me where she wants me.

I pull away from her sensuous mouth to bite her ear. "What do you want, baby? Use your words."

Her hips chase me again as she whimpers, "Y—you. I want you."

I chuckle and lean back to look at her needy face, "You already have me, Shchenok."

Slight irritation creases her brows as she looks into my eyes, making me smile wider.

"You know what I mean, Gabe."

I hum, "I don't think I do. Tell me."

"I want you to fuck me, Gabriel. Ple—"

She doesn't need to say please. I slam into her before she even finishes and I watch with deep satisfaction as her head snaps back and her eyes roll.

"Is that what you wanted?"

She nods, her eyes squeezing closed as I pull out slowly, pushing back in just as slow. I chuckle when she groans and reaches down to dig her nails into the skin of my ass. She tries to move me against her, but I resist her needy actions and continue to move slowly. When she cries out a whimper and opens her pretty eyes, I give her what she wants. I pound into her with every ounce of anger and fear I have in me.

I hold myself above her so I can watch her tits bounce freely. Her nails continue to claw at me and a growl slips from my throat at the sting they leave behind. I put a hand beneath her hips, tilting them upwards for a better angle.

"Gabe.. oh my god.. Fuck.."

I smirk down at her, "That's it baby, call out for me."

Her walls start to close in around my cock and I have to bite my tongue to not cum at the sensation. *She's so fucking tight..*

She says my name again on a broken cry as I thrust into her without remorse. A tear slips from her eye and I lean forward to lick it off her face with a moan she matches.

"Come on, Elizabeth. I know you have another one in you. Come for me like my good little slut. Let me feel how tight you can squeeze my cock."

Her eyes roll back and her back arches further as her orgasm finally rocks her body. I close my eyes at the sensation of her squeezing me so tightly I can barely push back in. Before she's finished, I follow after her. Whisper her name like it's my saving grace.

I lay on top of her, still buried deep in her sinful pussy, as we both come back to earth. I place gentle kisses over her face while I tell her how much she pleased me, how good she did. Her smile tilts the edges of her lips so smally but so prettily. With a final kiss to her puffy lips, I pull out and roll to my side to hold her against me.

I hold her closely, shoving my nose in her hair and breathing in the lavender scent of her shampoo. She holds me just as tightly, her nose shoved into my chest. We lay like that until I'm on the brink of sleep, and I feel her starting to move away. I pull her back against me, not bothering to look at her as I shove her head in my neck and talk.

"Where are you going, moya lyubov'?"

Her fingers run gently over the sensitive skin of my abs, causing them to flex.

"I was going to go clean up."

I shake my head, holding her closer, "No, you're going to sleep with my cum dripping out of you like the good girl you are."

Her fingers freeze their exploration as her breathing picks up. Her next words come out softly, slightly embarrassed.

"But it's going to make a mess on the sheets."

"I'm not worried about the sheets, Elizabeth. Go to sleep."

It takes her a couple seconds before she finally gives up her fight and snuggles into my tight embrace. A rightness settles deep within me as my breathing evens out and I drift off to the thoughts of Elizabeth's smile and perfect heart.

Chapter Forty Five

Elizabeth

I WAKE UP IN THE MORNING to fingers trailing over my back and lips to my forehead. I smile against Gabriel's warm chest, giving him a kiss right back.

"Good morning, lepestok." His voice causes butterflies to erupt in my stomach. It's rough from sleep and deeper than usual.

"Good morning." I smile against him when a thought occurs to me. *He keeps calling me things, and I still don't know what they mean.* I think of what we're going to be doing tomorrow night, and it makes me want to say everything I haven't—to do things we haven't had the chance to do yet.

I lift my head to ask him, but his lips meet mine in a gentle kiss. He lingers against me, longer than a normal peck, so I push against his mouth a little harder before pulling away with a smile and half open eyes. The smile he gives back to me is nothing short of contentment.

"Can I ask you something?"

He nods, leaning his head back to lay on the pillows, "Of course."

I chew on my lip as I break eye contact. I'm not sure why I hesitate, but I don't really want something he calls me to negative and I'm a little scared that it is.

"What names do you call me in Russian? You say them often and I still don't know what they are."

His chuckle bounces my resting chin and I finally look back to his shining field eyes. His smile is broader but still relaxed as he traces a soft finger down my spine.

"Well, lepestok means petal. Sometimes I say little petal."

I nod, a small smile building, "What about the other ones?"

"Shchenok, means pup."

My brows crease, "You've used that one since I met you that first night. Why pup?"

He shrugs, pulling me impossibly closer, "You reminded me of one when I ran into you. You looked terrified, and were running from something... You trusted a stranger with your safety."

I think back to that moment. I was pretty scared of Ben catching me. I know he wouldn't have been nice if he caught me, and when I ran into Garbiel.. he felt safe. There was a certain protective energy that was coming from him that I was drawn to and immediately trusted.

I give him a shrug with a smile, "You felt safe. Safer than the guy chasing me."

He chuckles lightly, his eyes brightening as they look over my face. "I'm glad. YA nikogda ne pozhaleyu, chto pomog tebe toy noch'yu."

I give his side a pinch. "Hey! What did you just say?"

He laughs harder as he pinches me right back, causing me to squeal.

"I said, you little brat, that I will never regret helping you that night. It led to this, and I've never been so happy someone almost knocked me on my ass on the street."

I laugh loudly at that. We did almost fall over, I ran into him pretty fast and hard. We laugh and talk for a little while longer before finally getting up to eat some breakfast.

He lets me clean up from last night on my own as he goes to start the food. When I make it downstairs, he's looking delicious in low hung sweatpants and no shirt—the muscles in his back shifting as he stirs whatever he's making.

I sit down at the counter as I talk over the sound of the sizzling food, "What are you making?"

He keeps his eyes on his task as he answers, "Some scrambled eggs and sausage. I'll get you some lemonade in a second, lepestok."

I nod though he can't see me and just smile as I watch him. My eyes start to burn when I think about having to go to that meeting with Murph, all the things that could go wrong, but I shove it away when Gabriel turns around to plate the food and bring me a glass of lemonade.

We eat in a comfortable silence, occasionally sharing a smile around our forks. All my life, I've only ever had my foster mom to eat with and love. She was the only person I was ever able to let my guard down around, to freely laugh with or cry with. But, now I have Gabriel. No matter how tomorrow night goes, I'll always have him.. and he'll always have me.

When both our plates our empty, Gabriel takes them to the sink and returns to his seat looking nervous and a bit shy. My brows furrow as I tilt my head at him. I can tell he's wanting to talk about something, and is working up the nerve to actually say it. He doesn't need long before he gives me a soft smile and turns his chair to fully face me.

"You told me about your foster mother the other night.. and your sorry excuse of a father. Now, I want to tell you about my mom, and my father."

I give him an encouraging smile and nod. I wasn't sure if he would talk about them since I know his mom is such a sensitive topic. He mentioned she was murdered, and after that, I didn't want to bring it up again.

"For starters, I don't talk to my father. I have no idea where he is or what number wife he's on. And I'm happy to keep it that way.

He was an abusive asshole to both my mom and I, while also being a drunk. He might've been in the mafia, working occasionally with Dominic's father, but he wasn't even liked by *them*. He would come home from whatever shady shit he was doing, and find some reason to hit me. My mom would always try to protect me, to stand in his way and aim his anger towards herself.." He smiles sadly, tears starting to glaze his eyes.

"She was so strong. She tried so hard to be everything I needed. Then she started getting into pills. The older I got, and the worse my father got, she dove deeper into the drugs and was rarely ever sober. Then he left us for a young mistress. He might've been a shitty person, but sadly she still loved him. One day, one that I replay often, she came home sober. She sat me down and told me that she was going to do better, she was going to be better. She never touched pills again."

I smile smally, reaching forward to hold his hand as my eyes burn for him, "She sounds like she really loved you. Sounds like you were her whole world, Gabriel."

He gives me a tiny nod, "I was, and she did. She was better.. healthier. She was working at the library, and that's how I got to know Natalie. My mom loved that job, loved working with Nat. She started talking to a man, but didn't tell my anything about it. When she started going out and wearing makeup and looking light on her feet, there wasn't anything I could do but be happy for her. Then one night, she didn't come home."

I suck in a sharp breath, my hand squeezing his tighter as the first tear falls down his face.

"She was murdered in a dirty alley. Shot up with some kind of drug that she OD'd on. I wasn't sure who did it, but I knew it had to be someone in the mafia and connected to Dominic. I knew she *never* touched anything with a needle, and that she hadn't touched drugs since the day she sat me down. I started running around with red vision, killing men I didn't know and causing havoc while Dominic and Rick were trying to clean up the city. Then I met them."

I smile and wipe the second tear from his face, "That's how you got so close to them. They helped you solve your mom's murder."

He nods, kissing my palm before holding it in his lap. "Yeah. Rick, Natalie, and I got close while a whole bunch of shit was happening. Long story short, Rick became like my brother *and* he became my legal guardian for my birthday."

"I'm so sorry, Gabriel." I don't know what else to say. Hearing his story hurts my heart. His mom sounded like such a loving and gentle woman, someone who shouldn't have been taken from him so soon. He deserved to keep her in his life, to mend that little boy that was broken so young.

He pulls me from my seat and into his lap to cradle me against him. "Why are you apologizing, moya lyubov'?"

I hold him tightly, falling into the warmth of his skin, "I just.. it's such a sad story. You didn't deserve to have your mom ripped away from you like that."

"Neither did you, baby."

He held me in the kitchen while we both tried to heal from our losses. When I was finally able to move, I led him back to our room and to our bed. We fucked two times before Dominic finally called to tell us they were coming back over. Reluctantly, we got dressed and my jello muscles moved me downstairs where Dominic and Rick were walking through the front door.

I greet them both with a slight smile, eyeing Rick a little longer. Neither of them look remotely nervous. When Rick gives me a nod and a tight smile, I nod back and follow behind them to Gabriel's office. Dominic and Rick sit in front of the desk, Gabriel in his chair. I stand to the side awkwardly, not sure where to sit where I can still be involved in the conversation.

Gabriel eyes me, holding out his arm and gesturing with his hand for me to sit with him. My cheeks heat but I walk over anyway to settle down in his lap. Only when I'm settled does Rick start to talk over the plan while Gabriel's thick fingers rub circles on my leg.

"So, we're going to be at Murph's at nine tomorrow. I'm going to stay in the car until you guys are inside just in case he has men waiting. When his guard is down and Elizabeth moves to go with him, I'll take my shot."

Dominic continues where he lets off, "I'm going to be helping Rick after that with whoever else is in the house. Gabriel, you're going to be getting Elizabeth back to car. When everything is clear, we'll leave. The days following that will be going after the rest of Murph's men who aren't willing to back down. It's going to get bloody and it's going to get crazy, all the women and my daughter will be in lockdown until everything is settled."

Gabriel's body is relaxed behind me but his words are tense, "How do we know that Murph isn't just going to kill us while we're there?"

I shake my head, eyeing Rick before looking to Gabriel, "He wants me back too much. I don't think he's going to risk killing you guys with me in the way."

Gabriel's jaw ticks as he looks over my face. I try to give him a reassuring smile even though there's so much inner turmoil that I can hear the blood rushing through my veins. He finally nods and turns back to the guys. I don't listen to what else they're talking back as I look over Gabriel's face, smiling softly to myself. They must've asked me a question I didn't hear because Gabriel looks to me with a squeeze of my leg.

My brows rise as I look between the three of them, "What?"

Dominic snags my attention with his deep voice, "Are you going to be ready for tomorrow?"

I nod, determination settling in my bones, "Of course. I'll be ready."

Chapter Forty Six

Gabriel

ELIZABETH AND I SPEND the rest of the day sparring, watching TV, and with me taking the opportunity to fuck her on every surface available. I can't keep my hands off of her. When she smiles brightly at me or laughs, my chest lightens and my lungs constrict. She's absolute perfection, and I can't wait to be able to have her to myself without death looming over our heads.

I finish the dishes from dinner and walk back up to our room to find her in the bathroom, about to step into the shower.

She jumps at the sound of my voice, "What, no invite?"

She smiles and laughs lightly, walking further in to get under the spray, "What, I have to actually ask?"

My smile tightens my cheeks so much they hurt. I've never smiled so genuinely than when I'm with her. Taking her unspoken invitation, I strip from my clothes and step into the shower. I walk up behind her and wrap her wet body into my arms, sticking my face into her neck. I hum into her, already smelling the flowery scent of her soap filling the air.

When I slip my hand over her stomach to go between her legs, she pushes her hips away from my touch, her ass pushing harder against my growing erection.

"Gabe, we've had sex like a million times today already."

I lick up her neck, biting her ear as she gasps, "And it's not nearly enough, Shchenok."

She doesn't fight me again when I reach to play with her clit. After a few heavy circles, her hips start to rock with my hand as she chases her high. I bite down harshly on the curve of her neck right as I shove two fingers deep into her needy little pussy. Her hands reach down to claw at my arm and I groan at the sting they give. I roll my fingers against that precious spot I know makes her knees weak as I rub my thumb over her clit, basking in her breathless moans.

"Are you going to come for me, baby?"

She nods, her walls pulsing against my fingers as she continues to rock herself against my hand. Her legs start to shake, her weight falling back against me for support and I tighten the arm wrapped around her stomach. Her head falls back to my shoulder and I lean over her for a kiss.

It's sloppy and slightly awkward from the angle of my face, but no less satisfying. I bite her plump bottom lip before sucking it into my mouth to lick away the sting I know I left behind. As her breathing goes choppy and her eyelids flutter, I move my arm from her waist to squeeze her throat. Her eyes pop open when I cut off her air.

"Come on, Elizabeth. Show me how good I make you feel. Show me just how much you're *mine*."

She cums with her hazel eyes on my face with an open mouth and no air. I smirk down at her drunken gaze and release her neck when she starts to come down. She sucks in air through her pink lips, her knees twitching with the effort to hold herself up. I barely let her recover before I wrap her hair around my fist and shove her to her knees.

"My turn, pretty girl. Open."

She doesn't hesitate to open her sweet mouth and lean towards my leaking cock. I grant her a few bobs on her own, to taste what I'm offering her. When her eyes close and her moan vibrates against me,

I tighten my hold in her hair and shove myself as far back into her mouth as I can. Her fingers reach for my thigh as her eyes open and start to water. I hold myself perfectly still, letting her feel me twitch in her throat.

"Fuck, Elizabeth. You should see how pretty you are with my cock in your mouth."

I pull out slowly, her nose sucking in air loudly. I give her a hungry smile and a wink before thrusting into her greedy mouth with such speed it doesn't take long before tears start to leak down her cheeks, mixing with the water dotting her flushed skin.

Release is so close there's already a warmth tingling up my spine. My head falls back as my eyes close and I focus on how good she feels. Her soft tongue, puffy lips, and gargled moans around me. When I look back down, I notice her eyes still haven't left my face. I groan loudly, putting my free hand against her cheek as her pupils dilate further.

"Such a good girl, so perfect with this sinful fucking mouth. Fuck, I love this mouth."

Her whimper is what sends me over the edge. I cum to the sight of her watery eyes and brutalized mouth stretched around me. As I slow my thrusts and twitch against her tongue, she closes her eyes and drinks from me eagerly. I moan when I feel her swallow around me and let go of her hair to massage her scalp and wipe her tears.

She pulls off of me and smiles, like she's proud of herself, and I can't help but to smile back. I bend down and stand her up, kissing her forehead, nose, then mouth.

"You did so good, moya lyubov.'"

Her cheeks flush further as she leans up to give me another lingering kiss. I sigh against her and then pull away to wash off her addictive body.

If I die tomorrow, at least I'll die with my heart in her delicate hands.

Chapter Forty Seven

Gabriel

ELIZABETH HAS BEEN on edge all day, and I don't blame her. She's barely let me touch her besides a quick kiss or when I cuddled her as she woke up. We're getting everything ready to leave and I watch her sitting on the stairs, twiddling her fingers in her lap. I move to walk over to her when Dominic suddenly slaps a heavy hand on my shoulder and asks me to help him with something. I give one last look to my little petal, catching her looking up at Rick as he walks closer.

Dominic drags me to the SUV that we'll be taking to Murph's house and leans against the side facing away from the front door. He crosses his arms over his chest and looks to me with intense features.

My brows furrow as I raise my arms slightly, "What?"

"How are you feeling?"

I shrug, "Fine. I'm ready to get this shit over with."

He nods, looking me up and down quickly. "Good. You need to be able to show Murph you're willing to let Elizabeth go."

My muscles tighten. He has rights to doubt me when it comes to that. Even if I don't plan on actually letting her go, it's going to be hard to pretend that I am. Murph knows by now that I'll do anything to keep her with me. Me 'giving her up' tonight needs to be believable. He needs to trust that we don't want her anymore, and that's he's free to go.

"I've got it handled."

He looks into my eyes for a few more seconds before nodding and telling me to get everyone in the car. I watch him slip into the driver seat and take a deep breath to get my emotions under control before I grab Rick and Elizabeth.

I've got this. I don't have any other choice.

The drive to Murph's is silent. None of us saying anything as we drive down dark roads leading further into the thick forest outside of the city. Dominic is driving, with me in the passenger seat, and Elizabeth in the back seat. Rick is sitting in the trunk area, getting our guns loaded and ready. Dominic and I will have a hidden one strapped to us, but Elizabeth won't have one. Murph would be able to see it on her when she gets close enough and we don't want to risk him doing something stupid.

The road starts to get bumpy and I look up from my lap to see Dominic driving down a skinny road towards a simple looking house. It looks old, like it was built somewhere around nineteen-twenty. The paint is chipping off different spots, and some of the windows are boarded up from the inside with cracks spiderwebbing over the glass.

"What a lovely house."

Rick's rough sarcastic comment has a single laugh barking from my throat. He always tries to lighten moods like that, and I appreciate him for it right now. The air in the car is thick with anxiety, almost suffocating.

Dominic parks and shuts off the car. There's no sign of anyone but Murph being here, with his stupid bright red car sitting ahead of us. There could be people inside, but we won't know for sure until we go in. I'm the first to open my door and step out, opening Elizabeth's door for her and helping her out. I stop her with a hand around her wrist when she starts to walk away. I keep my face emotionless, for the camera, as I look her over.

"I might say some stuff in there that I don't mean, Shchenok."

She smiles tightly before dropping it quickly, "I know, Gabriel."

Nodding, I drop her arm and step around her, already starting to act that I don't give a shit about her. Dominic and I walk in front of her, still trying to shield her a little bit. I knock tightly against the old wood door, double checking that no emotions are showing on my face.

One of Murph's men opens the door and leads us inside without a word. He takes us through a small entryway, a tiny sitting room, and into another hallway going to the back of the house. There's a big open space here, looking newer than the rest of the house like it was built recently. The floor is concrete with some questionable spots on various areas. The walls are wood like the rest of the house but brighter in color, confirming this is a new room. There's folding chairs stacked against the farthest wall on the right, and one big couch on the back wall where Murph sits.

I do my best to look around without being obvious. There's two windows facing what would be a backyard, but no other ones. The only way Rick is going to be able to do anything is if he can get a shot through the windows. Murph smiles greasily towards Dominic and I without standing.

"Welcome to my home, Mr. Mortelli." He looks to me, "Gabriel."

Neither of us say a thing or acknowledge his welcome. He's trying to pull a power move, but from what I see, we're still above him. Elizabeth shuffles behind me and I have to shove my hands in my pockets so I don't hold her to my back.

Murph drops the smile and looks directly at Dominic, "My sunshine said you'll let me leave with her. I'm already getting a place set up in another country, so I hope she isn't lying."

Dominic looks way too relaxed as he replies, "She was right. I'm willing to not kill your pathetic ass if you leave. Of course, you're not allowed to come back once you're gone."

Murph nods, and waves his hand in the air, "Fine, fine. As long as I get to take her with me, I don't care." He tries to look around my broad shoulders, and I have to bite my tongue so I don't try to block Elizabeth from him. "Come here, sunshine."

Elizabeth steps out from behind me, looking more calm than I know she is. She holds her head high as she moves to stand a decent ways in front of Dominic and me. I make sure not to look at her as Murph looks between us.

"Gabriel, I'm surprised you're giving her up."

I shrug with a forced chuckle, "She was just a toy. I played, I used, I tarnished. Now I'm done. You're more than welcome to have her back."

Elizabeth's shoulders tighten, but I ignore it as Murph tenses in his seat. He takes a big breath before plastering on a fake smile and standing. He walks closer to Elizabeth, and I continue to force my eyes to stay on him instead of her. She does good at not flinching when he reaches out to tuck her hair behind her ear. Me on other hand, I'm struggling. I want to break his fingers before I cut his hand off and shove it down his throat. He softens his smile on her and steps even closer to talk in her ear, his eyes on me.

"You're mine now, sunshine. And I can do with you what I wish."

My jaw starts to clench, the only sign I don't like what's happening. Murph notices it and smirks at me from over Elizabeth's shoulder. Before we're ready, he twists Elizabeth around until her back is smashed against him and a gun is to her temple. Dominic and I immediately draw our own guns, aiming them towards him without a clear shot.

Where the fuck *is Rick?*

Murph laughs when he sees us ready to take her back. "Well, I guess I *can't* really have her, can I?"

Dominic's voice is tense but low as he speaks, "What's your plan here? It's two against one.

"Ah, but you won't shoot me if you have to go through her."

My jaw locks as a protective snarl lifts my lip. Two men barrel into the room behind us, shoving a gun against both mine and Dominic's head. My hands tighten around my gun as I finally look to Elizabeth. Her eyes are wide and watery, looking only at me. A single tear falls down her cheek and I want nothing more than to tell her everything will be okay. Murph squeezes her tighter against him as he gestures with his head to the men behind us.

"It's three against two now. Make a single move, and I shoot her."

My single word comes out on a growl, "*No*."

He cocks his head at me with a smug look, "Oh, yes. Now, lower your guns."

"No!"

Murph's man behind me presses the gun harder against my head, Elizabeth's tears now freely flowing down her face with panic in her eyes. He'll shoot her even if we put our guns down just to torture me. I know he will. I refuse to let her die, I refuse to lose her.

Her voice is broken and soft, but I hear it clearly through the roaring in my ears, "Gabriel... Let me go.."

I shake my head, my face set in determination as I look to her scared face, "Not even in death, Elizabeth."

She smiles shakily and my stomach sinks at the goodbye in her eyes. My head is already shaking as terror rushes through me. Her lips move with silent words, but I hear them nonetheless.

I love you.

Her next words aren't silent, but they are heartbreaking. "Then I'll let go for the both of us."

One second, Murph's gun is at her temple.

The next, their bodies are falling backwards as Elizabeth pulls the trigger with the barrel pointed at her chest.

Someone roars loudly. *It might be me.* Murph stumbles to his ass, the gun sliding across the floor, as Elizabeth falls on her side—her eyes already closed and tears still running down her puffy cheeks. My voice is distant as I yell her name. Rage is all I feel as I twist out of the way of the gun at my temple, slamming the arm over my shoulder to twist their wrist and firing my gun into the blank face behind me.

I don't hear their body hit the floor as I shoot the man struggling with Dominic. My feet rush forward, bypassing Elizabeth's body until my hands are wrapping around the throat of Murph, who's scrambling for his gun. I pick him up by his neck, slamming him into the ground underneath me.

"What the fuck did you do?!"

I continue to squeeze, hoping his head will pop like a balloon, and slam his skull into the concrete ground over and over again. Even when his eyes go blank, I can't pry my hands from crushing his throat. Hands are pulling me off, my body fighting the pull so I can keep cracking Murph's skull until I see his brains spilling out.

An arm wraps around my throat, cutting off my air and pulling me backwards. I struggle to get out of the hold, ready to fight them off me until I hear Dominic yelling in my ear.

"Enough! Gabriel, enough! He's dead!"

My chest heaves with frantic breaths, my arms falling to my sides as I stand on weak legs. My vision starts to clear and I see Murph sprawled on the ground. His eyes are barely in their sockets, his throat crushed, and his head split so wide at the back there's a puddle of blood beneath it. When Dominic feels me relaxed he finally lets go and I fall to my knees.

My head whips towards where Elizabeth is still on her side in her own puddle of blood. A broken cry rips from my throat as I crawl towards her on the dirty floor. I pull her into my arms, cradling her head in my neck and crushing her to my chest, soaking my shirt in the blood pouring from her. Hot tears sear my skin as I cry out her name, my body rocking back and forth as my chest tightens and my heart shatters. Dominic doesn't come to pull me away as I rock her limp body. I pull her head away to look down at her pale face and closed eyes. There's no more tears on her cheeks, no more air flowing from her lungs, no more light in her hazel eyes. My bloody hand runs over her cheek as I cry harder, tainting her perfect skin.

My throat is sore and tight, my eyes stinging as I continue to look at her, not wanting to look at the wound that took her from me.

My words are broken, and empty, "Please.. please.. Don't leave me. You can't leave me, Elizabeth. I *love* you.." My next word is barely audible, coming out on a sob, "*Please.*"

Dominic's hand lands on my shoulder and I shrug it off, not looking away from the one person who owned my soul. I feel Dom squat down by me, but he doesn't try to touch me again. My eyes close as my sobs wrack my chest. I lay my forehead against hers, feeling the warmth there slowly drifting away. Someone comes running into the room but I ignore it as I hold Elizabeth tighter.

They're panting as they come closer, and I hear a drag in their step until they stop in front of me and drop to their knees.

"Gabe..."

I look up at the sound of Rick's voice. *He was supposed to shoot Murph. He failed. He failed* her. When my watery eyes meet his, they widen slightly at the sight. He looks almost as bad as when he was abducted a couple years ago. His forehead and lip are bleeding, one of his eyes is swelling, and his nose looks broken.

He looks down to Elizabeth, his face falling at the sight of her lifeless body in my tight arms. His head starts to shake side to side as he looks back to me.

"I'm so sorry.. There were four men at the back of the house. I tried to be here as soon as I could..."

My jaw locks as my tears dissipate. My brother tried to get here. He almost died to be here to help. I can't be upset with him for almost dying. I give him a tight nod and look back down to my lifeless little petal. Tears threaten to rise again but I push them back as I cradle her in both my arms so I can stand. I stumble slightly, but Dominic rights me with a tense hand to my shoulder.

With a deep breath, I walk out of the house with Elizabeth in my arms—my heart following after her soul.

Chapter Forty Eight

One week later
Gabriel

I HAVEN'T LEFT MY HOUSE since Dominic and Rick took Elizabeth's body from my arms. They didn't tell me where they were taking her, even when I asked. That was the last time I spoke to them. I don't remember getting home that night or how I made it to the room Elizabeth chose when she first moved into my house. But I found myself standing in the middle of that room, surrounded by her things and her soft flowery scent.

I lost myself in that room.

I broke everything in sight, screaming until my throat was raw and there wasn't a clean area on the floor. I haven't gone back in there this whole week. There isn't a reason for me to see the destruction of my heartbreak. I'm on my second glass of whiskey in ten minutes, sitting in my office with my feet on the desk. The black screen of my monitors reflects the empty feeling inside my chest. Stubble lines the bottom of my face, my hair is messy, showing how much my fingers have been running through it and pulling the strands in all different ways. I'm about to chug the whole glass that's warming between my palms when there's a knock at the door.

The glass pauses at my lips as I think about answering. I haven't spoken to my family in a week, I'm sure they're here to check and make sure I'm not dead. I don't feel like moving, so I decide to speak loudly, barely lowering the glass from my mouth as I yell.

"I'm alive. Go away."

There's no response, then they knock again. I groan, slamming my glass on my desk as I stand. They knock again as I step from my office and I roll my eyes at their impatience. My steps faulter when I see the figure through the panes of the door. It doesn't look like Dominic or Rick, and they wouldn't send one of our men to check on me.

I stay by the office door as I speak loudly, "Who is it?"

They don't answer, only backing up a step from the door. *Okayyy, not getting a good feeling.* I allow my mind to stick to the current situation, grateful I have a reprieve from my dark thoughts. I walk back into my office, grabbing the gun hidden in my desk, and walk back to the door.

I open it a crack to see someone I don't recognize. He looks at me through the small opening, his face blank but his eyes vengeful. Looks like Dom and Rick are slipping up in their cleanup of Murph's men. We knew some would probably retaliate after Murph died, but I haven't been keeping track of how it's going. I haven't been able to do much besides replay Elizabeth dying over and over in my mind—reliving my heart shattering.

Guess it's time to change that.

I give the stranger a forced smile, speaking in Russian as I ask, "Are you here to kill me?"

He doesn't respond, and I notice the quick twitch of his brows like he's trying to hide that he doesn't understand me. I smirk and take a quick look to his empty hands. A weapon might not be there, but he could still have one on him.

"How can I help you?"

His throat bobs with a quick swallow, "Just checking in."

I nod with a hum, opening the door wider and motioning for him to come inside. He hesitates, looking over my smiling face, before stepping over the threshold and walking inside. I shut the door behind him, looking over his form from the back. There's a gun tucked into his waistband, and the edge of his pantleg is caught on the sheath for his knife. I have to resist rolling my eyes at the pure amateur shit I'm having to deal with.

Before he has a chance to turn around, I send a shot into each of his knees from the back, laughing darkly when he falls to the floor with an agonized scream. His palms are flat by his head, trying to push himself back up. So, I shoot both of his hands. He screams again, looking to me with rage and panic in his wide eyes. My smile grows as I crouch down in front of him.

"You know, I think this is exactly what I needed."

I don't let him open his mouth. I smack my gun into his temple, knocking him unconscious. My sigh is the only sound in the otherwise empty house as I stand straight and cock my head as I look him over. He seems pretty heavy.. I'm not looking forward to moving him. There's a hidden basement through the living room, I need to put him down there before he ruins my floors with his bullet wounds.

Putting my gun on the table by the door, I bend down to wrap my arms under his and over his chest. When I stand up, an involuntary grunt rumbles from my throat. Definitely a heavy dude. I drag him into the living room, flinching when I notice the blood trail following us. Probably going to have to call in our professional cleaner for my floors, but that's something to worry about later.

I manage to get him to the basement without dropping him. Well, without *accidentally* dropping him. I might've let him roll down the stairs to make it easier for me. When he's tied tightly to a chair in the middle of the soundproof room, I stand back and admire my rope work. I've definitely gotten better at it. I decide to let

Dominic know what's going on, breaking my silent no contact rule. It's a simple text.

Murph dog at my house.

He doesn't need anything else, I'm sure he'll come and bring Rick with him. I leave the nameless guy in the basement as I walk back to my office to grab my whiskey. I'm not going to waste it, it's the good shit. I relax back in my chair as I wait for the guys to show up, sipping my drink and enjoying the way it warms me. I've been cold since Elizabeth was... Taken. Alcohol has been the only thing to bring life back into me. That, and now my new toy in the basement.

I'm not sure why I haven't joined Rick in taking out the rest of Murph's sad example of a mafia. It would definitely be cathartic, and I could get the remaining rage out of my system with bloodshed.

Within fifteen minutes, both my brothers walk through my front door. First they see the blood, then they see me. I hold my arms out wide with a big—almost drunken—smile on my face.

"Hey guys! You ready to play?"

They give a look to each other, neither of them saying anything as I stand from my chair to join them in my bloody foyer. My smile is loose but broad thanks to the alcohol in my system. I give them both a shoulder pat before motioning with my head for them to follow me. When I look back to make sure they're following me, I see the worried look they share at the trail of blood leading to my living room. Once we step in, and they don't see any guy, I realize they don't know about my secret basement. I chuckle as I open the hidden door and gesture to the stairs with a tingling hand.

"He's down here."

Again, they give each other that look, still staying quiet, and I follow them down into the basement, shutting the door behind us. They make their way over to the guy I have perfectly tied into the chair who's starting to regain consciousness. I slap my hands together as I walk in front of the him.

"Great timing, he's waking up."

Rick finally speaks, "He just showed up here?"

I nod, walking over to a table full of different weapons, "Yeah, knocked right on my door. I swear, Murph chose the stupidest fucking guys to work with."

When I turn back around with a mallet hanging from my fist, both my brothers are looking at me with a questioning furrow between their brows. My own raise towards my hairline.

"What?"

Dominic asks the next question in a careful tone, "How have you been doing? We haven't heard from you this whole week.."

I shrug, passing the mallet between my hands, "Not great. But I'm starting to feel better. I decided I wanna help with whoever is left of Murph's men."

Dom says nothing else, taking a couple seconds before nodding. He gives a quick side eye to Rick, which he returns. My anger is rising quickly as I walk over to where they're standing.

"Look, I lost the person I never wanted to live without. I'm allowed to handle that in my own way. If you don't want my help, and aren't going to help me now, you can leave."

My knuckles pinch with how tightly I hold the mallet, my brows set in determination, and my mind being the clearest it's been all week. I need this outlet. This emotional release. If they don't understand that, that's fine. But I don't need babysitters while I take care of business. So what if I want to torture a guy for a little bit? I'm grieving.

With a roll of my eyes I twist away from them and towards the guy slowly coming back to consciousness. I don't think about anything else besides the placement of my swing. I don't want him to start bleeding internally. With as much force as I can muster, I swing down the mallet right above his knee, breaking the bone with one hit without risking rupturing an artery. His eyes pop wide as he screams out his pain. Another smile threatens to tilt my lips, but I suppress it. As soon as his scream is finished, I do the same to his other leg. Satisfaction fills me when tears start to pour down his sweaty face as he screams again. I feel Dominic and Rick move to a different spot in the room, not worrying about them as I plan my next hit.

Maybe the mallet wasn't the *best* first choice. I could do too much damage too quick if I choose the wrong spot or miss by even an inch. Throwing the mallet to the floor, I squat down until I'm eye level with the guy and give him a smile that promises death.

"Good morning, sleeping beauty. You ready to have some fun?"

His breathing is fast, spit dripping from his mouth, his voice soft but angry, "F—fuck.. you.."

I chuckle deeply as I stand back up and hold my hand towards where Rick stands at the table full of violent toys. He hands me my next tool, a pair of pliers. I think about using them on his fingernails, but there's no point in that since I shot his hands and they won't have any feeling. So, I decide on the next cliché. His teeth. Without looking to Rick, I ask him to hold the guy's head. He does without hesitation. I press into each of the shitbags cheeks until he opens his mouth, then I hold tighter until my fingers are hooking onto his bottom teeth through the thin skin and muscle.

I begin pulling his top teeth, moving from the left to the right—using his agonized, choking sounds as background music. When his last tooth is removed from the top row, I release his jaw and Rick backs up from holding his head. His chin falls down to his chest as he falls unconscious once more, and I sigh.

"Well, that sucks." I look to Dominic who's leaning against the table with a look of almost boredom. "Can I have the knife to your left, please?"

He grabs it without looking, walking over with a blank face to put the handle in my waiting palm. When I close my fingers around it, he holds my closed hand tightly and leans to talk close in my face.

"Are you about done with your little game."

My eyes roll as I pull my hand away, "What do you think I'm using the knife for?"

He eyes me for a little longer, then steps away, nodding at me to continue. With growing numbness in my muscles and my dark thoughts starting to resurface, I stab the knife into the side of the guys throat until the handle sits flush with his skin. I twist it harshly before pulling it out to let it clatter to the floor.

I'll admit, I feel less angry and a little better. My mind is a little more clear, but the flashes of Elizabeth's pale face and bloody chest still pop into my head. I want to yell, I want to break something, I want to hurt someone, I want to feel better..

I want her back.

Chapter Forty Nine

Gabriel

RICK AND DOMINIC TAKE care of the dead guy, telling me to go take a shower. When I'm out, feeling only slightly refreshed, I find them both in my office. I sit in my seat with a sigh and lay my head back with my eyes closed. Whatever they were talking about, they aren't anymore. I'm not sure what they wouldn't want to talk about in front of me, but I can't find any shits to give in this moment. We're all silent—me because I only feel half alive, and them because I'm sure they're worrying about my mental health.

Rick is the first to break the silence, talking lowly, "You and I are going to be spending tomorrow going after the last group of Murph's men that have been hiding out in the warehouse district."

I nod against my headrest, "Sounds good."

They don't say anything else and I finally tilt my head straight to look at them. I doubt I look great. I have a week's worth of stubble, bags under my eyes, and today was the first shower I took in two days. I pinch the bridge of my nose before leveling them with a mask free face. Rick's eyes tilt down, his lips turning into a soft frown. Dominic looks just as unaffected as always, with only a slight frown.

"Elizabeth is—"

Dominic cuts Rick off, "She's someone who we will all miss. Not like how you do, but we do nonetheless. Both Elliana and Natalie have been worried about you, please try to call them at least."

I'm shocked that I heard 'please' from his mouth. "Yeah, sorry, I'll make sure I call them."

Dominic nods and stands, looking down at Rick with set brows and a tick in his jaw. Now I'm even more confused about what's going on. Rick gives me a forced smirk as he stands and walks over to me. He leans down to grab my neck and hold our foreheads together, and I copy the well-known gesture.

"I've missed you, brother."

I swallow thickly, my eyes and nose starting to burn, "Yeah.. I've missed you too."

He gives my neck a tight squeeze before letting go. I watch them leave with limp muscles and stinging eyes. I've missed them, I just haven't really been able to function. All I've been able to feel this week is the pain from losing Elizabeth.

But I guess it's time to do something instead of letting grief and depression eat me from the inside, out. It's time to step up into the roll that Dominic gave me, and be the right hand I'm supposed to be. I've been strong my whole life. I survived through a drunk, abusive father. I survived through my mom's drug problem and her murder. I *need* to survive this. Not just for myself, but also for my family.

I grab my phone from my pocket and pull up Natalie's contact. I'm sure she's been more worried than anyone. It barely rings once before she answers with hope ringing clearly in her voice.

"Gabriel?"

I smile smally, "Hey, Nat."

I can hear the relief in her sigh. I close my eyes at the new ache twisting my chest. I'm the one who made her worried, and she doesn't deserve that.

"How.. How are you?"

I shrug, "Not great, trying to do better. I'm sorry I haven't called yet. I've been... In a dark place."

"Yeah.. I know.. Is there anything I can do to help? Maybe make you the fried rice you like so much?"

My chuckle surprises me, and I smile a little more genuinely, "Sure, I'd like that. I haven't really been eating."

I hear her gasp, "You? Not eating? What, did hell freeze?"

My next chuckle doesn't surprise me. I knew calling her first would be a good idea. She knows me too well not to take my mind off where it shouldn't be.

"I guess so. I'll come over tomorrow night and help you make it, if you want?"

Her hair tickles the phone speaker in what must be a nod, "I'd love that. I'll see you tomorrow."

"Bye, Nat."

I hang up and revel in the tiny genuine smile on my lips. Maybe my survival will be a higher percentage if I let my family back in. One phone call, and I feel so much better than I have all week.

The next morning, I wake up to a door slamming. I jolt out of bed, grabbing the gun that's behind my headboard and stand ready as I walk out of my room. When I get to the top of the stairs, I look down to see Rick leaning against the front door with crossed arms and a smirk.

"Hey there, beauty queen. It's time to get to work."

I rub a hand over my face as I lower the gun to my side. "Jesus, man. I could've shot you. Why are you slamming my door?"

He shrugs, pushing off the door to come upstairs, "Had to wake you up somehow, thought this would be entertaining. And you didn't disappoint. You should've seen your tired ass face trying to aim."

He laughs as he winks at me and I flip him off with a small smile. *Fucking dick.* He follows me back to my room, plopping down on the edge of my bed as I get clothes out to change. With my brain still waking up, I start changing in the middle of the room. When my pants hit my ankles, Rick whistles from his spot on the bed and I groan, pulling on my boxers quickly.

"Damn man, good thing Natalie never wanted to date you. I wouldn't have even compared after that thing."

I laugh and flip him off again, "Oh, I know you wouldn't have. I've seen your dick, remember?"

He tilts his head as he thinks before he widens his eyes and gives me a wolfish grin. "Oh yeah, how could I forget about that."

I laugh again, finishing getting dressed and walking into my bathroom. When I'm all ready, I follow Rick to his SUV but don't get in. He gives me a questioning look and I tilt my head to my garage.

"I think I'm gonna take the bike. You have all we need?"

He nods, "Yeah. Go for it, just don't fly past me. *Actually* stay with me."

I solute him with two fingers as I walk to get my bike, "Sir, yes sir."

He laughs behind me as he slides into his seat. I open the garage from the outside and falter in my step when I see the two helmets sitting on the shelf by my bike. Swallowing thickly, I do my best to not look at the helmet Elizabeth used as I grab my own and my gloves. Rick waits for me to pull out and shut the garage before he takes off. I do what he asked and stay with him the whole time, not speeding down the street like my body screams at me to do.

Maybe I'll take a cruise before going to make dinner with Natalie.

Twenty five minutes and we're pulling into the warehouse district. Rick stops us when we're a building away from Murph's and walks over to me as I take off my helmet and gloves. He takes the gear from me, tossing it into his open trunk, and proceeds to hand me my weapons. I get two guns, an extra clip, and two different knives that I strap to the outside of my thighs. When we're both armed and ready, we slink closer to Murph's warehouse. There's no windows in this building, which is both helpful and annoying. We could probably take out some of the people in there without going inside if we had windows to use.

We make it to a side door and Rick gives it a test pull. Of course, it's open. Like I said before, Murph chose the stupidest fucking people to work for him. The hallway we walk into is barely lit and quiet. The walls are damp and I have to breathe smally so I don't smell whatever questionable scent is in here. The hall comes to a two way split, and Rick motions for me to go left. We know this way will lead to the bigger space of the building while his way leads to another hallway with closed off rooms. I can't decide who's direction is the easier one to handle.

I stop at the doorway to peak my head around the corner. I blink quickly against the bright florescent lights and look over the unusually quiet area. There's only one guy I can see from my vantage point and he's leaning against the farthest wall doing something on his phone. I raise the gun with the silencer attached and line him up with my sight before pulling the trigger. He falls with a hole in his forehead and a spray of blood staining the wall.

With light and careful steps, I walk further into the room towards a huge stack of crates. I pause there to listen, hearing possibly two sets of boots shuffling on the dirty concrete floor. I peek around the corner and spot them walking around another stack of crates, talking quietly and headed right to where the first guy was. They're too busy with their conversation to notice him and I take it as the perfect opportunity. I shoot the taller guy first, getting a perfect hit, but when I go to shoot the second, he's ducking and running.

He starts yelling at whoever else is around and I groan. *Guess I got the more difficult route.* I sprint towards another stack of crates and start to climb on them to get a higher view but leaving myself enough to duck behind. I peak over the top and look down to find the guy I couldn't hit leaning against the crates across from me, waiting for more gun fire. Without a second thought, I aim and fire a perfect shot.

A thrill starts to course through me as my adrenaline spikes. A part of me has thoroughly missed the action. I pop my head up a little higher and look around, hearing a few more people running around the echoing space. My gun stays propped up in my hands as I twist back and forth over the area I can see. Right before I look past another set of crates, another guys fat head pops out from the side to look around. My finger pulls the trigger, my arms moving again before he even hits the floor.

An alarmed yell bounces off the walls, not giving me a clue as to where it came from. I don't have a chance to keep looking before a hand grabs my ankle. I flip over to kick them off but stop when Rick's focused face comes into view. I scowl at him and pull my ankle roughly from his hands.

My voice comes out as a rough whisper, "I almost kicked you in the face."

He smirks at me with a gesture to climb down, "You could've tried, kid."

I roll my eyes as I climb quickly off the crates. He still calls me that even though I'm going to be twenty three in a couple months. When my feet are back on solid ground, he leads us around the crates to another pile that still has netting holding it together. We both look around the corners, my side coming up empty but I hear the soft sound of Rick's gun firing. I pull back around to look at him, and he gives me a nod. We move from around the stack and rush forward, guns at the ready.

He downs two more frantic guys while I get one before a boot connects to my wrist and I stumble, my gun clattering to the floor. Before I can grab my extra, the same boot lands harshly to my ribs. I fall to my side, rolling in order to stand back up and face my opponent. Relaxing my body when I see they only have a knife and no gun, I cock my head as I look them over. I think I recognize him, and when he speaks, I'm sure I do.

"Morozov. Just needed to end it all, huh?"

I smile lethally, pulling both my knives out and squatting slightly to ready myself, "Ben, right? You were Murph's favorite little bitch."

He snarls at me, only getting my muscles more excited for the fight. He comes at me with impressive speed, but sloppy form. I dodge away from him, letting the tip of one my knives slice into his bicep. Surprisingly, he only lets out a deep grunt at the wound and I silently applaud him for it. There's gunfire in the background where Rick is, but I ignore it and focus on Ben.

We start to circle each other when he smiles at me, a fire tinting his eyes. I could throw a knife at him and end this quicker, but he seems like a fun fight. He flips his knife in his hand casually as he speaks.

"How's your little whore of a girlfriend?" I practically snarl at him as my fingers tighten around the handles of my knives. He cocks his head at me, his smile widening. "Oh, wait. She's dead."

I rush him, rage fueling me as I dodge his wide slice and slam a blade into his thigh. I pull it out as I spin away, the spurt of blood shooting from the wound giving me deep satisfaction as he falls to his knee. I step behind him with both knives against his throat, leaning over to talk in his ear.

"You're right. And you're next."

I slice through his neck from both sides, the wound wide and messy. Blood pours from his open throat as he falls forward. He tries to hold the blood in for only a few seconds before they fall to his side and his eyes go distant. Boots pound against the ground to my right and I look quickly to see a sweaty twig of a man running towards me. I grab the extra gun from my back and shoot him before he makes it another foot.

My breathing is heavy as I lean down to Ben and wipe my knives off on his pants, sheathing them before walking away. I keep my gun lowered but ready as I creep around different stacks of crates. When I turn a corner, I hold my gun into the face of whoever ran into my path, only to receive one in my face too. I pause, looking around the barrel to see who it is, and see Rick looking back at me with his usual vicious mask. I roll my eyes, dropping my arms.

"How many times are you going to come close to dying by hands today, Rick?"

He chuckles, pulling me in with an arm around my neck, "Hopefully that's the last time, kid."

I shove him away with a smile, dropping it when I start to look around us. "That everyone?"

He nods in my peripheral, "Yeah. Five dead in the back, the way I went. The rest of them were out here."

I breathe deeply and look to him with raised brows, "Now what?"

He gives me a charming smile that doesn't match his words, "Now, we burn this shithole."

I chuckle, following him back to the door we came in to get whatever supplies we need from the car.

Chapter Fifty

Elizabeth

I WATCH GABRIEL WITH tears streaming down my face and a sharp pain in my heart. He doesn't deserve to go through this after everything else he's been through.. but we don't have a choice. If Murph survives, he'll keep coming for me. Even if he's dead, his men will likely retaliate and use me as a bargaining chip. I don't have any other option but to make this decision for everyone.

Something Gabriel doesn't know, is that Rick knew this was my plan. He took a little convincing, but he ended up agreeing it would be best—even if painful—this way and helped me with the details. Gabriel wouldn't be able to focus on the small war ahead if he had me to worry about. He would do what he could to stay with me, to protect me. Rick and Dominic are going to need his help after tonight to totally end this, and finally get their city back to the way they want it. Under only Dominic's control.

I don't want to do this. I have to do this.

I just hope that he can forgive me for it.

He doesn't want to let me go, and I don't want to let him go.. but I'm going to.

I mouth the three words I've been too scared to tell him, and watch the pain and terror rise in his soulful green eyes.

"Then I'll let go for the both of us."

My eyes close as I use what I've learned from Elliana and Natalie to take control of Murph's gun. I aim it towards my chest—from the farthest distance I can hold it—knowing this is going to hurt like a bitch, and I pull the trigger. My lungs fail me as I fall heavily to the concrete floor, my eyes closing tighter against the pain radiating from my chest. I feel the blood running out, noticing how oddly warm it is.

I didn't think it would hurt so much.

My muscles grow weak, my eyes refusing to open, my heart noticeably slowing. I hear Gabriel screaming and want to cry for him, but no tears threaten to sting my eyes—I'm too far under. Something is cracking loudly, soon becoming a wet smacking sound that rolls my stomach. My chest is now barely moving, my body no longer functioning, and every factory almost completely shutting down.

This is it, this is the terrifying moment I knew was coming. I hear someone yelling Gabriel's name but it's muffled, like it's coming from far above my drowning body.

Forgive me, Gabriel.

Chapter Fifty One

Gabriel

I'M ON MY WAY TO RICK and Natalie's house for dinner after going home to shower. I let the wind flow over my arms as my mind drifts to the ride I took with Elizabeth. She held on so tightly at first, but it didn't take her long to let go and start to really enjoy it. *I never got to take her on another ride.* I know she wanted to go again, and I wanted to take her out of the city. We would've stopped in the middle of the forest to look at the stars before riding back into town, to go home and fall into each other as we laid in bed...

Before I know it, I'm parking my bike in front of Rick's house. I stay seated as I pull off my gloves and helmet, noticing Dominic's car is also here. I wouldn't be surprised if Natalie invited them since I'm actually out of the house. I still feel bad for making her worry so much about me, and for doing that to Elliana too.

I throw my leg over the empty passenger seat as I hop off, swallowing tightly so I don't think about Elizabeth again. When I stop at the front door, I take a deep breath to prepare myself. I know they don't expect me to be all smiles and laughs like I normally am, but I can't be in my head and zoning out the whole time. I came tonight to show them that I'm alright, I'm alive—not to show them that I can barely function past the basic necessities.

Rick opens the door when I knock with a small smile. I try to return it but know it wasn't too convincing. There's a tightness to his shoulders that I don't know how to place as I follow him into the library where everyone is sitting and drinking. They all grow quiet when I walk in, standing from their seats to look at me. I stop abruptly with all their eyes on me, feeling a little uncomfortable. I give a small wave and smile.

"Hey guys.."

Natalie rushes over to me and throws her arms around my waist. I freeze for two seconds before I hug her tightly, laying my chin on her head.

"It's good to see you, Gabe."

I nod against her, "Good to see you too, Nat."

She pulls away with a watery smile, biting her lip as she walks away with her eyes on the floor. My brows crease as an uneasy feeling settles over me. Everyone is being so weird, there must be something going on. I look to Elliana as she walks over to me with the same look that Natalie walked away with. She gives me a tight hug which I return.

She whispers as she pulls away, "You have to keep being strong, okay?"

Again, I'm a little confused but I nod anyway and let her walk back over to Dominic. He only gives me a tilt of his lips in what should be a small smile, and a nod. I nod back then look to Rick who's still standing by the doorway.

"What's going on? Why are you all acting so weird?"

Rick clears his throat, gesturing with his arm for me to take a seat. I walk over to one of their new chairs and plop down, looking over all their worried faces. Before I can ask again what's going on, Rick stands in front of me and starts talking with a careful tone.

"There's some news we need to tell you that we've been keeping a secret. Everyone thought it was best to not say anything until all of Murph's men were either gone or dead. It's been a hard time watching you go through this, especially alone. I never planned on this, and I never wanted it to hurt you this bad."

My ears start to ring as my breathing picks up. I want to ask what he means, to get to the fucking point, but my tongue is too heavy and my mouth is too dry. When he hesitates to continue, looking sorrowful, Nat touches his arm to give him strength. Something is seriously wrong if Rick isn't sure what to say...

"When Elizabeth brought up the idea to use herself in the meeting with Murph, she made each of us promise not to mention the full plan. She thought she was protecting all of us with her decision, even if it was painful."

I barely recognize my voice when I question, "What the fuck are you talking about, Rick?"

His chest moves with a deep breath, "Her plan was what happened, but she didn't think Murph would threaten to kill her from such a close range..."

What? She knew she was going to die? And she chose to do it anyway?

"I don't understand..."

Dominic steps closer, grabbing my full attention, "She convinced Rick to put her in a bullet proof vest lined in real blood, to fake her death. Rick gave her a drug to slow her heartrate so she would look truly dead once her body felt the impact of the shot to the vest..."

I'm shaking my head, looking between the both of them. My body keeps flipping between a pile of mush and rock—flexing and going numb all at once.

Rick continues, his voice soft, "She was shot too closely, and actually took some damage, but it was closer to her shoulder than her heart."

There's a tense pause, the next words hanging in the air baiting me with false hope until I fully hear them. But no one says anything. Everyone starts to split apart, as someone walks into the room and closer to where I'm sitting. My eyes are blurry from unshed tears, taking too long to focus on the curvy figure gliding towards me. My body locks when they stop a short three feet away.

She's alive.

Elizabeth stands in front of me with a nervous smile, a sling around her arm, and tears in her big hazel eyes.

I can't breathe. I can't move. I can barely think.

She's here, she's alive.. she's fucking *alive*! Joy is the first thing to restart my heart, but then the anger comes. She faked her death. Made me believe that I had lost her forever. Made me *grieve* her, only to be safe and breathing. My nostrils flare, the only sign of my anger. I try to stay calm, and think over what my brothers were saying. She was trying to protect *me*. She knew with her being alive, even if Murph wasn't, she was a liability to have around. She would've been their first target so they could hold her over our heads. So, she chose to take herself out of the equation.

Slowly, my anger melts, but it doesn't fully go away. I'm still very much pissed off that she didn't come forward sooner. It's been a full agonizing week of thinking she was gone. That I would never have her in my arms again.

My heart feels like it's fully functional for the first time since that night. The air is lighter and my shoulders no longer burn from the tension in them. I look her over slowly, not sure exactly what my face looks like. She's wearing a pair of green shorts, a baggy black shirt that's tighter because of her sling, and her hair is up in a messy bun. Her cute little feet are bare against the floor. Every inch of her skin that I can see looks just as flawless as when she 'died'.

I look over her face, seeing tears slowly fall from the corner of her eyes and her teeth torturing her plump bottom lip. I'm sure she's waiting for me to say something, or to move to her.. but my brain is still trying to process that she's standing here with a beating heart.

"Gabe?"

Her voice nearly stops my heart. Not only because I've missed hearing it, but because it sounds so scared and unsure.

"Get out."

Everyone locks up at my rough, deep tone. Hurt and heartbreak flood Elizabeth's eyes before she looks to her feet and starts to turn away. My hands close into fists on top of my thighs, my jaw clenching before I try to speak softer and fail.

"Not you, moya lyubov'. Everyone else, get. Out."

Elizabeth's shocked eyes swing to mine and I hold them hostage as everyone leaves slowly. Elliana lingers near the doorway, like she's unsure if she should leave me alone with Elizabeth. I don't rush her to shut the door though. I keep my sight set on the woman who stole my heart, shattered it, and brought it back to life again.

Only when the door clicks shut do I speak again, choosing to talk in a whisper so my words aren't so harsh. "You're alive."

She nods, looking over my face and taking a tentative step closer to me. Her eyes are watering again, making the green in her irises stand out.

"I... You..."

I don't even know what to say. My mind is a Rubik's Cube of thoughts that I can't put together. I'm angry, I'm hurt, I'm happy, I'm... I'm so madly in love with her..

I stand quickly causing her to jump, but I ignore it as I lung at her and pull her into my arms to crush her into my chest. Her immediate tears soak into my shirt as her delicate hands clutch the fabric at my back, her arm sliding out of her sling. My eyes squeeze closed as I shove my face into her hair, inhaling the lavender scent I've been missing. I breath out a long sigh, like I had been holding it in since the night I lost her. Her quiet sobs shake her body as she holds me just as tightly as I hold her. My chest gets tight as my nose burns, and I don't stop the tears that push through my closed eyes.

My knees grow weak and I collapse onto the floor, taking her with me. She wraps her legs around my waist, forcing her arms through mine to throw them around my neck. I cradle the back of her head with tense fingers, shoving her face into my neck as I fall into hers. My nose rubs against the soft skin under her jaw and I let out a shaky breath, my tears slowing now that I know she's back in my arms.

"I love you, Elizabeth. You hold my heart in your hands, my soul in step with yours." I crush her closer when she sobs, giving her jaw a kiss before continuing with scratchy words, "You are the reason I breathe, my heartbeat is synced with yours..."

Her words are broken but happy as they rush out over my skin, "I love you, Gabriel."

I let go of her head to cradle her face in my hands, brushing our noses together with a sloppy smile. "Never do that shit again.. Never leave me again. I won't survive it."

She nods in my hold, pushing forward until her lips brush over mine, "I swear."

Our mouths crash together like a star being born. A rightness rushes through my veins, my body finally at ease with my soul back. I kiss her until we're panting and her lips are swollen and a beautiful shade of pink. I pull away with a nip to her lip, laying our foreheads together to look into the eyes I thought I would have to live without.

The smile that tilts my lips feels happier than any of the ones before, hers reflecting mine back to me.

My sweet little petal. My love. My life.

Epilogue

Three months later
Elizabeth

IT'S GABRIEL'S BIRTHDAY today. The first birthday of his that I'll be a part of. I want to make it special. I want him to feel just how much I love him and his existence today, how grateful I am to his mom for putting him into this world.

What better way to start your birthday than morning head? I have to leave in three hours to get the cake with Natalie and pick up one of his presents. Knowing him, I'm going to be running late once I start this. But I totally don't mind.

I lift the sheet up so I can slide under, grateful he let me out of his death grip at some point in his sleep. I carefully straddle his legs without waking him, coming face to face with his long and thick cock that's resting against his muscled stomach. Lightly, I run my nails over his abs, watching as he starts to grow hard. He groans, flexing his stomach as his hand comes under the sheet to run over where I scratched.

He only has a semi, but I know that's all I'm going to get until he's a little more awake. I snake my hand around his base, still shocked that I can't wrapped my hand fully around it. Giving him slow but firm strokes, my tongue teases his tip with heavy circles until he's a little harder. His legs start to move between mine, the sign he's

339

waking up, and I take that moment to shove him into my mouth until I gag around him.

His breathless curse causes my stomach to clench and I moan around his length, bobbing my head slowly with hollowed cheeks and a flat tongue. Arousal starts to slip from between my legs, my clit already throbbing for attention. His voice is rough from sleep, and I suck harder at the sound of it.

"Fuck.. Elizabeth.."

He pulls the sheet from over me, and I look up to find his half lidded green eyes burning down at me. His big hand finds its way into my hair to hold it away from my face and I smile around his tip while licking over his slit to taste the precum already gathering there. I bob down quickly to come back up slowly, letting my teeth lightly graze him—my eyes never leaving his face.

His words come out on a growl, his fingers tightening in my hair, "Goddamn, baby. You're getting too good."

I hum around him, finally closing my eyes and placing both of my hands on his hips, showing him I want him to control my movements. I love when he fucks my face. And he loves making me cry from it.

He doesn't miss my gesture, picking up where I left off with a push to my head and a deep moan. His hand moves me quickly for a few strokes before holding me still. I feel his muscles flex beneath my fingers as he starts to lift his hips, thrusting into my mouth with impressive speed and hitting the back of throat with each one.

Tears start to gather in my eyes and I whimper around him, almost choking on the sound.

"Look at me, Shchenok."

My eyes immediately open to find his heated gaze. My legs push into his and he smirks down at me. He rests his hips back down to slowly shove my face until I'm gagging and can't breathe, arousal slipping down my leg as I shuffle my hips above him.

He hums and I feel it all the way to my toes. "Such a needy little slut. Swallow my cum and then maybe I'll help you."

A silent whimper moves my throat as he pulls me off to piston into my mouth again. Drool flows from my mouth as tears fall from my eyes, my clit thumping in time with my rapid heartbeat. He takes only a few more forceful thrusts before he's pulsing against my tongue. He pushes me down until his cum is squirting into my throat. I close my eyes and swallow every drop, enjoying the salty and sweet flavor of him. When he's done twitching and there isn't a single drop left, he pulls me off and pulls me up his body by my hair.

He gives me that orgasm-worthy smile, rubbing his nose against mine before licking my remaining tears from my heated cheeks. He flicks his tongue over my cheekbone then kisses his way to my ear.

"Such a good girl for me. Fucking perfection, lepestok."

I hum and shift my face to give him a soft kiss and speak against his lips, "Happy birthday, love."

He smiles against my mouth, his eyes shining brightly, "Happy birthday indeed."

A squeal tightens my throat as he rolls over and slips between my legs. I have no idea how he's still hard, but I'm definitely not going to complain. He rubs his length against me, spreading my arousal around, and leans down to lick and suck my painfully hard nipples. My eyes fall closed on a moan as my back arches. He kisses a path up to my neck and I claw his back in return. His tip rests against my entrance as he speaks against my sensitive skin.

"Best gift I could get, is you, moya lyubov."

Just as his teeth sink into the curve of my neck, he shoves himself in to the hilt. My eyes roll back, my mouth opening on a silent cry. He doesn't give me any time to adjust, thrusting in and out with such speed, my breasts move between us with a slightly painful bounce. My hips can't keep up with him, so I settle for tilting them upwards for that perfect angle.

"Fuck yeah, lepestok. This pussy is mine." His next words come out with each thrust of his hips, "You. Are. All. *Mine*."

His mouth crashes to mine on a growl, his teeth biting at my lip, my tongue getting sucked into his mouth. His name rushes from me like a prayer. Heat starts to build at my toes, goosebumps peppering over my arms.

"Shit.. that's it, baby. Come for me like the good girl I know you are."

Gabriel leans on his forearm by my head, one of his hands reaching to squeeze my throat until breathing is no longer an option. My orgasm builds quickly the longer my air is cut off, my walls closing around his thick cock tightly.

"Fuck, Elizabeth.. So tight.." My nails claw at his back, my vision slowly going black around the edges as I climb higher. Right as I feel myself reaching the peak, he slams into me harder and whispers darkly into my ear, "You come, you breathe."

I crash into harsh waves beneath Gabriel's hard body. My walls clamp around him as my orgasm wrecks me, his fingers loosening from around my throat as he follows close behind. I can feel each jet of his cum, my pussy closing around him tighter like it wasn't to squeeze out everything he has.

My name flows from his lips on a whisper as he slows his hips until he rests his solid weight on top of me. When both our bodies come down, and we melt into the black silk of his sheets, he peppers sweet kisses over my neck, up my cheeks, down my nose, and finally my mouth. We both sigh into the kiss, our lips and tongues meeting in lazy hello's.

"I love you, moy malen'kiy lepestok."

I smile against him, opening my eyes to look into the grassy fields of his, "I love you."

He gives me another kiss before rolling from my sweaty body to leave me cold in the bed. It doesn't last long. His strong arms cradle me as he pulls me from our bed and carries me to the bathroom. My stomach starts to twist as I think about the present I'm giving him. *Well, one of them.*

He sets me gently on the toilet, backing up to start the shower. I watch his firm ass as he moves. It's so unfair for him to have such a nice ass. His thighs flex as he leans into the shower to turn the handle and I bite my lip when his arms flex, moving around the veins that snake over them. With the water running, he walks back over to me, squatting down until we're eye to eye.

Now I bite my lip with nerves. We've never talked about this, so I'm scared how he's going to take this present. I tilt my head towards the counter where there's a dark green box waiting.

My voice comes out hoarse and full of nerves, "Your first present is over there."

He quirks a brow at me as he stands to grab it, "*First* present?"

I nod, though he's no longer looking at me. I stand from the toilet after wiping and move to stand at his side as he lifts the lid to the box. Inside is a pair of baby socks and a positive pregnancy test.

His body locks, his fingers tightening around the box. I keep my eyes on his hands, not strong enough to look at his face as I talk.

"Congratulations, you're going to be a dad, Gabriel..." He still doesn't move or speak, so I start to ramble, "We never used condoms and you never asked if I was on any birth control. I honestly forgot to talk about it, myself. I'm not even sure if you want kids. But if you don't want to be a parent with me then—"

He cuts me off by dropping the box and picking me up. My legs wrap around his waist on instinct as my arms fall around his shoulders. I look to his face with wide eyes and a racing heart. I wasn't sure what to expect, but I definitely wasn't expecting the wide smile stretching his lips or the glaze in his eyes like he's trying not to cry.

His voice is rough but excited, "We're having a baby?" I nod with a watery smile. "I'm going to be a dad..."

It wasn't a question but I nod anyway. His big hand cradles my cheek as he leans forward to kiss me. I sigh against his mouth, my arms tightening around his neck. He chuckles against my mouth and I smile. When he pulls away, he brushes our noses together—his bright grassy eyes shining.

"Luchshiy podarok v moyey zhizni.[*] I love you so fucking much, Elizabeth. I can't wait to raise our child together.. To give them all the love they could ever ask for."

My inner child melts on the spot, loving what he's implying... Giving our child what we never truly got—unconditional love from both parents.

Bonus Scene

When Gabriel finds out Elizabeth is alive
Elizabeth's POV

I CAN HEAR RICK AND Dominic starting to explain what happened, why I made the choice I did, and why I haven't confessed sooner. Before they can fully confirm what they're hinting to, I walk with shaky legs into the room. Everyone parts as I walk closer to Gabriel. The look on his face has pain and regret stinging my chest. Tears line his eyes, the green of his irises dark and haunted.

I'll never forgive myself for doing this to him, for causing him this pain.. but it wasn't any less necessary. If I showed up on his doorstep sooner, he still would've been in a dark place and I still would've been healing. Natalie wanted me to wait until I was mostly better and Gabriel was no longer floating in darkness.

Tears I didn't know were there fall down my face as I look him over. Black jeans and a black shirt hug his muscular body. His hair is messy and there's some stubble on his flawless jaw. Even with tears in his eyes, his shoulders slumped but tight, and an almost raging look on his face, he's beautiful. I start to fear that he won't want me back after what I did. That he lost his love for me when he thought I died.

It doesn't even seem like he's looking at me, but rather through me. He doesn't look happy to see me. He looks pissed. I swallow thickly and speak through my slowing tears.

"Gabe?"

His chest moves with a breath. "Get out."

I flinch, my eyes burning even more. I wasn't sure how he would react to seeing me, but I didn't think he would tell me to leave without even listening to what I had to say. I turn to leave when his dark, deep voice surrounds me.

"Not you, moya lyubov'. Everyone else, get. Out."

I freeze, watching as everyone tentatively leaves us alone. Elliana lingers at the door like she's unsure about us being alone, before finally shutting it. I'm left alone with the man who owns every part of me. The man that I've always belonged to.

His words come on the softest whisper, "You're alive."

I nod, taking a small step closer as tears threaten to fall again. My heart gallops in my chest like it wants to break free and fall into his rough hands.

"I... You..."

I jump when he lunges for me. He pulls me tightly into his strong body and I clutch him without hesitation. My arm slips from its sling, my shoulder giving a twinge, but I ignore it as I sink into his embrace. His nose pushes into my hair, and I hear his deep inhale. Sobs start to wrack my body out of nowhere, falling apart in his arms. I didn't think I could miss him so much when I first met him—didn't think I would grow to love him so strongly.

His legs shake before finally giving out and I follow him to the floor, wrapping my legs around his waist. My shoulder gives another pinch as I move my arms to hug his warm neck. I feel the tears that made their way to his neck as he cradles the back of my head with a tense hand—shoving my face against the damp skin until his pulse beats wildly against my nose.

His wet nose rubs under my jaw as he speaks shakily, "I love you, Elizabeth. You hold my heart in your hands, my soul in step with yours." An unexpected sob shakes my body at his words, and he holds me tighter. He gives my tight jaw a kiss before continuing, "You are the reason I breathe, my heartbeat is synced with yours..."

I speak quick and roughly against him as I push past my tears, "I love you, Gabriel."

My chest lightens and warms as he cradles my wet face to brush our noses together with a wild and messy smile. "Never do that shit again.. Never leave me again. I won't survive it."

I nod with a small smile, pushing against his tight hold until my lips brush his as I speak, "I swear."

Neither of waste another second, our lips come together with a hungry intensity. He kisses me like it's the last and first time he'll be able to. I kiss him without reservation, telling him without words how sorry I am for what I put him through—how much I love him with every cell in my body. We kiss until we're panting and our eyes are dry, a heat developing in my stomach as his erection pushes into me through his jeans. He gives me a playful nip as he pulls away to lay our foreheads together.

I lose myself in the depths of his bright green eyes. The smile he gives me is filled with love and happiness. I reflect his smile back at him. I don't hide just how much he means to me, shoving that feeling forward until it shines from every pore on my body.

I shine for my greatest and only love.

The man that saved me. The man that broke me. The man that will always be there to put me back together.

[*] Shchenok—Pup

[*] YA by pomog, nesmotrya ni na chto, Shchenok.—I would have helped regardless, Pup.

[*] moy malen'kiy lepestok—my little petal

[*] to, chto ya khochu sdelat' s toboy, lepestok—The things I want to do to you, petal

[*] Yesli by ty tol'ko pozvolil mne prikosnut'sya k tebe, kak ya mechtayu—If only you would let me touch you like how I dream of.

[*] YA budu yedinstvennym, s kem ty kogda-libo budesh' katat'sya, Lepestok.—I will be the only one you ever ride with, petal.

[*] YA ne zabyl, lepestok. Teper' ty moy.—I did not forget, petal. You are mine now.

[*] Ty budesh' moyey posledney zhenshchinoy.—You will be my end woman.

[*] Vsegda, lepestok—Always, petal

[*] malen'kaya lisa—little fox

[*] Pozhaluysta, ne ostavlyay menya—Please don't leave me.

[*] Mne ne men'she zhal'—I'm no less sorry.

[*] Yesli by ya mog dobit'sya svoyego pryamo seychas, ty by krichal i prosil poshchady.—If I could have my way with you right now, you would be screaming and begging for mercy.

[*] YA ne ozhidal, chto ty budesh' takim napryazhennym. Mne ne terpitsya pogruzit'sya v etu shelkovistuyu pizdu.—I didn't expect you to be so tight. I can't wait to sink into this silky cunt.

[*] Ideal'nyy malen'kiy lepestok—Perfect little petal.

[*] Ty vyglyadish' takoy krasivoy, kogda plachesh' vozle moyego chlena.—You look so beautiful when you cry around my cock.

[*] moya lyubov'—my love

[*] Ty dlya menya takoy osobennyy.—You are so special to me.

[*] YA iskrenne veryu, chto ty sozdana dlya menya.—I truly believe that you were made for me.

[*] Vy sovershenny dlya menya, moy malen'kiy lepestok.—You are perfect for me, my little petal.

[*] YA lyublyu tebya, moy sladkiy lepestok.—I love you, my sweet petal.

[*] Luchshiy podarok v moyey zhizni—The best gift of my life.

Also by J.N. Crump

All Mine series
Arranged or Destined
Affected or Desired
Accidental or Designed